*To my sweet,
my darling daughter,
Nora Lee*

Books by William Lashner

Falls the Shadow
Past Due
Fatal Flaw
Bitter Truth (Veritas)
Hostile Witness

Coming Soon in Hardcover

Marked Man

WILLIAM
LASHNER

FALLS THE SHADOW

HarperTorch
An Imprint of HarperCollins*Publishers*

Grateful acknowledgment is made to reprint the excerpt from "The Hollow Men" in *Collected Poems 1909–1962* by T. S. Eliot, copyright 1936 by Harcourt Inc., copyright © 1964, 1983 by T. S. Eliot, reprinted by permission of the publisher.

◆ HARPERTORCH
An Imprint of HarperCollins*Publishers*
10 East 53rd Street
New York, New York 10022-5299

Copyright © 2005 by William Lashner
ISBN-13: 978-0-06-072158-9
ISBN-10: 0-06-072158-8

First HarperTorch paperback printing: May 2006
First William Morrow hardcover printing: May 2005

HarperCollins®, HarperTorch™, and ◆™ are trademarks of HarperCollins Publishers Inc.

Printed in the United States of America

Visit HarperTorch on the World Wide Web at www.harpercollins.com

10 9 8 7 6 5 4 3 2 1

CHAPTER

1

Unlike the rest of you, I cheerfully admit to my own utter selfishness. I am self-made, self-absorbed, self-serving, self-referential, even self-deprecating, in a charming sort of way. In short, I am all the selfs except self-less. Yet every so often I run across a force of nature that shakes my sublime self-centeredness to its very roots. Something that tears through the landscape like a tornado, leaving nothing but ruin and reexamination in its wake. Something like Bob.

Take, for example, the strange happenings one night when I brought Bob to a bar called Chaucer's.

Chaucer's was strictly a neighborhood joint, prosaic as they come, except for the name. The narrow corner bar had rock posters glued to the walls, Rolling Rock on tap, a juke-box stocked with Jim Morrison and Ella Fitzgerald. It was the kind of bar where you drank when you weren't in the mood to put on a nicer pair of shoes.

"My, what a colorful establishment," said Bob as we stepped inside.

"It's just a bar," I said.

"Oh, it's more than that, Victor. A bar is never just a bar. It is like a watering hole on some great African plain, where all creatures great and small sit by clean blue waters to relax and refresh themselves."

"Don't get out much, do you?"

"Look around. Can't you see the cycle of nature revolving before your very eyes?"

I looked, but there wasn't much cycling to see. A quartet of college kids were laughing in a booth. A mismatched couple was arguing at the bar. An old man was nursing a beer and complaining to another old man, who showed little interest in anything but his Scotch. The usual weeknight crowd at Chaucer's.

We took a table by the window. I flagged the waitress, ordered a Sea Breeze for me, and looked at Bob for his order.

"J&B on ice," said Bob, "with a twist."

About right, I figured, the last part anyway. At first glance, Bob didn't appear to be worth a second. He was short, soft and pudgy, with heavy black glasses that slipped down his nose and made him look like a fumbling schoolboy. Even with a five o'clock shadow worthy of Fred Flintstone, there was something sexless about him. Women scanning the watering hole for men scanned right past Bob. Their gaze would catch on leering hyenas from South Jersey, on lummoxes from South Philly, on old lemurs with expensive haircuts, on empty chairs, but not on Bob. He was of less interest to them than the furniture. They knew the type right off: the guy who works to fit in, who doesn't make waves, who accepts the world as it is, the guy who watches television on Saturday nights because he has nothing better to do, the guy with a hobby. And they would be right, sort of. I mean, it turned out he did have a hobby.

"I used to fish as a boy," said Bob, after I asked what he did with himself after work. "Yellow perch, caught with fathead minnows. But with the condition of the Schuylkill, that's impossible here. So nowadays I simply try to help."

"You say that a lot," I said. "What exactly do you mean? Do you volunteer?"

"In a way."

"Community service? Outreach for the homeless? Crisis hotline?"

"It varies. I lend a hand where I'm needed."

"Freelance do-gooder?"

"Yes, I suppose. Something like that. Do you do much good in the world, Victor?"

"Not intentionally."

"Unintentionally, then?"

"I'm a lawyer, I represent clients, and I do that to the best of my ability. If any good comes out of what I do, so be it."

"Like the murder case you're trying now."

My ears pricked up. "That's right."

"A bit bloody, isn't it, representing murderers?"

"That would make it right up your alley, no?"

He clapped his hands and laughed. Bob laughed like a car alarm; when first it goes off, you don't mind so much, but after a while you want to choke someone.

"You're right," he said when the siren calmed. "I'm not one to squeal at a little spill of blood. And sometimes, as you well know, it's more than a little. But do you think any good will come from you putting your client back on the street?"

"Honestly? No. I don't like him much and trust him less."

"And still you represent him."

"He paid me a retainer."

"A rather mercenary approach."

"Is there any other?"

"Sure there is. A far better one. Maybe I'll show you. Pay attention now. Did you see that couple at the bar?"

"The one that is fighting?"

"Very good, Victor. I'm impressed. Well, the fight has escalated and he has stormed off toward the restroom. They've been together for a while but are now going through a rocky patch. You know the point that a couple gets to, where they must decide to either break up or get married? That's the point they've reached."

"How do you know that?"

"I've been watching, listening. People, I've found, are so transparent. She is upset, and she's almost finished her beer." He snatched up his drink, downed it, slammed the glass back on the bar. "You stay here. I think I'll buy her another."

I was about to say something about how it didn't seem the most opportune time to hit on her, but he was already out of his seat, on his way to the bar. While his back was turned, I used a napkin to lift his small glass, dump the ice and lemon rind into my now empty Sea Breeze, and deposit the glass into a plastic bag I had brought just for the occasion. Surreptitiously, I placed the bag in my jacket pocket.

Bob leaned on the bar, a few stools away from the woman, turned his head toward her once, twice, and then called the bartender over and placed an order. The bartender came back with a J&B on the rocks and a fresh Corona, which the bartender took to the woman.

She looked up, surprised, and then turned her head to Bob and nodded. He smiled back. He slid over until he was standing next to her, and he began to speak.

I couldn't hear what he was saying, he kept his voice low, but it was having an effect. She was listening, and nodding, and at one point she even smiled. The woman was small, with brown hair and a pinched face, she didn't seem the type who was often bought drinks by strange men in bars, and she was flattered and wary both, as Bob leaned toward her. His eyes, behind his glasses, were the eyes of a mesmerist. And slowly, visibly, you could see a connection develop. Her posture eased, her smile grew, she even laughed at one point, for a moment placing her hand on Bob's arm.

Son of a gun, I thought. That bastard was going to get

lucky. Bob was going to get lucky. At my local bar. Bob. I wanted to choke him, yes I did, I wanted to strangle him until his eyes bulged. And that was before she said something and he started in again with his laugh.

He was still laughing when the boyfriend returned.

I had said before that the couple was mismatched, and what I had meant was the almost comical size disparity. She was small, slight, mousy; he was big, broad, bullish. And from the look of him, coming back from the bathroom, angry already from the argument, now staring at the little guy in glasses hitting on his girl, he was seeing red.

"Who the hell are you?" said the boyfriend.

Bob looked up at him without an ounce of fear or worry on his face. He smiled unctuously and reached out a hand. "The name's Bob," he said.

"Get lost."

"Calm down, Donnie," said the woman, her voice dismissive. "We were just talking."

This was the moment when Bob should have backed off, apologized, this was the moment when Bob should have realized he had broken the unspoken code of men in bars and slunk away to leave the two of them alone to work out whatever they needed to work out. But that's not what Bob did. What Bob did was take a step forward.

"If you'll just excuse us for a moment, Donnie," said Bob, emphasizing the name as if it were an insult. "Sandy and I were having a rather personal discussion."

"Sandy and you? Personal? I don't think so."

"Donald, stop it now," said the woman. "This is ridiculous. He just bought me a drink."

"Shut up and let me deal with this jerk."

"That's no way to talk to a lady," said Bob cheerfully. "In fact, I think it would be better for everyone if you would just go home now and leave us be."

"Is that what you think?"

"Absolutely," said Bob, a peculiar smile on his face, peculiar because it wasn't meek or conciliatory in the least, which made it all the more infuriating.

The man took a step forward.

Sandy shouted out, "Donald, no."

The man cocked his fist.

I rose from my seat, ready to do what I could to stop the massacre. Fricasseed Bob, no doubt about it. We'd be scraping him off the walls.

But then Bob shifted to his left, bent down, and exploded upward, slamming his elbow smack into Donnie's face with a crack that sounded like a line drive to center field.

There was a crystalline moment of stunned silence in the bar when everything stopped, when everyone froze, when nothing yet had been sorted out and the disastrous possibilities seemed endless.

And then a shriek, a holler, and the scrape of a chair skidding away as Donnie collapsed to the floor, hands over his nose, blood leaking through his fingers.

Bob reached a hand out to Sandy.

She slapped his hand away, dropped down to minister to Donnie, cradled his head in her arms. "Sweetie? Donnie? Are you all right, Donnie? Sweetie? Say something, please."

"My nose," moaned the boyfriend. "He broke my nose."

Bob took it all in impassively. When the bartender reached over the bar to grab for him, Bob shrugged him off. He backed away, winked at me, and left the bar, vanishing before anyone could stop him.

The bartender and I both rushed outside after him. We scanned the streets veering away from the corner, first Lombard, then Twentieth. Empty, vacant, Bobless.

"Who the hell was that?" asked the bartender.

"That," I said, "was Bob."

Back inside, Donnie was still on the floor, sitting up now, one hand over his nose, his white shirt splattered with his own blood. Sandy was holding him, hugging him, straightening his hair.

One of the old men leaned over. "Let me see it," said the man.

Donnie removed his hand. His nose was an amorphous blob.

"It's broke," said the man, his voice high with delight. "Broke, broke, broke. No doubt about it. I seen enough of them. The hospital's just down the street. You ought to get that thing fixed."

We helped him onto his feet, helped him out the door. He pushed us away when we tried to help him further, and he and his girl, both of her arms around him now in support, walked slowly toward the bright lights of the emergency room.

I paid the bill, searched the area to no avail, shrugged, and went home. Bob was waiting in front of my building. He leaned against a wall, his arms were crossed, he seemed to be insufferably pleased with himself.

"Are you insane?" I said to him.

"I just did Donnie the biggest favor of his life."

"You weren't interested in Sandy?"

"Please," said Bob. "I prefer a little more substance on the bone."

"So then it was all a setup."

"Their relationship was in dire straits, it needed some juice. Years from now, when the two of them are celebrating their wedding anniversary, with their children all around, they'll think back on the most important day of their lives, the day they recommitted themselves to their future together. The day he fought for her, the day she rushed to his aid."

"You set him up and then you broke his nose."

"I try to help," said Bob.

"But you broke his nose."

"That, I'm afraid, wasn't part of the plan. Accidents happen, Victor, remember that. Sometimes even the best of intentions go awry. But often the accidents work out for the best. Think of Donnie with his new nose. It will enhance his features, don't you think? Lend his face the character it was sorely lacking."

"What gave you the right?"

"We are all fellow travelers. We don't have the right to turn away."

"So you step in whether they want you to or not?"

"I do my part."

"You are insane," I said.

"Like a rabid fox," said Bob. "But let me ask you this, Victor. Whom did you help today?"

As I said, he had a hobby. And he was right, I hadn't done a teacup's worth of good that day. And he was probably right about Donnie and Sandy, too. They had seemed closer, with Donnie holding back the blood from his nose and Sandy wrapping her arms about him, much more the loving couple. And the broken nose probably would improve Donnie's appearance and, after it was set, maybe improve his sinuses, too. Who knew, maybe Bob was just what they both had needed. But still, I saw the blood leaking between Donnie's fingers, the blood splattered on his fine white shirt, dripping onto the floor. And I couldn't help but wonder if the answer I was looking for, the answer to a killing I was still trying to solve, was there in the blood.

I was just then in the middle of the François Dubé murder case, and I sensed that Bob was somehow in the middle of it, too—that was why I had taken him to the bar, why I had swiped his fingerprints. The Dubé case was the usual type that falls upon a lawyer's desk, a case of murder, of protested innocence, of history and dentistry and the best of intentions gone all to hell. Not to mention the gratuitous sex and the gratuitous violence. Not to mention.

Yet for me it was a case about more than a lone woman dying in a whirlwind of her own blood. It also started me to thinking about the benefits and costs of involving yourself in other people's lives. When are we compelled to help? When does a helping hand turn meddlesome? And when does meddling turn murderous? The questions proved to be more than idle, they proved to be a matter of life and death.

Mine, for instance.

But it didn't start with Bob, no. His role would be crucial, yes, but he would appear later in the story, he was not there at the beginning for me. No, for me it started with a cashier's check in the amount of five hundred dollars from another self-centered son of a bitch, François Dubé.

"Thank you so much for coming, Mr. Carl," said François Dubé in his strong French accent. "Can I call you Victor?"

"Sure," I said. "Knock yourself out."

"Vic?"

"Victor."

"I am so grateful that you came."

"You sent us a cashier's check for five hundred dollars to pay for this meeting," I said. "We're not here as a favor."

"But still, Victor. I feel better already. It is as if hope has returned to my life."

"I'm just a lawyer, Mr. Dubé."

"But where I am now, I do not need a priest, I do not need a doctor. Where I am now, only a lawyer can help."

I'll give him this, he was right about that.

François Dubé looked like the scruffy college professor all the girls fall in love with their sophomore year. Maybe that's why I was wary, because he was better-looking than me, but I don't think so. Or maybe it was because he was French and had all those curlicues and accents attached to the letters of his name, like some baroque affectation, but that didn't seem to be it either. No, I think it was a visceral reaction to his very persona. I could feel the danger in him, the violence. It was in his eyes, pale blue and unaccountable, with a bright golden flaw in his left iris that seemed to light demonically. It was in his scarred hands, clutching each other as if to keep them from lurching angrily about. Yes, true, it might also have been the prison jumpsuit, I am not immune to such subtle cues, but for the record let me state, something about him put me on guard. And did I mention he was French?

"You need to know, Victor, that I did not do what they say I did. I loved my wife. I could never have done such a thing. You must believe me."

But I didn't believe him, did I? And what I didn't believe was not that he didn't kill his wife, because that early in my involvement in his case, how could I know such a thing? Or that he loved her, because who was I to peer into another man's heart? No, what I didn't believe was that he could never have done such a thing—could never have slipped into his wife's apartment and shot her through the neck and left her on the floor to die as the blood gushed and spattered— and I didn't believe his earnest, pleading words because I felt the violence in him.

We were in a small, windowless conference room at Graterford Prison, a bleak old complex that sits on a rise overlooking the Perkiomen Creek. The main walls at Graterford are thirty feet high, which is about as high as prison walls go, and considering who was inside, the worst of Philadelphia's criminal population, every foot was welcome. François's overalls were maroon, the conference room was slate gray, the air was stale. My partner, Beth Derringer, and I were seated across from François at a metal table, bolted onto the floor so it couldn't be raised on high and used as a weapon. Just then I was glad for the precaution.

"It doesn't matter what you did or did not do, Mr. Dubé," I said. "And it doesn't matter what I believe. I'm not here to pronounce judgment. That's already been done by twelve of your peers."

"They were not my peers," he said. "They were fools, and they were wrong."

"A jury is like an umpire at a baseball game. Even if the pitch is a foot outside, if he calls it a strike, it's a strike. Do you understand?"

"I do not know baseball," said François Dubé. "All I know is the truth."

"The truth of the thing, whatever that is, doesn't matter. The law said you were guilty. The law sentenced you to spend the rest of your life in this prison. The law gave you the right to appeal, and you exercised that right, and your appeals were all denied. The law says you are screwed."

Maybe I was coming on too strong, maybe I should have shown him a little more sympathy. I mean, there he was, locked away in that hellhole with a life sentence shackled around his neck. He was about my age, he once had a life outside those thirty-foot walls that I would have envied: a restaurant of his own and a reputation as the city's hot young chef, a pretty wife, a young daughter. His fall had been spectacular. I'm a lawyer, my instinct is to reach out to those in the deepest of troubles, and he certainly qualified. But there was something about François Dubé that was keeping my empathy at bay, or maybe it was just that I had enough problems of my own right then, including something seriously wrong with a tooth, to get all worked up about his.

"I expected innocence to matter in America," said François Dubé with undisguised bitterness. "But when the Supreme Court refused to hear my case and my lawyer said all my chances were finished, I wrote to you. There must be a way for you to help." He searched my face and then Beth's. "Is that not why you've come?"

"We came because you paid us," said Beth. "This meeting is exploratory only. We haven't agreed to get any more involved in your case."

"You will not help?"

"Based on what we could glean from the newspaper reports, we don't see any immediate grounds for a new trial," she said. "You need something on which to base the request. Are there new DNA results?"

"No," he said.

"Has a new witness come forward?"

"No."

"Is there a piece of previously undiscovered forensic evidence?"

"Nothing like that," said François.

"Do you have something you want us to examine?"

"Everything."

I threw my hands up in exasperation. "Which means nothing," I said. "There has to be something new that will convince the trial judge to go through it all again. What should we tell him?"

"That I did not do it," said François Dubé.

"Innocence is not a basis for a new trial, Mr. Dubé. You claimed innocence at your original trial and failed."

"I did not fail," he said. "My lawyer failed. He was terrible."

"So you want us to claim ineffective assistance of counsel?" said Beth.

"Will that get me free?" said François, his face suddenly lit with hope.

I shook my head. "That and a quarter will get you fifteen minutes on a meter, not a new trial. Your lawyer was Whitney Robinson, right?"

"A doddering old fool," said François. "His idea of a strategy was no strategy."

I narrowed my eyes. "Whitney Robinson, besides being a dear friend of mine, is a crackerjack trial attorney."

"Maybe at some point in his career, but not for me. For my case he was too old, too distracted. Almost senile. He retired right after the Supreme Court turned its back on my hope. It is his fault I am here."

I felt for my sore tooth with my tongue. Ouch. Yeah, sure, blame the lawyer, blame the jury, the judge, the D.A., blame everyone except the guy who shot his wife point-blank in the neck. I had seen her picture in the newspaper accounts. Leesa Dubé had been young and beautiful, with a marvelous set of teeth. And then she married François.

"Let's go over the facts," I said. "From what I understand, the murder weapon was registered in your name."

"But I left it with my wife when I moved out. For her protection."

"It was found, wrapped within a shirt of yours, covered with your wife's blood, on the floor of your closet."

"I do not know how it got there. The police, maybe. The detective was a lying bastard."

"Your fingerprints were found at the crime scene."

"It was my apartment, too, before I moved out. Of course they would be there."

"You had no alibi."

"I was alone, asleep. Is that a crime?"

"And an eyewitness spotted you coming out of your wife's building the night of the murder."

"He was mistaken. It was not me."

"Even the best lawyers, including Mr. Robinson, are limited by the evidence available to them. But the truth is, Mr. Dubé, no one cares about the reasons you lost, just that you did. To get another trial now, you need new evidence, new test results, a new witness. You need something fresh, something new and startling. The legal standard is very high."

"That is why I need your help. To find it. I read about you in the paper, that thing with the Supreme Court justice and the boat. And one of your clients works with me in the kitchen. He speaks most glowingly about you."

"But that he's here should clue you in to the fact that I'm not a magician," I said. "I can't create evidence out of thin air. If you don't have anything I can take to the judge, there is nothing I can do."

"Can you at least take a look at my case?" said François. "Can you at least see if you can come up with something?"

"Mr. Dubé, that would be a waste of everyone's time. To be honest, you have the time to waste, but unfortunately we do not. Unless you have a compelling piece of new evidence, there is nothing we can do."

"I need your help, Mr. Carl. I am desperate. I have a daughter. I have not seen her for three years. My wife's parents won't let her near me."

He glanced at Beth with glistening eyes. She stared back for a moment and then placed one of her hands encouragingly over one of his.

"It's okay, Mr. Dubé," she said.

"Call me François, please. And you are Beth?"

"That's right. How old is your daughter?"

"She is four now. I have not seen her for three years, since my arrest. It is breaking my heart."

"I'm so sorry," said Beth.

"I have not hugged my daughter for three years, Mr. Carl. I am asking you as a father. Can you help me, please?"

It might have tugged at my heartstrings, his touching little plea, except I had no soft spot for the tiny bundles of snot that others went mushy for, and my own father had never been one for hugs.

"No dice," I said. I took hold of my briefcase. I stood at the table. "Good luck, Mr. Dubé. Really, I mean that. But there is nothing we can do."

"Maybe we can look," said Beth.

I stopped and gaped at my partner. She was still seated, still with her hand over his. This wasn't unlike her. Beth Derringer was the patron saint of lost causes, which was one reason our finances were always on the precipice. And for some reason, which I couldn't yet fathom, she seemed ready to take on another.

"Beth, it won't do any good."

"We can't promise anything," said Beth to François. "But maybe we can look. When Victor is on the trail of evidence, he's like a bloodhound. If there's something to be found, he'll find it."

"I don't think so, Beth," I said.

She looked up at me. "Victor. Please. We should help him. He hasn't hugged his daughter in three years. He needs our help."

"There's nothing we can do."

"But can't we try?" she said, her hand still over François's hand, her face suddenly younger, like a little girl's. "Please?"

"No."

"What can I do to convince you?" said François.

"You can't," I said.

"How about if I arrange for you to be paid whatever money you require?" he said.

"Up front?"

"Of course."

"It might be a lot."

He shrugged.

"Say, ten thousand dollars?"

"Not a problem," said François.

I sat right down, gave him a grin. "Okay then, Mr. Dubé. I'm convinced."

See, sometimes it is just that easy to fall into a hole.

Outside Graterford Prison, as we walked to my car in the parking lot, I asked Beth what her little outburst in the interview room was all about.

"I don't know," she said. "Something just came over me. He seemed so lost, so helpless. He misses his daughter, and she misses him."

"Does she?"

"Of course she does."

"You talk to her lately?"

"I couldn't stop thinking of her waiting for her daddy to come home. We couldn't just do nothing."

"Yes we could."

"We had to do something."

"No we didn't."

"He needs our help. Isn't that enough?"

"See, that's the problem with you, Beth. You view the law as a helping profession. Me, if I want to help, I help myself. That is the capitalist way, and I am a freedom-loving capitalist of the first rank: All I lack is capital."

"Sometimes you're a creep."

"That may be true," I said, "but I'm never as creepy as that creep in there."

"Who? François?"

"Yes, François. I didn't like him from the get-go. Frankly,

I have no great belief in his innocence, and I have no burning desire to reunite this convicted murderer with his young and innocent daughter."

"Then why did you take the case?"

"You're my partner, you wanted the job, and there was the promise of ten thousand dollars. The combination was enough for me. If lawyers only defended those they liked and admired, the species would be endangered. I figure we'll cash the check and spend the retainer preparing the motion for a new trial. Then we'll stand stoically in court as the judge denies it. *We did what we could*, we'll tell François. *We're sorry it didn't work out.* Easy money."

"Is there such a thing?"

"This," I said.

"You don't think we have a chance?"

"There is no way, no how a judge will give that guy a new trial. He's got nothing, nothing but the money he's going to pay us, and pretty soon he won't have that either."

"I'll go to the clerk's office tomorrow and get the file. I assume reviewing the record will be my job."

"Right you are. Last thing I want to do is bury myself for a month in his paperwork."

"In exchange, then, you can handle this pro bono case I was assigned by Judge Sistine."

"I don't think so. I've told you before, I'm not one for causes."

"It's not a cause, it's a kid. We're representing a young boy whose mother has been neglecting him."

"Pro bono, Latin for 'empty bank account.' Couldn't you have just said, 'Sorry, but we're too busy'?"

"No, and neither would you have."

"I think the reason we've stayed together so long, Beth, is that you still have no idea who I really am."

"So let's keep it that way," she said. And then she added, "I thought he was cute."

"Who?"

"François."

"Everyone looks cute in prison maroon."

"You didn't think he was insanely handsome?"

"In a Charlie Manson sort of way."

"There was something in his eyes."

"The mark of Satan?"

"You know, Victor, when he said he didn't do it, I almost believed him."

I stopped, stared at her for a moment until she stopped, too. She turned to face me, and there was that same little-girl look in her eyes. She had said something came over her, and I could see that maybe it had, but what it was, I had yet not a clue. Part of it was the romanticism of a client she believed in, of a cause worth fighting for, sure, but there was something else, too, something that involved this man in jail and his daughter, whom he hadn't hugged in three years. I didn't understand yet what it was, the something, though I would discover it later, yes, I would, discover it from Bob, as a matter of fact.

"He's a convicted murderer," I said.

"He's a human being, too."

I pulled out my phone. "Let's find out."

"Who are you calling?"

I held up a finger, said into the earpiece, "A Chestnut Hill address. The name is Robinson, Whitney Robinson." Then I looked at Beth. "You want to glimpse the rotting cesspools in the soul of a man, just ask his lawyer."

4

The term *WASP* was coined by a Philadelphia professor who grew up among the city's aristocracy and went on to write learned treatises about his clan. Even if he had never met Whitney Robinson III, the professor would have recognized as a brother the man who answered the door of the rambling stone house in the swankiest section of Philadelphia. Chestnut Hill was a place of great stone houses and ornate swimming pools, of horses and cricket clubs and tweed jackets. If you played tennis in Chestnut Hill, you wore whites and played on grass and wondered why anyone would play the game on anything else. Tall, gray, elegantly stooped, with argyle socks and a dignified sprinkling of dandruff on his dark jacket, Whitney Robinson, now in his seventies, seemed the very personification of the type of Philadelphia patrician who had inherited his seat at the Union League and his sinecure at the family firm. His nose was straight, his face was long, his step light, his manners perfect. I should have hated him as a matter of principle, but I never did.

"Victor, how nice," said Whitney Robinson in his lock-jawed drawl. "So good of you to come."

There they were, those perfect manners, making it seem as if I were doing him the favor even though I had asked for the meeting. Manners go further than you could imagine in defusing the natural animosities of class.

"Hello, Whit," I said. "It's nice to see you again."

"And I you, my boy. You've become quite notorious in the last few years. And about that, I say good for you. It is always better to be notorious than ignored. I thought we'd sit out back, if that's all right with you."

"Of course."

"Come along, then," he said as he turned to lead me through the center hallway of his house. "I've made my famous lemonade."

"Pink?"

"You know me, Victor, I wouldn't have it any other way."

Whit still maintained his chair in the Philadelphia Club, an organization that would sooner disband than admit the likes of me, and his locker at the Germantown Cricket Club, where he was three-time club tennis champion, but he had long ago turned down a partnership in the law firm founded by his great-grandfather a century ago with the sole purpose of ensuring that its rich clients stay that way. Fresh out of law school, he had decided, much as I would decide decades later, to hang out a shingle and make it on his own in the wilds of criminal law. In the course of his colorful career, Whit became a Philadelphia legend, representing high-society murderers and lowborn politicians on the take, socialist terrorists in the sixties and corporate swindlers in the eighties. And through the course of his career, he generously reached out to befriend and mentor scores of young attorneys trying to make it on their own, including a bitter young lawyer of no discernible talent or evident prospects.

"How goes the firm, Victor?"

"We're still around."

"Good for you. Surviving is always nine-tenths of the battle."

"Maybe," I said, "but it's that last tenth that's killing me."

"Yes," said Whit, "the final bit always proves to be the devil."

I had never been in Whit's house before—we didn't socialize in different circles, more like different planets—and so, as we proceeded through the house at Whit's typically brisk pace, I swiveled my head to take a gander. Whitney Robinson was always full of life, he was still, but there was something aged and forlorn about the interior of his home. It was furnished as one would expect of a Robinson manse, old American chairs, French divans, urns, the odd baroque piece up against the wall, but the house looked like it had been set up decades ago and not touched since. The walls were dingy, the fabric dull and faded, the carpets threadbare. There was a thick scent of must, and something else, too, something out of place. It smelled strangely medicinal, like an old hospital where doctors in dark suits sawed at gangrenous legs as blood spurted onto their shirtsleeves. When we passed a doorway, I glanced in and spied, through a dark dining room, another room, and in that room the corner of a hospital bed, a nurse in white leaning over it, a rigid figure rocking back and forth under the sheets.

"Through here," said Whit, opening one of a pair of French doors leading to a stone terrace at the rear of the house. The lemonade pitcher was sweating on a round table, green-striped cushions rested on the seats of wrought-iron chairs, birds twittered about us. We sat, he poured, the lemonade was sour enough to pucker my cheeks.

"You're wincing," said Whit. "Not enough sugar?"

"No, it's perfect," I said when my face and jaw had recovered from sour shock. "I'm just having problems with a tooth."

"That explains the swollen cheek."

"Is it that bad?"

"Oh, yes. You should have that looked after."

"You're right," I said, "I should."

"I wanted to thank you for the note about my wife, Victor. It was very kind of you."

"She was quite a woman, had to have been to put up with you for forty years."

"You have no idea," said Whit.

"I couldn't help but notice the hospital bed."

"My daughter lives with me. That she is still alive is a miracle, but she is very ill and needs constant care. It has been hard since my wife's death, but one manages, and after a while, dealing with adversity becomes less a struggle than a habit."

"You were always your best under pressure."

"I used to think so. But now, Victor, while I might have time to putter and reminisce, you are quite the busy man these days. So?"

"François Dubé."

Whit turned his head away from me for a moment, turned toward an expanse of grass that led to a dense wall of rhododendron. It seemed, if only for an instant, that he spied something lurking behind the greenery and among the thick woody stalks.

"Whit?" I said. "Are you okay?"

His head snapped back in my direction. "Yes? Oh, my. Sorry, Victor. What do they call those, 'senior moments'? When you get to my age, sometimes the memories seem more real than the reality. François Dubé, you say?"

"He was a client, I believe."

"Yes, he was. Sad story, really. What's this about?"

"He wants me to ask for a new trial. I'm trying to figure out if there is anything there."

"I wouldn't think so, though I wish him all the luck."

"What was the story?"

"He was in the middle of an ugly divorce. There was a daughter involved, custody was at issue. It was a pity, the whole thing. They made such a beautiful couple, but that might have been the problem, don't you think?"

"Fortunately, I've never had to suffer the torments. So the divorce was getting out of hand?"

"Charges flying back and forth like eggs on hell night, splattering everyone who got close. But this one had a particularly ugly edge. He accused her of rampant drug use, argued she was an unfit mother. She claimed that he had sexually abused their daughter."

"A pleasant time for all."

"Yes, well, unfortunately, such accusations were a common tactic for a while back there. Things were getting very heated, all of it reaching a fever pitch, when they found the wife dead. Shot through the neck, blood everywhere. A brutal crime."

"Who was the lead detective?"

"Torricelli."

"That lunkhead?"

"He searched François's apartment and found the murder weapon rolled up in a shirt covered with her blood."

"Convenient," I said.

"Certainly was. And of course François's fingerprints were all over the crime scene. It was grim for him from the start, yet I think I could have dealt with all that. As you know, there are always ways. But there was another most intriguing piece of evidence not found by Torricelli. In her death throes, the wife—her name was Leesa, I think—the wife grabbed something and clutched it in her hand. By the time they found her body, rigor mortis had set in. They had to pry her fingers back at the morgue. And there it was."

"What?"

"I did everything I could to exclude it, called it unduly prejudicial, called it hearsay, everything. But Judge Armstrong let it in, found it to be a dying declaration, and that was the case right there."

"What was it?"

"A picture she had kept, a picture from happier times, a picture of François."

"Like a message from the dead."

"That's what the prosecutor argued. In fact, it was our estimable district attorney, trying her last case before she ran for the big seat. Oh, she had a grand time marching back and forth in front of the jury with that creased and bloodied photograph. The jury returned in less than a day."

"The newspaper accounts said there was a witness that put him at the scene."

"Yes, a young man. He testified he had seen François leaving the apartment building on the night of the murder."

"Any way to discredit him?"

"We asked for everything the state had on him, and nothing came up. But I don't think he had much impact. He wasn't the real problem."

"Then what was?"

"Besides the photograph? There were no other suspects. There was no one else who would have done it. There was no robbery, there was no rape, there was no string of burglaries in the neighborhood. Whatever I argued about the evidence being weak, or planted, or explainable, there was no other theory of the murder I could put forward that would have been believed. It became a reasonable-doubt case, and those are very hard, especially when you have a message from the dead."

"I can imagine. What was he like, your client?"

"Have you met him?"

"Yes."

"Then you know. Difficult, manipulative, arrogant. Very smart, but not as smart as he thinks he is, obviously."

"Obviously?"

"If he was as smart as he thought he was, he would never have gotten caught. Why are you taking his case anyway?"

"He's paying me," I said.

"Of course, what better reason is there? I'm sure you two will work fine together, though I wouldn't start racking up the billables until the money is in the bank. After the trial I ended up prosecuting his appeals pro bono. By then he had no funds left, as far as I could tell."

That was interesting and disheartening both. How did François get the five hundred he had paid me for the meeting, and how was he going to get me my retainer? I hadn't asked in the prison—he'd said he could pay me, so I just assumed he could—but as always, when it came to money, it was wrong to assume anything.

At that moment, still thinking about the money, I glanced behind me, to the rear of the stone house. Ivy was climbing the walls, digging into the crumbling mortar for purchase. And framed by a tiny square window was a face, long and pale, with a white nurse's cap pinned atop its dark hair. The mouth was a thin, straight gash, the eyes were black and staring, staring at me. When I cocked my head out of curiosity, the face disappeared.

"So, Victor," said Whit, dragging my attention away from the window, "what grounds are you considering for the new trial?"

"I don't know yet. We're still looking into it. I'll of course want to talk to the witness."

"That might be difficult. He died a few years back."

"How?"

"A tragedy, really. Shot during a drug deal, apparently."

"Was he on drugs at the time of the trial?"

"Not that I knew of, and like I said, we asked for any information the police had on him. He came back clean. Quite the wholesome young man, so we all thought." He glanced over his shoulder for a moment, as if to that window. "Not much there, I'm afraid."

"I suppose then I'll have to comb through the record for something else to hang our hat on. And my partner, who's also working on the case, thinks we should, well, you know . . ."

"Blame me," said Whit, nodding with a touch too much enthusiasm. "Of course she's right, you should. Anything for the client. I'll help out, too, if you want. Put me on the stand, I'll have a senior moment for the judge. You can claim me as senile."

"Some things, Whit, are too beyond belief for even me to argue."

"Oh, Victor, I doubt that." He laughed. "I doubt that very much."

On our way out, we passed again through the faded hallway of his house. The medicinal smell leaked from the side room like a dark secret. With the front door open and the two of us in the entranceway, he put his hand on my shoulder. "Victor, really now, you must take care of that tooth. Let me give you the name of a dentist."

"I'm not much for dentists," I said.

He took a card and pen from his jacket pocket, scribbled a name and a number. "He's a miracle worker, trust me."

I reached for my tooth with my tongue as I looked over what he had written. A name, Dr. Pfeffer, and a phone number.

"Give him a call." He smiled at me and nodded, and just then a scream came from the back room, and the sound of something crashing to the floor. I glanced at Whit. Some strange emotion played itself on his face, something fearful, shameful.

"My daughter," he said. "I should go to her."

"Of course you should. Thank you, Whit," I said, shaking his hand. "Thank you for everything."

"Keep me informed of Mr. Dubé's status."

"I will."

He started away and then stopped, turned toward me, al-most lunged as he grabbed my shoulders and leaned into me. I recoiled from him, thinking for a moment he was going to kiss me for some reason, but that's not what he did. He grabbed my shoulders, leaned close, and whispered in my ear as if cadres of eavesdroppers were close by.

"Leave him where he is, leave it be. For your own sake. You can't imagine the price."

Then he let me go and lurched off down the hallway and was gone.

CHAPTER

You know that stuff they sell in drugstores, the goop you put into your mouth to stop your toothache? Well, it doesn't work. I know this because I slathered three times the recommended dosage onto my throbbing tooth, hoping for just a moment of relief, but the pain was getting worse. It was as if a mole were burrowing into my gum, digging and chewing. But the goop, all it did was numb my tongue, leaving me to talk as if sky high on paint thinner.

So I was sprawled on the couch, a towel full of ice on my jaw, drooling from my numb tongue, looking every inch the suave man-about-town, when the phone rang.

"He likes you," said Beth from the other end.

"Who likes me?"

"François. He called me from the prison today while you were out at Whit's. He said he's very grateful you agreed to take the case and that he likes you."

"That makes my day."

"What's wrong with your voice? What are you, drunk?"

"Hardly. I'm having a situation. Remember when that thug socked me with his gun on that old boat? My teeth have never quite been right since."

"You should have them looked at. I know a dentist—"

"Yes, it seems everyone knows a dentist." I took out of my

pocket the card Whit Robinson had given me and thumbed over the name. "If it gets any worse, I have someone to see. I hear he's a miracle worker. But I'm sure it will take care of itself."

"A bit of dentophobia, Victor?"

"Hey, nothing wrong with a healthy fear of men with hairy forearms who want to stick sharp metal implements into your gums. What did Shakespeare say, 'First thing let's kill all the dentists'?"

"I don't think that's quite it. Anyway, I called to remind you that you have that hearing in family court tomorrow."

"I know. I talked to the boy's mother on the phone and arranged to meet up with her before we go to the judge."

"Good. You'll be in and out. Judge Sistine told me the case shouldn't take much time."

"And it pays so well, too. Pro bono, Latin for 'no cable.' "

"Doing a little good in the world will do wonders for your soul."

"My soul's fine, it's my wallet that's a little thin. Since you spoke to your boyfriend—"

"Stop it."

"Did he say when he was going to get us our retainer?"

"He said soon."

"Because the word is, he couldn't pay for his appeals. The word is, François Dubé doesn't have a cent to his name."

"Where did you hear that?"

"Whit."

"Did he say anything else of interest?"

"Not really, though our meeting ended a little strangely. But he did mention that François ran out of money at the end of the trial. So I'm naturally wondering how the jerk is going to pay us."

"I don't know. He didn't say."

"Be a dear and find out next time he calls, won't you? It

would be nice if we got paid for something some time this month. The landlord has been leaving notes."

I hung up the phone and looked again at Whit's card. Dr. Pfeffer, miracle worker. Just then things weren't going so well in my life. My business was precariously perched on the brink of bankruptcy, my anemic love life was the stuff of a Sartre treatise—*Being with Nothingness*—my car could use a tune-up, my apartment could use a scrubbing, my body could use some exercise, though who would give it that was a mystery to me. I was too young to feel old, and yet there it was, the despair of middle age, hanging around my neck like a noose. And now I had a client who couldn't pay me but who was calling my partner from prison to say how much he liked me. Let me tell you, hearing from a convicted murderer serving a life sentence in an all-male prison that he likes you doesn't exactly make your day. And on top of it all, there was a mole digging a burrow into my jaw. My life could sure use a miracle. If my tooth didn't get any better soon, I was going to have to give that Dr. Pfeffer a call.

But first, lucky me, I had an appointment in family court.

Philadelphia Family Court sits in an old neoclassical building on the Benjamin Franklin Parkway, just next to the main library, which is its exact double in architecture. The buildings were modeled after twin palaces at the mouth of the Champs-Elysées, built by ambitious civic leaders determined to turn Philadelphia into the Paris of America.

Talk about missing the mark.

On the third floor of the Family Court Building, I stepped warily into a large, beat waiting room outside Judge Sistine's courtroom. The room was as noisy as a day-care center at recess. In one corner was a carpet with a few sad plastic toys strewn upon it. Young children, placed with desperate hope on the carpet by their mothers, looked around and screeched as if to say, *Is that all there is?* Older children sat sullenly on the molded plastic chairs and mouthed off, infants cried, mothers fussed, men eyed the nearest exit as if waiting for their moment to dash for it.

I checked in with the clerk and then went around the waiting room asking each of the women there if she happened to be Julia Rose. She wasn't.

The slim file in my briefcase told the story. An anonymous complaint had come into the child welfare department concerning the treatment of a young boy named Daniel

Rose, age four. After an investigation it was determined that the boy's interests might best be represented by his having his own lawyer. This was not a case designed to make me rich or put my mug on the front page of the newspapers, and so my plan was to get in and get out as quickly as I could. The social worker at child welfare, a woman named Isabel, had assured me the boy was in no apparent danger. I figured the judge would lay out a series of concrete steps for the mother to follow, the mother would agree, and that would take care of that.

Julia Rose's not being in the waiting room wasn't helping my get-in-and-get-out strategy.

I slumped in disgust on one of the hard plastic chairs and gently rubbed my swollen jaw. You can imagine my delight when a woman with an infant sat down right next to me, the baby crying and slobbering, drool flying as the baby shook in its mother's arms. I pulled my suit as far out of harm's way as I could. Sitting across from me, a skinny old man in a bow tie and a black porkpie hat was jiggling his leg. I caught his eye, and for an uncomfortable moment we fell into an impromptu staring contest. I lost, turning my attention to the side of the room, as if something of great import were happening there. As surreptitiously as possible, I glanced back at the old man. He was still staring, a bent smile of victory on his narrow face.

This, I thought, as I leaned away from the baby and pretended that I hadn't noticed the old man's stare, as children ran and squealed around me, as the smell of an unchanged diaper wafted from behind, this, I thought, was why I became a lawyer.

"Daniel Rose," called out the clerk.

The old man glowered at me as I stood.

It was less a courtroom I entered than a small, shabby conference room. Judge Sistine, a large woman with the forearms of a wrestler and reading glasses perched on her nose, sat at the head of the table. To the judge's right was a file clerk, to her left was the child-welfare social worker, the woman I had spoken to on the phone, Isabel Chandler, who turned out to be tall and stern and quite pretty. I sat at the far end of the table, feeling uncomfortably like I was on trial.

"Have you met your client yet, Mr. Carl?" said the judge.

"Not yet, Your Honor."

"Don't you think you ought to?" said Judge Sistine, peering at me over her glasses.

"I was hoping to meet him today. I called the mother, and she assured me she would show up at this hearing."

"From what I can tell, her assurances don't mean much. That's why we're here. Miss Chandler, have you been able to contact the mother today?"

"No, Judge."

"I'm concerned about this report. I'm concerned that we can't get a grip on the conditions in which this boy is living. How many times have you tried to visit the home, Miss Chandler?"

"Twice, Judge, both times unsuccessfully. Miss Rose continually apologizes and promises to be at home and then misses her appointments."

"The anonymous report mentioned a boyfriend," said the judge. "I want to talk to him, too. See if you can get him in, Miss Chandler."

"Not likely, but I'll try."

"Mr. Carl, the truth is, Miss Chandler has a caseload that would choke an elephant. There is only so much she can do. You are this boy's lawyer. I'm going to expect you to have some answers for me, and soon. I would hope you'd give this boy the same attention you give your corporate clients."

"I don't have any corporate clients, Judge, though if you see a herd wandering around, I'd appreciate your driving them my way."

Isabel Chandler bit her lip to stop a smile, but the judge was having none of it.

"Do your job," she snapped. "If you can't handle this, let us know, and I'll find someone who can. We'll reschedule this matter for three weeks from today, at nine o'clock. If the mother doesn't appear on that date, I'm going to issue a bench warrant. You tell her that, Mr. Carl. And I expect you to get the whole story from your client."

"He's four years old, Judge."

"Then speak slowly."

Outside the courtroom Isabel Chandler shook her head at me as if I were a troublemaker who was once again in some kind of trouble. She was thin and dark, with the kind of sharp, cool beauty that was like a driver's-ed movie, so shocking you couldn't look away.

"Judge Sistine doesn't have much of a sense of humor, does she?" I said, trying to ingratiate myself.

"She was quite jolly when she started in family court six months ago, but I wouldn't test her patience anymore. In fact, the most fun she's had this month was reaming you."

"I'll be sore for weeks."

She fought a smile again. "What's with your cheek?"

"A bad tooth."

"You ought to get it looked at."

"So I've been told. But the lady at the insurance company acted like I was Cedric the Entertainer opening a bottle of beer when I asked if I had dental coverage."

"She laughed?"

"And not just her. She put me on speakerphone, and soon the whole floor was guffawing."

"So no coverage?"

"Bare naked."

"That's a shame. Look, if you want, I'll schedule another home visit and we can go see the Roses together."

"That would be great."

"I'm not quite sure what's happening with Daniel, and all we're really going on is the anonymous report, but we ought to find out what we can. I'll give you a call."

"Thank you."

"How'd you get this case, anyway?"

"My partner dumped it on my desk."

"You ever do one of these before?"

"No."

"Having fun yet?"

I was watching her walk down the hall when I heard a sharp bark of a voice from behind me.

"It's a double shame, yes it is."

I turned and saw the skinny old man who had been staring at me in the waiting room. His porkpie hat was still on, as was his scowl.

"What's a shame?" I said.

"That someone ugly as you can be plain stupid, too."

I must have misheard. "I'm sorry?"

"Don't you be apologizing," he said, accenting the consonants with a snap of his voice. "It's not your fault you had a mama as ugly as my foot."

"Excuse me?"

"Or a daddy as dumb as my other foot."

"Now, stop that," I said. "I'm the only one who's allowed to insult my daddy."

"You're so ignorant, I bet you think you got a shot at that there girl."

I looked back at Isabel. "And you don't think I do?"

"Son, you got a face good for catching hardballs, and that's about it."

I turned and grinned at him. "I've got a better chance than you, old man."

He took off his hat, spit on his palm, rubbed his hand across the shiny pate of his head as he whistled out of the side of his mouth. "Don't bet against me."

"Victor Carl," I said, reaching out my hand.

"I know who you are, boy," he said as he slapped my hand away. "You think I just insult any damn fool who steps in my way?"

"Why, yes," I said. "I do."

"The name is Horace T. Grant. My friends call me Pork Chop. You can call me sir."

"You were in the army, I suppose."

"Hell yes, but I wasn't a commissioned officer, if that's what you're thinking. I speak out from my mouth and fart out my asshole. With those mixed-up bastards, it was the other way around."

"So what can I do for you, sir?"

"You can buy me a cup of coffee," he said.

And so I did.

Now, this is strange, but absolutely true. I looked up *irascible* in the dictionary and found a picture of Horace T. Grant in his porkpie hat.

"You call this coffee? This isn't coffee. I've had ground donkey bladder tasted better than this."

"Maybe you need a little more sugar."

"Sugar's not going to help this, fool. You ever put sugar on a load of crap?"

"No."

"Well, let me tell you, it doesn't turn it into cake. That's experience, boy, hard won. Now, you might get me one of those muffins if the thought strikes, though I bet it's a rare occasion when a thought strikes your sad excuse for a brain. I bet there's celebrating in the streets, banner headlines, dancing girls up and down Broad Street."

"Do you want the donkey-bladder muffin or the horse-shit muffin?"

"Blueberry. And if they don't got blueberry, cranberry. And if they don't got cranberry, then the hell with them, they don't deserve my business."

"Your business?"

"Get a move on, boy. I don't got all day."

"Yes, sir."

"And another cup of coffee while you're at it."

Why was I subjecting myself to Horace T. Grant when I could find pleasanter ways to bide my time, like wrestling porcupines or pouring hot coffee down my pants? Because I had screwed up. The judge was right to lash my scrawny back with her fierce words. Even if I had never met him, even if he was too young to know who I was or what role I was supposed to play in his life, even if I had never wanted his case in the first place, Daniel Rose was my client and I owed him more than a cursory phone call the day before a hearing. Yes, I had relied on the mother, but if the mother was reliable, I wouldn't be needed in the first place, would I? So I escorted Horace T. Grant to a quaint little storefront in the charming residential area behind the courthouse, I treated him to a coffee, and I now jumped up with alacrity when he asked, in his own sweet way, for a muffin. Partly it was a form of penance, suffering Horace's slings and arrows was surely a penance, but partly it was something else, too. Because Horace had known my name.

"What kind of muffin you say this was?" said Horace T. Grant.

"Cranberry."

"I don't see no berries. Where are the berries? All I see is little red spots. This might as well be a chickenpox muffin. I'm not eating no chickenpox muffin," he said as he took a bite off the muffin top. "Next time you take me someplace right."

"Next time?" I said.

"Oh, yes. You got to make it up to me, taking me here to this hole. I got standards."

"I bet you do. Why don't we talk about what you wanted to talk to me about?"

He looked up at me as he took a sip from his coffee mug. "I got nothing to say to you."

"Then why am I treating you to coffee?"

"Don't ask me. You the one can't wait to flash your wallet, show everyone how fat it is. 'Look at me, look at my wad, see how much I got.' "

I took out my wallet, as thin as a slice of bologna. "That look fat to you?"

"Now you're blaming me for your struggles? It's not my doing you can't make enough money to buy yourself a decent suit. And look at that tie."

"What's wrong with my tie?"

"It's an embarrassment. There's a word you might not be familiar with. Style. It means not that tie."

"Here's a word for you, sir: Daniel Rose."

For the first time in our short acquaintance, Horace T. Grant was close to speechless. But only close. He looked at me, he looked away, he took a swig of coffee and winced at the taste. And then he said, "We talking flowers?"

"No, little boys. Daniel Rose is my client, as you very well know. An anonymous report was made to child welfare about him. I figure it was you who did the reporting. You might pretend to be a hard act, but you cared enough to make the report, and you cared enough to keep up with the proceedings. That's why you were there in the courthouse, that's how you knew my name. You saw me searching for his mother in the waiting room."

"Looking every inch the fool, you were."

"So I'd appreciate your telling me what you can about the boy's situation."

"See, here's the thing about anonymous reports that might have escaped your sterling perspicacity, Mr. Carl. They're anonymous. That's another word, like *style,* that you must have no idea the meaning of."

"So why would the person who made the report want to remain anonymous?"

"Where'd you grow up, boy?"

"Philadelphia."

"Now you're lying to me. Dumb and dishonest, no wonder you're a lawyer."

"Well, to be honest—"

"Don't strain yourself on my behalf."

"I grew up just north of the city, in a little place called Hollywood."

"The suburbs." He exhaled dismissively. "A wasteland for the congenitally unfit. I could tell just by looking at you that you was dumber than an ear of corn. They grow them stupid out there, don't they? Boys from the suburbs can't understand what it's like in the city, how close we all live, one next to the other. How delicate are the relationships between neighbors."

"So you're scared."

"Don't be a pinhead. You seen what I seen in this world, it's not scared you get. But maybe Mr. Anonymous is simply cautious."

"All right. And maybe who he's cautious about is Daniel's mother's boyfriend."

"Listen, fool. Whoever made that report might not know for sure what is going on, might not have any proof of anything. There might simply be concern, a cautious concern."

"Based on what?"

"Neighborhood history. The dramatis personae. You know what that means, or is them words too big for you, too? Well, I'll help you out. Dramatis personae. It means if you're so damn interested, you ought to go visit the boy for yourself."

"I intend to," I said. "But that won't be so easily accomplished. Apparently every time an appointment is set up, the mother isn't home."

"Well, that pretty social worker, each time she shows up, might be going to the wrong house."

"The mother takes the son somewhere and hides to avoid the visit, is that it?"

"Don't be getting any thoughts that you are suddenly some genius, now. Remember your limitations."

"And you might know where she goes to hide?"

"I know a lot more than you'll ever fit in that cement head of yours."

"That I believe," I said, smiling into his scowl. "Can I get you something else, sir?"

"Yes, you can. It's the least you can do, an ungrateful suburban pinhead like yourself. But no more pastry like childhood diseases for me, no chickenpox muffin or measles muffin for me. And no mumps muffin neither, you understand. Next thing you know, my cheeks will be swelled and my thing will fall off, and then I'd be no better off than you."

I bought him another muffin, bran because I thought he could use the fiber, and then I sat and listened to his insults until he decided it was time to give me an address.

I don't usually care much about the package in which money comes. Give it to me in a fancy embossed envelope, a brown paper bag, a check that doesn't bounce, give it to me any way you want, so long as you give it. But I have to admit that when I returned from family court and found a package of money waiting for me in my office, it was the package itself, rather than the cash, that really caught my interest, being it was five foot eight and blond.

She was waiting in the little waiting area in front of my secretary's desk, sitting like a mannequin from Nordstrom. Her back was straight, her ankles crossed, her handbag matched her pumps matched her pearls, oh, my. In her beige linen suit and freakishly unfurrowed brow, she looked cool as cash, even in our overly warm offices, even on the rickety plastic chairs we left out for those waiting to meet with us. Her hair was done the way they do it in only the best cutting joints, as if each strand had been individually washed and colored and trimmed. In all my life, I'd never been as pampered as one lock of her hair. And her lips were plummy.

"Mr. Carl," she said in a soft, breathy voice, standing up when I entered the offices.

"That's right."

"Do you have a minute?"

"Yes, I do."

"Could I meet with you," she said, glancing toward my secretary, Ellie, "in private?"

"Yes, you can," I said, and then I gave Ellie a raise of the eyebrows, a look-what-the-cat-dragged-in look.

The woman's big blue eyes took in the whole of my office as she sat in one of my client chairs. There wasn't much to see. The walls were scuffed, the large brown filing cabinet was dented, piles of files teetered in the corner. Behind where I sat, the small framed photograph of Ulysses S. Grant was askew. In front of me, my desktop was its usual haphazard heap of paper. My first impulse was to apologize for the state of my office, but I stifled it. A woman like this would have been welcome in any lawyer's office in the city, no matter how ritzy the digs or high the hourly fee. She had chosen mine to step into, and it wasn't because of the décor.

"Mr. Carl, you had a meeting two days ago."

"I had a number of meetings two days ago," I said.

"This was one in which a sum of money was discussed."

"You'll have to be more precise, Miss . . ."

"Mrs.," she said.

"Yes," I said. "Of course." The ring was the size of a small dog. "But I didn't catch your name."

"No, you did not," she said, and as she said it, she crossed her legs and smoothed flat her linen skirt. That's when I noticed the tattooed vine of thorns that wound around her ankle.

I liked it, yes I did. I should say that I was more than impressed by the whole package, even if it was obviously out of my league, but it was the tattooed vine of thorns that really got me going, and not just because it was quite the nice slim canvas on which the artist had worked. That it was still there, for me to see, amidst the rest of her high-priced look, was a statement in itself. The tattoo was from an earlier, wilder time, but she hadn't had it removed. It was her way of saying to the world that her voice might not be. naturally breathy, her hair might not be naturally blond, her lips might not be naturally puffy, her eyes might not be naturally blue, there might not be an inch of her body that wasn't varnished and buffed to perfection, but there was still some part of her untamed by money.

"You had a meeting two days ago," she said, "in which you agreed to represent a certain party on condition of the payment of a retainer."

"You're talking about François Dubé."

She pulled the handbag onto her lap, opened it, lifted out a rather thick envelope, and plopped it onto my desk. "I hope this is sufficient."

While restraining myself from grabbing the envelope and dancing a jig as I threw the money up in the air so that it fell gaily all about me like confetti, I said, "Is that the ten thousand?"

"Nine thousand nine hundred."

"My price was ten."

"I didn't think a hundred mattered."

"Oh, it matters," I said.

She let a trace of amusement curve her lips and then reached into her handbag for her wallet. From the wallet she pulled out five new twenties as if she were pulling out lint and gently tucked them inside the envelope.

"Although, to be honest," I said, "I'd prefer a check."

"Really? I thought you'd be a cash-and-carry type of fellow."

Suddenly I wasn't so entranced. Some people act like they're doing you the favor of your life when they pay you what you're owed.

"You thought wrong," I said. "Cash creates all kinds of accounting problems, cash deposits and withdrawals make the bank uncomfortable, as you surely know, since you withdrew only as much as you could without triggering the bank's reporting requirements. But whatever you might have thought, we run an honest business here. We like our funds accounted for. I'll need a check."

"Will a cashier's check do?"

"Personal check."

"That won't be possible."

I sat back, lifted a foot onto the edge of my desk, looked at her very carefully. She had been rude to me, and I didn't like that, but she wasn't enjoying herself. There was something wrong. "Who are you to François Dubé?"

"It's not important."

"For me to accept the funds, I need to know why you are paying his retainer."

"I have my reasons."

"You're going to have to tell them to me."

She lifted the envelope off the desk. "I'm not here to talk. Here's the money, Mr. Carl. Take it or leave it."

"I think I'll leave it."

She threw her head back as if she had smelled something repugnant. Me, I supposed.

"It was a pleasure meeting you, Mrs. Whatever," I said, dropping my foot down, turning my attention to the mess on my desktop. I pulled out a piece of paper, some meaningless letter, and took a pen to it. "My secretary will see you out."

"But what about your client?"

"He's not my client until I get paid."

"And I'm trying to pay you."

I looked up. "But you're not trying hard enough. Why don't we start with names? Welcome to the firm of Derringer and Carl. I'm Victor Carl, and you are . . ."

"Velma Takahashi," she said.

I leaned back. "Very good. Takahashi, huh? How do I know that name?"

"My husband's deals are often in the papers."

"Samuel Takahashi, the real estate mogul?"

"Not quite a mogul."

"Quite enough. And you don't want to pay with a check, which means you don't want a record of the payment that might get back to your husband."

"Did someone beat you in the face with a clever stick, Mr. Carl? Is that why your cheek is swollen?"

"This is fun, isn't it, communicating like human beings? I ask pertinent questions, you give me reasonable facsimiles of answers along with your insults. Next thing you know, we'll be square-dancing together."

"I don't do-si-do."

"People do all sorts of things they never expected. Your being in my office, for one. Now, Mrs. Takahashi, what is your relationship with François Dubé?"

"I have no relationship with François Dubé. He's the worst type of scoundrel."

"But you're paying ten thousand dollars to get him out of jail."

"My feelings for him, however bitter they may be, are beside the point. I was a friend of Leesa's since well before her marriage."

"And you think it a friendly gesture to pay for the defense of the man convicted of her murder."

"I think it's what she would have wanted."

"Now, that's a lie. I don't half believe a word you've said from the moment I laid eyes on you, Mrs. Takahashi, including the Mrs. and the Takahashi, but *this* I know is a lie. Leesa Dubé was in a bitter custody fight; she was making brutal accusations against her husband. The one thing that would have cheered her about her own murder was that because of it her husband was sentenced to spend the rest of his life behind bars."

"You didn't know her, Mr. Carl. She wasn't like that. In the end it was bitter, true, but he was the father of her daughter. She was too sweet to have wanted him in prison forever for something he didn't do."

She was right about one thing, at least, I didn't know Leesa Dubé, didn't know the first thing about her, and was wrong to imply a viciousness that might not have been there.

"So if this is what Leesa would have wanted," I said, "then for some reason you must believe he's not guilty?"

"I'm running late."

I leaned forward, examined her closely. "You really do, don't you?"

She snapped her bag closed, stood. "I have an appointment. Take the money, Mr. Carl. Do what you can for François."

"You know something."

"I need to go."

"Tell me what you know."

"I can't, please, believe me. I simply can't."

And it was there, just for a single precious moment, there, behind the mask, the swollen lips and frownless forehead, the perfect hair, the perfect skin, the blue contact lenses. There, behind the finest facade that money could buy, I saw something striking. It was the woman she had been, the woman who had gotten the tattoo and palled around with Leesa Dubé before falling into a morass of money that seemed to have swallowed her whole. This woman was wild, wildly ambitious, this woman was too smart by half for what she had become. And there, yes there, I could spy some terrible burden in her eyes. Was it sadness? Was it regret? Was it, perhaps, a crushing guilt that was tearing her apart?

It would be interesting to find out, wouldn't it?

I reached over, took the envelope, riffled through the bills.

"You understand, Mrs. Takahashi," I said as I performed my quick count, "that this retainer covers only our motion. If we are successful, we'll need another retainer to handle the trial."

"Then let's hope we meet again."

"Yes," I said. "Let's hope." Let's hope indeedy. "My secretary will give you a receipt for the cash."

"I don't need a receipt."

"Maybe you don't, but I still need to give you one. We have a rule here, anyone who drops off a load of cash and isn't given a receipt gets a free frozen yogurt his next visit."

I walked her out of my office, waited behind her while Ellie typed up a receipt, smelled her rich, sweet scent, felt myself swoon. See, even with all the lies she had told, even with all the enhancements to her beauty, I couldn't help but breathe in her fragrance and feel my stomach flutter. Let me tell you true, the only thing more enticing than raw natural beauty is rampant, raging artificiality.

Back in my office, I pulled the wad out of the envelope, fanned the bills just for the feel of it, and then performed a more careful count. I wasn't beyond running down the street, calling out *Oh, Mrs. Takahashi, Mrs. Takahashi* if she was so much as a twenty short. But she wasn't short. Ten thousand dollars. Not a bad way to start the day.

I pulled a card out of my shirt pocket. My share would be enough to pay for a visit to the dentist, I figured, even without insurance. I could now afford to have Dr. Pfeffer, miracle worker, perform a miracle on my tooth. But wouldn't you know it? My tooth was suddenly feeling so much better. Money has that way, doesn't it, of easing your worldly pains? So maybe the ache was more existential than dental, maybe it had less to do with the condition of my tooth and more with the sad condition of my life. And the answer might be to dig into the past of the very wealthy Velma Takahashi instead of digging into my gums. I put the card away and put in a call to my detective, Phil Skink.

It was getting interesting, this case I didn't want, this futile motion on behalf of a defendant I disliked. First Whitney Robinson had grabbed hold of me at the end of our meeting and, whispering as if every word he said were being overheard, had begged me to leave this case be. *For your own sake,* he had said, whatever that meant. *You can't imagine the price*, he had said, though he didn't say the price for whom. And then Velma Takahashi, as pretty and as false as the Vargas pinups I had drooled over as an adolescent, Velma Takahashi had dropped a wad of bills on my desk and begged me to help François Dubé, even as she held back, for reasons of her own, a secret about the murder. It was getting oh, so interesting. All I needed now was a way to convince the judge to overturn a guilty verdict three years old, the appeals of which had all been denied, and where no new evidence or new suspects had emerged. It would be a hell of a trick.

And damn if I didn't know where to start.

"His name was Seamus Dent," I said to Beth as we drove north through the city. "He was the witness who put François Dubé at the scene of the crime."

We were heading into an insular, working-class part of town. North of Kensington, south of Center City, hard by the river, a piece of Philadelphia but a place all its own. The name pretty much said it all: union town, scrapple town, tavern town, Fishtown.

"I thought you told me he was dead," said Beth. "It sounds like whatever use he could have been to us in getting a new trial died with him."

"You would think. Except Whit told me something that grabbed my attention. Apparently Seamus was killed during a drug deal not too long after he testified. But drug use wasn't brought up in his cross-examination."

"You think your friend Whit might have missed something at trial?"

"I don't know. The kid had no record, but you're not clean one day and mixed up in some drug deal gone bad the next. Why was he on the street that night? What was he looking for? Was he using at the time? All that stuff could have destroyed his credibility on cross. And because he was admittedly in the neighborhood, and maybe desperate for a fix, he might have become a suspect himself."

"But even if true, that won't be enough to get François a new trial, will it?"

"That's the thing. The case law is pretty clear. You can't use new evidence that might have affected the credibility of a witness to get a new trial."

"So what's the point?"

"Something just doesn't seem right here, does it? Why didn't Whit know? Who was hiding what? I have a feeling, that's all. Do you have a better place to start?"

"No," she said, shaking her head. "But it's not much of a start."

"Well, Beth, to tell you the truth, it's not much of a case."

We pulled into a narrow residential street with mismatched houses jammed cheek by jowl into an eclectic row. I checked the notes I'd made, searched the addresses on the buildings, found the house I was looking for. I parked right in front.

As I was ringing the bell of a small gray row house, a woman sitting on a stoop three doors down called out, "Who you here for?"

I stepped back, eyed the gray house up and down as I said, "We're looking for a Mrs. Dent."

"What you want with her?"

"We've got some questions."

"What about?"

I turned to the woman who spoke to me, annoyed at her prying. She was young, heavy, wearing a blue smock. Beside her sat another woman, rail thin, with short red hair, her elbows on her knees, staring at me with unblinking eyes as she smoked a cigarette. A third woman sat on the step above them. Three nosy neighbors, spending their days talking about laundry soaps and passing recipes, neighborhood gossip, the occasional bottle. I squinted and considered them carefully. A regular coffee klatch, sometimes just the thing when you're looking for information.

"We want to ask her about her son," I said, glancing once more at the nonresponsive house before walking over to them, Beth at my side.

"Good Lord," said the heavy woman. "What kind of trouble is Henry in now?"

"Not Henry," I said. "Seamus."

"Seamus is dead," croaked out the woman with the cigarette and the short red hair, and there was something in the way she said it, something bitter and sad and not matter-of-fact at all.

Beth heard it, too, because she said, "Are you Mrs. Dent?"

"What are you, cops?" said the woman sitting behind the other two. She was small, with nervous hands and bright eyes. It was still morning, but it didn't look as if that had stopped her.

"Do we look like cops?" I said.

"She does," said the third woman, pointing at Beth.

I stepped back, turned toward Beth, crossed my arms, and examined her as if I were examining a sculpture of Beth as created by Duane Hanson. "Really, now? And what makes her look like a cop?"

"That station-house pallor," said the nervous woman.

"Excuse me," said Beth.

"And those eyes."

"What's wrong with my eyes?"

"You might be right," I said. "She is rather pale, and her eyes are shifty."

"My eyes are not shifty, they're attractively cautious. What about him?" said Beth, sticking her thumb at me.

"He's too soft," said the woman. "He looks like he sells insurance."

"Or maybe a high-school guidance counselor," said Beth. "Does that fit?"

"Could be. Is that what he is?"

"No," said Beth.

"You aren't Mrs. Dent, are you?" I said to the woman with the cigarette.

She looked at me a long moment, took a last drag, dropped the cigarette, and crushed it beneath her sneaker. "No," she said. "Betty's away on vacation."

"Any idea where?"

"She has a sister in California."

"How long is she supposed to be gone?"

"She didn't say, but I wouldn't hold my breath, if I was you."

"Henry's looking after the house," said the heavy woman, "which is like letting a fat swine run free in your garden."

"Henry's a big guy?"

"Oh, he's hurly-burly, he is."

"And he's trouble, is that it?"

"Double trouble. All them Dent boys were."

"Including Seamus?" I said.

The woman with the red hair lit another cigarette. "The worst of the three, you ask me," she said.

I looked at Beth, raised an eyebrow.

"Him and his friends," said the third woman. "They were like a pack of wolves."

"Who, the Dent boys?" said Beth.

"No, Seamus and his two friends, the second Harbaugh boy, Wayne, and then Kylie."

"Seamus, Wayne, and Kylie," I said. "The terrible trio. What kind of things did they do? Pranks and stuff? Light bags of dog poop on fire and then ring the doorbells?"

"That the kind of stuff you did as a boy?" asked the red-haired woman.

"I just did that yesterday in Chestnut Hill."

"Aren't you something wicked."

"They were just bad, those kids," said the nervous woman

sitting above the other two. "Sneaking places, stealing, sex and drugs. Even when they were young, they were trouble. But the drugs, well, you know, that just ruins you." She spoke like she remembered what she was talking about, like she wouldn't mind a drink to forget.

"The police had them in their sights, I suppose," I said. "Always coming around."

"Not till the end. Them kids was too smart to get caught, even when everyone knew it was them."

"And Seamus was the ringleader," I said.

"No," said the red-haired woman with the cigarette. "It was Kylie."

"Any idea where we could find her, this Kylie?"

"None," said the woman. "She's gone."

Again there was that thing in her voice, like a bitter lozenge that had been stuck in her throat for a decade. I looked closely at the woman, she looked away. "You're Kylie's mother, aren't you?" I said. "I can tell just by the way you speak about her with so much affection."

"We have history."

"And you have no idea where she is?"

"Don't care neither. But I can tell you this, mister, wherever she is, she's on her back."

"Sweet. Member of the PTA, were you?"

"Who'd you say you was?"

"I don't think I did."

"Why are you so interested in Seamus?" said the heavy woman.

"It's my profession to be interested. I'm a lawyer, that means I'm greedy and I'm nosy."

"Then you'd fit right in around here," she said, and the three of them laughed.

"How about that Wayne you mentioned? Is he still around?"

"He works at the church," said the third woman.

"What is he, the priest?"

"The janitor."

"I suppose you have to start somewhere. You mentioned that the police didn't come around until the end. What did you mean, the end?"

"After Seamus was killed," said Kylie's mom. "A detective come around to talk to Betty. I think his name was same as the fat guy on that old TV show."

"Detective Gleason?"

"Right. He told Betty they had found the guy who did it."

"Was there a trial?"

"Wouldn't have been much use, seeing as the one who did it ended up with a bullet through the head."

"About time the cops did something for this neighborhood," said the heavy woman, laughing, and the other two joined in.

That was enough for me. Good, sweet neighborhood ladies laughing about a bullet in the head. If I ever spent my life sitting on a stoop, spilling gossip to the passersby, you might as well save the bullet for me.

I thought about what they had said, turned to look at the empty Dent house once again. "She go away much, this Betty Dent? Always traveling?"

"Nope," said the heavy one. "Barely left this street the whole of her life."

"So how'd she get to California? She drive?"

"Flew. I drove her to the airport myself."

"When?"

"Just a day or two ago."

"She say how she got a ticket?"

"Said she just got it."

"Nice for her." I took out three cards from my wallet, passed them out. "My name is Victor Carl. Anything you can remember about Seamus, about the things he did or any troubles he had with the police, especially that, I'd appreciate hearing from you."

"Don't hold your breath on that one neither," said Kylie's mom.

We could hear their cackling as we walked away.

"Why do I feel," I said, "like I just walked out of a scene from *Macbeth*?"

CHAPTER 10

"**How long do** you suppose they've been sitting on that stoop?" said Beth as we drove through the narrow streets of Fishtown.

"From the dawn of time," I said. "They've buried kings, presidents, husbands, Seamus Dent. And they'll bury us if we give them half a chance and half a bullet."

"It took us, what, about thirty seconds to pry the Seamus Dent story from them?"

"If that. Another twenty minutes we would have had the sexual history of the entire block, and the parish priest, too."

"So why didn't Whitney Robinson come down here and ask those same ladies about Seamus Dent before François's trial?"

"Good question," I said. "Whit was a sharp lawyer and knew what he was doing. Maybe he did come down, learned what he could, and decided it wasn't reliable or admissible."

"But he didn't tell you about it."

"No, he did not. So that's one puzzle we need to figure out. And I sure would like to know who sent Betty Dent a plane ticket to California right after we took the case. That's the church over there."

We parked on Gaul Street, just across from the church, a Romanesque stone structure with the requisite stained-glass window showing Jesus first carrying the cross and then nailed to it. On our side of the street was the school and a shrine to Our Lady of Knock. I was about to make a crack to Beth about the name and then stopped, because the shrine was beautiful and heartfelt and I'd heard enough jokes for the morning.

The church inside was tinted with the blues and reds from the stained-glass window. Heavy columns ran down both sides of the interior, leading to a lovely painted altar. The pews were burnished wood, the confessionals were not too ornate, the wood beneath the flickering candles was spattered with wax, and there was that solemn hush that always follows you into an empty church.

A woman was in the front, straightening the altar. She watched us as we entered, watched as we walked up the aisle toward her. She was older, with curly white hair, a long skirt, and sneakers.

"Can I help you?" she said.

"We're looking for Wayne Harbaugh," said Beth.

She tilted her head and looked us up and down for a moment, gave me an extra eyeful, like she knew my type, and then asked us to wait.

"I always feel weird in a Catholic church," I told Beth as we sat side by side in the front pew. "Like I'm infiltrating behind enemy lines."

"It's just a church."

"To you maybe, yes, raised as you were in the warm embrace of Christianity. But to me, I'm always wondering when I'll be identified as a Jew and beaten about the head and shoulders until I run out screaming."

"The Inquisition ended"—she checked her watch—"something like five hundred years ago."

"Still," I said, "it's been known to happen."

"What do you think, Victor, people look at you and only see a Jew?"

"I swear that lady was giving me the eye."

"She's a nun, she gives everyone the eye."

"Don't they have to wear those habits?"

"Not anymore."

"Is that fair? How can we tell who's who?"

"For your information, then," she said, standing and indicating a ruddy-faced man coming into the chapel, his collar turned around, "that is a priest."

"Yes, hello. Welcome to the Holy Name. I'm Father Kenneth. And what, pray tell, can we do for you today?"

Father Kenneth was short and solid and energetic, with a ready smile that put you immediately at ease. He didn't look at me like I was an infiltrator, he looked at me like I was a friend waiting to do his parish some great good.

"We understand a man named Wayne Harbaugh works here," said Beth.

"Yes, that's true. Wayne is an employee."

"We were hoping we could have just a few words with him."

"Is there a problem of some sort?"

"Is he here today?" said Beth rather curtly.

"Yes, he is," said the priest, still smiling. "He is currently at work in the school." He paused for emphasis, widened his smile. "With the children, you see. Has Wayne done something wrong?"

"No, not at all," I said, giving Beth a warning look. There was no need to come on like, well, like cops. Maybe she did have more of the cop in her than I had imagined. I introduced Beth and myself, gave the priest a card.

"So you're lawyers," said Father Kenneth. "It's never a good sign, is it, when a lawyer steps through your door?"

"I could have news of a huge bequest left to Wayne in a will."

"But you don't, do you, Mr. Carl?"

"No. We just want to ask him a few questions about an old friend of his."

"And who is the friend, may I ask?"

"Seamus Dent."

The father nodded, pressed his thin lips together. "Poor Seamus. He was baptized here, along with his brothers. He was actually a sweet boy, if you got to know him. You should have heard him play the guitar. Magic. What happened to him was a tragedy."

"You mean his murder?"

"Yes, and before that, too. His problems. The way his life veered off track. Although it looked as though things were coming around just before he died."

I glanced at Beth, puzzled. "How so?"

"He looked to be clean, Mr. Carl. He was the one who brought Wayne here and convinced me to give him this job. Seamus had rededicated his life, he told me, for the good of the world. A bit ambitious, but we all need ambition. So for him to lapse like he did, and then be murdered like he was, made it doubly tragic."

"Could we talk to Wayne about Seamus?" said Beth.

The father pressed his hands together, pressed his forefingers into his lips, considered. "Why are you interested in Seamus?"

"We represent a man who was convicted of murder, partly on Seamus's testimony," she said. "We're investigating every aspect of the case, and that means we need to learn as much about the witnesses as we can."

"This man you represent, is he currently in jail?"

"With a life sentence," said Beth.

"Of course, yes, I see now the cause of your concern. That's why you are such an adamant young woman. Okay, Ms. Derringer, I'll have Wayne brought around. Do you think he ought to have a lawyer of his own present?"

"That really won't be necessary," I said. "We just want to talk about Seamus. To get a sense of him. Wayne is not personally involved at all."

"You won't mind, though, of course, Mr. Carl, if I sit in just to be sure."

"Do you know anything about the law, Father?"

He winked. "Everything I know about the law I learned from *Matlock*."

"Funny," I said, "same with me." I glanced at Beth and then shrugged. "Be our guest, Father."

He brought us into a dark, book-lined room off to the side of the altar. A series of robes hung on hooks along one wall, a semicircle of leather-upholstered chairs was set up in front of a small desk against another. He bade us sit, made a call, then sat behind the desk and stared at us. He leaned forward slightly and opened his mouth as if to say something, as if to start some sort of conversation, and then gave a shrug. What was there to say, after all? We waited quietly until the door opened.

The man who came in was painfully thin, with dark, sunken eyes and a scraggly beard. He was wearing jeans and a T-shirt, a blue baseball cap. When he saw Beth and me, in our suits, sitting with Father Kenneth, he took off his baseball cap and clutched it with both hands, tucking his jaw in to his shoulder at the same time. He looked like a boxer on shaky legs, awaiting the knockout blow.

"Wayne," said Father Kenneth, "these people are lawyers and want to ask you a few questions."

"I didn't do nothing."

"We know that, son. Why don't you close the door behind you and take a seat."

Wayne Harbaugh glanced uneasily at us before shutting the door and sitting on the edge of one of the chairs, still clutching his hat.

"Wayne," said the father, "they want to know about Seamus."

"What about him?"

"He testified at the trial of a man accused of murdering his wife," I said. "Do you remember that?"

Wayne looked even more uneasy, if that was possible. "Yeah," he said. "I remember. He told me about it."

"What did he tell you?"

"Just that lawyers made him nervous."

"Like we make you nervous?"

"Sort of."

"I wonder, Wayne, if you could just tell us a little about Seamus. Was he basically honest, dishonest? Did he tell the truth most of the time?"

"Go ahead, Wayne," said Father Kenneth. "Tell Mr. Carl if Seamus told the truth most of the time."

"I suppose he did," said Wayne, "but not when it counted."

I sat forward, glanced at Beth, who looked back with wide eyes.

"What do you mean?" I said.

"When it counted most, he was the biggest liar there ever was."

"Wayne?" said Father Kenneth. "He was your friend, son. Your oldest friend."

"But he said we was in it together, and that was a lie, wasn't it, Father Ken? He betrayed you, didn't he, by getting back in it? And he betrayed me just the same."

"Why don't you tell us about it, Wayne?" I said.

"From when?"

"From the start," I said.

He looked at Father Kenneth, who stared at him closely for a moment and then nodded.

"Then I'll have to talk about her," said Wayne.

"Go ahead, son," said the father.

Wayne closed his eyes and paused for a moment, and when his voice came out, it was stronger now, younger. "Because it was really about her, all about her," he said. "Everything was always all about Kylie."

And then he told his story, hesitant at first, later less so, as if there was some compulsion to get it off his soul. As he sat in the vestry, with Father Kenneth nodding, it flowed out almost like a confession. And to tell you the truth, I wasn't surprised to hear Kylie's name arise like a specter to haunt the dramatic twists and turns of Wayne Harbaugh's story. I had heard what the witches on the stoop said of her, I had met her mother. I didn't yet know the role she would play, Kylie, sweet Kylie, but I sensed from the start that whatever had happened to Wayne and Seamus, she was in the middle of it.

But there was someone else involved in the story, too, haunting the edges, shaping the outcome like a demented director with his clapboard and megaphone. I didn't yet recognize him there. How could I? My first meeting with him was still in the future. But there he was. Look close as the tale unfolds. Do you see him? Do you see Bob?

CHAPTER 11

His earliest memories were of the three of them, running through the streets, the alleyways, playing hand games during church, rock paper scissors, the slap of Seamus's two fingers on his wrist during the homilies, the feel of Kylie's whisper in his ear as she plotted some daring piece of mischief. His mother surely suckled him, his father surely beat him, his sisters surely teased him and tickled him till he cried, but his family was something he suffered through until he could be with his friends. It was Seamus, Kylie, and Wayne, the three of them, always and forever, the trio at the heart of his life.

And he remembered, too, when they first discovered the old textile plant on the other side of the railroad tracks, in the shadow of the highway. As second-graders, they found that the plywood on one low window was shattered enough to climb through, and they spun around on the filthy factory floor, spinning in freedom with their arms stretched wide, until they were dizzy and collapsed laughing.

"Don't tell anyone," said Kylie. "This will be ours."

"Our secret fort," said Wayne.

And Seamus nodded, and Kylie laughed, and so they laid claim to the dank old place, and it became more home to them than their homes. Clubhouse, playground, sanctuary. The fort. The roof had collapsed, letting in, along with the pigeons, sufficient daylight so they could see comfortably during the day and allowing the smoke from their fires to rise out at night. And this is where they went, the three of them, Seamus, Kylie, and Wayne, to laugh, to play games, to tell stories, to smoke cigarettes when they were older, to drink beer and blow dope when they were older still.

Wayne was the wiry one, the funny one, quick with the joke or the rib. Seamus was bigger, yet meeker, less physical, more sensitive. Ashamed of his teeth, he would never smile, and with the dark beneath his eyes, he always appeared on the verge of tears. Kylie was the spark, pretty and slight. With her dark hair and darker eyes, she was the one with the ideas, the one who could make things happen, a girl full of fun and guile, able to look like the sweetest, most innocent thing on the outside while full of troubling schemes on the inside. And she liked to steal, shivered at the thrill.

She was the one who started them on shoplifting at the corner store, getting Wayne and Seamus to divert the old storekeeper while she stuffed cupcakes and candy down her skirt. And she was the one who started them on stealing bicycles from any kids who happened to leave them lying around unlocked. There were a dozen bicycles, useless and rusting, their tires flat, their bars covered in pigeon dung, leaning against the walls of the fort, a futuristic sculpture of decay. And she was the one who convinced Seamus to stand like a ladder before the open windows of empty houses so . she and Wayne could slip in at night or during the shank of the afternoon to grab anything they found lying around. That's how Seamus got the guitar he played incessantly back at the fort, how Wayne got the leather jacket that was way too big for him, how Kylie got hold of her first pack of cigarettes, swiping a whole carton from a kitchen on Palmer Street.

You could tell she was troubled, Kylie, the way she

never ate and got all scrawny, the way she came to the fort with scabs up and down her arms. The first time, she said it was an accident, and after that first time they didn't talk about it anymore. And you could see the need in her in the way she smoked her cigarettes. Once they got that first pack, and she felt the nicotine rush flow through her like a gift, she was obsessed with getting them, lighting them, smoking them. She inhaled so furiously it was as if she wanted to turn her whole body into ash. There was always a cigarette between her fingers, and she was always scrounging around for another one, and she always needed money to buy them, always.

Then, when they started with the beer, stealing first a couple bottles from Wayne's father, it wasn't long before Kylie, her eyes rimmed dark with mascara, was waiting in front of the Chinese take-out place, asking the male customers if they'd take her money and buy her a six-pack. Kylie liked to drink, she drank fast—while they were still cold, she said—and often until she got sick. One corner of the fort, next to the bikes, held a veritable mountain of cans and bottles.

But it was the reefer that changed everything for Wayne. And not just because it turned out to be the best of all ways to waste their days. Or because it started to get expensive, which forced them to be more brazen in their thefts. Or because Kylie took to it as if in marihuana she found what she had been looking for all along. No, for Wayne it was the reefer that changed everything, because it was under its influence that he first realized the truth of their relationship, one to the other.

They were the best of friends, that's how they saw themselves, more like a family than their families themselves, brothers and sister to one another. And they discussed openly among themselves their boy-girl escapades. Seamus was pretty much useless with the opposite sex, but Wayne was sort of dating Erin McGill and had already been to third with her in Palmer Park. And Kylie always had boys chasing her, boys she would tease and play with and let play with her and then mock back at the fort with Wayne and Seamus as the three got wasted on beer.

But reefer felt different. They were twelve the first time they tried it, when Henry had given Wayne a couple of joints to get him started, and when they lit the first one, Seamus and Kylie went off into a fit of giggling, which pissed Wayne off, because nothing seemed to be happening to him. But the second time, when he hogged the reefer just to make sure it would have some effect, it hit him hard, the dizziness, the fear and paranoia. He closed his eyes, felt the world shift beneath him, feared he'd never recover, that what he had done to himself was permanent. He tried to get control, to fight off the nausea, and when he did, finally, when he opened his eyes, finally, it was as if the world had indeed changed.

He could see things he had never seen before. Kylie looked different, her pretty dark eyes, outlined by the mascara, were sadder than he ever remembered. And Seamus looked different, too, bigger, more handsome, as unreal as a movie actor, playing his guitar as if it were a part of him. And strangest of all, the air between them seemed to shimmer, as if something never before glimpsed had turned hard and real. When Kylie looked at Seamus, and Seamus looked back, it was as if Wayne could see exactly the emotion running between them, and he knew what it was, instantly. It was love. Seamus loved Kylie; Kylie loved Seamus. And the reality of it seemed to settle like a sharp pain into Wayne's chest. And that was the first time, believe it or not, that Wayne realized, Erin McGill notwithstanding, that he himself was helplessly and hopelessly in love with Kylie, and that Seamus was not just a friend but an adversary.

He couldn't tell her. How could he tell her? Kylie was his friend, more sister than his sisters, and then there was Seamus, who was always around when Wayne was with her. And what would he say anyway? So he didn't tell her. Instead, back at the fort, they got high, or wasted on beer when they couldn't afford the dope, and listened to Seamus play, and rolled around laughing at the rest of the world or poked sullenly at the fires they built at night.

The new plan for getting dope money came to them out of the blue. Kylie was waiting outside the Chinese joint, searching for someone to buy a six-pack for them, when the guy she propositioned, propositioned her right back. Her mind was quick enough to figure out the angle straightaway. She motioned to Seamus and Wayne before leading the man down the street, around the corner, over the railroad tracks, to the fort. And then, just when the creep thought he was going to get some underage action, the boys went at him, Wayne especially. They sent him away, bloodied and broke, and split between them two hundred dollars. It was so simple, so obvious, so safe, because the mark could never go to the police, could he? The next time it didn't just happen, the next time Kylie cast her gaze like a weighted bass plug and reeled in a mark, and it went off as smooth as the pale skin on her lovely cheek.

And the thing of it, for Wayne, was that it excited him more than he wanted to admit, even to himself. Yes, he liked the huge boom box they bought with the money and kept down at the fort, and yes, he liked being high, like, all the time, but it was the thrill of it that hooked him, different from the other thieving they had done. The angry spurt of jealousy he felt when he saw the mark trying to make his Kylie. The fear that roiled his stomach as he and Seamus followed them across the railroad tracks to the patch of weeds outside the fort, not ever sure how the violence would unfold. The raw thrill of saving Kylie, the girl he loved, from some older man who was putting his hands on her, pulling her close, stroking her hair and rubbing her thigh and bringing his crusty lips close to her innocent mouth. And the fear on the mark's face, yes, that, too, when they pulled him away, and began to rain on blows, and stripped him of his wallet, and stripped his wallet of cash.

And Wayne would always remember the look on Kylie's face, flushed and triumphant and proud, and maybe disappointed, too, though that he didn't understand. And then the way they sat together around the fire at the fort and smoked and laughed and hugged and were as they always were.

Until the one time it didn't play out like they had planned. When they followed Kylie and the mark, and the mark started fiddling with her hair, started stroking her leg, drew her close, bent down to bury his face in her neck. They rushed in to pull them apart, but she stared at Wayne and Seamus, stared at them with dead eyes, and mouthed to them, clear as chalk on slate, "Go away." And they did what she said, as they always did what she said, they left, the two of them, left her with the man, left like whipped dogs.

Wayne wanted to go back, to stop it, to stop her, but it was Seamus who kept him away. "It's what she wants," he said.

"She doesn't want him," said Wayne.

"Or us, or anything," said Seamus. "She wants only nothing. This is just like the cutting and the drugs. But there's nothing we can do about it, Wayne. There never has been."

And so they stayed back, out of sight, just hearing the rude calls of the mark who wasn't a mark anymore but had become a john. And when it was over, Wayne followed him back across the tracks and fell on him like a wolf and beat him bloody, beat him unconscious, beat him until Seamus pulled Wayne and his red fists off the lifeless figure.

That got the police involved. The man wasn't dead, but it

was close, and all of Fishtown was talking about it. And what they were talking about was that it was the three of them, the trio of degenerate friends, that had done it. The police brought them in, and put them in separate rooms, and laid into them like they were cop killers on the lam. But they said not a word. Wayne's knuckles had been scraped playing basketball. Seamus had been playing basketball with Wayne that afternoon when Wayne fell on the concrete and ripped up his hand. Kylie didn't know anything about it. And the guy was an outsider, and pretty soon some other horrific act of violence came to sweep up the neighborhood's attention, and that was that. Nothing but suspicions.

But that was the end of them, the end of the trio, the end of the fort. They all knew that something had turned, and now beer or reefer or even sex wasn't enough. So Kylie went off in search of something harder to help her escape from what had become of her life, something that would more easily take her out of herself, and Seamus and Wayne, they went along for the ride. For if that's what she wanted, self-obliteration, that's what they wanted, too.

And it wasn't so hard to find.

CHAPTER

12

"After a while we sort of drifted apart, the three of us," said Wayne. "The connections just seemed to disappear."

"What were you on, son?" said Father Kenneth.

Wayne rolled his shoulders guiltily. "Everything. Pills, cocaine, reefer laced with embalming fluid we swiped from the funeral home."

"My God," said Father Kenneth.

"Not bad, actually, if you could get over the taste," said Wayne. "And then heroin."

"Was Seamus on heroin, too?" I asked.

"We started together. That's what made what happened so strange."

"Him getting killed by a drug dealer? That doesn't sound so strange at all."

"No," said Wayne. "Before that."

I looked at Father Kenneth. Through the whole of Wayne's sad, lurid tale, I had been expecting the father to explode in some sort of righteous condemnation. But that hadn't happened. Instead he had kept a benign expression on his face, showing only the measure of disapproval required of his position at the more troubling points, enough to say that the story had registered, not so much to discourage Wayne from continuing. He was good, the good father, I had to give him that. Probably had plenty of experience in the confessional, but still it was impressive.

"Tell us about it, Wayne," said Father Kenneth. "Tell us what Seamus did."

"There was an addict name of Poison, a big guy with this sort of electric gaze that drew to him the most desperate losers on the street. Which is how I fell in with him. He had contacts with some dealers, and he could keep you supplied so long as you stayed with his program. But his program was mostly about following his orders and taking the risks for his risky schemes and letting him hit you when he wanted, which was pretty much all the time. But you couldn't just walk away from Poison. Once you were in, that was it, he'd kill you sooner than let you walk away, and he had done it once, right in front of us. Stuck his knife into some guy's gut.

"Now, I hadn't seen Seamus for over a year. I had heard things, though. I heard some old poof had sort of taken him up, was keeping him off the street. He even had arranged to get Seamus's teeth fixed. It sounded worse than Poison to me, and I didn't know that Seamus was like that, a boy toy. But, you know, when you're desperate like we were, anything goes, and I figured he had followed Kylie down that route. So I had written off Seamus. I figured I'd never see him again.

"And then one night we were in the fort, Poison and his crew. It was a cold snap, and I had showed Poison our old place so we could build a fire to stay warm. And we were huddled around this fire, the crew, strung out, talking about our next scam, when this shadow just appears in the doorway. You couldn't make out anything but the outline. It was tall, wide, and it was wearing this long coat that almost reached to the ground. And then the shadow talked.

" 'I'm looking for a piece of scum called Poison,' it said.

"Poison scurried out of the light of the fire and said, 'What do you want with him?'

" 'I have a proposition,' said the shadow. 'It can be worth some money to him.'

" 'Go ahead,' said Poison.

" 'Not until I know who I'm dealing with,' said the shadow.

" 'All right,' said Poison, and he was standing now, with his hand in his coat pocket, and he stepped forward until his ugly, scarred face was lit by the fire. 'How much?'

" 'Five hundred dollars,' said the shadow.

" 'All for me? What do I need to do for it?'

" 'Nothing,' said the shadow. 'I just want to take away one of your gang without you giving me trouble.' And the shadow stepped forward into the circle of light from the fire, and it was Seamus. Like he was stepping toward me from out of a dream. And he said, 'I want to take away Wayne.'

"Poison looked over at me with a sneer and said, 'Wayne's with us.'

" 'Not anymore,' said Seamus.

" 'Do you have the money on you?' said Poison.

"Seamus took an envelope out of his pocket. Poison stepped forward to reach for it. Seamus jerked it back. 'Do we have a deal?' he said.

" 'We'll have to discuss it some,' said Poison with an eerie smile plastered on his ugly face, but just as he said it, his hand jerked out of his coat pocket and he charged at Seamus, the fire shining in the knife's long blade.

"Seamus turned sideways and kicked him in the face. Poison went spinning to the ground, his knife flying out of his hand. When Poison raised himself onto his knees, Seamus kicked him in the face again. Jesus, he just wiped him out. Then he looked around at the crew, saw me, and said, 'Let's go, Wayne.' And I went. And he brought me here, to you, Father Kenneth. Do you remember?"

"I remember," said Father Kenneth, nodding. "And we cleaned you up, bought you some clothes, and got you into a treatment program. But it was you who did the hard work. It was you who stuck with it."

"Because Seamus visited and told me I had to. Because Seamus told me there was something golden on the other side."

"And was he right?" asked Father Kenneth.

"What do you think, Father?"

"I think you've come a long way."

"But if it was so golden, why did Seamus get back into the life? Why did he get himself killed like that?"

"I don't know, son," said Father Kenneth. "I don't know."

"And that's why you think you were betrayed?" I said.

"He left me here alone," said Wayne. "Without him."

"Who was the old man who had helped him?" I said. "Did you ever find out?"

"No," said Wayne. "He didn't want to tell me anything about him, and I understood. That kind of thing, who would want to talk about it?"

"Was Seamus always a good fighter?"

"Hardly. He was one of those big, timid guys."

"It didn't sound like he was timid when he took on Poison."

"It was like he was a different person, like he had turned into some sort of comic-book hero."

"Was he ever arrested by the police, do you know?"

"Not that I was aware of," said Wayne. "Not when he was hanging with me."

"You have any idea what happened to Kylie?"

"She disappeared. Maybe you should ask her mom."

"I tried," I said, "but she didn't know. She's been too busy picking up her Mother of the Year award."

"Is there anything else you need for that legal case of yours?" said Father Kenneth.

I looked at Beth, she shrugged. I slapped my knees and stood. Beth stood, too. "I think we're through here, Father. Wayne, it was a pleasure meeting you. Thank you so much for your time. And good luck."

"Give me a minute, Wayne," said Father Kenneth before he led us out of the small room.

He was quiet for a long moment as we walked up the church aisle. "I don't know if that helped," he said finally, "but if you need anything more, give me a call, and I'll do whatever I can."

"Thank you, Father."

"Now let me ask you, Mr. Carl. After hearing all that, is Wayne in any legal trouble?"

"I wouldn't think so. All this happened a while ago. The statute of limitations on most everything he might have done would have already run."

The priest glanced back toward the still-open door. "That's good to know."

"It looks like he's trying," I said.

"Oh, he is, Mr. Carl, believe me. But it will be a struggle still for a long time to come. Sometimes confession alone isn't enough. Sometimes you can't move forward until you've gone back to take care of the past. It would help him, I think, if we could find Kylie. And that man he beat up. He didn't seem like a nice man, but even so, maybe I'll find out his name. Maybe Wayne will find some way to make amends. You'll keep me informed of anything more you find out about Seamus?"

"Sure, Father, if that's what you want."

"Oh, I do, yes. And best of luck in saving your client in that prison."

"Thank you, sir," I said. "We'll certainly need it."

13

"Quite the story," said Beth as we wended our way out of Fishtown.

"Yes, it was," I said.

"Three old friends, descending into the maelstrom of crime and drugs and prostitution, their bonds seemingly obliterated. And then, out of the blue, like some superhero with a cape, this Seamus Dent emerges to save his friend before succumbing to the dark side once and for all. But does anything we learned help François?"

"Not yet," I said.

"Then what's the point?"

"Most of the facts behind the murder of François Dubé's wife were fully presented in court. They will become relevant if we get to try the case again, but not when we're fighting to get a retrial. For this we need something new, something that will pique the judge's interest. Seamus Dent's story is exactly that."

"But you said facts that might have affected credibility aren't enough to get a new trial."

"The facts themselves, no. But who else knew those facts? If the police were aware of his background, then the prosecutor might have known about it, too, and her failure to turn over the information to Whit would be a *Brady* violation."

"Let's subpoena her records."

"They won't show anything. Whatever anybody knew wouldn't have been written down. We're going to have to make the connection ourselves."

"How do we do that?"

"I don't know."

"Victor, we're not getting anywhere." There was something in her voice, a line of frustrated desperation.

"Calm down," I said slowly. "Don't take this all so personally. It's just another case. It's been three hours today already, times two lawyers, times our usual fees, plus expenses, including mileage on the car. We've got a retainer to run through, and with our morning's work we're making a good start."

She laughed. "My God, you get more cynical every day."

"It's just that over the years I've learned that most people in prisons deserve to be there."

"I don't believe that of François."

"And you could tell by looking in his eyes."

"Yes."

"See, but you can't. That's just the way of it, Beth. He might be innocent, he might be guilty, he might be a saint, he might certainly be a sinner, but whatever he is, you can't tell by looking in his eyes. The eyes aren't the window to the soul, they are just sacks of jelly."

She stayed quiet for a moment, unhappy, I could tell, with her cynical partner.

"You want to stop for lunch?" I said.

"And charge it to the client?"

"Sure, but we'll consult about the case over Cokes and a burger. I could use a burger."

"Victor."

"All right, no lunch, but we still have one more visit."

"Where?"

"The intersection of Whitaker and Macalester, just next to Juniata Park," I said.

"What's there?"

"Someone who might know how Seamus Dent was killed."

The sergeant sat hunched at his desk, heavy eyebrows raised wearily. He looked as tired as the entire squat brick building, swamped as it was with a steady torrent of crime. There are twenty thousand auto thefts a year in Philadelphia, twenty thousand a year, every year, year upon year. And against all odds, the great majority of these cars are recovered. What condition they are recovered in is another story, but they are recovered still, and the center of this Sisyphean effort is the Philadelphia Police Department Auto Squad.

"Did you file a report with your local district?" said the sergeant when he saw us walk in the door.

"No," said Beth.

The sergeant breathed in heavily. He seemed too exhausted to get upset at this failure of protocol, too exhausted even to shrug. "You have to file a report with the local district."

"I don't want to file a report," said Beth.

"You don't got no choice. It's procedure."

"But my car wasn't stolen."

The sergeant scratched his nose with his thumb. "This is the auto squad, lady," he said. "We don't do televisions."

"My television wasn't stolen either."

The sergeant wiggled his eyebrows. They looked like caterpillars sliding along a pale leaf. I almost felt sorry for him.

"The way I remember it," I said, leaning on his desk, "it was Who on first, What on second, and I Don't Know on third."

"Mister," said the sergeant, "I might have some idea of what you're talking about, except I don't speak Greek."

"I'll make it easy on you." I slowed down my speech, as if I were talking to a Frenchman. "We're looking for Detective Gleason."

"Well, why didn't you say so from the start?"

"You didn't give us a chance," said Beth. "Is he in?"

"Yeah," said the sergeant, picking up his phone. "Elvis is in the building. Who's looking for him?"

"Tell Detective Gleason that Victor Carl is here for a visit. That will be sure to make his day."

"Hey, hey, hey," said Detective Gleason, not deigning to rise from behind his desk and greet us. "My old bad-luck charm, Victor Carl, here to ruin an already lousy day."

"How have you been, Detective?"

"Taking care of business," he said, his voice deep and slightly southern. "I haven't seen you since you called me a liar on the stand in the DeStafano murder trial."

"Nothing personal," I said. "Just doing my job."

"That's all right," he said. "Nothing personal on my side either, when I called you a scum-sucking piece of crap with his head up his ass, to that reporter waiting outside the courtroom."

"I wanted to thank you for the plug," I said. "They spelled my name right, which is all I care about. You're looking swell."

"I got lucky. After ten years of humping homicide, I finally pulled a cushy spot here in the auto squad. Two years to my twenty, and then I can sit back, smell the roses. Can't you see how happy I am?"

"You're positively glowing." Except he wasn't, was he? Beyond the false smile, I could sense something defeated in him. He was a tall, thin man with arrogant sideburns that tapered wide at the base, but there always seemed to be something anxious in the surface of his hatchet face. With his bulging eyes, he had never presented the cocksure arrogance of the usual homicide dick. Instead he had the perpetually startled expression of a man who had just accidentally swallowed a squirrel. And it looked as if the squirrel had finally gotten the best of him.

"Can we sit?" I said.

He stared at me as he rubbed his mouth with the back of his hand, and I caught a brief whiff of something sweet, sweet as bourbon. The thing about Gleason was that, despite his dated style and startled expression, he had always been a pretty sharp cop, first on vice and then at homicide. But there was something going on with him now, something not right. Maybe he had started drinking and that had thrown him off his game, or whatever had thrown him off his game had started him to drinking. It didn't matter much, did it? He rubbed his mouth with the back of his hand and then pointed at a couple of chairs in front of other desks.

I pulled two around to face him, and we sat. "Detective Gleason, I'd like you to meet Beth Derringer."

"Hello, little darling," he said. "How's the world treating you?"

"Other than the fact that I'm not little and not a darling," she said, "it's treating me just fine."

"Relax," he said. "I didn't mean nothing. Prickly, isn't she?"

"Beth's my partner," I said.

"Well, that explains that. So who are you here for today, Victor? Another drug dealer? Another leg breaker? Or is some hard-luck angel looking to slime his way out of grand theft auto?"

"Today it's your garden-variety murderer," I said.

"Homicide's in the Roundhouse."

"We're in the right place."

"Is that so? The perp anyone I know?"

"François Dubé," said Beth.

Did something flit through his eyes at the name, some fearful sense of recognition? Or was I only imagining it? It wasn't easy to tell with his strangely haunted expression.

"I remember the Dubé case," said Gleason, leaning back in his chair, crossing his hands over his chest. "Wife killer, tried about three years ago. Went down hard, I believe. Life. That was Torricelli's case. Talk to him."

"But Seamus Dent was yours," I said.

It looked for a moment as if the squirrel he had swallowed was trying to scamper back up his throat. "There's no connection," said the detective.

"Sure there is. Seamus Dent testified at the François Dubé trial, put the defendant smack at the scene of the crime."

"Oh, yeah, right. There might have been something about that in the file. But it didn't have anything to do with what went down with the kid."

"What did go down, exactly?" I said.

"Not totally clear. It happened in a crack house in Kensington, one of the floaters that flit from abandoned house to abandoned house. There was a rip-it-up about something. One rumor said it was over territory, another said it was over money, another said it was over a girl. Or maybe it was just because. There's always a reason, isn't there? It's hard to find out what's happening when the only witnesses are addicts, who scatter like cockroaches at the first pop of pistols. But we got a pretty good description of the fight before the shot."

"Who was arguing?"

"The victim, Dent, and some self-styled gangster and rap impresario, went by the street name of Red Rover. There were hard words, hard knocks. Then, as Red Rover took a swing, Dent side-kicked him in the face. Hurt him bad, but not bad enough. On the floor now, Red Rover rolled over, pulled a Glock 9 from his belt, and shot Dent in the forehead. Western Unioned him to Nothingville."

"And what happened to Red Rover?"

"He was tracked down at his mother's place in Logan."

"He say much when they found him?"

"Enough. He was told to put his hands up and surrender. He pulled out a weapon instead. Three in the chest."

"So you never got a statement?"

"You're catching on fast. We figured the way he played it was confession enough."

"Maybe so, but you know the way we defense attorneys are, with all our hang-ups and all. We like the execution after the trial, not before. And a statement would have made things clearer. Anything dirty about the shooting?"

He shook his head. "Righteous. He was a hood, he killed that boy, he pulled a weapon. Not too many cops lost any sleep over it."

"You learn much about the victim?"

"We knew he was dead, which was pretty much all we needed."

"What did the autopsy show?"

Gleason leaned forward, curled half his upper lip in a sneer. "What'd I say? The autopsy showed a bullet through the forehead."

"What I was asking, Detective, is whether or not the victim was clean at the time of the shooting?"

"Does it matter?"

"Yes, it matters."

"There was evidence of past drug abuse."

"But his blood came up clean, is that it?"

"So they said."

"You figure that one out?"

"Maybe he was strung out, maybe that's what made him

so ornery. Maybe he was looking to score, and Red Rover told him to pound asphalt. It doesn't matter what he was on with a bullet in his head."

"We heard that before he was killed," said Beth, "Dent was taken up by some older guy. Someone who was trying to clean him up, straighten him out. It might have been a sexual thing, but apparently for a time he was straightened. Did you hear anything like that?"

"No."

"Did you try to find out Dent's situation at all?"

"Well, he wasn't a sweet Leilani, if that's what you're saying. Look, we did what we needed to do. We investigated what we needed to investigate, we found the shooter, we took care of it. Now, I appreciate the visit, but I got work to do. In the time I wasted with you, another two cars were stolen off the street."

"It's nice to see they keep you busy."

"If any other questions come up," said Beth, "would you mind terribly, Detective, if we give you a call?"

"Do me a favor, little sister," he said, "and don't."

CHAPTER
15

It was the last sentence of Detective Gleason's that stuck in my mind for some reason. His voice, like I said, was deep and southern, and he gave that last word a melodious lilt that struck me as something strangely familiar.

I let it rattle around in my head as I drove Beth back to the office. She wasn't so encouraged by our outing, Beth, and not so happy with me, I could tell, and I could tell why, too. She was like my seventh-grade gym teacher who told me, when I refused to climb the rope, that he didn't like my altitude. Well, Beth didn't like my altitude either.

"Dent's dead," she said, "his killer is killed, that line of inquiry is buried. It was a wild-goose chase from the start."

"I like wild goose. A nice pudding and some cranberry sauce and it's like we're in the middle of a Dickens novel."

"Not to mention the billable hours."

"Not to mention."

"We don't have anything, do we?"

"I told you at the start it was useless."

"But still you took his money."

"It wasn't his, but yeah, I took the money. And if it's hopeless, it's not our fault. He's the one who killed his wife."

"Did he? Are you sure?"

"In the eyes of the law and jury, that's just what he did.

But see, look at me, I can cheerfully say I don't give a damn. I don't have to believe in my client; I just have to believe in the legal tender he's tendering. A lawyer is really nothing more than a mechanic. Bring in your life, with all its troubles, and I'll open the hood, poke around, see if any of the legal tricks at my disposal can fix the problem. It isn't personal, I don't make judgments about the quality of the car. I just roll up my sleeves. When was the last time your auto mechanic took it personally when your engine needed a valve job? He shakes his head, sure, clucks his tongue, and says all the right things when he tells you the bad news, like an oncologist with really dirty hands, but trust me, he doesn't take it personally. Instead he takes Visa or Master-Card."

"I didn't go to law school to be a mechanic."

"Yeah, but Atticus Finch was fiction and Darrow is dead. Ow."

"What's wrong?"

"Your self-righteous whining is starting my tooth to aching."

"Good. Want me to give it a twist?"

That's how we left it, with my tooth throbbing and the cracks in our relationship starting to show. And the truth was, I didn't understand for certain where the new tension was coming from. I was the same cynical, opportunistic asshole I had always been. Since when had it bugged her so?

I thought about that some, and then, back in my office, I thought some more about Detective Gleason. There was something in the story he had told, in that desolate building and futile department in which he now worked, something in the way he defended the killing of Red Rover, something in the way he protested Beth's insinuations about Seamus Dent's sexuality. And somehow it was all contained in that last sentence, in that very last word.

Do me a favor, little sister, he had said, *and don't.* Don't. That's what he said. Each time I held that word in my mind, it seemed to sing to me. And then, quick as a "Hey, baby," I listened, and the raw possibility came clear.

So I called up Torricelli. Tommy Torricelli was a lunkhead, absolutely, and we weren't exactly buddy-buddy, but he was the homicide detective who had investigated the Leesa Dubé murder, who had found the bloodied shirt and gun, who had concluded that François Dubé was the killer, who had testified convincingly at the trial in which François Dubé was convicted. He would be oh so delighted to learn that I was looking into his case. But before I told him that little gem, perfectly designed to make his day, I had a few other questions.

"How you doing there, Detective?" I said.

He wasn't inclined to tell me. He wasn't inclined to tell me anything except to get lost, which is exactly what he did. I had never worked one of Torricelli's cases before, but we knew each other enough to be wary. I was a criminal defense attorney with sharp teeth and a well-honed shamelessness. He was a cop known to cross a line or three in order to get the results he was looking for. Not quite oil and vinegar, more like fertilizer and diesel fuel.

"I only called to say hello," I lied, "and to give you some news that might interest you. But first I thought we'd gossip a bit."

Torricelli lied back when he said he wasn't one to traffic in gossip. Torricelli trafficked in gossip like I-95 trafficked in cars.

"I was just at the auto squad on Macalester," I said. "Ran into Detective Gleason. How'd he end up in that backwater?"

He told me.

"Wow," I said, acting surprised. "But they didn't pull his badge?"

He told me that they hadn't, that everything had checked out, but still the transfer.

"Well," I said. "At least it turned out okay. What's with those sideburns, though? Yeah, and that southern twang in his voice?"

He laughed and made a snide comment.

"Right," I said, "more like South Street. You have any idea where he drinks?"

He gave me the name and a description of the place.

"You're kidding," I said. "I didn't know they had a place like that outside of Memphis. You ever go down there, have a drink with him?"

He said no, he said they couldn't drag his fat Italian ass into a place like that with a team of horses.

"I don't doubt it," I said.

He growled something at me.

"You know, Detective, I've been thinking about you. We ought to have dinner sometime. Someplace nice. Candles and violin music. Someplace romantic that makes up a nice pasta fazool. My treat."

He was quiet for a long moment and then let out an expletive I have tactfully deleted.

"And maybe we can talk about a new client I've just been hired to represent. François Dubé. Remember him?"

I held the handset away from my ear to save my eardrum the wear and tear as he told me, in his own way, that yes, he did remember François Dubé and how delighted he was that I had decided to take up his cause. That was one of my favorite things about my job as a defense attorney, the way I was able to create pleasant and meaningful relationships with the noble members of the city's police department. But even as I suffered the detective's abuse, I still felt the shivery thrill of discovery, the same thrill you get when you slide in the final pieces of a jigsaw puzzle. It was coming clear for me, the story of Seamus Dent, not all of it, I would learn more in the course of my investigation, but now maybe just enough was coming clear to get François Dubé that new trial he so desperately sought.

It was late already by the time I figured it out. Beth was gone, my secretary, Ellie, was gone, it was just me in the office, the sole representative of the law firm of Derringer and Carl, but I was enough. I sat in Ellie's chair, took out a blue-backed document, rolled it into the typewriter my secretary used to fill the blanks in preprinted documents, hunted and pecked, whited out the mistakes, hunted and pecked some more.

And then I put on my jacket, stuffed the document into my jacket pocket, and drove out to the Great Northeast to have myself a drink in the shadow of the King.

CHAPTER
16

King's Dominion was not the kind of joint people stumbled into by mistake. If you weren't looking for it, you'd never find it, but then again you wouldn't want to. I parked in the lot of a small shopping center just off Roosevelt Boulevard. There was a Radio Shack, a T.J. Maxx, a dry cleaner, a vacant storefront, a CVS, a dollar store. Scintillating, no? The number I was looking for was taped onto a glass door next to the dollar store. I pushed open the door and was immediately hit by a deep throb of bass that resonated in my bad tooth. As I climbed the stairwell, I passed a series of signs tacked to the wall.

NO SNEAKERS

CHECK ALL GUNS

PEANUT BUTTER AND NANNER SAMMICH—75¢

Not my kind of place, exactly. I just hoped they served Sea Breezes.

Beside the closed door at the top of the stairs, an old man sat on a stool, clipboard in hand. He was tall and stooped, his shoes were white patent leather, and it looked like a gray poodle was perched on his head. When I tried to walk past him, he shot out a bony arm and stopped me cold.

"What's your song?" he said.

"I'm just here to see a Detective Gleason," I said. "Has he shown up tonight?"

"Do I look like a matchmaker?" he said.

"Hello, Dolly," I said.

"The name's Skip."

"Kept that from summer camp, did you? I like your shoes."

"Dancing shoes. I know a guy what knows a guy what gets them direct from Hong Kong."

"Maybe he can get me a pair."

"You want a pair?"

"Nah. So is Gleason in?"

"Yeah, he's in."

I gave the old man a wink, and started again for the door, and again the bony arm barred my way. I looked at it for a moment and then at the old man.

"What, is there a cover?"

"No cover," he said. "But it's karaoke night."

"Just my luck. I should have come tomorrow."

"It wouldn't do no good," said the old man. "Here, every night is karaoke night. What's your song?"

"I don't sing."

"Sure you do, if you want in. Everyone sings, at least once. Makes you part of the show, keeps it festive." He cocked his head, the poodle shifted, his eyes brightened crazily. "It's karaoke night."

"I know 'Feelings.' Should I sing 'Feelings'?"

He looked at me, looked at his clipboard, paged through the pages, looked back at me. "We don't got it."

"How about 'Kumbaya'?"

He looked back at his clipboard. "We got 'Kismet,' we got 'Kiss Me Quick,' we got 'Ku-u-i-po,' which is pretty close, but no 'Kumbaya.' "

" 'Satisfaction'?"

"None."

"You don't got much, do you?"

"Only everything he ever sung."

"Ah," I said. "Now I get it. Why don't you pick something for me."

"How's your pipes?"

"Not so good."

"Then stay with something low, something easy. I got one here that usually works for first-timers. There's a slow part you can talk your way through."

"Done."

"What's your name?"

"Franz."

"Funny," he said as he pulled a white slip from his clip-board, filled it out, handed it to me, "you don't look like a Franz. That will be ten bucks."

"Ten bucks a song?"

"Just for the first song. After that it's free."

As I pulled out my wallet, I said, "Good thing you boys don't charge a cover."

I stepped through the door and into a neon-lit room, ringed with everything Elvis. Velvet paintings glowing with black light, guitar clocks, gold records, ceramic busts, framed photographs from each Elvis era: Elvis impossibly young, Elvis impossibly handsome, Elvis impossibly svelte in black leather, Elvis impossibly bloated in a white jumpsuit. There were tables, about half full, in the center, bars around the edges, booths in the back. Waitresses dressed like schoolgirls with high hair carried drinks on circular trays. On a narrow stage in the front, a redhead in a ruffled shirt, looking a little like Ann-Margret, belted out the first verse of "Viva Las Vegas" as the words rolled up a television screen and the crowd hooted and clapped along.

A man in dark glasses greeted me with a bright smile. "Welcome," he said in a deep voice. "Slip?"

I handed it over. He gave it a look.

"Good choice, Franz," he said. "You want some company tonight?" He thumbed toward a trio of women at the bar with bouffant hair and low blouses. They were nice-looking women once, but once was enough.

"No thanks," I said. "I already had my fiber today."

I scanned the scene, found whom I was looking for in a booth in the back. He was sitting alone, hunched over a drink, something dark and almost gone in his glass. He wasn't viva-ing to Ann-Margret. I wondered if my visit that afternoon hadn't ruined his day. Knowing what I knew now, I didn't doubt it.

Gleason glanced up when I sat down across from him, didn't seem one bit surprised to see me. "How'd you find this place?" he said.

"Torricelli."

He nodded, he understood. Torricelli hadn't just told me about the bar, he had told me about the shooting, too. "I should hang up a sign," he said. "Do not disturb."

"You know that piece of gum you step on and can't get off your shoe?" I said. "It ends up on your hand, your other hand, your nose. That piece of gum? That's me."

"I was thinking of something else that sometimes gets on my shoe. What do you want?"

"I want to know if you were the one to teach Seamus Dent karate."

His eyes widened a bit, as if he were about to say something, but just then one of the waitresses with the schoolgirl skirt and high hair came to our table. Her eyes were rimmed dark, her lips were red as paint.

"Anything, boys?" she said.

"My treat," I said.

"Wonder of wonders," said Gleason. "I'll have another bourbon, neat."

"Can I have a Sea Breeze?" I said. "With lime?"

"Closest thing we have is a Blue Hawaii," she said.

"What's that?"

"Vodka, pineapple juice, crème de coconut, and blue Curaçao."

"Aloha," I said.

"Thanks, Priscilla," said Gleason before she swished away.

I raised an eyebrow. "Priscilla?"

"They're all Priscilla," he said. "How'd you know about the karate?"

"It made sense. From the stories I'd been hearing, Seamus Dent, big as he was, was never a fighter. Then suddenly he starts giving side kicks like he's Jackie Chan. Somehow he learned. And then you have this whole Elvis thing going with the sideburns, the little southern twang you give your voice even though you grew up in Manayunk, not Memphis. And the way you described Seamus's fight with that drug dealer. You seemed to even know the type of kick he used to send him to the ground. It just added up."

"Aren't you clever."

"Well, you know. Deal with cops long enough, it rubs off."

"Why the hell do you care so much about Seamus?"

"Because he testified against François Dubé."

He stared at me for a while, saw something in my eyes that made him turn to look at the stage, where the woman was swinging her arms as she wailed the final chorus.

"She's not bad," I said. "And she does look a little like Ann-Margret."

"But not the Ann-Margret of *Viva Las Vegas,* more like the Ann-Margret of *Any Given Sunday.*"

"Can't have everything."

Okay, folks, said the DJ, the man who had taken my slip, speaking from off the stage, so his voice was like a disembodied presence. *Let's hear it for the scintillating Elvira.* The audience cheered. *Next up, Harvey from Huntingdon Valley, doing a little blues number from 1957.* A young man with blue-black hair in a duckbill and a face like a punching bag stepped up to the stage, took the microphone off the stand, cleared his throat, mumbled, "Let's get it this time." After a short blues intro, he started in with a gravelly rendition of "One Night."

"It wasn't like your partner was saying," said Gleason after we both listened a bit to Harvey from Huntingdon Valley, who was not too awful at all. "There wasn't anything sexual about it."

"You don't have to hitch up your pants and talk about the Eagles. It doesn't matter much to me."

"But see, that's the thing. Everyone thinks they understand when they think the worst. But the worst isn't always the truth."

"So what was the truth?"

"He was a kid in trouble. I was trying to help." Gleason finished off his bourbon. "And that, my friend, is the whole sordid story."

There was something in his voice that didn't seem to care whether I believed him or not.

"How'd you meet him?" I said.

"There was a killing in Juniata. We crashed a drug house, looking for a witness. Seamus was cowering in a room up the stairs, hugging his guitar. I put away my gun, asked him if he could play that thing. He showed me."

Priscilla came back with our drinks. I told her to make up another round and to run a tab. Gleason took a gulp of his bourbon and winced, more from the memories, I thought, than the drink. The Blue Hawaii was cold and too sweet, but it looked good in the glass. The thing I love about a blue drink is that it isn't pretending to be anything other than a prissy, made-up concoction for people who can't drink their whiskey straight. A cocktail with the courage of its lack of conviction.

"Was Seamus good at the guitar?" I said.

"Better than good. You ever hear any recordings of Robert Johnson playing his old Kalamazoo archtop?"

"No."

"Then you wouldn't understand. Physically he was a mess, filthy, strung out, a black eye, but he could play some blues. So I took him out of there and bought him a cup of coffee. He told me all about the drugs, the things he had done with those friends of his, everything. It was a brutal, sad story, but I saw something in him. He was really sorry. In my racket it's rare to see it like that, sincere and not put on as a show for a judge. So I got him treatment, got him a job running files. And when it started working out, I helped him even more. Let him stay at my place. We used to play guitar and sing together. Spirituals, believe it or not. I did what I could for him."

"Like fixing his teeth."

"God knows he needed it. I found a dentist to do it for free. Some guy who had come to the station, passing out his card, looking to do a little public service."

"And the karate?"

"A boy that big, not able to defend himself. It wasn't right. I asked myself, what would Elvis do? He'd teach him karate, so that's what I did. I'm a third-degree black belt, I help out at an inner-city dojo on weekends. I brought him along. After enough years in homicide, you get tired of helping corpses. It was nice to help a boy still with some hope. And I was helping, I could tell. He cleaned up quick."

How to get down with the King, Harvey from Huntingdon Valley. There was clapping, whistles. *Next we have a first-timer. Let's hear a warm welcome for Franz. Come on up, Franz, and do your thing.*

"If he was so clean," I said, figuring I could ignore the DJ, "what was he doing in the crack house where he was killed?"

Gleason closed his eyes for a moment. "I don't know."

"You ever find out?"

"I tried."

Come on, Franz, no hiding. Let's hear it for Franz, every-body. The crowd started chanting, "Franz, Franz, Franz!" *Where are you, Franz?*

"It's hard to find the truth with a bullet," I said.

"I didn't go out there to kill that man, not that he didn't deserve it. I was just looking for answers, but maybe, yeah, I was looking a little too hard. I saw Seamus's body and I went a little over the edge."

There you are, Franz. Sitting with our own Patrick Glea-son. Franz, Franz, Franz. *Come on down, Franz.*

Gleason looked at the stage, then at me. "You're Franz?"

"That's my nickname in the lawyers' bund."

"It's your turn then, big boy. Go on up."

"I didn't come here to sing."

"You don't have any choice," said Detective Gleason. "Everybody sings. It's karaoke night."

17

I was caught in a trap. I couldn't walk out. So instead I snatched down the rest of my Blue Hawaii, marched right to the stage, hopped on up, grabbed the mike, shielded my eyes from the spotlight. Sometimes there's nothing to do but barrel forward with misplaced confidence.

"This is for the ladies out there," I said, loosening my tie. "Just toss on up those hotel keys."

That got a laugh, which was good, because then the music started.

A numb, dumb silence fell across the crowd at the first note. Jaws dropped and stayed dropped, eyes glazed, thumbs reached for ears. I don't know if it was the beat, the tone, the key, maybe it was the lack of all three, but as I sang out on "Suspicious Minds," I could feel the recoil of the audience. And there were grimaces of horror when I shook my hips, gut-wrenching, bladder-loosening horror. I was the Texas Chain Saw Massacre of karaoke night. At one point, during the chorus, I thought a cat was screeching somewhere in the corner of the room, and then I realized it was my voice coming out of the speakers.

Thank you, Franz, for that interesting rendition of a number one hit from 1969, said the DJ as the music faded out. *It used to be one of our favorites.*

I again shielded my eyes from the spotlight. "That seemed really short, didn't it?"

Not to us it didn't, Franz, said the DJ as heads shook in agreement across the club. *Thank you so much for coming on down, and take care of that head cold.*

"But there are more words scrolling up on the screen," I said. "And what about the slow part? I was really looking forward to that slow part."

And so were we, Franz, but trust us, there's only so much damage a song can take. Next, all the way from Mantua, singing one of the good old old ones, and good advice for Franz on his singing career, let's hear it for Marvelous Marv, performing "Surrender."

An old bald man with a bent back and gnarled hands climbed onto the stage. His ears came up to my hip. He grabbed the mike out of my hands, shooed me away. "Get off my stage, you butcher," said Marv in his rasp of a voice. "Let me show you how it's done."

And he did, the little crapper.

When I got back to the booth, Gleason was collapsed on the table, his head resting on his arms. I thought for a moment he had passed out, drunk with sorrow over the sad fate of Seamus Dent, but then I noticed his shoulders shaking with laughter.

"I told you I didn't come here to sing," I said.

"Is that what you call it?" He lifted his head, his cheeks wet with his tears.

"Was it that bad?"

"Like the bleat of a goat in heat."

"Cute. You ever bring Seamus here?"

"Oh, yeah." He smiled at the memory.

"How'd he do?"

"Seamus could sing. He did a version of 'American Trilogy' that would send you right straight to the army recruitment office. And his 'In My Father's House' would bring even an atheist to tears."

"So what happened? What was he doing with Red Rover? What was the fight about?"

"I don't know," said Gleason. "I just don't know. I traced that bastard Red Rover back to his mother. I went alone, that was my mistake. My partner was on something else, and I should have waited, but I wanted to know. I knocked on the door. The mother answered. I was just identifying myself. Next thing I know, the bastard runs over me on his way out. I charge after him. He stops, whirls, pulls something out of his waistband. I didn't have any choice."

"Was there an investigation of the shooting?"

"There always is."

"What did they find?"

"I came up clean."

"What did he pull out of his waistband?"

"A knife."

"And you standing there with your revolver."

"He whirled. He pulled something out of his belt. I wasn't waiting to see if it was a cell phone. I came up clean."

"But still you're in the auto squad."

"It made the papers, the shooting, and Internal said I was wrong to have gone there without backup. The brass transferred me to the auto squad to get the stink out of homicide. So now I chase cars. Like a dog."

Just then Priscilla returned to the table. "Nice job, cowboy," she said as she placed another Blue Hawaii in front of me.

"I'll be here all week," I said.

"Let's hope not," she said. "It would be hell on tips."

I took a long draft of the blue drink, winced.

"What's the matter?" said Gleason.

"I got this tooth. . . ."

"You ought to get that looked at."

"So I been told."

"The guy who took care of Seamus did an amazing job."

"I have someone in mind," I said.

"Think about it. Seamus's teeth were like Stonehenge before, and after they looked pretty damn good."

"Was he grateful for what you did?"

"Oh, yeah. That was the thing. He was a good kid and appreciated everything. The more you did for him, the more you wanted to do."

Thank you, Marv, that was beautiful and heartfelt. The ladies here would surrender to you in a minute. A squeal went up. *Let's give Marvelous Marv a hand. Next up, the always popular, always terrific, our own Officer Patrick Gleason, singing something from the King's 1968 Comeback Special. Come on up, Patrick.*

Gleason downed his bourbon, belched to clear his throat, gave me a wink before standing and walking with authority to the stage. On his way up, he motioned for the three sirens at the bar, with their rising hair and plunging necklines, to follow, and they did, climbing to the stage with him, forming a row behind.

"This is for a kid I used to know," said Gleason.

He lowered his head, shook his knee, waited as the music started, a muted trumpet, the humming of his background singers swaying slowly in their row, a slip of strings floating over the bridge.

When Gleason raised his head, his eyes were now focused high and there was something different about him, something transported. He began to sing in a lovely and deep gospel voice about lights burning brighter and birds flying higher, about bluer skies and better lands and brothers walking hand in hand.

It was a sappy song, maudlin and obvious, without a hint of irony. And here was this Elvis wannabe, standing on a karaoke stage, in a pathetic tribute bar, singing to a sparse crowd already punched into submission by the likes of Harvey from Huntingdon Valley and Marvelous Marv, by the likes of me. Yet with the emotional music, the background singers, the way Gleason's voice roughed with passion as it strived to reach the high notes and higher emotions, it also seemed, for a moment, as true as pain. And his apparent belief in every word shamed me.

See, Gleason was a cop, and sometimes cops become cops because they like the power, the guns, the adrenaline rush of being on the front lines of someone else's tragedy. And then sometimes they become cops because it's a tough job that doesn't pay near enough but needs doing and allows the men and women who take it up to maybe make a real difference in the world. It's not always so easy to tell one from the other.

"You're pretty damn good," I said when he sat back down at the table. "You ever sing professionally?"

"Remember there was this rockabilly trend a couple decades back. The Stray Cats. Robert Gordon. The whole 'Gene Gene Vincent, we sure miss you' thing. Some of us just out of the academy had a group. I fronted and played rhythm guitar."

"What were you called?"

"The Police Dogs. Played some of the bars around here. We were pretty good. Had offers from clubs in New York. But it was just a hobby. I always wanted to do what I was doing."

"Police work," I said.

He shrugged.

"It was a good thing you tried to do for Seamus."

"He was a good kid."

"Not everyone steps out to help like you did."

"It wasn't anything."

"But I'm troubled here. You knew about his testimony in the François Dubé case?"

"Yeah."

"And you knew that the defense would be interested in knowing about his former drug use, his misspent youth, how he was found by a cop in a drug house during a raid? You knew all that would be relevant, didn't you?"

"I know the way it works. You guys on the other side take any little thing and twist it into something else."

"That might be true, Detective. We all have our jobs to do. But when you learned he was slated to testify, why didn't you tell anyone what you knew?"

"No one asked."

"And you didn't volunteer. You didn't think Torricelli would be interested? Or the D.A.? They were basing part of their case on the kid's testimony. You didn't think they would want to know about his past?"

"He was cleaning up," he said. "His future was bright. No one needed to know everything he had gone through."

"Or about your relationship with an ex–drug abuser."

"I told you, there was nothing wrong in it."

"Maybe there wasn't."

"I was just trying to protect him."

"Or maybe you were just protecting yourself. Like you said, everyone thinks they understand when they think the worst."

He didn't answer, he didn't have to, the truth of it was writ upon his face. But if he had spoken up, things might have been so different. The D.A. would have turned over the information to the defense, she would have had to, and it would have been rough for Seamus on the stand, sure. It might have made a difference in the François Dubé case, sure, but it would have made a difference to Detective Gleason, too. Because if his commanding officers had known of his relationship with Seamus Dent, he never would have been assigned Dent's homicide, he never would have rushed off rashly to confront Seamus's murderer, he never would have killed the man, never would have been booted down to the auto squad. And he never would have been in this situation now, right now, with his fate in my hands.

"You should have told them," I said.

"I know it now."

"If they find out, they're going to look again at that shooting."

"Most likely."

"It's going to appear less like self-defense and more like a dark vigilante form of revenge."

"It was what it was," he said.

"But still."

"Yeah, I know."

"It's going to be bad."

He shrugged.

"You understand I don't have a choice."

"I was just trying to do something good."

"But that's the way of it, Detective," I said as I pulled out the subpoena I had typed up in my office and placed it gently before him. "No good deed goes unpunished."

He didn't look at it, he didn't have to.

I emptied my second Blue Hawaii. The alcohol puckered my throat, the pineapple juice jabbed like a steel pick into my tooth. For a moment my jaw trembled and the blood in my head drained and the world grew pale.

Gleason reached out a hand and grabbed my shoulder. "Sakes alive, boy. What's going on? Are you drunk?"

I shook my head and immediately regretted the action, the pain burrowing deeper with each shake.

"It's your tooth, isn't it? Let me give you the name of the dentist I was telling you about."

"I have a name," I said, grabbing into my jacket for the card Whit had given me.

"But you should give this guy a chance. He's supposed to be relatively painless."

"It's the relative part that has me worried."

"You need help, son. Really. I could give him a call."

I put the cool of the glass against my jaw. "Who is he?"

"Pfeffer," he said.

My eyes snapped open at the name.

"Dr. Pfeffer," said Detective Gleason. "He's the one who helped Seamus, and believe me when I say, based on what he did for Seamus, he's an absolute magician."

18

"Oh, Mr. Carl," said Dr. Pfeffer's receptionist, "we're so glad you've come in for a visit. You're looking
well, I must say. And such a nice tie. The doctor is seeing another patient right now, but he's certainly expecting you. If
you could just fill out this new-patient questionnaire, we'd
be so very grateful."

It was bright in Dr. Pfeffer's flat beige waiting room, too
bright. The colors of the magazines laid out in perfect rows
on the side tables were washed by the relentless incandesce-
cence of the fluorescent lights overhead, the air itself was
conditioned by the jaunty Muzak pumping loudly through
speakers in the ceiling. And then there was the pretty young
receptionist herself, with her daunting cheerfulness, her own
wondrous smile, her lies about my tie. Her perk made my
aching tooth ache all the more. Walking into Dr. Pfeffer's
waiting room was like walking into a timeless, context-free
capsule of dental cheer. We could as easily have been soaring to the moon as in a building in Philly, but wherever we
were, we would show off our pearly whites and be jolly.

As I took the clipboard with the questionnaire, I noticed
something strange on the wall beside the reception desk.
Hanging in their wooden frames were an array of smiles,
photographs of gleaming, perfect sets of teeth one above the
last, just the smiles, nothing else, a sort of hall of fame of

happy dental hygiene. I looked at all those perfect mouths, rubbed my tongue along the rows of my ragged teeth, and then retreated to one of the generic beige chairs and started on the questionnaire.

NAME: Sure.
DATE OF BIRTH: Getting a bit far away.
EDUCATION: Too much.
INCOME: Not nearly enough.
FAMILY HISTORY: Murky, at best.
HEALTH HISTORY: Surprisingly good, except for a tooth.
NATURE OF PROBLEM: Dental.
CURRENT MEDICATIONS: Sea Breezes at dusk.
HEALTH INSURANCE: Deficient.
DISABILITY INSURANCE: Why does this question make me
      nervous?
LIFE INSURANCE: Yikes.
GREATEST ACCOMPLISHMENT: Huh?
GREATEST DISAPPOINTMENT: Excuse me?
DARKEST SECRET: You're kidding, right?
PERSON YOU'D MOST LIKE TO MEET: A dentist. I have a
      toothache and I'd like to meet a dentist.
ARE YOU CURRENTLY IN A FULFILLING SEXUAL RELATIONSHIP?

That last question sent me back to the receptionist. "What is this all about?" I said.

"It's the new-patient questionnaire, Mr. Carl. Every new patient fills it out."

"But it's getting a little personal. Like this question here about current relationships."

"Well?"

"I don't understand the relevance to my sore tooth."

"Dr. Pfeffer takes a holistic approach to the practice of

dentistry. You don't just treat a tooth, he likes to say, you treat a person."

"How about if the person only wants to treat the damn tooth?"

She sighed cheerily. "That's fine, Mr. Carl. Only answer the questions you are comfortable with, so long as you put down all your insurance information."

"I don't have dental insurance."

"Then we take Visa and MasterCard."

"Of course you do."

"Just give us your card number and the expiration date. But remember, Mr. Carl, as Dr. Pfeffer constantly reminds his patients, every tooth is connected to a nerve, and every nerve is ultimately connected to every other nerve in a series of switches we don't yet fully understand." Her bright, cheery smile was suddenly not so cheery. "You wouldn't want to cure the tooth only to find something else stops working."

I smiled politely back until it hurt, sat down, read again question sixteen.

Are you currently in a fulfilling sexual relationship? How does one answer such a question? Do I talk about my past affairs, my hopes for the future? Do I discuss the dates I had been on in the last couple of months, the prospects I was prospecting for as we spoke. And what does fulfilling mean, anyway? Can a sexual relationship be equated to a brisket, where after your third portion you push away from the table and say, *No more, thank you, I'm fulfilled*? By and large, my fulfilling relationships had not been sexual and my sexual relationships had not been fulfilling and that seemed to me exactly the way the world worked. So I thought about it some more, all the twists and turns, the ambiguities inherent in the question, when a door opened.

A woman holding a file strode out, her smile blinding in its whiteness, its width, its perfection. She was tall, thin, her ginger hair straight and silky, her eyes blue. She was dressed like a high-fashion model on a runway and was every bit as lovely.

I watched as she handed the file to the receptionist.

"How did it go, Ms. Kingsly?"

"Fine, Deirdre, wonderful." She rubbed her tongue, pink and glistening, across her upper teeth. "He has such gentle hands."

She glanced my way. I tried to smile. She turned back to the receptionist as if my chair had been empty.

"The doctor wants to see me in four months. A Wednesday would be best. In the afternoon."

They chatted a bit more as the receptionist went through the book and staked out an appointment. Ms. Kingsly leaned forward to reach for a pen. Her supple body formed a dancer's line with her arched back, her raised leg, her pointed toe. When she stood straight again, her nose wrinkled and her pretty teeth bit down on her lower lip as she wrote out her address on an appointment-reminder postcard.

I looked down once more at question sixteen. "No," I wrote.

"Victor Carl," came a voice, strong and Germanic. It was a voice that brooked no possibility of dissent, the voice of a leader of men. I rose instinctively, stood at attention, looked around for the voice's source. She was standing tall in the doorway, dressed in white, holding a file to her chest. Her shoulders, her breasts, her hands were all strangely outsized. She looked like she could wring me out like a damp rag and that, quite possibly, I'd like it.

"Y-yes," I said.

"We are ready for you, *ja*," she said without a breath of emotion flitting across her stony face. "I am Tilda, Dr. Pfeffer's dental hygienist. We are very pleased that you have come to us. This way, and bring your questionnaire."

I glanced nervously at Deirdre and Ms. Kingsly. They both looked back, widening their eyes encouragingly. Gentle hands.

"Sure," I said. "Yes."

Tilda, the hygienist, stepped aside as I walked past her into the hallway. Her scent was woody and strong. The brightness from the waiting room dimmed. The Muzak hushed when she closed the door behind us both.

"You will be in examination room B, *ja*," she said.

Well, I thought, that sounds cheery. Examination room B. Transpose the letters and it spells Maximum Pain. Doesn't it?

She led me to a clean, brightly lit room down the hall. Arrayed around a large orange examination chair were drills and lights, X-ray guns, sinks, flat trays full of barbarous instruments. She ordered me into the chair, and I complied, lying back as she jacked it up and down and up again. My vertebrae bounced against the orange leatherette.

"Comfortable?"

"Put on some Jimmy Buffett, give me a margarita, and I could be at the beach."

"*Ja*, well," she said, clearly not amused. "This is not the Costa del Sol. Wait here. The doctor will be with you shortly."

"That's exactly what I was afraid of."

A few minutes later, he swept into the room, the doctor. I could tell he was the doctor because he wore a doctor's mask over his mouth and a doctor's scrub cap over his hair and the lettering on his white linen doctor's jacket read DR. PFEFFER.

"What have we here?" He picked up my file, scanned quickly through the new-patient questionnaire. "Victor Carl, yes. And you are having some sort of problem?"

"My tooth."

"That's good," he said. "If it was your foot, I'd have to say you're in the wrong place." He laughed. "Tell me about this tooth."

"It hurts."

"A lot?"

"Oh, yes," I said.

"Was there any precipitating event?"

"I'm not sure, but a short while ago I got socked on the side of my jaw with the barrel of a gun."

"A gun? Oh, my. Was it an accident?"

"No, he meant it, all right."

"How interesting. Someday you'll have to tell me the story. Every detail. I'll be fascinated. But I suppose now I should take a look."

He went to the sink, scrubbed his hands, took two rubber gloves out of a box on the counter. "Where is this tooth of yours?"

"Lower side, Dr. Pfeffer, on the right."

"Oh, we're not so formal here," he said as he fitted the gloves onto his hands. "Why don't I call you Victor?" He tightened a glove with the snap of rubber. "And you can call me Bob."

CHAPTER

19

"**I am very concerned,**" said Judge Armstrong from high on his bench, shaking his big round head with great concernedness, his voice falsetto high. "Very, very concerned."

I leaned over to Beth at the counsel table in Judge Armstrong's courtroom and said, without moving my swollen jaw, "I think he's concerned."

"What?" she said.

"Forget it," I said.

"What?"

This is what happens when a tooth is pulled out in pieces and half of your jaw swells to the size of a grapefruit: No one can understand a word you say.

My visit to the dentist ended with Bob pulling my tooth, a grisly event that I still shudder to recall, which was why it was Beth who had put on the evidence at François Dubé's hearing for a new trial and why Beth had made the argument. On one side of her sat François, in his prison jumpsuit, looking ever suave in maroon. I sat on the other, offering encouragement and trying not to spit blood onto the courtroom floor.

"The Supreme Court has said repeatedly that impeachment information can be crucially important to a fair trial," said the judge. "In light of the circumstantial nature of the evidence in Mr. Dubé's trial, the testimony of Seamus Dent, putting the defendant at the scene of the crime, was particularly significant. If the information about his drug use had been available to the defense, his credibility could have been shattered."

"But, Your Honor," said A.D.A. Mia Dalton, standing for the District Attorney's Office, "in light of the fingerprint evidence, in light of the motive evidence, in light of the photograph of the defendant grasped in the victim's hand, the proof in this case remains—"

"I know the evidence, Ms. Dalton. I sat through the trial, remember? The standard is whether the impeachment information could reasonably be taken, in light of the whole case, to undermine confidence in the jury's verdict, and I believe Ms. Derringer on that point is persuasive."

"We respectfully disagree," said Dalton, standing straight, if not tall, at the prosecution's table. Mia Dalton, all five foot one of her, was a hard woman in a tough spot. The François Dubé case had not been hers when it was originally tried, but the prosecutor who had handled it was now the elected district attorney, and so Dalton was saddled with the burden of defending her boss's handiwork. "Even without Seamus Dent's testimony, the prosecution would have no trouble proving guilt beyond a reasonable doubt."

"Well, Ms. Dalton, you may have the chance to show us. I think my responsibility here is clear. The impeachment information was both material and in the hands of the police at the time of the trial and therefore was required to be handed over to the defense."

"But it was not in the hands of the prosecution, Judge." Dalton turned and glared at Patrick Gleason, who was sitting behind her in the courtroom. "Detective Gleason failed to inform the acting detective, Detective Torricelli, or the prose-

cutors of what he knew of Seamus Dent's past. How can we
be held responsible for Detective Gleason's failure?"

"I'm not saying your office did anything wrong here, Ms.
Dalton. Like I tell my daughter over and over, it's not all
about you. We're talking François Dubé's constitutional
rights."

"What about the rights of Leesa Dubé not to be shot in the
neck?"

"Are you being argumentative, Ms. Dalton?"

"Being as this is argument—"

"The Court in *Brady* says it doesn't matter if the prosecution's failure to turn over impeachment information was in-
tentional. And in *Kyles v. Whitley* the Court reaffirmed that
the prosecution has a duty to learn of any favorable evidence
known to others acting on the government's behalf, including the police."

"That puts too high a burden on our office."

"No, it doesn't, Judge," said Beth, standing now and entering the fray. "Any other rule would allow the police, not
the prosecutor or the courts, to make the determination of
what evidence should be turned over to the defense. Which,
I might add, is exactly what happened here."

"Absolutely right, Ms. Derringer," said the judge.

Dalton glanced over at Beth with something close to ad-
miration in her eyes and then down at me. As I grinned at her
as best I could, she puffed out one cheek, aping my swollen
jaw. Sweet.

As the argument continued, I turned to take in the rest of
the courtroom crowd. A few reporters, a few bored lawyers
looking for some entertainment, and then those with a more
direct connection to the case. There was an angry claque
sitting together on the prosecution's side of the courtroom,
leaning on one another, offering support. In the middle,

stone-faced, sat an older couple, both looking like they were trying hard not to burst a vein. It is a common sight in a murder case, the victim's family and friends putting on a show of support for the dear departed. The older couple were Leesa Dubé's parents, guardians now of Leesa and François Dubé's four-year-old daughter, who was not in the courtroom. I smiled at them, they studiously avoided looking back.

Detective Gleason was sitting up front, taking his medicine with a mournful, startled expression. Things would not be going well for the detective; two Internal Affairs officers had been in the courtroom during his testimony, taking notes. But to the detective's credit, he didn't hem and haw up there on the stand as Beth questioned him about Seamus Dent. He swore his oath to tell the truth and then followed it like a path to redemption, a rarer event in the criminal courts than you would imagine. I also couldn't help noticing that his southern drawl was replaced with a flat Philadelphia accent, as if the Elvis had been knocked out of him by the troubles I had brought down upon his head. Which was a shame, I thought, because if ever he needed a little Elvis in his life it would be over the next few months.

Behind our table Whitney Robinson nodded at me, something wary in his eyes. Beth had also wanted to argue ineffective assistance, and Whit would have gone along, testifying to all his mistakes in the first trial if we had asked him. But I convinced her against it, partly because it would dull our argument that the failures were the government's fault and partly because I didn't want to tarnish Whit's legacy. He deserved better, I figured.

And then in the back, arms crossed, luscious lips pursed, sat Velma Takahashi in a smashing turquoise suit. I was surprised to see her, actually, but there she was, making sure she was getting value for her cash retainer, no doubt. She was looking pretty good, was Velma, she was money, all right, and we would have to have another chat soon. Maybe as soon as the judge ruled.

"As I stated before," said the judge, scratching now his scalp as if to scratch up an answer, "I am concerned, very concerned. I remain horrified at the depravity of this crime and am aware of the importance of finality of judgment. At the same time, I am duty bound to follow the dictates of the Constitution."

"Can I say something, Judge?" said François Dubé, standing as he spoke. It was the first time he had said anything at the proceeding, and to hear his reedy French voice in the courtroom was jarring.

This was not good, this could only hurt his cause. I grabbed at Beth and shook my head. Beth leaned over and said something into his ear. He gently pushed her away.

"Judge," he said, "can I please say something?"

"You are entitled to your say, Mr. Dubé, but it looks like your counsel is trying to prevent you from speaking, and I recommend you listen to your counsel."

"No one today has said anything about whether I did or didn't do what I am accused of."

"Convicted of," said Dalton.

"I want you to know, Judge," said François before he turned to face the angry claque on the other side of the courtroom, "and I want Leesa's parents, Mr. and Mrs. Cullen, to know that I did not kill Leesa. I loved Leesa. We were having our problems, yes, but I loved her, and I always will."

The old woman in the middle, her face set, her jaw clenching as if she were cracking chestnuts, said in a low voice, "Sit down. God, do us all the favor and just sit down and shut your mouth."

"Quiet now, everyone," said the judge. "Your protestations of innocence have no effect on the matter currently before me, Mr. Dubé. You made the same protestations at your trial, and they were not believed by the jury."

"But I didn't do this," said François Dubé. "I'm an innocent man. And *ma mère, papa,*" he said, facing again the Cullens who were swearing at him with their eyes. His use of the familiar paternal and maternal forms of address brought a gasp from the courtroom. "I want to see my daughter. Please let me see my Amber. Please."

At that moment, Mrs. Cullen stood, swallowed a sob, and quickly slid past the other people in her bench before rushing out of the courtroom. One of the younger women in the claque stood, glared at François, and then followed her out. Mr. Cullen continued staring with a hatred that could have smashed boulders.

François turned back to the judge. "That's all I have to say."

"I think that was quite enough," said the judge, with a bite of anger in his voice. "Now, sit down, and not another word. The Cullens have endured a great tragedy. There is nothing you can do to assuage their pain, Mr. Dubé, but I won't let you make it any worse."

"Your Honor," said Beth, "Mr. Dubé was only—"

"I know what he was trying to do, Ms. Derringer. But it is your responsibility to control your client. He has made this decision ever more difficult, but I find I have little choice. Mr. Dubé, I'm granting you your new trial."

There was a gasp, a series of exclamations of incredulity and anger from the crowd. François Dubé stood again and hugged Beth. Mia Dalton shot up and said, "But, Judge—"

Judge Armstrong slammed his hammer twice, the bailiff yelled out, "Quiet." The noise in the courtroom ceased.

"We'd like the opportunity to brief the issues raised in the hearing," said Dalton.

"No, I don't need your briefs." The judge put his hand on a stack of paper two feet high sitting beside him on the bench. "You've all written enough briefs on this matter to kill a forest. I'm as disappointed as you, Ms. Dalton, but I read every case you both cited, and I don't see that I have a choice. Don't look to me, look to Detective Gleason. Are you prepared to go forward and prosecute this case again without Mr. Dent's testimony?"

"Absolutely, Your Honor," said Dalton.

"Who's trying it for the people?"

"I am, Judge," said Dalton.

"Need much time, Ms. Dalton?"

"No, sir."

"How about you, Ms. Derringer?"

"The sooner the better, Judge."

"Good. Put on your seat belts, people, because this case isn't going to sit. I'll hear you on bail, Ms. Derringer."

As Beth stood and began to speak, trying to get François Dubé out of jail pending his trial, I looked back at the courtroom, saw the resigned weariness on Detective Gleason's face, the sad compassion on Whit's—compassion for whom, for me? I saw the anger and bereavement flood through Mr. Cullen's eyes. And I spied the slender turquoise high heel, the narrow back, and the glistening blond hair of Velma Takahashi as she exited the courtroom door.

Like a mongrel chasing a purebred bitch in heat, I followed.

CHAPTER

20

I caught up to her at the elevator. She smelled rich, like a lilac bush. On a citrus farm. In spring. With a servant serving cocktails and a light breeze coming off the sea. Yeah, like that.

"Did you enjoy the show, Mrs. Takahashi?" I said.

"No, I've never been to Tallahassee, Mr. Carl, why?"

"Who said anything about Tallahassee?"

"I'm not sure I understand a word you are saying. Are you inviting me to Tallahassee? That's quite forward of you."

I pushed my tongue through the gap in my molars, rubbed it along the scab where my tooth had been. Dr. Bob had told me under no circumstances should I disturb the scab with my tongue, which was why I couldn't stop myself.

"Is something wrong with your head?" she said. "It appears today to be particularly misshapen."

"I lost a tooth."

"Yes," she said, "I think the truth is always best, don't you?"

I slowed down my speech, enunciated as precisely as I could in my current condition. "I lost a tooth."

"Ah, I see," she said, pushing the elevator button. "That would explain the drool. Well, let's hope you find it."

"Do you have a minute?"

She looked at the elevator door as if hoping it would open

and save her, but when it did, instead of getting on, she let it close without her and stepped to the side. She seemed quite uncomfortable to be there, in that hallway, with me. Funny, having seen my grossly swollen jaw in the mirror that morning, I could understand. I was tempted to give her the whole *I am not an animal, I am a human being* speech, but I worried that she might just think I was inviting her to Cleveland.

Speaking as clearly as I could, I said, "I mentioned before that we would need an additional retainer if we succeeded in getting Mr. Dubé his new trial."

"So you did. But can we discuss this at a different time and place?" She glanced over her shoulder, I turned to follow her gaze. Mrs. Cullen was staring at us from just outside the courtroom door. Interesting.

"Sure. I was only reminding you. Anytime that's convenient would be fine, as long as it's soon. Preparing for a trial requires a big commitment of both time and money."

"And you prefer checks."

"You remembered, how sweet. The judge is probably going to set bail for François. It will be high, but reachable for a Takahashi. Are you willing to put up what's necessary?"

"No."

"Cash would work, but some sort of guarantee could be arranged, too."

"Backed by my signature?"

"Or your husband's."

"I won't put up a cent. Tell François to raise the bond money on his own. Maybe his father-in-law will help."

"Somehow I don't think so. I don't understand, Mrs. Takahashi. You're willing to pay for his defense, but not his bail?"

"At least your hearing is clearer than your speech. François has spent three years behind bars. I think he can handle a few months more."

"Just so long as your husband doesn't learn of your assistance to the cause."

"Is that all? Can I go now?"

"Someone's been laying flowers at Leesa Dubé's grave. Every Thursday. Quite touching, actually."

"Her parents loved her very much."

"I'm sure they did, but it is not the Cullens leaving the flowers. Every Thursday afternoon your driver takes you to the cemetery. You step across the other sites, kneel at Leesa Dubé's grave, and lay a single white rose on the grass above her coffin. Then you stay there awhile, smoothing out the grass, cleaning off the leaves, taking away last week's offering."

"She was a dear friend," said Velma Takahashi.

"Weekly visits and tears three years after the fact are not the acts of friendship. They are acts of something else. Love, perhaps. Or guilt."

She looked at me, something dark and fierce in her eyes, and then she stepped away to the elevators. She punched the down button, crossed her arms, tapped a tidy toe, before stalking back to me.

"You had me followed."

"But only out of a deep and abiding affection," I said.

"Don't forget your place, Mr. Carl. And be certain of one thing: Whatever you do, you will leave me out of it."

The elevator doors opened. She reached out and sharply pinched my swollen jaw before marching off into the elevator, leaving me collapsed against the wall in pain.

It was the second time she had treated me like someone she had bought and paid for, someone whose sole purpose of existence was to serve her own mysterious ends. It was the second time she had treated me worse than a dog.

This was starting to be fun.

*   *   *

Mrs. Cullen now stood directly between the courtroom and me. She was a solid, pale woman with short white hair and navy shoes to match her stolid navy suit. Altogether formidable, and not looking too kindly at me as I made my way toward her. That's one of the things I've always loved about courtroom work, the gentle feelings of all the participants, one to the other.

And if you think divorce cases are tough, try murder.

"I'm sorry, Mrs. Cullen," I said slowly and clearly as I approached. "I know how difficult this is for you."

"Do you now, Mr. Carl?"

"No, I suppose I can't. Not really."

"She was my youngest daughter, my last child. She came late, a gift from God."

"We don't mean any disrespect toward your daughter. We're only trying to ensure that Mr. Dubé gets the fair trial he deserves."

"He got everything he deserved, trust me on that, young man. And what did my daughter deserve?"

"She deserved better than she received," I said.

"I saw you speaking to Velma Wykowski."

"Wykowski, huh?"

"That was her name when she roamed about the city like a feral goat. What business could you have with a woman like her?"

"Whatever it is, it's my business," I said.

Mrs. Cullen let out a perfect middle-class humph. "She's a molten one, isn't she? Warming to look at, but dangerous to the touch. You know, she was with him first."

"With whom?"

"Your client. But he wasn't rich enough for her tastes, so the tramp tossed him and his toys to my Leesa."

"Toys? What toys?"

"It's not important. What is important is that she sent him my daughter's way. I'll never forgive her that."

"Velma seems to have genuinely cared for your daughter."

"Not enough to keep Leesa away from the French snake who became her husband. He's a bad man, a charmer to be sure, but bad. A man can be a snake and a charmer both. He charmed my daughter, yes, but all the time I knew. I told her so, but Leesa wasn't one to listen. So, against our best judgments, we gave him our daughter, and look what happened. I knew it, from the first. I could see the darkness in him."

"And what does that look like, Mrs. Cullen," I said, "the darkness in a man?"

She took a step closer, grabbed the fabric of my sleeve. "A flash of light where there should be none. Look in his left eye, Mr. Carl. It is there to be seen."

"The flaw in his eye?"

"A sign."

"But that doesn't mean he murdered her."

She let go of my arm, turned toward the courtroom door. "Maybe not, but it means he had it in him."

Funny, I thought, that was exactly the way I felt about François Dubé, too. Except that wasn't what he was on trial for. Sometimes I had to remind myself of why I ended up a criminal defense attorney. It wasn't the money, really, because, truth be told, I wasn't making enough, and it wasn't because I believed that my clients were ultimately good souls wrongly accused, because generally they were neither good nor innocent, they were a bad lot, and François Dubé might just have been one of the worst. No, the root reason I was a criminal defense attorney was that I was always most comfortable on the side of the guy everybody else was against.

"You can be assured," I said, "that Ms. Dalton, who will be prosecuting the case, is a highly competent trial attorney. If there is enough evidence to convict Mr. Dubé again, she will get it done. My job is just to make sure that the trial is fair."

"That's a lie, Mr. Carl. I know what your job is. Your job is to disseminate the perjuries he gives you, to make the truthful look false, to spread doubt like a farmer spreads manure."

"We all need to have faith in the system, Mrs. Cullen."

She lowered her head so that she was peering angrily at me from beneath her brow. "That's not where my faith lies."

There was something interesting in the malevolence she aimed at me just then. "If you can see darkness in François Dubé, what do you see when you look at me?"

She took a step forward, reached out a hand as if pulling a message from my soul. "I see something missing, is what I see."

"Any idea what?"

"Well, for starters," she said, a smile breaking out on her face, "a tooth."

I gave her a small laugh, nodded, and started toward the door, but before I got past, she grabbed my arm again.

"He's a charmer, like I said, and a snake, too, Mr. Carl. You should be on alert for who he's charming now."

It was sort of creepy, my hallway discussion with Mrs. Cullen, which might explain the strange image I carried in my head when I opened the door to the courtroom. In fact, I almost expected to see in the courtroom a giant cobra with a flaw in its eye, waving back and forth as it rose out of its basket, itself wearing the turban, itself playing the pipe, not itself subject to the beck of a charmer but looking to do some dark charming of its own.

What I saw instead was François Dubé, standing at the defense table, a sheriff with one hand on François's shoulder, his other hand on François's arm, about to step François back and take him off to prison. But François wasn't looking at the sheriff, no. The sheriff was behind, and François was looking forward, directly into the eyes of my partner,

Beth. He was holding her hands and gazing into her eyes, and speaking as calmly and softly as a hypnotist.

And my partner, Beth, God help her, was looking back and listening both and seeming to fall ever deeper under his spell.

I suppose at this point I need to recount the first of my visits to Dr. Bob. Remember I mentioned gratuitous violence?

"Uh-oh," said Dr. Pfeffer cheerily as he peered into my mouth. "I see an abscess. And that's not the bad news."

With his hands still in my mouth, I replied, "Arruuuarrheearrgh."

"It's cracked, you see," said Dr. Bob. "Your lower-right first molar. This one there."

He gave it a tap with one of his instruments and I tried to kick out the fluorescent lights in the ceiling.

"It must have been the gun across your jaw that broke it. The crack is what's causing the abscess, bacteria crawling like hungry spiders down the gap until they find a cozy home in your gums. I would love to save it, nothing I like better than a good endodontic procedure, but what can I do with a cracked root? Out it must come." He gave a pickpocket's giggle when he said this last part, delighted by the possibility of separating my tooth from my mouth. "Is that okay with you, Victor?"

"No chance to keep it?"

"On a chain around your neck, possibly," said Dr. Bob, "but not in your mouth."

"What about the gap?"

"Oh, we'll take care of that, don't you worry."

"Too late."

He pulled back, his eyes narrowed behind his glasses. "Do you want us to get another opinion? I could ask Tilda, but she usually agrees with me."

He laughed, that car-alarm laugh. I glared.

"Really, Victor, don't look so worried. It's all quite routine, and there really is no choice."

"I suppose if you say there's no choice."

"That's right, Victor. We all must do what we must do."

"Okay, then."

"Good. Great. Yes. And there is no reason to wait, is there? No time like the present to take control of a situation. Lucky for you I have a hole in my schedule."

"Lucky for me."

"Let me call in Tilda, and we'll begin."

Almost immediately the massive figure of Dr. Bob's hygienist appeared in the doorway, like some dental Valkyrie sent down to gather in my mortally wounded tooth. Behind me I could hear the unnerving clank of metal, the fitting of fixings, the ominous taps as a syringe was filled.

When all his preparations were complete, Dr. Bob gave a nod. Tilda leaned over me and gripped each of my biceps with her huge hands. Her woody scent covered me like a blanket.

"This part won't hurt much," said Dr. Bob. "You'll only feel a little pinprick."

He jabbed a sliver of metal deep into my gum and jabbed it again and then again as I writhed beneath him on the examination chair and my gum and lip turned to slack, lifeless rubber.

"Calm down," said Tilda as she pressed my arms hard into the chair and smothered my upper body with her chest. "Don't be such a silly man, *ja*. This is the easy part."

*   *   *

Dr. Bob, in the middle of my extraction, was in the middle of a story, and neither was going well.

The story was about a farm family in Colombia, whom he had happened to meet while doing volunteer dental work in Bogotá. The daughter was a beautiful fourteen-year-old who had caught the eye of a local drug lord. The drug lord had demanded that the family deliver the girl up to him when she turned fifteen. The father had complained, the drug lord had shown little patience for complaints, the father came to Dr. Bob because half his teeth had been knocked out by a baseball bat.

"His mouth was a mess," said Dr. Bob. "Worse than yours, if you can believe that. I speak Spanish fluently, and still I could barely understand a word he was saying."

Maybe it was because your hands were in his mouth, I thought but didn't say. First, I didn't say it because his hands were in my mouth, and second, I didn't say it because the extraction wasn't going well at all and I was too terrified to speak. At the outset he had gripped my tooth with his pliers, prepared to start muscling it out of my jaw, and after the first hint of pressure, something came free. Boy, that was easy, I thought, remembering what I had heard about Dr. Bob's gentle hands, and then it came again, the "Uh-oh," and a nervous giggle.

I proceeded to search the walls for diplomas.

"It's fallen apart, Victor. Your tooth, it has come undone. The damage was worse than we thought. This makes it a little more inconvenient. Tilda, I'll need the narrow forceps, please."

And then the rocking began as Dr. Bob, hairy forearms flexing with effort, gripped the disparate parts of my shattered tooth with pointy-nosed pincers and pulled and yanked and heaved and hauled, all the time continuing with his story.

"It was a sad tale the father told, so sad that I could not stand by and do nothing. I had to do something. I felt obligated. I guess it's just the way I am wired. And so, after I fixed up his teeth as best I could, I took a week of vacation and had him lead me to the lair of this drug lord.

"A day on a bus, a day on a mule cart to get back to his farm, a full day in the blinding heat to climb the mountain to the east, to descend the other side, and to hack our way through the jungle. It was a struggle for me, I am used to cold weather, but I soldiered on. At the edge of a clearing, we crawled as close as we dared. Through binoculars I could see a road and a wall and a gate and a château perched on the edge of a hill. There was a picnic with children going on behind the wall. Men with machine guns patrolled, fancy cars drove in and out. There were balloons, I seem to recall, and a plane. Aha."

His hands jerked out of my mouth. In the teeth of his pliers was a bloodied sliver of bone and root.

"We're making progress," he said as he dropped the sliver into a metal tray with a clink, "though it's hard to see with all the blood. Spit."

I spat. Leaning over the no-longer-white sink, I took the opportunity to rub my tongue over the half-extracted tooth. Like Dresden after the bombing, shattered walls, narrow shards of chimneys rising above the smoking wreckage.

"Once more into the fray," said Dr. Bob as he reached into my mouth. Tilda gripped my narrow shoulders with her massive hands. Dr. Bob placed his foot upon my chair for leverage. "Let me see, what next? Ah, yes." I felt something clamp onto my mouth, my jaw shivered from the pressure.

"I was also at the time doing dental work in the American embassy," said Dr. Bob. "The usual services for embassy personnel, you understand, scaling and filling, picking out bits of jalapeño. Foreign Service types tend to trust only Americans with their teeth, and it merely takes a few brisk walks in Bogotá to understand. After my visit with the farmer, I began sifting through my embassy clientele. You get a sense of a person when he or she is in the chair. Grip a tooth, I often say, and you get a grip on a soul. Steady now, yes."

My head rose up under his pull, my neck strained to stay attached, and then my head snapped back into the headrest. Another sliver of bone, another clink.

"I knew what I was looking for. A certain nonchalance, a certain lack of evident responsibility, usage of last names only in hearty greetings, oversize laterals and cuspids. It didn't take long to find him. A doughy-faced man with a rumpled suit and blasé gaze, who said, whenever he spied me, 'Good to see you again, Pfeffer.' We got to talking, the usual dentist-to-patient pleasantries, as we are doing now, Victor. Offhand conversation about the weather, the wine. And then I mentioned a trip I had recently taken, a hike and a climb, a chance to see the real Colombia. And a strange sight I had come upon, a clearing, a château heavily guarded, trucks rumbling in and out at all hours—yes, that part I added, a little color to keep up interest—and a plane. Let me tell you, Victor, his gaze wasn't so blasé anymore. Brace yourself, boy."

A grunt from me, a gasp of satisfaction from him. Clink.

"Open up, open up, we're almost done. Yes. I see you." He dug once again into my jaw. "When he left the office, his teeth were bright and shiny, and in his shirt pocket lay a map, complete with GPS coordinates. And so I had done all I could do. Nothing left but to hope. Hold tight. Ah, yes."

Clink.

"We're almost done. I see another shard. Hold on, this

one's deep. Just before I was about to leave Bogotá, the farmer came back to have his teeth inserted. He was very happy with his new mouth and happy that the problem with his daughter had been solved. Apparently there had been a secret military operation, bombs had been dropped—bombs, Victor, and napalm—the entire clearing had been turned to cinder. The drug lord's reign of terror was over, and the farmer's daughter was now engaged to a local butcher. To show his gratitude, the farmer brought me a sack of green coffee beans and a live chicken. Have you ever tasted chicken, Victor, cooked up just moments after it has been killed and cleaned? It tastes different, richer. A little like snake. Grab hold, Tilda, I need some help."

It felt like a winch was raising my jaw. My eyes rolled, I almost blacked out before my head snapped back. Clink.

"I think we're done. Open up once more and let me check. Yes. Yes. Clean. Done. And the blood is flowing nicely. That wasn't so bad, now, was it?"

I was about to answer with a spicy bit of invective when Dr. Bob said, "Spit."

I spat.

"This is why I became a dentist. To be able to aid patients in need, to stop their suffering, to make their lives just a little bit better. I want you to know this, Victor, I need you to know this. All I ask for in the world is a chance to help. You'll have to come back in a week."

I tried to say something, but it came out like mush, and after a while I just stopped.

"Absolutely," said Dr. Bob, as if he had understood every word. "Now, Victor, I need to warn you. The blood will clot over the hole. That is good. It protects the wound, it aids in the healing. Do nothing to disturb the clot, or the consequences can be dire. Do not prod it with a toothpick, do not worry it with your tongue. Cigarettes, alcohol, carbonated beverages like pop can all disturb the clot. Do you understand?"

I nodded, felt for the wound with my tongue.

"Good," he said. "Tilda will finish up. See you in a week."

He ripped off his bloodstained gloves, tossed them gallantly into the biohazard bin on his way out of the office.

Tilda, whose broad back was to me as she worked over a counter, spun around. In each hand, wielded like weapons, were little boxes covered in cellophane.

"Stop your whimpering and make a decision, *ja*," she said. "Which color for your toothbrush, green or blue?"

I was still licking my wound, literally, when the social worker assigned to my pro bono case, Isabel Chandler, pulled up in front of my office building in her jaunty yellow Volkswagen. She smiled brightly at me and said those sweet words all men are longing to hear.

"What happened to your face?"

"Let's just go," I said.

We were off to visit my four-year-old client, Daniel Rose, and his mother, Julia, to check out their living conditions, to ensure that Julia was taking proper care of her son, and to impress upon her the need to show up in court at the assigned times and to follow all recommendations of Children's Services.

"She should be home this time," said Isabel. "I called just before I left to make sure she remembered. She said she's waiting for us."

"Which means she won't be there," I said.

"Excuse me?"

"She won't be there," I said slowly.

"What's with your mouth?"

"I lost a tooth."

"You ought to find it, before the rest of your mouth collapses."

"Thank you for that."

"Julia better be there," said Isabel. "The judge is losing patience."

"I'd say the judge's patience with Julia is already lost."

"I meant with you," said Isabel.

"Hey, I'm here, aren't I?"

"The judge wants more from you in this case than just showing up. She wants you to give her a solid recommendation about what's best for your client."

"I'm having a hard enough time keeping my own life straight. How would I know what's best for a four-year-old?"

"That's the trick, isn't it?"

"I'll just do whatever you tell me to do."

"No, see, Victor, that's not good enough. I have to consider the best interests of everyone involved, including Julia and the state. You, on the other hand, have only Daniel's interests to consider. And you have enough time to learn what you need to learn, that is if you're willing to put in the effort. Are you, Victor?"

"He's my client," I said.

"What does that mean?"

"Pretty much everything," I said.

"Okay, then. So this tooth thing, did it hurt much?"

"Like two squirrels fighting in my mouth."

"Yikes."

"Yeah," I said.

We weren't headed too far away, just over the Schuylkill River, past the University of Pennsylvania, into the heart of West Philly.

Isabel parked on the street, near a small bodega and a Chinese take-out place, its counter swathed in Plexiglas. It was a crowded, jaunty West Philly neighborhood, some of the row houses cracked and run-down, some brightly painted, with AstroTurf on their porches. Kids played, old ladies sat on folding chairs and surveyed their domain, a dragon on the sign of a tattoo parlor sneered at passersby.

Down the street we walked together, in our suits, with our briefcases. We would have looked less out of place in hula skirts.

"Here," she said when we reached a corner bar called Tommy's High Ball.

"What, are we going for a drink first?"

"That might not be a bad idea, but no." She motioned to a door next to the tavern entrance. "Julia lives with her boyfriend and Daniel in a single room above the bar."

"Nice wholesome environment."

"It's a home," she said as she rang a buzzer beside the door.

While Isabel waited for an answer, I opened the door to Tommy's High Ball and glanced inside. Not too crowded, not too smoky, not too dark. It wasn't quite a clean, well-lighted place, but it seemed friendly enough. A few men sat at the bar, a group of men played cards in a booth in the rear. And just to the left of the door, beneath the neon signs in the window, two men hunched over a chessboard while a third man stood and watched. One of the players pushed a piece forward before turning his head and looking at me.

Cragged face, red bow tie, black porkpie hat. Horace T. Grant. Of course it was.

I was about to raise my hand and shout out, "Hey, Pork Chop," when Horace T. Grant did something strange. He looked at me, raised one eyebrow just enough to let me know he recognized my face, and then turned back to the board without a word.

Well now, I know how to take a hint, and I remembered what Horace had told me about anonymity as he devoured his chickenpox muffin, so I didn't yell out or wave or even wait there for him to look again my way. I turned back to the bar, nodded at the too-tall bartender with the shocking white hair who was giving me the eye, and slipped back outside, where Isabel still waited at the door.

"She's not answering," said Isabel.

"She's not there," I said.

"Maybe the buzzer's broken."

"It's not broken. Did you try the door?"

She looked at me, looked at the door, pressed it open.

We climbed the stairs, dark and damp, the smell of stale beer and cigarettes leaking in from the bar, and reached a painted wooden door on the second level.

Isabel rapped the door lightly with her knuckles. Rapped it again.

Nothing.

I knocked less lightly, pounding at the wood with the bottom of my fist. "Ms. Rose," I yelled. "I am Daniel's court-appointed lawyer. We have come for a court-ordered visit. Ms. Rose, you need to open up."

Nothing.

"She's not here," I said.

"But she promised. She said she was waiting for us."

"She doesn't want us in her life. Or maybe, more interestingly, somebody else doesn't want us in her life."

"Too bad," said Isabel, taking out a phone.

"What are you doing?"

"I'm calling the judge. She'll issue a bench warrant."

"And then what? How soon do you think the police will get around to looking for her? And when they do start looking, and if she does get picked up, then what? What happens to Daniel?"

"What would you have me do?"

"Follow me," I said.

"Where to?"

"Just follow."

I climbed down the steps, pushed through the front door. Isabel hesitated a moment before following.

At the corner Horace was leaning against the brick wall of the bar, a chessboard and box in his hand. I walked by him without so much as a nod. I knew where I was going, I had already traced the route on a map in my office. I turned right, turned left at the next intersection.

These were all row houses now, more in disrepair than those on the commercial street, cracked porches, peeling paint, trees shriveling in the little plots of land between the cement of the sidewalk and the asphalt of the street.

And there it was, a quiet house on a quiet block, shades drawn, lights out, nothing.

"Go on up and knock," I said to Isabel.

"Who's in there?"

"Go on up and see."

She gave me a look, as if I had grown antennae, as if I had transformed before her very eyes into a different species, and then headed up the stoop. This time I followed her. From inside we could hear a television going.

Isabel rang the buzzer, waited a bit, then rapped her knuckles gently on the door. She looked at me, I showed her a fist, she gave the door a bang.

A woman answered, T-shirt and jeans, short dark hair, dark eyes, a crying baby on her hip. With the door opened, she shouted into the house, "Turn down the damn TV," before turning her attention to us. "What you want?" she said angrily, and then grew quiet when she took in exactly who was there before her, Isabel with her suit and briefcase and me standing beside her.

"Hello, Julia," said Isabel.

"Crap," said Julia Rose.

CHAPTER

23

Daniel Rose slumped on a couch in the living room, his fists balled, his features impassive, his stare intent on the cartoon playing on the television set. He was a stocky, towheaded kid with pale skin and slip-on sneakers, and he was doing his best to ignore me, which is pretty much par for the course with my clients.

In the kitchen Julia Rose and Isabel were having a face-to-face. Isabel was not too pleased with Julia or her explanations. Julia's friend had to run an errand, and so Julia had been forced to watch her baby daughter, which was why she hadn't been at her apartment that day or the other times Isabel had tried to visit. Julia had no way to get to the parenting sessions she had promised Isabel she would attend because she couldn't find the bus schedules. Julia had missed her appointment with the doctor because Daniel was too sick to go out.

There was a technical legal term for what Julia Rose was shoveling to Isabel. The whole scene was enough to weary a saint, and I wasn't a saint, so instead of letting her toss shovelfuls onto me, I'd left the kitchen and sat myself beside Daniel on the couch.

"Daniel," I said, trying to speak over the sound of the television, "do you know what a lawyer is?"

Daniel stared at the screen and said nothing. I was

tempted to switch the TV off so he'd give me his full attention, but if I switched it off and he ran away screaming, that
would end my chance to speak to him that day. And I didn't
mind that the sound of the television was keeping our conversation private from Julia in the kitchen. So I waited for
him to respond to my question. When he didn't, I answered
it for him.

"A lawyer is someone who helps people who might be in
trouble. I'm a lawyer."

No response, no reaction, but he did chuckle at a pratfall
on the screen.

"Today, Daniel, the person I'm here to help is you."

I waited. No response. I hadn't had much real experience
with children, and I wondered if a four-year-old kid could
understand anything I was saying. Probably not. I was about
to give it up and go back to Isabel's conversation with Julia
when Daniel, still staring at the television, finally spoke.

"You talk funny."

"Well, you look funny."

I thought he'd laugh at that, or smile at least, but he didn't.
He tightened his lips and kept his gaze glued to the television. I licked the scab in my mouth. How do you talk to kids
anyway?

"The reason I talk funny," I said, "is that I lost a tooth. You
want to see?"

He nodded.

I opened my mouth, pulled down the edge of my lower lip
so the gap was clear. He turned to look at it, nodded, turned
back to the television.

"Did it hurt?" he said.

"Not really."

"I didn't do nothing."

"Anything, son. You didn't do anything, and I know that."

"So I'm not in trouble."

"But you still might need a lawyer, and that's why a nice judge lady hired me to help you. How does your mother treat you?"

"Good."

"Well. She treats you well. That's good to hear. Does she give you enough food?"

"Yeah."

"Does she give you baths?"

"Sometimes."

"Does she read to you?"

He shrugged, twisted up his fingers.

"Does she ever hit you?" I said.

"When I'm bad."

"How often are you bad?"

"I don't know."

"Does it hurt when she hits you?"

"Not really."

"Do you like watching TV?"

"Yeah."

"Do you watch a lot?"

"My mother lets me."

"Do you ever play with friends?"

"I don't know. I'm watching."

"So am I, but we can still talk."

"I can't hear."

"Sure you can, Daniel. Do you have many friends?"

"I don't know."

"Who are some of your friends?"

"Can we be quiet now?"

"Not yet. Do you ever go to the park?"

"Yeah."

"What do you do there?"

"The big slide."

"Who watches you in the park?"

"My mom."

"Does your mom have a boyfriend?"

He waited a moment without saying anything and then picked up the remote control, increased the volume.

"What's his name, your mother's friend?" I said.

"I don't know."

"Sure you do."

"Randy."

"Randy. Good. How does Randy treat you?"

"I don't know."

"Does he play with you much?"

"No."

"Does he read to you?"

"No."

"Does he give you baths?"

"No."

"Does he ever hit you?"

He picked up the remote, raised the volume again.

"Turn it down in there," shouted Julia Rose from the kitchen.

Daniel lowered the volume. He was pretty good with the remote, was Daniel Rose. I didn't know if he was good with LEGOs, with puzzles, I didn't know if he liked to turn the pages of picture books, but he was pretty damn good with the remote.

"Hey, Daniel, would it be all right if someday, with your mom's permission, I took you to the park?"

"I don't know."

"I could buy you some ice cream. What kind of ice cream do you like?"

"Chocolate."

"Okay. Good. Do you like sprinkles?"

"Yeah. The pretty ones."

"All the different colors? Okay, chocolate ice cream with

rainbow sprinkles. Just do me one favor, Daniel. Can you smile for me? A big smile? Give me a smile to let me know we're friends and I'll leave you to watch the television all alone."

He turned his head and faked a big smile and then turned back to the cartoon, and my throat tightened on me.

"Julia has agreed to go to the parenting classes," said Isabel when I returned to the kitchen, where the two women were sitting. Isabel was now holding the neighbor's baby. "No excuses, right, Julia?"

"That's right. I promise."

"I'm going to make sure the judge keeps you to that," said Isabel. "And the doctor's appointment. You can't miss that. You understand, Julia, that this is getting serious? If these things don't happen, if you don't appear before the judge at your next hearing and follow all her recommendations, then we might be forced to take your son away and put him in foster care."

"You won't do that," said Julia. "Promise me. You won't."

"We will do what we have to do to protect Daniel."

"I'm going to follow all the things you told me to follow. And the doctor's visit you set up. I will, I promise."

"And you know how to get to the courthouse?"

"The bus is expensive," she said. "That's why I missed it last time. I wanted to show up, but the bus is, like, a couple bucks each way, and they make me pay for the baby."

"How about if I pick you up and drive you to the hearing?" I said. "Would that work?"

"Okay. Yeah."

"I'll pick you up at your apartment, you and Daniel and Randy."

Her head snapped, her eyes widened. "What? No. Not Randy. He can't make the hearing. He works."

"Where?" I said.

"I don't want to talk about him. What does he have to do with Daniel?"

"Doesn't he live in your room above the bar?"

"Not really. Not no more. He left. He's gone."

"He's out of your life?"

"Yeah, out of it. Good riddance, the creep. Just don't bring him in it, okay?" There was a fear in her eyes that I didn't like. "I'll do whatever you tell me to do, but he don't want to be involved in my mess."

Isabel looked at me. I shrugged.

"Okay for now," said Isabel. "Let's see how you do before your next court hearing. If everything's going well, we'll create a new action plan then. Do you have anything else to add, Victor?"

"Yeah, I do," I said. "What's up with Daniel's teeth?"

"How did you know she'd be there?" said Isabel as we made our way back to her car.

"I have my sources."

"So you're not just showing up."

"What did I tell you?"

"That he's your client. But I'm not sure what that means?"

"Why'd you become a social worker?"

"To help families in trouble. To make a difference, I suppose."

"See, that's where we diverge. I'm not out to save the whales, or save the planet, or save the children. Frankly, I don't want to make a difference in the world, because I'd probably just screw it up. I'm only a lawyer trying to do his best for his clients. Daniel Rose is a client, four years old or not, and so he gets everything I've got. It's that simple."

"Even if the file was dumped on your desk and you're not getting paid?"

"That's the part that sucks."

"I don't know if I find you admirable or appalling."

"When you figure it out, let me know. So what do you think about my client?"

"I think he's a little kid living with a mother who doesn't know what the hell she's doing."

"But do you think he's in danger?"

"Of getting messed up by his mother? Sure, like every other kid in America."

"I could tell you stories about my childhood that would leave you weeping," I said.

"But I don't see any reason to pull the mother and son apart. You do that, there are always scars, and good foster homes are scarce. But I want to keep an eye on her and the boy. It seems like a fragile situation. And you're right, those teeth are a problem. We'll have to get a dentist involved."

"Which is always bad news," I said. "And the boyfriend still troubles me."

"Julia said they broke up."

"Yes, she did, and she was so truthful about everything else there's no reason to believe she wouldn't be truthful about her boyfriend."

"Did Daniel say anything about him?"

"He seemed like he was too scared to talk."

"You're going to have to learn more about him," she said.

"How?"

"He's your client," she said. "You figure it out."

Figure it out indeed. I thought about the boy, the mother, the boyfriend, Randy, thought how I could find what I needed to find out, when Isabel let out a gruff "Hrumph."

"Excuse me?" I said.

"That's all right, Victor. I've heard a belch before."

"I didn't belch. You said something."

"I didn't say anything."

I stopped, looked around, saw the front brim of a black porkpie hat peeking over the railing of a porch.

"Why don't you go on ahead," I said to Isabel. "I need to make a call."

When she was far enough down the block, I took out my

phone, wandered over to the edge of the porch, leaned against the brick, pretended to make a call.

"Was that you clearing your throat," I said into the dead phone, "or was someone plunging a stopped-up toilet?"

"Watch your mouth afore I smack it closed," said Horace T. Grant from behind me. "Although it sounds like someone else done that already. I see you found the place. How was your visit?"

"Fine."

"Twenty minutes is all you give it and you come out saying, 'Fine.' You on a tight schedule, boy? Got you a pedicure appointment you don't want to miss?"

"We were there for an hour," I said calmly. "We set up parenting sessions and a doctor's appointment, and I'm going to personally drive Julia and Daniel to the next court hearing. Does that meet with your approval?"

"It's not up to me to approve, which is about the only reason you still breathing, other than a nose that could fit on Mount Rushmore."

"Why, thank you."

"It wasn't a compliment."

"She knows we're all looking over her shoulder," I said. "That should help things from here on in. Though there might be something else of concern. What do you know about the boyfriend? His name is Randy."

"I know his name, fool. Which is more than I want to know."

"That bad."

"Like a bunion on the foot on the face of the world."

"I get the idea. They're still together, Randy and Julia?"

"Like shit and Shinola."

"What does that mean, actually, not knowing shit from Shinola?"

"It means you're a lawyer."

"Horace, your wit is surpassed only by your pleasant manner. You know where this Randy works?"

"What am I, the Yellow Pages? You were inside for a so-called hour, why didn't you ask that woman?"

"She wasn't so willing to discuss her boyfriend."

"Then maybe I'm not so willing neither. You mention my name in there?"

"No, sir."

"Good."

"Okay, I understand."

"What do you understand? You understand less than a bloodworm on a hook, wiggling yourself free even as the largemouth bass comes looking for dinner. You understand? A thumb in my eye, you understand. I bet you didn't even find out nothing about the daughter."

"The daughter?"

"There you go, see? You're like a jalopy without an engine, ugly and rusting on the outside, empty on the inside. What good are you?"

"Julia has a daughter?"

"You so lost, how you fall out of bed and don't hit the ceiling is beyond me."

"Where is she?"

"Now you're getting to the root of it, boy. Now you starting to ask some questions."

"You don't know where she is?"

"You stupid sumbitch. If I knew where the hell she was, would I be dealing with the likes of you?"

"No, sir," I said. "I don't think you would."

"First sensible thing you said all day. Now, get on going, there's work to be done."

I pushed myself from off the porch railing, started walking toward Isabel without looking back. He was such a pleasure to deal with, Horace T. Grant, and unfortunately, from what I could tell, he was almost always right, which meant there was more work to be done. So Julia Rose had a daughter somewhere, my client Daniel had a sister somewhere, and no one knew enough to even search for her. Which meant that I might have to.

If I had a dog, I would have kicked it just then. I was falling deeper into something that I didn't understand, that I wasn't qualified to handle, and that wasn't going to pay me a cent.

Pro bono blows.

CHAPTER

25

This is how I ended up flat on my back, mewing in agony, reaching for the white light in the distance.

We had gotten François his new trial, now it was time to devise some devious way to win it. The best route, I figured, was to ride François's Gallic charm as if it were a surfboard on a six-foot swell. But to do that he'd have to testify, so it was time for him to finally answer our questions. It was hot in the prison interview room, Beth was quiet, I was sweating, and all the time François was answering, his eyes were saying, *How can you doubt me, Victor?* How could I? Because his tongue was moving. But it wasn't the lying so much that got to me, I'm used to clients lying—what would I ever do with a client who told me the truth?—more it was the insouciance with which he told his lies, as if he was so charming he didn't have to try too hard. It was all enough to send me sucking on my scab.

"Tell us where you met your wife," I said.

"There is a place called Marrakech owned by Geoffrey Sunshine."

"The guy whose name is always in the papers?"

"That is him, yes," said François. "The second floor of the building was a club. It was fun, this club, a spectacle. There was a restaurant, too, and Geoffrey was a friend of sorts. He was always trying to get me to cook for his restaurant, which was why I was often there. He would invite me to the club, introduce me to the girls. Quite nice. One of the girls he introduced me to was Leesa. She had a bit of a reputation, but there was something in her that I admired. A spark of freedom, I think, and a sweetness. At first it was just, you know, playing around. But after a while it became something else, if you understand."

"Why did you marry her?"

"Why else? I loved her."

"So what happened to the marriage?"

"It is hard to say."

"Try."

"Things change with a child. Amber was a beautiful baby, yes, but things changed. It was a difficult delivery, and Leesa was in quite a bit of pain for a long time afterward. The baby was crying, shrieking, always seemed hungry, and Leesa was depressed. The doctor said it was a normal thing, the depression, but that did not make it easier. And I had my new restaurant. I was obsessed with starting it right and so could not be around as much as maybe I should have been. With Leesa's pain and the depression getting worse, the doctor finally prescribed some medicine."

"What medication?" I said.

"Something about an ox, I do not know. It fixed the pain, yes, but it had a bad effect on Leesa. She became moody, manic, or depressed, depending on the hour. She did not seem to bond with the baby. And we began to fight. She said she felt smothered, chained, and abandoned all at once. And it was not only her, I was feeling a little trapped, too. After a while we were like strangers. And then she accused me of cheating."

"Did you?"

"Is that important?"

"Yes."

"Maybe then I did, yes. Nothing extraordinary."

"With whom?"

"None of your business."

"Believe me when we tell you this, François, everything in your life has become our business. Whom?"

"There was a customer. There was a girl on a bicycle. What do you want, Victor? I'm French."

"I'll need names," I said.

"Who can remember? Katherine? Lorraine? Yes, Lorraine." A smile followed by a dismissive wave. "And then there was someone from work. Darcy. Darcy DeAngelo. That was maybe a bit more serious. But it was not the affairs that caused the end of us. They were just . . . affairs."

"What was it, then?"

"We were both unhappy. That was it. We began to make each other miserable. Therefore, I left. I thought that was best, but Leesa evidently disagreed."

"The divorce proceeding wasn't amicable, I presume."

He gave a French snort of derision. "I wanted it to be. I was worried about Leesa and concerned about Amber, but Leesa decided nothing would be easy. She went crazy with revenge, she showed no concern for Amber. It was the drug still, I thought. I tried to get her off the pills, but the only way to talk to her now was through the judge. So that is what I did. For some reason, me bringing the drugs into the court case only made the situation worse."

"Funny how that works," I said. "Where were you the night of the murder?"

"In my apartment. I had worked lunch and then the dinner shift also. We had a drink or two after closing, but I was too tired to stay long. I was exhausted. I still had my chef's coat on as I walked home. I collapsed into the bed. I was asleep when the police woke me up with the news. I let them search my apartment. I had nothing to hide. That is when they found the gun and the blood."

"How did it get there?"

"I do not know. I still do not know. It was the fat detective that found it."

"Torricelli?"

"Yes. Maybe he brought it over in his briefcase to frame me. It is always the husband, right? He wanted to be sure."

"I wouldn't put it past him."

"He did not seem to me, that detective, to be so bright."

"Bright enough to put you in here. Did he arrest you right then?"

"Yes, of course. That very morning. I have not been out of jail since. I would have had another drink that night if I had known."

"What happened to all the stuff in the apartment?"

"I stopped paying the rent when I was in jail. I do not know where everything is. My clothes, my books and pans. Who knows? Who cares? I have not lately had much use for a copper salmon poacher."

I had been pacing back and forth, sucking on my wound, as I asked my questions. Now I sat down right across from him, looked at him carefully as I said, "Why is Velma Takahashi paying for your defense?"

"I do not know."

"I don't believe you."

"But you must, Victor. I do not know. Truly. She came to visit me. I knew her, she was a friend of Leesa's from her days at Marrakech, and we maybe played a bit, if you understand, but we were never really friends. In fact, I always thought she resented me."

"Why?"

"I broke up the team. They were quite the team, and a

team after our separation, too, if you listened to the rumors. So I was surprised that she came to visit. She said she only wanted to see how I was getting along. I lied to her and said I was fine. But I was not fine. Who is fine in this place? And I think she could see that. And somehow it affected her, I do not know. She looked at me, I had a bruise on my face from something that happened in the shower, and I could see tears in her eyes. Like somehow the bruise, it was her fault. And then she told me she would help me any way she could, that she would pay for a new lawyer if I needed."

"How did you light on us?"

"I saw your name in the paper, Victor. I asked around. When I thought you were the one, I decided to write. I have done some fishing in my life. You catch nothing with an empty hook. From what I heard about you, I knew what I needed to get your interest. I called Velma and asked for a check."

"As bait?"

"Yes, of course. Dangling on a hook. And here I am with another chance at life." He grinned, like a cat with a fish tail sticking out of its teeth. "And it worked, did it not?"

"I guess it did."

"Anything else?"

I thought a bit. "There is one thing more that has been bothering me. Why do you chef guys always undercook my steak?"

"You must be careful with the meat," said François. "There is a point where the taste and texture are perfect. You go beyond that point, the muscle it clenches and everything is ruined. It is like eating leather."

"But what if I like it well done?"

"Then you, Victor, are a barbarian."

At least he wasn't lying about that.

*   *   *

"He'll make an awesome witness," said Beth after they had taken François Dubé back to his cell. We were still in the room, both of us standing now, waiting for someone to lead us out.

"Sure he will," I said.

"The jury will eat him up like a crème brûlée."

"Maybe, if they go for that French thing. Personally, I find it annoying, like a cat in the corner coughing up hair balls and meowing orders."

"A cat?"

"Don't the French remind you of cats? Insufferably superior, willfully independent. And they lick themselves clean after they eat."

"Stop it."

"No, I've seen it, really."

"He'll do great," said Beth. "If he's telling the truth."

"The big if."

"He admitted the affairs," she said.

"With a great amount of pride, I might add."

"And if he had really used the gun, why would he bring it back to his apartment, and why would he consent to the search?"

"I don't know."

"Maybe he is telling the truth. What do you think, Victor?"

I felt the scab in my mouth with my tongue. I had worried it so hard during the interview the edges had come loose. I had been playing with my scab because the whole interview had made me itch all over. Every answer only raised more questions. Like his alibi on the night of the murder, which was no alibi at all. Like his story about how he met his wife, and his relationship with Velma Takahashi, both of which seemed to contradict what Mrs. Cullen had told me outside the courtroom. And his side of the separation seemed a little too pat, didn't it? But then again the strange sadness he had seen in Velma's eyes matched what I had seen there, too.

"He's lying," I said. "He's hiding something, I just don't know what."

"Always the skeptic."

"Come on, Beth. You've heard it enough from me. What's the first precept of the legal profession?"

"Clients lie."

"Very good. There are some things I'm going to want to check out."

"Like what?"

"Like the records of the divorce proceeding. And I'll need to visit that club he talked about, Marrakech."

"You think you might find something there?"

"No," I said, "but it sounded like a pretty good place to pick up women."

Beth laughed as I fiddled with the scab.

"But first," I said, "what we need to do is to talk to Mia Dalton about . . . arrgh."

"Victor? What is it, Victor?"

I gagged on something and searched around futilely for a tissue. In desperation, I spit whatever had come loose into my hand. I couldn't help but give it a look.

An uneven circle of blotchy scab, about the size of a tooth.

"Victor, are you okay?"

I gagged again before gaining enough control to say, "I think so." I took a deep breath and a pure, scorching pain buckled my knees.

"Victor," said Beth, rushing over to me. "What is it?"

I grabbed hold of her arm and felt the blood rush from my head as a great white wooziness overtook me.

Next thing I knew, there was music, lush and ethereal, and a white light lay an arm's length before me, like a vision of another and better world.

And strangest of all, it shone into my mouth.

CHAPTER

26   **"A dry socket,"** said Dr. Bob. "See, the clot is gone, and now the bone of the jaw is exposed, with all its jangling nerves. I warned you, Victor. Didn't I warn you? But apparently you were too bullheaded to listen. Now we have a problem. You were worrying the clot with your tongue, weren't you?"

"Arrghighahoo."

"Of course you tried not to, everyone tries not to, but some are too weak to resist. You had a soda pop, I'd wager, or a beer. Didn't I give you explicit instructions? Even with my best efforts, the failures of others sometimes get in the way and the unexpected happens. It is hard to describe how frustrating that can be. Yet this, too, can be solved, have no fear."

Telling me to have no fear while in a dentist chair was like telling Marley's ghost to look alive.

"Any changes in your medical or personal situation since last we met?"

"Ayyaaw," I said.

"Other than the pain in your jaw, of course. No? Good. So I assume that means you still are not in a fulfilling sexual relationship. I know, these things take time, but maybe I can help. Open wider. We'll need to clean the hole before I apply the dressing. The water might tingle a bit. Yes, yes, very

good. Why is your leg shaking like that? That didn't hurt too
much, did it? Stop nodding your head, please, you're making it hard for me to see. Now, let me just dry it with a quick
burst of air."

He reached in with his air nozzle and blew dry the hole.
My shoe flew against the wall.

Dr. Bob turned his head to inspect the scuff mark. "Second time that happened this week."

He opened a small, squat jar, and the smell of cloves
wafted through the room. He took a long piece of gauze off
his tray with a metal forceps, dipped the whole thing in the
jar. It came out smeared thickly with a brown ooze.

"Now open wide, this is sometimes a bit tricky. Yes, I've
managed to help many of my patients find more than just a
bright, shiny smile. Hold on, now, I have to pack this tightly
in, section by section. The smell is rather nice, but the oint-
ment tastes suspiciously of earwax. Tense your neck as I
push down. Excellent. I'll wipe away the tears from your
cheek. It will be over very soon."

He turned toward his tray, fiddled.

"I've had some success in matching up my patients. It is
not something I do as a matter of course, I am not a busy-
body, heavens, but I do like to help. And I must admit, from
my chair has dropped more than one acorn that has grown
into the mighty oak of marriage."

He leaned over me, brushing my chest as he adjusted the
light. "Open up now, let me get a good look. Ah, yes. Now
tense that neck." As he worked, all ahs and ohs, my head
bobbed up and down like a baseball giveaway.

"I had a patient in Baltimore with a rather unfortunate
overbite who was, as one would expect with such a mouth,
a rabid Republican. Whenever we talked, as I worked like an
overmatched jockey to rein in his teeth, it was all politics
politics politics, and always mindlessly doctrinaire. It was

like having the Fox News Channel in my chair. Except for his bite, he wasn't a bad-looking man, but needless to say he didn't date much."

He took out his hands, adjusted the light again, peered so closely into my mouth I could count his nose hairs.

"Nice. Okay, almost finished. Tilda," he called, "can you come in, please?"

The hulking figure of the hygienist appeared in the doorway. "Yes, Doctor."

"I'm almost through here. Get Mrs. Winterhurst ready, please."

"Very good, Doctor."

"Make sure her entire dress is covered with toweling. She's a bleeder, and we don't want to ruin another Givenchy. And, Tilda, I think we'll need to paint that wall again."

She leaned inside, observed the scuff on the wall, my shoe on the floor. She sneered at my weakness before she left.

"Open wide," said Dr. Bob. "At the same time, I had a patient with two impacted wisdom teeth. A small woman, always angry. She, too, would constantly discuss politics, but she was a raging liberal, a bleeding-heart Democrat to the core, and incensed at everything the Republican Party had perpetrated—her word—upon the country. And she seemed very anxiety-struck about the deficit for some reason. Her calendar, too, was pathetically empty."

"Ayaheeay," I said.

"Absolutely. I'm not much one for politics, it all seems so grubbily self-interested. And it tends to take on the reflexive quality of rooting for a sports team, don't you think? Democrats hate the Republican Party the way Phillies fans hate the Mets. Not much considered thought in that, is there? Although how a mere political party could be more loathsome than the Mets is beyond me."

"Ayahee."

"And don't get me started on Don Young."

"Ooh?"

"I said don't get me started. One person's miracle is another person's disaster. I could hear the groaning from my backyard. But both Baltimore patients had answered question sixteen much as you did, Victor, and I could see in each, along with the loneliness, a certain overwrought sensitivity. They were, perhaps, made for each other. But how to get them together, how to get them past the blindness of their politics?"

Another press into my jaw that sent my neck into spasm.

"I think we're pretty much done," said Dr. Bob. "How does that feel, Victor?"

I rubbed my neck, took a deep breath, gently rested my tongue against the now dressed wound, pressed harder. "It feels fine," I said, slightly shocked that it actually did. "The pain is gone."

"That's the point. It's rather simple, really. Now, try not to disturb the dressing, though I know it might be hard for someone such as you. And under no circumstances should you eat lamb's bladder."

"Why? Will that hurt the wound?"

"No, but it's disgusting, don't you think?" He laughed, I winced. "And now, Victor, it's time to decide how to handle the missing tooth on a more permanent basis. What I'd like to do," said Dr. Bob, "is to drill into your jaw."

"Oh, I bet you would," I said.

"I would drill a hole and screw in an implant. If all goes well, the implant will graft solidly into your bone, something called osseointegration. After about three to six months, depending on the success of the integration, atop the abutment I would attach a restoration, which is that part of the implant that looks like a tooth. It is the most permanent solution. It's also the most painful and most expensive."

"Why am I not surprised? And it takes six months?"

"Some dentists will put the restoration on right away, but the chances of failure are higher that way."

"What about option two?"

"A fixed bridge. It's easier, less painful, less expensive."

"That sounds right by me."

"But its long-term prognosis is not quite as good."

"Still, I find myself strangely attracted to easier, less painful, and less expensive. Am I alone in seeking in dental reconstruction the same traits I look for in a woman?"

"I noticed you don't have dental insurance."

"That's right," I said.

"Still, you mustn't think of dental work the way you think of suits, Victor. Cheaper is not always better. But okay, then. We'll go with the bridge. Next time we'll get started with the grinding."

"Grinding?"

"Don't worry, Victor, it's relatively pain-free."

"Relatively?"

"I'd like to take another set of X-rays to see how the bone looks without the tooth. Tilda," he called.

She appeared quick as a ghost in the doorway, her huge hands dangling like boiled hams at her side.

"A set of bite wings and a periapical X-ray, please, Tilda. Make sure to get a good shot of the lower right."

"Of course, Doctor," she said. "Anything else?"

"No, that's it, thank you," he said, standing. He ripped off his gloves, tossed them into the container, took up my chart, and started scribbling his notes. "Victor, I'll see you in another week."

"Thanks for taking me on such short notice."

"We all must do our part," he said.

"What happened to them, the Baltimore people?"

"Married," he said. "Two children. They're as happy as

mussels. Don't you find the mussel a far more cheerful bivalve than the clam?"

"How did you get them together?"

"Oh, you know. I have my ways. What's the Latin expression? *Minutus cantorum, minutus balorum, minutus carborata descendum pantorum.*"

"We didn't learn that one in law school."

"It means: 'A little song, a little dance, a little seltzer down your pants.' I push here, pull there, I reach in and help mold the clay of reality. It is what I do when I am not molding teeth. I slip horizontally through people's lives and change them for the better. Check your shirt pocket, Victor."

I patted my pocket, reached in, pulled out a slip of paper. On it was written "Carol Kingsly" in script and then a phone number.

"You saw her in the waiting room," said Dr. Bob, "remember? She's a lovely woman, with very refined tastes, not your normal cup of tea, I suppose, but a woman who, fortunately for you, also answered question sixteen in the new-patient questionnaire with a no. She's waiting for your call."

"My call?"

"Yes, your call, Victor. Do try to be pleasant, won't you? And take my advice, dress sharp and never ever talk politics on your first date."

As I watched him leave, Tilda stepped forward. She draped my chest with a heavy lead apron. I pulled it low enough so that it covered my groin. Tilda noticed the gesture and shook her head.

"What kind of men do you fancy, Tilda?" I said.

"Hockey players and prison guards," she said.

"I guess I'll have to lose a few more teeth."

"It can be arranged, bucko. Now, open up, *ja.*"

I opened my mouth. She slipped a white piece of plastic-covered film over my teeth.

"Close."

I closed. The edges of the plastic bladed painfully into the floor of my mouth. Tilda wrapped my face in her muscular hands and twisted my head until my neck cracked.

CHAPTER

27   **Inside the old** YMCA building that served now as the district attorney's offices, I pulled at my lower lip to expose the gap in my teeth. Beth, sitting next to me, grimaced at the sight. Mia Dalton leaned over her desk to get a better view.

"It's gone, all right," said Mia Dalton. "What's the brown gunk in the hole?"

"A dressing. I accidentally removed the scab and exposed the bone."

"Does it hurt?"

"It did, like someone jabbing a red-hot knife into my chops. But not anymore. My dentist took care of that."

"He any good?" said Detective Torricelli, standing behind Dalton's desk. "I might be in the market for a molar masher."

Detective Torricelli was short and round, with the pug nose and swollen eyes of an angry porker. He had looked at my display with enough interest, and he was running his tongue along the inside of his cheek with enough determination to indicate that he might indeed have dental problems of his own.

"Oh, he's terrific, Detective, absolutely," I said, putting on my most trustworthy expression. "And painless, too."

"Painless?"

"Oh, yes. Painless. Such gentle hands. You should give him a try."

"Tell me why I don't swallow the painless part, Carl?" said Torricelli.

"Because you are a cynic with an irrational fear of dentists."

"I might be a cynic," said Tommy Torricelli, "but ain't nothing more rational than my fear of dentists."

"Do you mind if we get down to business?" said Beth. "We want to know if you've given any consideration to a plea offer for François."

"What are you looking for?" said Mia Dalton.

"Something that would take into account the constitutional violation that underlay his prior conviction," said Beth, her voice stellar with righteous indignation, "that would take into account the years he spent in jail as a result of the unjust conviction only a few days ago reversed by Judge Armstrong, that would recognize the price he has paid and allow him to walk out of jail with a sentence of time served."

"Yeah," I added, "something like that."

As Beth spoke, Mia Dalton began hunting around her office, as if she had misplaced an item of great importance.

"What are you searching for?" said Beth with some impatience.

"The reporters that must be hidden here. Or why else would you be giving me a speech."

Torricelli snorted. Beth's features collapsed with disappointment.

"You're not going to let him plea his way out of jail?" she said.

Mia leaned back, crossed her arms. "Look at my face."

We both did. Mia Dalton was short and stocky, with the sharp eyes of a fighter. She had worked her way up the lad-

der in the district attorney's office, from municipal court
bench trials to homicide, based not on her flirtatious manner,
because it wasn't, or her pleasing personality, because she
was more sandpaper than silk, but instead on her sheer
willpower and dogged determination to prevail. The cops all
hated working for her, because she worked them as hard as
she worked herself, but they still fought to have her assigned
to their cases, because she would invariably give them a win.
In the hard-knuckled world of criminal law, nothing succeeded like success, and Mia Dalton was still rising. She was
honest and smart and generally intolerant of fools, which
was why I always felt a little uncomfortable in her presence.

"Do I look like François Dubé's fairy godmother?" she
said.

"I don't see a wand," I said.

"Then there you go. Second-degree murder, twenty years,
out in thirteen, three of which he already served. Let me
know within forty-eight hours."

I turned to Beth and raised an eyebrow.

She shook her head. "I can let you know right now. He
won't accept it. He wants out now."

"Then I guess we're going to try this puppy," said Dalton,
not visibly displeased. "In all the time I've known Victor
here, we've never gone up against each other in front of a
jury. It should be interesting."

"We'll need to examine the physical evidence as soon as
possible," I said. "That is, if you haven't lost it after all these
years."

"It's all there," said Torricelli. "Good to go."

"You both are welcome to examine it at your leisure," said
Dalton. "Everything that was let in in the last trial will be
presented here."

"Except for Seamus Dent," I said, "your crucial eyewitness."

"Not so crucial, but still, nice job on that, I must say. I was almost impressed."

"We aim to please."

"And, Beth, your argument was quite solid. I spoke to the boss about you. We have an opening in the law department if you're interested."

"And leave Victor? I couldn't do that."

"Silly me, I thought leaving Victor here was the main inducement of the offer."

"Speaking of Dent," I said. "What's happening with Detective Gleason?"

"Nothing sweet," said Torricelli. "You lit him up but good, Carl. They took away his gun, put him on the front desk at the auto squad until Internal Affairs finishes its investigation of the shooting. Don't know if he'll weather it. The dead guy's mother just filed a civil suit against the city. Wrongful death."

"Of course she did."

"I was shocked when I saw the pleading," said Mia Dalton, a smile slipping onto her face. "Shocked that your name wasn't on it, Victor. You're slipping. Time was, you would have been the first one knocking at her door, contingency fee agreement at the ready."

"I'm getting old," I said. "Or maybe I believed the detective when he said he had no choice. He tried to do something good for that kid, Dent. It didn't work out, but still."

"Without the eyewitness," said Mia, "we're going to concentrate more on the motive evidence. The prickly divorce. The fight over custody and assets. The girlfriends."

"Excuse me?"

"Detective Torricelli has been busy. Your client had a number of affairs. It will be detailed in our trial memo."

"You care to give us the names now?"

"No, I don't."

"Darcy DeAngelo?" said Beth. "The girl from the restaurant?"

Dalton's eyes widened.

"He told us about her," said Beth. "He told us everything, including that he didn't kill his wife."

"Well, it won't be the first time," said Torricelli.

"The first time for what?" I said.

"The first time a client pulled your chain," he said.

"You don't know the half of it."

"Anything else?" said Mia Dalton.

I took a document out of my briefcase, gave it a quick scan, and then tossed it across her desk. "I have a question about this."

She looked it over. "An inventory of what was seized during the initial search of Mr. Dubé's apartment. The search was done with the defendant's consent and incident to a valid arrest. What of it?"

"What happened to my client's stuff?"

Torricelli stepped forward and took hold of the document. "Everything we wanted, we took and inventoried," he said. "Besides the gun, the bloodied shirt, the bloodied boot, there wasn't much else of interest. We just left it there. I assume your sleazeball client took care of it."

"Apparently the landlord sold it off," I said. "But some stuff appears to be missing, even in your initial notation of what you found in the apartment. There's computer cables but no computer. There's a full-size video camera, with a tripod and lights, but no videotapes. And there are no toys."

"Toys?"

"Yes, toys." Mrs. Cullen had mentioned toys outside the courtroom, but none had been found in Dubé's apartment. Not even kid toys for the daughter.

"I don't know about no toys," said Torricelli. "Maybe he

wasn't a toy kind of guy. Maybe he pawned off what he had to raise biscuit for his legal beagles."

"Maybe, maybe, maybe," I said, grinning. "That's no way to prosecute a murder case."

"What we saw, we noted," said Torricelli, tossing the paper back onto Dalton's desk. "What we took, we inventoried."

"Everything?"

"Everything. We did it by the book. End of story. Don't be making a mountain out of a dung heap, you gap-toothed worm."

"But that's my job."

"Let me straighten you out on something, my friends," said Mia Dalton. "The district attorney herself won this case before her election to be my boss. She expects me to win it again. You have never seen her when she is disappointed. Her nickname, 'The Dragon Lady,' is well earned. When disappointed, she eats the furniture, she flies around terrifying small dogs and grown prosecutors, she breathes a blue-hot flame. I do not intend to get a faceful of fire."

"Meaning?"

"Meaning don't expect any favors from me on this one. You had better come into that courtroom with more than a heartfelt plea of reasonable doubt, because I have every intention of serving that murderer's ass up to the jury on a silver platter. If you're going to have any chance in that courtroom, you better bring your A game."

"I don't think I have an A game," I said.

"That's what cheers me in the late hours of the night," said Mia Dalton. "I don't think you do either."

CHAPTER

28

Dawn shambled up the dark city street like an arthritic old man, arms pumping, gums working, a lot of action but not much forward movement. Yeah, sure, the metaphor is strained, but just then so was my bladder.

I was sitting in my car waiting for the day to break, and I was in pain. I had asked Phil Skink, my private investigator, if he had any tips on staking out an apartment. "Other than paying someone with half a clue to do it for you, mate?" he said. "Yes, Phil," I said, "other than that." Pro bono, Latin for "on the cheap." So this is what he told me. Make sure there is no way out the back door of the building. Check. Use a car that fits in socioeconomically with the neighborhood. Check. Reconnoiter the neighborhood to find the best place to set up. Check. Park in front of a store or a bar. Check. Sit in the front passenger seat so it looks like you're waiting for someone. Check. Sit low. Check. Have a cover story in case a cop or neighbor gets curious. Check. Buy your coffee small. Well, there was maybe where I might have messed up.

I started early, well before old man dawn even put on his surgical socks, and so a small cup of coffee was simply not going to do it for me. Grande or venti? What about big? Whatever happened to just plain big? Give me something big, I said to the barista, who was not young, pierced, and rude but was fat, Greek, and rude, who worked the counter of my diner, and who would have punched me in the face if I called him a barista. Something big, I had said, and now I was paying for it.

I jiggled my leg, thought about dry things, kept my eye on the door beside Tommy's High Ball on Daniel Rose's West Philly street. I was parked across from his building and down a bit, in front of a still-closed bodega. Nothing had yet gone in or out that door, but I knew, I just knew, that the instant I left that street to empty the soggy, storm-tossed sea that was my bladder, the door would open, the mark would exit, the morning would be lost. So I waited and watched and jiggled my leg and thought of desert sands, of camels and Bedouins, of all manner of desiccated things. Which was when I started comparing the dawn to Horace T. Grant.

I wasn't good at this, I was not the patient type, I wanted to go home and pee, but Julia Rose had said her boyfriend had moved out. I didn't believe her, and I didn't believe that she was lying because she wanted to. She was lying because someone else wanted her to lie. Daniel had said his name was Randy. Julia had said Randy didn't want to be involved. But he was already, wasn't he? If I was going to get a grip on Daniel's situation, I needed to learn what I could about Randy. His workplace was a start. Hence my stakeout.

It was a little after seven-thirty when the door beside Tommy's High Ball finally opened. The man who came out was medium height, thick-shouldered, with glasses and short blond hair. He wore a blue work shirt with a name stitched over the pocket and matching blue pants.

Outside, standing now in front of the door, legs spread, he shook a cigarette from a crushed pack, lit it, inhaled, picked a piece of tobacco from his teeth.

I slumped low in the car. The man exhaled through his nose. There was something dangerous about the way he held himself, in his big hands, in the two violent streams of smoke. He looked left, looked right, looked at me. And then he headed my way.

I slumped lower. My knees hit the dashboard. He kept coming.

I was trying to slink all the way beneath the seat when he knocked on the roof of my car.

I looked up through the window.

He smiled. "Hi," he said.

I waved back, sat up straight, opened the door so we could talk.

"Is there a problem?" he said.

"No, no problem. Just sitting here, in front of the store, waiting for a friend."

"The store's closed," he said.

"Then it might be a while."

"I've been watching out my window," he said, still smiling. "You been here for over an hour."

"Has it been that long?"

He pulled the door farther open. "Why don't you step on out for a moment."

"I'm fine."

"There are kids in this neighborhood, mister," he said. "We don't need perverts hanging around."

"I'm not a pervert."

"Then why's your leg shaking like that?"

"I have to pee."

He looked in the car, saw the blue paper coffee cup sitting in the cup holder. "You should have gotten the small."

"Tell me about it."

"Just get on out," he said, and I did. I gave him a close look as I stood before him, shifting my weight from one foot to the other. He was still smiling, but it wasn't a friendly smile. He had big teeth. The name stitched on his shirt was

RANDY, the store name on the other breast was WILSON PLUMBING SUPPLY.

"We got a quiet neighborhood here," he said. "Lots of families, children. We look out for one another. We don't like strangers with shaky legs hanging around. Give me your license so I can tell the police your name if I see you around here again."

"My name's Victor Carl," I said.

His smile faltered for just a second, just long enough for me to know he recognized it.

"That's right," I said. "I'm Daniel's attorney. And who I was waiting for, actually, Randy, was you. Do you have a moment?"

He leaned forward and then smiled again. "No," he said. "I have to get to work."

"You want a lift?"

"I'll take the bus."

"No, really. It won't be a problem. I'm very impressed with you acting to protect the neighborhood. It gives me more confidence about Daniel's situation."

He turned his head, looked at me sideways. "I'm just doing my part."

"You sound like you know how to handle yourself. Do you have a law-enforcement background?"

"I've had some experience." Pause. "I was in the army."

"It shows. Let me give you a lift."

He thought about it for a moment, glanced up at the window of his apartment, made his calculations. "Sure."

I stepped away from the open door and gestured him inside. "We'll stop for coffee. You know a place near here?"

"A couple."

"Good, but let's find one with a pot."

CHAPTER

29

"You don't need to be worrying about Daniel," said Randy Fleer—that was his full name, I learned—as I drove him to the warehouse in Northeast Philadelphia where he worked. "I'll take care of him. Julia, sure, she's a bit, well, yeah, right. I understand why the judge might have had concerns with just her around. But I'll take care of Daniel now on in. He's a good little guy, just needed a man in his life. And here I am, so he don't really need you no more."

"That's good to know, Randy," I said. "But I'm a little curious as to why you told Julia she should keep your name out of our discussions."

"She tell you I told her that?"

"It was pretty clear, the way she was acting. And she said you weren't together anymore."

"But you didn't believe her."

"No."

"Only woman I ever met who couldn't lie worth beans. Listen, I work. I got this job at Wilson's, and sometimes I help out a buddy who does contracting work. Drywall and stuff. I don't have time to sit all day waiting for some judge to tell me how I should be dealing with that boy. And even with all I'm working, I can't afford health care for us now. That's how come Julia and me, we aren't married yet. She's still on the state health-care program for herself and Daniel. I heard if they knew I was living with them, they'd kick them off."

"Are you living with them?"

"Off and on."

"Do you have a place of your own?"

"Not right now. It doesn't make sense, what with the money for rent they charge, even in that dump Julia's living in now, over the bar. But I have plans for us, for the three of us. As soon as I pay off some debt and get ahead of the game, I want to buy us a house. There's a nice neighborhood in Mayfair where some buddies from work live. I know what Daniel needs. I want us to be a family, I do. He deserves that. A boy deserves the right kind of family."

"There are things Julia has to do for Daniel," I said. "The judge has ordered her to attend certain classes, to show up at the hearings, and to take him to the doctor. And she has to do something about his teeth."

"They're a mess, aren't they? She spoils him. Her idea of raising a kid is to give him a taffy and leave him in front of the television. And at night he sleeps with a bottle in his mouth."

"Is that good for him?"

"It keeps him calm."

"Can you make sure she takes him to the dentist?"

"I don't know if the program she's on covers tooth stuff. It's just his baby teeth anyways."

"If I find you a dentist who will look at him without charging, will you make sure she takes him?"

"Sure, of course. Yeah. And I'll make sure of the other stuff, too. I've always wanted to have a son, someone to throw the football with, to watch the games with. Daniel's my chance, and I mean to do it right. You should see him run. Like the wind. He could be something. He's a good kid. I'll take charge of him."

"Okay."

"How long you going to be around?" he said.

"As long as the judge thinks I'm needed."

"Why don't you tell him that everything's okay now?"

"First, it's a her."

"Figures."

"Second, as long as there is some concern about Daniel's situation, I think she'll want me involved. I want to make sure his health is seen to, his teeth, and that his mother does all she can to take care of him."

"I told you, I'd take care of him."

"Were you ever in jail, Randy?"

"What the hell does that mean?"

"I was just wondering. The homemade tattoo on the back of your hand sort of gives it away."

"I was in for a check thing. Just a short stint. And then I was hanging with the wrong guys, and we got stupid. I mean, sure, I admit I have a past, I don't deny it. Except let me tell you, they say it's the army supposed to make a man out of you, but for me it was the joint. I want to make up for what I lost. Whatever I was, whatever I done, now I want to do the right thing by that boy. And Julia. I want us to be together, maybe have another one of our own. We're going to be a family."

"That would really be the best thing for him," I said.

"I know it."

"But I thought there were four of you," I said. "Doesn't Julia have a daughter?"

"Did she tell you that?"

"No."

"Then who did?"

"Does she or not?"

"No."

I kept driving. Sometimes, as a lawyer, you have to put

your finger in someone's face and call him a liar, and sometimes you just have to be quiet and let the silence talk.

"I want us to be a family Daniel can be proud of," he said finally.

"I don't know what that means."

"You don't have to. It ain't your family. You won't be living in Mayfair. You married?"

"No."

"Got any kids?"

"No."

"How was your family life growing up?"

"Crap."

"So what the hell are you talking about? You don't know nothing."

"Maybe not."

"My place is right up here."

We were on a busy street just off Roosevelt Boulevard. There was a brick showroom fronting a large warehouse and yard. Heavy pipes, bins, and boxes lay out in the yard, along with a forklift. Men in hard hats were standing around the forklift, drinking coffee, holding themselves in the blurry, motionless stasis that men fall into in the mornings, waiting for the workday to begin.

I parked the car. When Randy got out, I got out, too.

"Where you going?" he said. He had been pretty amiable through our chat, but something about my last couple of questions had withered our budding relationship, and there was now a bite of anger in his question.

"You don't mind, do you, Randy, if I ask your boss about your work history? The judge might want to know."

He glanced at the yard for a moment and then shrugged. "Go ahead," he said. "I work my ass off here, and I never miss a day."

"That's good," I said. "That says a lot."

He gave me a look, thought about saying something more, and then thought better of it. I watched as he walked away. Yeah, I know, I hadn't pushed it about the daughter and followed my unanswered questions with others that he would also leave unanswered. I hadn't done the whole cross-examination thing. But the line between anger and rage is a narrow one, and while I wasn't really concerned with weathering any storm I provoked, I wasn't living with him, was I?

But that didn't mean I didn't have questions still. *I want us to be a family Daniel can be proud of,* he had said. What the hell did that mean? I wondered. And even as I asked it, I was pretty sure I wouldn't like the answer.

CHAPTER

30

We were talking about Bob.

"I think he's marvelous," said Carol Kingsly as she picked at her salad. "Mystical, almost. When he works on my teeth, my jaw tingles."

"I'm not sure that tingle is the right word," I said.

"Oh, yes, yes, it tingles," she gushed, in a way that made me wonder if she was talking about more than her jaw. Dr. Bob? Yikes.

"How long have you been seeing him?"

"Only for a few weeks now. My yoga instructor recommended him. Do you do yoga?" she said.

"No, but I bend over sometimes to pick up a beer."

"You should do yoga. It's very spiritual. And so good for the skin. My instructor, Miranda, is fabulous. Amazingly limber. She would speak about her dentist in hushed tones, said his chakras were very open, especially his heart chakra. That's the energy source that reaches out to heal. How could I not give him a try? Before him, I went to a *Philadelphia* magazine top doc, one of the most respected in the region, but I never felt as comfortable in his chair as I do with Dr. Pfeffer. And with what he's done for my friend Sheila, I think he's something close to a saint."

"Is that possible for a dentist?"

"Why wouldn't it be?"

"I always thought dentists fell somewhere between blasphemers and sodomites in the seventh circle of hell."

"Victor."

"I have sensitive gums."

Carol Kingsly smiled and, all credit to Dr. Bob, her smile was fabulous.

I had fished her number from my shirt pocket, screwed up my courage, placed the call, and invited her to lunch. She was so happy to hear from me it was shocking. I repeated my name three times and carefully explained who I was, to be sure she didn't think I was some other man named Victor Carl. And now here she sat, across the table from me at some trendy bistro not far from Independence Hall, flashing that fabulous smile. But it wasn't only that smile I was interested in, or the lithe body, or the pretty eyes that were bluer than I remembered from the washed-out waiting room. No, I had an ulterior motive for asking Carol Kingsly out. I wanted to talk about Bob.

Who the hell was he? Where did he come from? What was he really after? *I like to help*, he had said repeatedly. Sure, and I like corned beef, but that didn't answer those questions or the big one that had sent me into his office in the first place: Was it merely a coincidence that Whitney Robinson, François Dubé's trial attorney, and Seamus Dent, the eyewitness with the troubled past who testified at François's trial, had both been patients of Dr. Bob's?

"Where's Dr. Bob from, do you know?" I said.

"I've heard Albuquerque, I've heard Seattle. He spent some of his childhood in Burma, from what I understand."

"But no one knows his hometown?"

"His history is a little vague, and I think he likes it like that. He only gives out bits and pieces to his patients. He practiced in Baltimore immediately before he bought a practice up here, I know that, and his diploma is from the

Karolinska Institutet in Sweden, but his name on it is smudged just enough to make one wonder." She smiled, licked her lips. "No one is certain of his details."

"An international man of mystery."

"Exactly. Can I ask you something, Victor, something that has been puzzling me?"

"Of course."

"That tie. Is it an heirloom?"

"No. Why would you think that?"

"I'm just trying to figure out why you would decide to wear such a thing. I could only imagine that it was some barbarous custom, passed down the generations, father to son, like a family curse."

"Alas, for a lawyer ties are part of the uniform."

"No, not ties in general. I think ties in general are wonderful things, anything roped around a man's neck is a step in the right direction. But why would you wear that tie?"

"It's very convenient, wash and wear."

"Do you know the number one fashion rule, Victor?"

"What is that?"

"Never wear anything you can clean in the dishwasher."

"I like my tie."

"Victor, don't be silly. After lunch we'll go to Strawbridge's and pick out something more suitable."

I rubbed my tie with my thumb, enjoying the way it crinkled at my touch, feeling the delicate ridges of the polyester. "You mentioned a friend of yours," I said to change the subject. "Sheila, was it?"

"Yes. She was also in class with Miranda. A nice girl, but a little sad, a little frumpy, you see. She was still pining over an ex-boyfriend who was always calling her but just wanted to be friends, and she was being harassed at work by her boss. Nothing was going right in her life. Miranda had been trying for years to open up Sheila's sacral chakra, the one that flows from the abdomen and has to do with emotional health and sexuality, but had been totally unsuccessful. She was just stuck. Then one of Sheila's wisdom teeth became impacted."

"Ouch," I said.

"And Miranda urged her to see Dr. Pfeffer."

"Double ouch."

Carol narrowed her eyes disapprovingly at me. "You are such a coward. We're going to have to do something about that. Anyway, she went to see Dr. Pfeffer, and it turned out that more than her teeth got fixed. It's been four months now and the change in Sheila has been astounding. She's more vibrant, more alive than ever. She lost weight and looks fabulous. Just last week she got engaged to a podiatrist."

"Every woman's dream."

"Oh, but it is, Victor. A podiatrist. Think of the shoes she now can wear."

"And you attribute this change to Dr. Bob?"

"I can't be certain, but it seems more than a coincidence, doesn't it? She visits Dr. Pfeffer, and the next thing you know the creepy ex-boyfriend stops calling. And when Sheila, ever the codependent, tries to contact him, he won't take the call. Strange, huh? And then the boss, the jerk who had been giving Sheila all kinds of trouble, gets transferred to Fresno. And guess who got his job?"

"I get the idea. And the podiatrist?"

"He's also a patient of Dr. Pfeffer."

"Of course he is."

"I mean, it's been astounding. And to top it off, Miranda says that all Sheila's chakras are blazing. So when Dr. Pfeffer called and asked if I'd be interested in meeting one of his patients, I jumped at the opportunity."

"Of course you did." Now I knew why she was so happy to hear from me.

"And I have to tell you, Victor," she said, flashing again that bright smile, putting her warm hand atop mine. "I'm very glad you called. I have a feeling this is going to be wonderful."

It wasn't long after we left the restaurant that I felt her warm touch on my neck, my collar, before I felt her loosening my tie.

"First we have to get rid of this monstrosity," she said as she undid the knot. When the tie was off my neck, she held it at arm's length with two fingers, as if holding the tail end of a dead possum, before dropping it into a trash can behind the department store's tie counter. "Then we'll find something that better suits your colors."

We had walked a few blocks north to Strawbridge's department store, where Carol had led me straight to men's accessories. With a calculating eye, she examined the silk ties arrayed beneath the glass. "May we see that one?" she said to the clerk, pointing at a wide, pale blue paisley. "And that one, too?" she said, indicating something yellow.

"I don't know," I said, "I sort of like my ties thinner."

"With those lapels?"

"And it's not really my—"

"Just try it, Victor. You won't believe what a difference the right tie can make, even to a boring plain blue suit like yours."

I ended up with the yellow one around my neck.

"Nice," she said as she backed away. "Very becoming."

Becoming what? I wondered. Really, now, a yellow tie. I was neither an investment banker nor an interior designer, and yellow does nothing to hide the inevitable gravy stains. Yet I had let her knot a yellow silk tie around my neck. Why? I'll tell you why. Because I liked the feel of her warm hands around my throat, I liked the way she bit her lower lip as she groomed me, I liked the mint smell of her sweet

breath as she leaned in close to be sure the tie lay cleanly beneath my collar. And the damn thing actually didn't look
half bad with my suit. It did make me look different, sharper.
When I examined my new look in the mirror, I had the sudden urge to say "debenture" and "taupe."

"Now," she said, "about that watch. Timex, Victor?
Really, now."

We were leaning over the watches, ogling the Movados,
when I said, "Wait here one moment. I've been looking for
a new wallet, and there was one that caught my eye."

I delayed my move until the salesclerk was showing Carol
something ridiculously slim and ridiculously expensive.
Then I slid over to the tie counter to rescue my thin red strip
of polyester from the discarded wrappings and receipts in
the trash can.

"Sorry, old friend," I said as I rolled it up and gently
placed it in my inside jacket pocket.

CHAPTER

"You look different today somehow, Victor," said Velma Takahashi when she entered my office after I purposely made her wait in front of my secretary's desk for a number of minutes. "Much more forceful. Did you get a haircut?"

"No," I said.

"A facial?"

"No."

"But you're positively glowing." Her puffy lips twisted into a smile as she sat before my desk. "Maybe it's like that commercial. Have you had your Viagra prescription filled, is that it?"

"No prescription, I'm still au naturel, but thank you for the compliment." I brushed flat my new yellow tie. "Can we maybe get down to business?"

"I brought your retainer. Your second retainer." She leaned forward to hand me something. It was all I could do to tear my gaze from her suddenly exposed, perfectly synthetic breasts to the envelope she was holding out for me.

"Excellent," I said. And I was pretty pleased with the check, too.

Velma was dressed for tennis, a low-cut white blouse, a short pleated skirt, peds barely exposed above her sneakers, with delicious little navy-blue balls at the heels waiting to be plucked like ripe blueberries on the bush. I'm no fan of tennis, I would rather watch a rotisserie infomercial than tennis on TV, and yet, with Velma in my office, in that outfit, I suddenly began to appreciate the sport's finer points.

"You play much?" I said idly as I opened the envelope and examined the check.

"Oh, yes," she said.

"Tennis, I mean."

"I know what you mean."

"I notice, Mrs. Takahashi, that there is no address on this check. Is this a new account?"

"It will clear, don't worry."

"I'm not worried. I'm just wondering when you're going to tell your husband that you are financing François Dubé's defense with his money."

"The terms of our marriage are not your concern. But have no doubt that my husband is getting good value for his money."

"My rates are rather reasonable, aren't they?"

She almost smiled and then thought better of it. "If that's everything?" she said. "I have an appointment."

"No, not quite everything. I'm a little curious about a few matters. Where did François meet his wife?"

"Somewhere, I suppose."

"He said a bar."

"Then a bar it was."

"Were you there?"

"Maybe."

"Why don't you tell me about it?"

"It was at a bar. I was with Leesa. François showed up. The owner introduced the two of us to him. What else do you want?"

"What bar?"

"The upstairs bar at Marrakech."

"And it was Geoffrey Sunshine who introduced you?"

"That's right."

"Who did François go home with that night?"

"Is this important?"

"Yes."

"Why?"

"Because the fun is over, Mrs. Takahashi. I'm now responsible for a man's life. The prime reason François went down the first time was that there were no other suspects in Leesa's murder. I need to find one."

"And since I'm sitting here in front of you, I'm convenient, is that it?"

"Yes, that's pretty much it. Why are you paying for François's defense?"

"I told you that already. It has to do with my friendship with Leesa."

"And I didn't believe you the first time you told me. Who did François go home with that first night? You?"

"Yes."

"Was Leesa upset?"

"No."

"She didn't feel left out?"

"She wasn't."

I cocked my head, Velma Takahashi laughed. It took me perhaps a moment too long to figure it out. François Dubé, that little devil.

"Is that all?" she said, arching one plucked brow.

"So how did lucky Leesa end up with him?"

"She fell in love, that was how. Victor, you have to understand, we weren't your usual sit-at-the-bar-and-hope-someone-notices-us type of girls. We were buccaneers when we were out together, in search of fun and profit. When we liked something, we went after it. When we both liked it, we shared. None of our victims complained, as far as I remember. And in the end, like good buccaneers, we divvied up what goods we plundered. Most of the men we tossed over-board, but François had certain talents, which Leesa found attractive. He never had enough money to suit my tastes, so I let her have him. At the time I was already being wooed by my husband."

"Did he know you were three-waying with François while he was courting you?"

"He knew what he was getting, and he couldn't wait."

"And François didn't mind you two women deciding his future?"

"He didn't have much choice, did he? But he was the fool who decided to get married. He told Leesa he wanted to save her from my bad influence. We laughed over that one, Leesa and I, but he did everything he could to separate us. And finally, after they married, he succeeded."

"So that's why you don't like him much."

"That's right."

"But it still doesn't explain why you put flowers on her grave every week."

"I need to go," she said, standing, pulling down the hem of her tennis blouse.

"Why do you feel guilty about Leesa Dubé's death, Mrs. Takahashi?"

"You'll let me know when you need more money."

"Count on it."

"Good day, Victor."

"You didn't answer the question."

"Your powers of observation, Victor, never fail to amaze me." And then she was gone, out of my office, down the hall, gone.

I leaned over to my window, saw her leave the building and wait impatiently until her limousine pulled up to the curb. The driver bounded out, opened the door. She slipped past him into the car, pulled her shapely legs in behind her. I waited there until the limousine drove off, and then I rushed out to my secretary.

"Did you get them, Ellie?"

"Yes, I did."

"Any good?"

"Not quite picture postcards," she said, "but not bad."

"Let me see."

Ellie handed me her cell phone. I paged through the photographs on her color screen. Velma Takahashi in her tennis outfit, sitting, legs crossed, looking off impatiently. Velma Takahashi talking on her own cell phone. Velma Takahashi in close-up, staring straight ahead.

"Did she know you were taking them?" I said.

"I don't think so. She doesn't seem the type to take much notice of the hired help."

"You're right about that," I said. "Can you get some prints made at a photo shop?"

"Why, Mr. Carl? To hang on your wall like a pinup?"

"Absolutely. But first I need to see a guy about a dog."

In Philadelphia, if you want to start a restaurant, first you buy a bank. Then you fire the tellers, tart up the place to fit your theme, hire a famous chef, stick the valet parkers out front, charge thirty-six bucks for a piece of fish, and away you go. That's the way it worked for the Striped Bass, for Circe and the Ritz-Carlton, and that's the way it worked for Geoffrey Sunshine, when he bought the First Philadelphia Bank building, with its soaring marble pillars and golden ceiling inlays. His supper club, Marrakech, was an exotic Moroccan fantasy for the discriminating diner, offering Mediterranean cuisine in an atmosphere of fluid lights and shimmering fabrics. The ceiling was blue, the upholstery golden, the tagines aromatic. Tables at Marrakech were booked months in advance, and still they made you wait when you arrived, just because they could. But the real action in the joint was not in the restaurant, it was upstairs, in the splendiferous El Bahia Club.

"She has a dinner appointment," I said to Beth as we stood together at the El Bahia bar, trying to grab the attention of one of the too-cool-to-care bartenders. "She's in public relations. But she said she'd join us here for a before-dinner jolt."

"So where did you meet her?"

"My dentist introduced us."

"Your dentist? I thought you hated the lot of them."

"I do. Savage little bastards."

"It's that tiny chuckle they give when they hit a nerve and you gasp in pain," she said, nodding. "It's the way they say, as if to a defiant child, 'Loosen your lower lip, you're fighting me,' and all I want to say is, 'Of course I'm fighting you, you sadist, you're scraping the flesh off my gums.' "

"Yeah, Dr. Bob does all of that."

"But still you trusted him enough to set you up?"

"Well, he's an interesting guy."

The bar of the El Bahia was jammed with quite the sharp-suited crowd. The place was decorated like a sultan's palace, inlays and mosaics, curtains and rugs and golden statues of naked women. Around the rollicking dance floor, heavy chairs and couches sat in intimate groupings on raised tiers. Tables filled with patrons surrounded the circular bar, there was a separate room in the back for the cigar smokers, the bartenders were crazy busy and they enjoyed ignoring your calls for drinks. And this was only a Wednesday. Saturday night the line to get in snaked well down the street.

Finally I caught the attention of a beefy guy behind the bar. He had a flattop and an earring and he wiped his hands on a rag as he came over.

"A Sea Breeze for me," I said. I looked at Beth.

"Beer," she said, "in a bottle."

"What kind?" said the barkeep.

"Brown," said Beth. The bartender looked at her for a moment, uncomprehending, before he shrugged and left to gather our order.

"You said your dentist was an interesting guy," said Beth. "How so?"

"He says he likes to help. I think it means he tries to meddle in people's lives in hopes of making the world a better and more peaceful place."

"And I suppose, as a dentist, he does it wearing rubber gloves and a mask, like Batman."

"I hadn't thought of it that way, but you're absolutely right. The Justice League of Professionals. Accountantman. Actuarial Woman. The Green Litigator. Gad."

"Who would your dentist be?"

"The Steel Pick, I suppose, scourge of plaque the world over, scaling great heights in the never-ending battle against tooth decay."

"With his archnemesis, the femme fatale Ginger Vitus."

"Ooh, I like that, sweet Ginger with her coffee-colored cat suit and faint aroma of decay."

"How'd you find him?"

"Whitney Robinson recommended him," I said. "And then I found out he was also treating Seamus Dent."

It was cute the way Beth's eyes bugged out at that one. "Does your dentist know anything about François?"

"I haven't asked him yet."

"Victor. Why not?"

"Because you don't go right at Dr. Bob. He's the kind of guy you have to come at obliquely. He's letting me know what he wants me to know in his own sweet way. Ah, our drinks."

The bartender slopped my Sea Breeze onto the bar, banged a Dos Equis in front of Beth, named his exorbitant price as if ransoming my firstborn. I reached into my jacket pocket and pulled out one of the photographs of Velma Takahashi that my secretary had snapped in my office.

"You see her around, ever?" I said.

"Nice," said the bartender. "What, is she missing?"

"Only her cellulite. You recognize her?"

He scratched his chin. "I can't be sure."

"You're a sweetheart, aren't you? What's your name, sweetheart?"

"Antoine."

"All right, Antoine. I'm running a tab for the drinks, but this"—I took a twenty out of my wallet, raised an eyebrow—"might be for you."

"You sure you can afford all that?"

"Screw it, then," I said, "I'll give it to a busboy." But before I could stuff the bill into my pocket, he snatched it out of my fist.

"Never saw her," he said. "And someone that well put together, I'd remember."

"Oh, I bet you would." I put the photo back in my jacket. "How long you been working here, Antoine?"

"A year and a couple of months," he said.

"Of all of the staff, who's been working up here the longest?"

"Celia started after me. Pinar's been here about two years, but he's about to go. No one stays too long because of the boss."

"You're talking about Mr. Sunshine?"

"That's right."

"Is he a tough act to get along with?"

"He's your best friend for a month or two, slapping your back, partying with you, giving you the best shifts, and then he becomes a sharp pain in your ass. It's a pattern of his. He says turnover keeps the atmosphere fresh."

"That and a little Air Wick."

"Plus there's his spy gadgets, hidden cameras and the like, all so he's sure we're not stealing him blind."

"Are you?"

"If we are, we're clever enough not to get caught by him. But the whole James Bond over-your-shoulder act gets old fast. And then there's the bounced checks."

"Really?"

"He said it was a mistake, and they've been good for a few

months now, but the résumés are out, you know what I mean?"

"So the only staff person who would have been here continuously for the last five or so years is the boss."

"You got it."

"He in tonight?"

"Not yet, but he will be. Eventually."

"Let me know when you see him."

"Sure."

I turned away to think on what Antoine had said when I saw her gliding toward me. Carol Kingsly. I wasn't yet sure how much I liked her, actually, but damn, she was good-looking. She was in work clothes, a gray suit, gray pumps, a silk blouse open at the collar, and a strand of pearls across her pretty neck. Accompanying her was a gelhead, one of those grossly handsome men with gleaming teeth and hair slimed back with massive quantities of some petroleum product. He was wearing a brown suit and a loud striped tie.

"Hey, you," said Carol, taking proprietary hold of my arm as if we had been an item for years instead of days. With her free hand, she smoothed down my tie. "You look great."

"It's my new fashion consultant. She's all the rage. You thirsty?"

"Parched."

After I ordered a round, we made the introductions and had one of those spineless conversations that awkward groups have at crowded bars where the music has grown a little too loud. The weather, the Phillies, the food downstairs, snide remarks about the latest celebrity scandal. Carol kept hold of my arm and was overly effusive toward Beth. Gelhead's name was Nick, and he seemed to have a thing for Carol. Beth, who usually had a thing for gelheads, didn't seem at all interested in Nick, but she couldn't stop staring at the way Carol flirted and clutched at me. All enough to give me a headache. I called Antoine over and ordered another round for the four of us.

Twenty minutes in, Nick glanced at his watch. "It's time," he said.

"Duty calls," said Carol. "Sorry to run out like this and leave you stranded."

"We'll manage," I said.

"The man we're meeting is very big in real estate," she said, her eyes widening at the word *big*. "It's all hush-hush, but this could be the break of our careers. One of his lieutenants is a patient of Dr. Pfeffer's. That's how he got my name. He told the doctor he was looking for a new public-relations firm."

"Convenient."

"He also told him they're looking for a new lawyer to handle some problem they are having. Should I give them your name?"

"We don't do real estate," said Beth.

"But we can learn," I said, handing Carol one of my cards.

She looked at it. "Derringer and Carl. It has a ring, doesn't it? Do you know anything about real estate?"

"Location, location, location," I said.

"That should be enough."

She yanked at the arm she had been holding, pulled me close, and as Nick looked balefully on, kissed me wetly on the lips. Our first kiss, but it was performed by Carol so matter-of-factly it was as if we had been intimate for months.

"It was so nice to meet you, Beth," said Carol.

"Likewise, I'm sure," said Beth.

"Bye, Victor. Be good. I'll call you when I get home, tell you what they said."

"So that's Carol," said Beth as we watched the two of them elbow their way away from the bar.

"That's Carol."

"Carol, Carol, Carol."

"She does yoga."

"I wouldn't put it past her," said Beth. "It seemed like you guys were pretty hot and heavy."

"So it did," I said.

"Are you?"

"I didn't think so, but I've never known what the hell is going on in any of my relationships. Why should this one be any different? I suppose by the time I get up to speed, she'll dump me."

"I don't think Slick Nick would mind that at all," said Beth.

"No, he seemed a bit smitten, didn't he?"

"You're not worried, your new girlfriend spending the night alongside handsome Mr. Nick?"

"With that tie? Please."

Just then Antoine stepped up and reached over the bar to tap me on my shoulder.

"There he is," he said, indicating a short, hunched man with wavy black hair and a pointed face. He looked like an overdressed ferret with bad posture as he made his way, meeting and greeting, across the club. A walking T-bone in a black turtleneck moved in front of him, wedging the crowd open as if for Caesar. "He generally holds court in the cigar lounge," said Antoine. "And he likes his privacy."

"Thanks for the warning," I said.

We stayed at the bar for a few moments longer, finished our drinks, paid our bill, watched as Geoffrey Sunshine entered the glass-walled, smoke-filled room. Geoffrey Sunshine, the restaurant mogul who had brought François Dubé, Leesa Cullen, and Velma Takahashi together, a combustible combination that ended in murder. I had a few questions for Mr. Sunshine.

"You ever smoke a cigar, Beth?"

"Not in this life."

"Time to start," I said as we fought our way to the cigar lounge and to Geoffrey Sunshine. "Off we go, into the miasma."

"You're the lawyers representing François,"
said Geoffrey Sunshine. He had heavy-lidded eyes and thin
lips, and every word that slipped out of his mouth had an
aura of corruption about it.

"That's right," I said.

"And you want to talk to me?"

"If your nanny doesn't mind," I said, directing my thumb
at the T-bone in the black turtleneck.

The moment we had stepped up to the corner of the
lounge where Sunshine was sitting, the bodyguard had in-
terjected his massive frame between his boss and us, as if
Sunshine was the president and our law firm's name was
Hinckley & Hinckley. We were talking now over the man's
broad shoulders as he restrained us with his outstretched
arms, readying to bum-rush us out the door.

Sunshine took a couple of puffs from his absurdly long
cigar as he eyed us and then said, "It's okay, Sean."

The bodyguard bared his upper teeth like a disappointed
dog before letting us by.

"How does it look for François?" said Sunshine, eyeing
his cigar and speaking as if he cared not a whit one way or
the other. "Are you going to get him out of jail?"

"We got him a new trial," said Beth. "Things are looking
better than before."

"Tell him there is always a place for him in my kitchen if you are successful." He showed his little teeth in an approximation of a smile. Something about his ferret face looked strangely familiar. "I could really use him, especially with the way my current chef abuses the turmeric."

"I'm sure François will be very grateful to hear it," said Beth.

"Sit down, both of you," said Sunshine, gesturing toward a couch set kitty-corner to his chair. There were two men in suits on the couch, overfed men with cigars, there to talk business with the mogul, but Sunshine gave them a brief nod and they jumped up with alacrity to give us the seats. It shouldn't have, but it felt damn good to see them scamper.

"Now," said Sunshine after we sat, "how can I help my good friend François?"

I took out the picture of Velma, passed it over. "Do you recognize this woman?"

He looked at it, squinted his beady eyes, looked at it again. I didn't remember ever meeting him before, but something about his sneer of a personality struck a chord of memory.

"It might be Velma," he said, "but she looks different somehow."

"I think she had some surgery."

"Well then, definitely Velma." He sucked at his cigar. "Velma Wykowski, one of the famous Wykowski sisters."

"I didn't know she had a sister."

"Leesa Cullen, I'm talking about," he said. "That's what we called them when they were both single, the famous Wykowski sisters. They didn't look anything alike, and that was the joke. They used to hang out at the bar when I was just starting. They were often the evening's entertainment."

"Karaoke?"

"More like carry out the door. They drank too much,

flirted too much." His eyebrows rose obscenely. "They did everything too much. This was before they met up with François. He broke up the sister act. Marriage seems to take the fun out of people, don't you think? Still, it was a tragedy what happened to Leesa."

"Yes it was."

"Whatever happened to Velma?"

"She got married," I said. "You know, Mr. Sunshine, you look familiar."

"Call me Geoffrey."

"Sure, Geoffrey. Do I know you somehow?"

He sniffed loudly, rubbed his pointy nose. "I don't think so."

"Where'd you go to college?"

"Temple," he said.

"Where'd you go to high school?"

"Abington."

"What year?"

He stuck his cigar in his mouth, rolled it around with his tongue. "So you're that Victor Carl."

I snapped my finger. "Jerry Sonenshein. Son of a bitch, I knew I knew you."

We each gave a couple loud "Hey"s and slapped each other on the shoulder and pretended we had been the best of friends in high school and could be the best of friends still.

"You've done all right by yourself, Jerry," I said as we calmed down.

"And you became a lawyer," he said, chuckling, as if by passing the bar I had fallen through an open manhole.

"Why'd you change your name?"

"In this business it helps to have a bright moniker. What could be brighter than Sunshine?"

"You were an AV guy, I remember, pushing projectors around the halls like you owned the place."

"And you wrote those stupid editorials for the newspaper. What was it?"

"*The Abingtonian,*" I said. "And they were supposed to be funny."

"They were stupid, Victor. Not funny. Stupid. All the AV guys were laughing at you."

"And you were all so full of yourselves, as if you were on some higher plane because you could run the film projector."

"We ruled the school."

"Except when the greasers were flushing your heads down the toilet."

"I don't recall you being on the football team yourself."

"You know what I also remember, Jerry?"

"The name's Geoffrey, Vic."

"I remember that I never liked you."

We stared at each other for a long moment, two high-schoolers again, murder in our eyes, facing off in dodgeball. And then we gave each other a couple more loud "Hey"s and a couple "Ho"s and slapped each other again on the shoulder, maybe a little harder this time, and pretended that our high-school animosity had disappeared over the years.

"Cigar?" said Sunshine.

"Sure," I said.

"Sean," said Sunshine, "bring us a selection."

It wasn't long before we were sitting back in our seats, the three of us, puffing away, a noxious cloud of smoke obscuring our features as Sunshine talked about François Dubé and the famous Wykowski sisters. Beth had opted for an Arturo Fuente panatela, thin and spicy with the delicate scent of nuts and sweet woods. I went with a Joya Antano Gran Consul from Davidoff, the King Farouk of cigars, I was told, short, fat, and potent. Beth seemed to be enjoying herself. I tried to keep a smile on my face, but King Farouk was doing calisthenics in my stomach.

"How'd you meet my client, Jerry?" I said.

"Geoffrey," said Sunshine.

"Whatever."

He glared at me, then calmed, looked at his cigar as he spoke. "I heard from my saucier that François, then sous chef at Le Bec Fin, was planning to resign to head his own kitchen. I was having trouble in the restaurant and was looking for a new executive chef. François would have been perfect. So I invited him up to see if we could work out a business arrangement."

Sunshine leaned over a small side table between chair and couch, tapped his cigar gently, and a roll of ash tipped into an ashtray. He looked absently at the single rose sitting in a black glass vase and then leaned back again.

"The famous Wykowski sisters were hanging around then, the absolute queens of the bar, scoring coke, flirting like mad, having sex in the bathrooms when it suited them, which it often did. They were out of control, but lovely, too, and frankly, they gave the place the kind of reputation that draws in a high-paying crowd. It was good to have them around. Fun, too." He puffed, he leered, I tried not to throw up. "So when François was due to arrive, I asked them to be nice to my new friend. I thought once he tasted the charms of the Wykowski sisters, saw how much fun this place could be, we'd be able to work something out. It didn't quite turn out as I had expected."

"What happened?" said Beth.

"The end of an era, that's what happened," said Sunshine. "First I caught my very popular bartender pulling cash from the till. When I sacked him, a large part of my clientele went with him. Not good. Then the famous Wykowski sisters just disappeared."

"Why?"

"They were a trio for a time, Leesa, Velma, and François. Then word was Velma got bored and she gave François to Leesa."

"Gave him to her?"

"Something like that. And right after, all three simply disappeared from the club. I heard Leesa was marrying François. I heard François was starting his own place, with his name on the window. I heard Velma had found other fields to plow. That was the end of everything. Without my bartender or the two girls, suddenly my club wasn't so hot. The nut on this place was killing me already, I had borrowed more for a redesign, and now I had a club that wasn't making the kind of money it had before. It took me three years to climb out of the hole."

"But it looks like you did," I said.

He grinned, his cigar pinned in his teeth. "Oh, yes."

"You ever see that Velma again?" I said. "She ever come back here?"

"No," he said as his eyes shifted back to that flower. "Leesa neither. I figured they were sort of embarrassed the way they behaved. What happened to Leesa I could follow in the paper, but Velma Wykowski, it was like she fell off the face of the earth. Who'd she marry anyway?"

"You don't know?"

"No. I never learned."

"Just some guy," I said. "Thanks for your help, Jerry."

"Whatever I can do for François, you let me know. He was a great chef. And I was serious about having a place for him."

"Thanks," I said. I took another puff, and suddenly I felt my stomach flip. One too many Sea Breezes, one too many cigars.

"What's the matter with your face there, Victor?" said Geoffrey Sunshine. "Suddenly, pal, you don't look so good."

I held my Joya Antano Gran Consul in front of me as the nausea sliced like a dull knife into my brain. "If you'll excuse me," I said as I smashed my cigar in the ashtray and stood weakly. "I need to find the bathroom."

Freaking King Farouk. The only good news was that none of it got onto my tie.

In preparation for my bridge, Dr. Bob was grinding two of my healthy teeth into nubby posts. He seemed to be enjoying his work. One could even say he was grinding with a certain gusto, which, while admirable in a stripper, is somewhat disconcerting in a dentist wielding a router in your mouth.

"So that must be the famous tie," said Dr. Bob over the whine of the diamond bur as it attacked my teeth. "Carol does have excellent taste. She just needs to lower her standards a tad. When we seek perfection, we always end up disappointed, but that's why you will be so good for her. We don't have to worry about perfection in your case, do we, Victor?"

"Aahohuu," I said.

"Shift over a bit and open your mouth a little wider. And stop your whimpering. I shot enough Novocain in you to stun a horse. If you don't calm down, I'll have to call in Tilda to assist."

I halted my squealing immediately. He changed the bur on his tool, delved back into my mouth.

"But you must be doing something right. She seems so happy. You look puzzled. Of course, Carol and I talk. The doctor-patient relationship can be more than a simple business transaction. I take a personal interest in all my patients.

We are, all of us in this practice, something like a family. Move your head this way, please. Yes, very good. I'm quite shocked, actually, Victor, but this is going smoothly. Rinse and spit, please."

I rinsed and spat. A white grit from my expectoration stuck to the edges of the porcelain bowl. I waxed nostalgic over what moments before had been my tooth.

He shifted the light above my head, peered into his tiny mirror to get a better view of the destruction, fired up the grinding tool once more. It sounded like a slot-car racer on steroids.

"Aahayyyaaaaeio?" I said.

"Of course you can ask a question. Is it dental in nature? Excellent. Then I might even be able to answer."

"Owioraaayayee?"

"Baby teeth? Very important. But you don't have to worry about that. Oh, you're not asking about yourself, are you?"

"Aiiah."

"A client. Interesting. How old?"

"Ooou. IoohiOhohoh."

"Four? And you represent him pro bono? I'm so very impressed. I think, in many ways, we are more alike than one would expect. Hold on while I grind out this ridge. So this is a four-year-old child with serious dental issues. Why don't you show me which teeth."

I rubbed my tongue all along my upper row.

"Ah, yes. Now that can be serious. Does he still use a bottle? Do his parents let him suckle himself to sleep with it?"

I nodded. He shook his head.

"I can't tell for certain without examining the boy, but it sounds like he is suffering from something called BBTD, or baby bottle tooth decay. Ooops. Sorry about that. When you keep fighting me by clenching your teeth, it makes it that much more difficult to get this right. Nothing serious, but suddenly there's a lot of blood. Rinse, please."

My God, it was Guérnica in the spit sink.

"Just a bit more and we're done. BBTD. A bacterium called *Streptococcus mutans* is feeding on the sugars in the milk or juice from the bottle, and its toxins are eating away at the teeth. If it progresses far enough, it can cause a serious infection that can enter the bone and permanently damage the adult teeth forming beneath the surface. This child should be immediately examined and treated by a qualified dentist."

"Aahilleyoo?"

"The standard treatment is to go into the affected teeth, excavate the decay, and then, in effect, mummify the damaged nerves. Caps are placed upon the teeth, which restore the primary teeth and allow the permanent teeth to come in without any additional problems. All very necessary. I hope the parents have insurance."

"Ayhaaahi."

"Nothing? That is a problem. You better rinse again, Victor. The flow of blood is stanching, but it's still pretty heavy."

Swirl, swirl, swirl, splat.

"Let me take another quick peek." He sprayed my teeth with warm water.

"How do they look?" I said. With his hands out of my mouth, I was finally able to pronounce consonants. I suppose consonants are like lower-right molars, we only really appreciate them when they are gone.

"Beautiful," said Dr. Bob, "round and even and beautiful. I could have been a sculptor, Victor. I could have been David Smith. I had the talent and the vision, but being locked away all day in a studio, the loneliness broken only by the occasional nude model, that wasn't for me. Instead I have the best, most noble job in the world."

He lifted up his diamond bur as if it were a torch of liberty and let it whir.

"Who knows what evil lurks in the teeth of men?" he proclaimed. "The dentist knows."

"You ever read comic books as a kid?" I said.

"Voraciously."

"You maybe take them a little too seriously?"

"Of course not. They were so unrealistic. Superman was a newspaper reporter; Batman, some millionaire socialite; Daredevil, a lawyer. Those are heroes? Please. Spider-Man, the part-time photographer; Iron Man, the industrialist; Green Lantern, the architect; Silver Surfer, some sort of Zen wanderer. Oooh, I'm impressed, Zen wanderer. Captain Marvel was a paperboy, for God's sake."

"But no dentists, is that it?"

"Tilda will take an impression for the lab, then I'll set temporary crowns on what's left of your teeth. When the full bridge comes back from the lab, I'll give you a call. Everything is going swimmingly, Victor. You should be greatly encouraged."

"Oh, I am," I said, rubbing my tongue along my lifeless gum. "One more thing. I was just wondering if . . ."

"The boy, is that it?" he said.

"Yes."

"I was curious as to when you would get around to asking. What is his name?"

"Daniel. Daniel Rose."

"Have Daniel's mother call me and set up an appointment. I'll do what I can. Pro bono. Just like you. You see, Victor, it is important for you to understand my mission in life. It is important for you to know what kind of person I really am."

"Why is it important what I think?"

"We are all one family. We should all understand one another. Tilda," he called.

She was in the doorway quick as the Flash. "Yes, Doctor."

"Let's finish up with Victor, shall we?"

She pressed a massive fist into her palm until the knuckles cracked. "With pleasure."

35 **Julia and Daniel** Rose's one-room apartment above the salubrious atmosphere of Tommy's High Ball: one unmade bed, one listing crib, a hot plate, a small refrigerator, a portable television, the faint smell of vomit. In the closet, above the piles of dirty clothes and dirty plastic toys, hung men's pants, men's shirts, a leather jacket twice Julia's size. Beside the closet was a small bathroom with a moldy shower stall. Not exactly the Ritz.

"How long has Randy lived here with you, Julia?" said Isabel.

"Off and on for about six months," said Julia Rose.

"Why did you lie to us and say Randy wasn't here anymore?"

"He said that because of his record, and his time in the pen, you might take Daniel away if you knew we was together."

"We don't want to take Daniel away from you, Julia. We only want you to take care of him as well as you are able."

"I'm doing the best I can," said Julia defensively. "And Randy helps. He's fine with Daniel. They get along real good. He takes him to the park, out to McDonald's. Randy's the closest thing Daniel's ever had to a father. And he didn't like it, you sitting outside spying on him, Mr. Carl. He didn't like that at all."

"I just gave Randy a lift to work, Julia. And I only did it

because I wanted to find the truth, and we weren't getting it from you. But I was impressed with him all the same. He gets up every day, goes to work, works hard. I admire the hell out of that. I agree with you, the best thing for Daniel would be to have a father in the household."

"Okay," she said.

But it wasn't okay, that we were there, that she had to answer to us, none of it was okay, and her sullen disposition let us know it clearly. She sat on the unmade bed, holding Daniel like a baby. Daniel looked up at me with big red eyes.

We had knocked on her door unannounced. That had been my clever idea, the only way, I assumed, we could be sure that Julia wouldn't bolt before we arrived, the only way we could check out Daniel's living conditions. We had entered the apartment like G-men, sniffing around, scanning it for evidence of a crime, and now we were standing there, in our suits, standing because there was no place to sit, standing as emissaries from a system that had somehow already failed this woman and her child. When first we showed, it had felt like we were being proactive, but now the unannounced visit felt presumptuous and creepy. Yes, I represented the little boy, yes, Isabel was just trying to be sure the child was cared for properly, yes, all of this was sanctioned by the court. But still I had to wonder what the hell I, a man who had no children, no experience working with children, who, to be honest, didn't even like the little smackers, what the hell I was doing here, judging the fitness of this hole they lived in, which was the most Julia could afford, judging her fitness to be a parent, when it seemed she actually was trying to do her best.

"How are the parenting classes going?" said Isabel.

"Good. Really good. I'm learning a lot."

"You missed Tuesday."

"Daniel had a fever."

"How is he today?" Isabel stepped over to my client and put her hand on his forehead. "He feels all right. Did you take him to a doctor?"

"No. It was just a fever."

"How do you feel, Daniel?" said Isabel.

Daniel didn't answer, he just tucked his head into his mother's shoulder.

"Has he been crying much?" said Isabel.

"Some," said Julia. "He's been having trouble sleeping."

"Does Daniel sleep in there?" said Isabel, indicating the crib.

"Yes, or in our bed if he's crying."

"With you and Randy?" I said.

"With me," said Julia, sticking out her chin.

"He might have an ear infection," said Isabel. "You need to get that checked out, Julia. You have to take him to the doctor."

"There's a copay at the clinic."

"Did you enroll him in the program I told you about?"

"Not yet."

"I brought some of the paperwork. We can fill out most of it today. But it has to get finished, Julia. These are things you have to do to properly take care of your son."

"I have an idea," I said. Daniel picked his head up and stared at me. I tried to put some false excitement in my voice. "While you guys go over the paperwork and get all the documents filled out, why don't I take Daniel over to the park?"

Julia looked down at her son, Daniel buried his head in her shoulder.

"Sure," said Julia, pushing him away. "That would be a big help."

It was just two blocks down from the apartment, a beat city park, surrounded by a metal fence. Black blistered rubber was set beneath a rusted jungle gym and a dented slide. Empty beer cans were strewn about the cement benches that surrounded the play equipment, a balled-up McDonald's bag, shards of green glass. It was desolate and ugly, but still, when Daniel approached it, after a slow silent trudge beside me, he couldn't help himself from breaking into a trot and then a run.

He jumped onto the rubber strap that served as a seat on the swing set. He grabbed the chains and said, "Push."

I pushed lightly.

"Harder," he said.

I pushed only a little bit harder, unsure of the government-approved safe pushing speeds for four-year-olds on rickety swing sets.

"Harder," he ordered.

I complied, and as he reached the pinnacle of his flight, he let out a squeal that told me I was doing it right.

After the swing he clambered over the jungle gym and slid down the slide and rode the bouncy woodpecker. I sat on one of the benches and watched. He went from apparatus to apparatus with a great seriousness, never smiling, giving me the eye now and then but continuing on his rounds, purposely avoiding me.

Eventually he tired and sat down on a different bench, his legs dangling, his Velcro sneakers swinging. I stood, ambled over, sat beside him. He slid away a bit but stayed on the bench.

"How's it going, Daniel?" I said.

He shrugged.

"Do you remember who I am? My name is Victor. I'm the lawyer. I'm here to help you. Do you remember that?"

"Mommy says I don't need no help."

"Any help, and I hope she's right. You were great on that jungle gym. You were like Tarzan out there."

"Who's Tarzan?"

"The king of the jungle gym. You don't know Tarzan?"

He shook his head.

"He was a kid, really a baby, that was flying in a plane with his parents. They were flying over the jungle when the plane went down, bang. Everyone was lost but the baby, alone in the jungle. Luckily for the baby, it was found by a family of apes, and the apes decided to take care of this little baby. So they fed him and cared for him, and the boy grew up playing with all the animals and swinging on vines. They called him the king of the jungle."

"That sounds like fun, swinging on vines."

"Yeah," I said.

"What's a vine?"

"Like a rope with leaves. I met Randy. Remember we talked about him before?"

Daniel nodded.

"You still like him?"

He shrugged.

"He doesn't hurt you, does he?"

He shook his head and then said, "What happened to the mommy and daddy in the plane?"

"Tarzan's mommy and daddy?"

He nodded.

"They died," I said.

"Oh."

"What happened to your father?"

"He's gone."

"Did he die, too?"

"No. Mommy says he's someplace called New Jersey. Is there a jungle there?"

"Sure," I said. "Newark. So it's just you and Mommy and sometimes Randy in your family, right?"

"And Tanya."

"Who is Tanya, Daniel?"

"My sister."

"Is she older or younger than you?"

"Older. And nice. And really pretty. She took care of me all the time, and we watched TV together."

"But not anymore?"

"No."

"Where's Tanya now?"

"I don't know."

"Where did she go?"

"Someplace. I don't know."

"Why did she go someplace?"

"I don't know."

"Do you miss her?"

"A lot."

"When did she leave?"

"After Randy came."

"Okay."

"He didn't like her."

"Do you know why?"

"Because she was Tanya."

"Okay."

"Can you find her for me?"

"Is that what you want me to do, Daniel?"

He nodded.

"How are your teeth doing?" I said.

He didn't answer, instead he pulled his mouth over his teeth so that his lips disappeared.

"Do you know what a dentist is?"

He shook his head.

"A dentist is a doctor who takes care of teeth. I found one to take care of yours. You get to sit in a chair, and there's this light and nice music, and the doctor looks in your mouth and fixes things. He said he could fix your teeth so you wouldn't have to hide them all the time."

"Will it hurt?"

"A little."

"I don't want to go."

"When something's broken, you have to fix it or it gets broken worse. It's the same with teeth. This doctor, his name is Dr. Pfeffer, he said he can fix your teeth so they won't get worse."

"I don't want to go."

"Daniel, you have to."

"No."

"How about we make a deal?"

"I don't want to go. I don't. I don't."

"How about this, Daniel? If you go to the dentist, I'll find your sister."

"Tanya?"

"Yes. How about that?"

He opened his mouth and rubbed his tongue over the blackened, irregular stubs of his upper teeth.

"He's a good dentist," I said. "He has gentle hands."

"I want to see Tanya."

"So we have a deal?"

Before he could answer, he swung his head around. I followed his gaze. Julia and Isabel were walking toward the small opening in the gate.

Daniel ran to his mother, buried his head in her thigh.

There was something about Julia that scared me as her son held on to her leg for dear life. She was a pretty woman, and sweet, too, without a hint of violence in her. She would never willfully hurt Daniel, that was clear. But there was something else in her along with the sweetness, a weakness, and it was the weakness that scared me. I had never been a parent, true, but I had been a son, and I knew how a mother's weakness could slice into a boy's psyche like a knife. She couldn't say no, Julia, she couldn't deny candy or a night bottle to a child whose teeth were rotting before her very eyes. She would rather ignore a problem than deal with it, and if pressed, she would rather run. That's why she had been avoiding Isabel, running whenever Social Services planned a visit. And that's what she would do if I started pressing her on her missing daughter. She'd run, and she'd take my client with her.

So when she came through the fence and Daniel ran to her, I didn't rush forward and start badgering her about her missing daughter, about Tanya, demanding to know what had happened to her, where she had gone, threatening to call the police. No, that's not what I did, even though it was a struggle to hold myself back. No, what I did instead was smile.

"How was he?" she said as I approached.

"He was terrific," I said. I tousled his hair. "He's a great kid. Julia, I spoke to a dentist about Daniel's teeth. He says you shouldn't give him a bottle in the crib before he goes to bed."

"It's the only way he'll sleep. He's been a bad sleeper since he was born."

"It's really terrible for the teeth. You need to stop. The dentist also told me you need to have someone examine Daniel."

"I can't afford a dentist."

"This dentist said he'd be willing to look at Daniel and treat him, if he can, and to do it for free."

I took a card from my jacket pocket, handed it to her. She looked at it, bit her lower lip.

"His name is Dr. Pfeffer," I said. "His office is in Center City, on Sixteenth Street. He's waiting for your call. He says if you don't do something quickly, there might be permanent damage. But he also seemed to think if you let him take care of it right away, let him put caps on the teeth, there's a good chance that Daniel's permanent teeth, when they come in, will be fine."

"Caps?"

"That's what he says."

"Daniel won't go. He's scared of doctors and won't let anyone touch his teeth."

"Oh, he'll go," I said. Daniel was looking up at me, fear in his eyes. "We made a deal. Didn't we, Daniel?"

He nodded.

"What was the deal?" said Julia.

I was about to say that it was between a lawyer and his client and hoped that covered it for her, but then Daniel spoke.

"He promised he'd get me some ice cream," he said.

I don't know if that was the moment I fell for my client, but it was certainly the moment I decided I was going to find Tanya Rose. Because with that little covering lie, Daniel had told me all he ever needed to about his plight in this world, and that of his sister, too. He loved his mother, of course he did, what child doesn't? But even at the tender age of four, he knew he couldn't trust her completely to take care of him or his sister. With one little covering lie, he told me he wanted me there, wanted me to help. Sometimes that's all it takes.

"What do you think?" said Isabel as we watched mother and son walk away from us and back to their sad little apartment above Tommy's High Ball.

"I'm worried about him."

"Any particular reason?"

"Well, the teeth, for one. We'll see if she follows through with Dr. Pfeffer."

"I'll make sure of it," said Isabel.

"And then there's the question about Daniel's sister."

"There's a sister?" She started searching through her file. "I don't see any indication of a sister."

"That's the point," I said. "I think I need to see the judge."

CHAPTER

36

We were swamped.

The François Dubé murder trial was coming fast, and there was still way too much to do. Every piece of evidence had to be examined, every piece of testimony offered at the first trial had to be carefully reviewed for weaknesses. The advantage of a retrial is that you have so much information to work with, pretty much the whole of the prosecution's case is open and available for your delectation. The disadvantage of a retrial is that you have so much information to work with, you can get buried in the details.

We had covered the conference-room table and floor with mounds of documents and files, all the pleadings and motions, all the testimony, all the police reports, all the forensics reports and crime-scene photographs. We had nicknamed the conference room, with its morass of paper, the Dubé Tar Pit, because we found ourselves stuck there all hours of the day as we tried to build some sort of defense. But as Beth and I worked our way through it all, and the shape of what we were up against became clearer, I began to feel uneasy.

"Something's not right," I said late one evening in the tar pit. In my hand were two photographs. The first was from the crime scene, it showed the body of Leesa Dubé sprawled across the floor of her bedroom, the walls sprayed with dark drops, the spill of blood like a halo about her head. She was wearing panties and a T-shirt, no rings, no jewelry, fresh out of bed. One arm was spread wide out to the side, the other was bent beneath her body. Her face was almost calm, pale above the bloody gash left by a bullet through her neck. The second photograph was of Leesa Dubé shortly before her murder, eyes bright, her smile dazzling and unforgettable.

"What did you find?" said Beth.

"Nothing, and that's just it. We're missing something here."

"A report Mia Dalton didn't give us? I thought we received everything."

"No, nothing like that. But still we're missing something." I dropped the photographs, gestured to the piles of paper. "All this stuff is what the prosecution is going to present. The last trial was fought right here, on this battlefield, and François lost."

"But they don't have Seamus Dent this time," said Beth.

"True, but Whitney Robinson said he wasn't that great a witness. His absence isn't enough to turn the tide. And remember, even though we get to see all of Mia Dalton's case, she gets the chance to correct all the mistakes the prosecution made before. Frankly, she's a better lawyer than her boss."

"So what do you want to do?"

"I don't want the fight to be about all this crap," I said. "I want to change the battlefield. What we need is another suspect. Someone to shoulder the blame. It's what Whitney said was missing in the first trial."

"We can argue it was a burglary gone bad."

"With nothing burgled? Break in, kill a stranger—no rape, just murder—and then run away without so much as grabbing a diamond ring? That won't fly."

"What else do we have?"

"Nothing, and that's the problem. Not a damn thing."

And I was right, we didn't have a damn thing. But we did have the bones of something. Velma Takahashi's apparent guilt. Geoffrey Sunshine's shifty eyes. The strange story of Seamus Dent's descent and redemption and death. And then there was the peculiarly coincident contacts of Dr. Pfeffer to Whitney Robinson and Seamus Dent both. I could spend every hour until the trial digging through the piles in the Dubé Tar Pit, but that wouldn't get me one inch closer to taking those bones and gluing them together and animating some credible creature we could put in front of the jury and blame for Leesa Dubé's death.

"You know what still puzzles me?" I said. "The stuff missing from François's apartment that no one could account for." It was the toys that were playing on my mind. Mrs. Cullen had mentioned toys. What kind of toys? Beanie Babies?

"François told us the landlord sold it off or threw it away," said Beth.

"That's what he said, but there was stuff missing even when the police searched his apartment."

"Why is it important?"

"I don't know. But it's a loose end. Our only chance is to find some loose end and pull it until everything unravels."

"If there was anything there, François would have told us."

"You think so?"

"Of course."

"It appears we have differing views of our client."

"You don't trust him."

"And you do."

She looked at me and there was something in her eyes. "Yes," she said. "I do."

And what I thought just then was "Crap."

My partner, Elizabeth Derringer, was the type of woman

whose beauty couldn't be captured in a photograph, with a glossy black ponytail and a smear of freckles across her broad cheeks. A picture showed a serious woman with serious glasses, the type that shushed you quiet in the college library. But a photograph couldn't catch the sharp humor, the abiding sweetness, the romanticism that hid like a virus in her heart. She still believed she could find something in the markets of Istanbul or along the rugged trails in Nepal that she couldn't find in Philadelphia. Dysentery was all, I explained to her, but still she often mused aloud of traveling the world and finding a richer self. Paying clients would be a surer route, I told her, and when I did, she would smile indulgently, as if I were a sweet little puppy who had just peed on her shoe. I was worried, just then, that her romanticism had gotten the best of her. And I had cause, didn't I?

"It's just another case, Beth," I said softly. "He's just another defendant."

"There's no such thing," she said.

"You know, Beth," I said in my best avuncular tone, "it's hard enough to determine innocence or guilt right after a crime has been committed, but this guy has been in jail—"

"I don't need a lecture," she snapped.

"Maybe you do. It is not our job—"

"Don't, Victor. Please. I know our job. He hasn't hugged his daughter in three years."

"It shouldn't matter."

"But it does." She slapped her notebook closed, stood up. "I'm tired," she said. "I'm going home."

I glanced at my watch, bolted to my feet. "Damn it, I'm late."

"Hot date with Carol?"

"Hardly," I said. "It's with Carol, all right, but tonight is all business."

Carol Kingsly was looking at the ground beneath my feet. I looked down, too. The interest with which she was staring down indicated that something quite special must lay there, the meaning of the universe, maybe, or at least a quarter. But there was nothing I could see, nothing at all, just the cement walkway outside the very fashionable, very trendy restaurant where she had set up a meeting with that rich guy who was thinking of hiring me as his lawyer.

"Are those your shoes?" she said finally.

"I think so," I said. "They're on my feet."

"They have a rather thick sole."

"Is that good?"

"On a dinner plate, maybe. Hopefully, no one will notice." She reached to my neck, fixed the knot of my yellow tie. "Just smile, try to be personable, and don't say anything intolerably rude."

"I'd rather change my shoes."

"Come on, you," she said, yanking me forward. "We're late." Carol didn't like to joke about business, which I found a little bit awkward, since the business portion of my professional life was pretty much a joke.

Inside, we were greeted as if we were actually important and led to a prime table right beneath the giant golden Buddha that gave the joint its name. Buddakan was bright and crowded, with varnished floors, high ceilings, onyx tables. The waitstaff wore pajamas, a too-hip crowd waited by the indoor waterfall for seating, and you had the sense, just by being there, that you were actually someone, actually somewhere, which was why, I suppose, so many people wanted in. Presiding over everything, on its bright red stage, was the aforementioned Buddha. He looked supremely happy, did the Buddha, content and satisfied, seemingly unworried about the soles of his footwear.

"I'm sorry we're late," said Carol when we reached the table. "Victor is preparing for a very high-profile trial, and it's keeping him crazy busy." She gave my arm a squeeze, looked adoringly into my eyes. "But that's the price of being so in demand."

A very lovely, very young Japanese woman said something in Japanese, and the middle-aged Japanese man beside her nodded.

Carol proceeded to introduce me around. There was Nick, her lovesick business associate, who gave me a sullen acknowledgment. Then the young Japanese woman, named Kyoko, who was apparently here as a translator. Next to Kyoko was the Japanese man himself, the apparent star of the evening, as round and as seemingly at ease as the Buddha over his shoulder. As Carol gave me his name, he stood and bowed and handed me his card, all of which was superfluous. I had never seen him before, but I knew who he was, right off. I could tell by the other woman at the table, the man's wife, Velma Takahashi.

Velma puffed out her puffy lips as we were introduced. "Pleased to meet you, Mr. Carl."

So that was how she was going to play it. Fine, I figured, I'd play along. I nodded at her and said something inconclusive, something like, "Nice to see you," and then glanced at Mr. Takahashi, who was watching me quite carefully as the lovely Kyoko whispered in his ear. Without taking his eyes off me, he spoke in quick Japanese.

"What kind of trial is it that keeps you so busy, Mr. Carl?" said Kyoko in a musical, heavily accented voice.

"A murder trial," I said. "A man is accused of killing his wife."

Kyoko translated. Mr. Takahashi nodded and spoke.

"What will be your role at the trial?" said Kyoko.

"I'm defending the husband."

"Then Mr. Takahashi is very glad to meet you," said Kyoko, without bothering to translate.

Everyone laughed heartily, Takahashi included, everyone but Velma.

They served some sort of pan-Asian cuisine at Buddakan, things like diced eel and miso tuna tartare and their famous angry lobster, all washed down with porcelain cups of heated sake. The food was actually pretty good, which was the saving grace of the evening, since it was one of the most awkward dinners I ever had the misfortune to sit through. Carol did her level best to keep the conversation flowing—I actually felt a great deal of affection for her as she struggled mightily against the forces of darkness—and I did what I could to help, but the thing just wasn't working. Desolation sat at the table as if it, too, had been invited.

First, Nick was moping. Gelheads should be full of silly banter and broad smiles, don't you think? Otherwise what good are they? But Nick just moped. He was in love, poor guy, and I just happened to be the one dating the object of his desire. By my book, that at least was something to drink to. Cheers. Across from Nick, Velma Takahashi sat at the table like a sullen fifteen-year-old, slurping ginger martinis instead of sake, barely touching her black cod with miso glaze. She wasn't enjoying herself at the fancy restaurant, seemingly jaded by all the fancy restaurants she had dined in since marrying Takahashi. So what was the deal with her deal? I wondered. This was exactly what she had sold herself for, dinners like this, so you would think she would at least try to enjoy herself.

But the truth was, I couldn't blame her for sulking, because right there at our table, Mr. Takahashi and his beautiful translator, Kyoko, were having what appeared to be, even in the midst of our little party, a private tête-à-tête. Kyoko, who was far younger than Velma, spoke softly into his ear, he responded lowly, they giggled like the teenagers one of them might actually still have been. She rubbed his neck; his right hand never appeared above the table. They were even sharing their food like lovers. I expected them to link arms as they slurped their sake.

While Takahashi and Kyoko were in the midst of their private conversation and Carol was trying to cheer up the morose Nick, I leaned over to Velma and said softly, "You seem full of good cheer tonight."

"I have so much to be happy about," she said.

"Your husband, at least, looks like he's having a fine time."

"He sees life as an oyster to be savored, then swallowed."

"And Kyoko?"

"Already shucked. I appreciate you not mentioning our other business with my husband."

"I thought it best to be discreet, considering this is something akin to a job interview."

"Let me warn you, he can be a tyrant."

"But you look so happy. Can I ask you a personal question?"

"Please don't."

"Was it worth it?"

"Was what worth it?"

"Marrying Faustus over there."

"I think you have the roles confused, but yes."

"Really?"

"He has made my life a dream."

"From the looks of it, though, it's wake-up time."

"He's entitled to his diversions."

"And you to yours?"

"No, that's not part of the deal."

"Too bad."

"You were hoping, maybe, for something more than a check?"

"One always hopes," I said while glancing across the table. Mr. Takahashi was staring at me. He smiled at me strangely and nodded. I nodded back. He said something in Japanese.

"Do you do bankruptcy law, Mr. Carl?" said Kyoko.

"Not really," I said. "I thought you needed a real estate lawyer."

A lengthy conversation in Japanese between Kyoko and Takahashi.

"We have real estate lawyers," said Kyoko. "New York real estate lawyers. Only Tokyo real estate lawyers have a sharper bite. But we might, in the future, have need of a bankruptcy lawyer with special talents."

"Are you having trouble paying your bills, Mr. Takahashi?"

Carol kicked me under the table. Takahashi stared at me as Kyoko translated. When she was finished, his eyes widened for a moment, and then he laughed in quick, angry spurts.

"It is not my bills I am worried about," he said through Kyoko. He stared at his wife for a moment and then said, "One of my investments is on the edge of failure. I would like to save something of it. We might have to push the business into bankruptcy court."

"I've never done bankruptcy law before, but I'm sure I can figure it out. Not much to it, from what I understand."

"It might not be as simple as you think."

"There's a book, isn't there?"

"You mean the Bankruptcy Code?"

"That's it. I'll just follow the recipes. A pinch here, a dash there, and bam, we have ourselves an involuntary bankruptcy."

Mr. Takahashi spoke and then raised his sake and smiled as Kyoko translated. "Excellent," she said for him as he bowed his head. "Then it is settled."

I lifted my own cup and bowed my head back. "To our future relationship," I said.

"To our success," said Kyoko.

"To the Bankruptcy Code," I said.

Carol put her hand on my knee, leaned her lips close to my ear. "He likes you," she said. "I didn't know you could be so effective in a sales environment." She leaned even closer and whispered, "I find business so hot, don't you?" before she squeezed.

My little reflexive leap was noticed. Nick stared balefully into his sake glass. Velma smirked.

Kyoko pursed her lips at me, tilted her head. "I like your tie," she said.

"Tell Mr. Takahashi I like his tie, too," I said.

"I wasn't translating," said Kyoko.

"I know," I said.

Kyoko giggled.

Later in the evening, I was in the bathroom, moaning softly as I drained the sake from my system, when the door opened behind me. I looked around. Takahashi.

I zipped up, turned, did the little bowing thing. Takahashi locked the door.

"Thank—you—for—the—dinner," I said slowly and loudly.

"You don't have to shout," said Takahashi in flawless English. "I'm not French."

I was so taken aback, I almost backed into the urinal.

"I went to Stanford, actually," said Takahashi, avoiding my eyes as he talked, staring at my still-clasped hands as if they were the maniacal tools of a homicidal strangler. "But when it comes to business, I'm more comfortable in my native language. This little meeting," he said, indicating our environs, "is personal. You know my wife."

I stammered something, but he waved me quiet.

"Don't bother denying it," he said, still staring at my hands. "I have her followed at all times. She has been in your office on two occasions. It is why I agreed to meet with you. Have you slept with her?"

"No, of course not."

"But you would like to. Of course you would, she has been sculpted to evoke that very desire. And, Mr. Carl, let me say this. You would do me the greatest favor if you did."

"Excuse me?"

"Between you and me, it is quite the experience. She is very talented. A night with her is enough to drive sane men to do insane things."

"Like marrying her?"

He laughed his hard laugh. "Why don't you wash your hands while I talk? Your standing there with them in front of you is enough to give me the . . ." He paused to get the slang just right. "The willies."

My hands were still clasped, and I realized that in all the surprise I hadn't washed them after urination. I jumped to the sink.

"Thank you," said Takahashi as I soaped and scrubbed. He took a paper towel from the dispenser, placed it against a tiled wall, leaned his shoulder onto the paper. "My marriage is over. Our differences are irreconcilable. Or maybe I should say our differences are existential. She continues to exist in my life. It happens. I would be upset at the prospect of losing her, but Kyoko is quite slim, don't you think? The lawyers are already involved. All that remains is determining the amount of the settlement."

"And you are telling me this why?" I said as I dried my hands.

"There was, of course, a prenuptial agreement," said Takahashi. "In the event of infidelity on my wife's part, her settlement is greatly diminished. It's not that the amount actually matters to me, it is the principle of the thing. And, I suppose, the amount. So any way I could prove infidelity would be most advantageous."

"What does your private detective say?"

"He has suspicions, but no specific proof."

"Then you need a better detective."

"You represent the chef she was sleeping with before she met me. Did she sleep with him after the marriage? Or does he know of someone with whom she did? If the answer is yes, and you have proof, it could be quite valuable to both of you."

"I don't want any part of this," I said. "It's your business."

"That is almost admirable, Mr. Carl, but if things go as we both hope, my business will soon be your business. I must say, I am somewhat surprised. Your reaction seems so out of character."

"And what do you know of my character, Mr. Takahashi?"

"You're a lawyer, for one thing," he said. "And you haven't cultivated the reputation of a priest."

"No, I suppose I haven't." I paused for a moment, thought. "Just out of curiosity, how much are we talking about?"

He laughed again. "Now I see before me a man with whom I can do business. Think about it. I am sure a clever man like yourself can come up with sufficient proof. You would not be disappointed in the result. As for the bankruptcy case, I will have one of my people send around the file shortly. I am certain you will be able to turn the entire situation around in no time. Will you be needing a retainer?"

"Oh, yes, indeed."

"As I expected."

"What kind of business are we talking about?" I said.

"My wife asked me to invest with an old friend whose business was failing."

"Are there assets?"

"A building, a business. Pots and pans. It is a restaurant, you see. My wife seems to have a thing for restaurants, but they never work out. This one is in an old bank building. It is called Marrakech. Maybe you've heard of it."

"Yes," I said, trying to remain inscrutable, even as my heart fluttered like that of a guy who has just hit trip aces on the flop. "I've heard of it."

"Good. The financial slide is getting more precipitous, and I have been having some disagreements with my partner, an oily little man who runs the place. His name is Sunshine. He is of the opinion that he has done me a great favor by taking my money. You must understand the way I do business. Financial success is only the penultimate goal."

"What could be more important in business than money?"

He smiled. "Spite." Takahashi shifted away from the wall. The paper towel drifted to the floor. He showed no intention of picking it up. "It would be quite acceptable for you to save my investment. It would be even more acceptable if you could cut off Mr. Sunshine's testicles."

"That," I said, bowing once more, "would be my pleasure."

CHAPTER

38

"**What can I** do for you, Mr. Carl?" said Judge Sistine when I stepped into her rather ordinary office. She barely glanced up at me as I entered. She was sitting behind her desk, law books piled all about her, scrawling on a legal pad.

"You look busy," I said.

"Always in this job." She dropped her pen, leaned back, beckoned me to sit.

I sat.

"I was a civil litigator before I became a judge. Personal-injury defense, medical-malpractice defense, you know the drill. Good money, but I was getting tired of the fighting, tired of the hours. When I ran for the judgeship, I thought I'd be able to relax a bit. No one knew more about civil litigation than I. I figured I'd be up to speed my first day, on cruise control shortly thereafter. So of course, the chief judge assigned me to family court, where I had never set foot my entire career. Six months, and I'm still struggling to figure it out."

"That's encouraging," I said, "because I'm totally lost. I came about the Daniel Rose case."

"Yes, of course. I've been getting reports from Miss Chandler."

"So you know the details of his situation."

"You misunderstand, Mr. Carl. The reports I've been getting from Miss Chandler haven't been about Daniel. They've been about you."

"Me?"

"Of course. I rely on the lawyers to keep on top of difficult situations, often volunteer lawyers like yourself. I can't do it, my caseload is ridiculous, and Social Services is swamped. If I trust the lawyer, then I can assume problems will be dealt with properly. But you worried me. Frankly, you looked to be lazy and uninterested, a disaster waiting to happen."

"That's our firm's motto," I said. " 'Derringer and Carl, a disaster waiting to happen.' "

"So I asked Miss Chandler to keep me apprised of your performance."

"That little spy. She said good things, I hope."

"I haven't replaced you yet. Is that why you are here? Do you want to be replaced?"

"No, ma'am."

"Good. Then what is it, Mr. Carl?"

"Apparently Daniel has a sister. Her name is Tanya. She is older than Daniel, and she's missing. Not just in her person but in the documents, too. She's not in the Child Services file. In fact, there is no record of her anywhere. But I learned about her from what I believe is a reliable source, and Daniel confirmed her existence."

"Daniel is how old?"

"Four. He doesn't say much, but what he says, I believe."

"Have you asked the mother about her?"

"Not yet. She's very skittish. Daniel's teeth are a mess. The mother has taken him to a dentist I found who will do the necessary work for free. The dentist is going to cement caps on Daniel's upper teeth in a few days, which is the only way he'll save the teeth. The mother is also cooperating with Isabel's parenting plan. But she has a tendency to disappear when things get difficult, and I fear that if I press her about the daughter too soon, she'll disappear with Daniel before all the work is done on his teeth. And with her gone, even if you issue a bench warrant, that will be the end of our ability to help."

"So what do you want to do about it?"

"I think you should appoint the missing girl an attorney, someone to find her and make sure she is all right."

She pinched her lip and thought about it for a moment. "We don't even know if she exists."

"That's the point, isn't it?"

"I agree. Good work. I'll find someone."

She leaned forward, started writing again on the yellow pad, noticed I hadn't moved. Staring at me over her reading glasses, she said, "Thank you, Mr. Carl."

When I still didn't move, she said, "Is there anything else?"

"Yes, Judge."

"Go ahead."

"I think you should appoint me."

"Don't you have enough on your plate? I saw your name in the paper in connection with the François Dubé case."

"That's right."

"I used to eat in his restaurant. He made a wonderful duck."

"I'll be sure to tell him."

"It sounds like a murder trial will keep you busy enough."

"I expect so."

"And still you want me to appoint you to represent this girl?"

"Yes, ma'am."

"Isabel said you and your client had started to bond."

"I don't really like kids."

"And that you keep surprising her with the fruits of your investigations."

"I've been lucky."

"Why you and not someone else with more time?"

"I promised Daniel I'd find her."

"You promised? That's a hell of an irresponsible thing to do."

"Yes, ma'am."

"You have no idea where she might be, or even if she exists."

"No, ma'am."

"We make a lot of promises to these kids, and sometimes we even keep them." She tapped her lip with the tip of her pen as she thought. "All right then, Mr. Carl. A promise is a promise. I'll have the paperwork taken care of. As of now you represent that girl."

"Thank you."

"What's her name again?"

"Tanya Rose."

"Very good."

She went back to her document. I stood and headed for the door, but before I got there, she stopped me.

"Mr. Carl," she said. When I turned around, I noticed that she had taken off her glasses and her expression was now devoid of the rigidity that had heretofore been its chief characteristic. There might even have been a blink of concern. "I appreciate your enthusiasm, and I hope you find that girl, but be careful. Emotionally, I mean. I haven't been doing this for too long, but it's been long enough to know that these cases very rarely work out as well as we would wish." She tried to smile and failed. "Hope for the best, of course, but be prepared, always, for the worst."

"Don't worry, Judge. Preparing for the worst is the first thing I ever learned in the law."

CHAPTER
39

Beth knocked hard on the brass front door of Marrakech. It was locked, as was to be expected that early in the afternoon for a restaurant that served only dinner. If anyone could hear us, we were being studiously ignored, but still she knocked.

"Maybe we should go around back," I suggested.

"I'm not done banging," she said.

"You're going to break your hand. Listen, Beth, we don't know where it will lead. Don't get your hopes up."

"He lied to us."

"It's little Jerry Sonenshein, the teacher's pet rat," I said. "How could we have expected anything different? One time one of the AV guys was showing a driver's-ed film, you know, the one with all the bloody accidents to try to scare you straight? Suddenly, right in the middle, while the Signal 30 soundtrack droned on, someone cut in a porn video that—"

"I don't want to hear old high-school stories, Victor. I want to know what he's hiding."

"So do I, but banging on a door like some demented tax collector is not going to help us. What's gotten into you?"

She let out a nervous breath. "This could be what he needs."

"I know," I said slowly, looking at her carefully. "That's why we're here."

She heard something in my voice, because she stopped the banging, backed away from the door. "All right," she said, turning from me so I couldn't see her face. "Finish your story."

"Okay, this is great. So the porn video went on for like five minutes, five revelatory minutes, before the teacher glanced at the screen and figured out what was happening. The AV guy got expelled, but word was, it was little Jerry did the cutting. He denied it, swore up and down, but there was some AV feud going on, a tussle for AV president, which is like a battle for king of the dung hill, and the porn video was enough to knock out his competition and for him to end up on top. He's always been that kind of guy."

"A liar?"

"Yes, and seriously creepy."

She sighed, looked down the street. "Let's go around back."

"Good idea," I said.

There was a truck in the alley offloading produce, shriveled tomatoes, wilted romaine, moldy onions, and spoiled leeks, the kind of produce you get when your vendors don't trust that you can pay and are certain you can't afford to go to someone else. I hated to even imagine the state of the meat they were getting.

"Where are you two going?" said one of the men lugging the wooden crates into the restaurant.

"We're here to see the boss," I said as we slipped past him through the door.

"He's busy," he called after us.

"He's not that busy," I said.

We entered a short hallway that led to the kitchen. The kitchen was empty, gleaming, the oven doors, the pots hanging from their racks, the service shelves. A man in blue pants and an apron was slowly mopping the floor by the ovens. He lifted his head.

"Is the boss downstairs?" I said.

The man slowly nodded.

"Which way?"

He indicated a door behind him, at the other end of the kitchen.

"Thanks."

"I don't think, meester," he said slowly, "you want to go down there right now."

"He's expecting us," I said.

"Not right now he not especting you."

"So we'll surprise him."

The man looked at us for a moment, turned slowly to look at the door behind, shrugged. As Beth and I passed by, he went back to his slow mopping.

The door led to a ragged wooden stairwell that tumbled into the basement. A single bulb hanging from a wire showed the metal door of a large freezer and an open storage room filled with sacks of couscous and spices, bins of onions and potatoes and garlic. On the other side was a door with a plaque that read OFFICE.

"That's it," I said. "You want to knock?"

"No," she said. "Why spoil the surprise?"

"Good plan."

I listened at the door. He was in there, all right. I heard him say something and heard some sort of noise that I couldn't make out. Like the rhythmic knocking of a radiator. Except it was too warm outside for a radiator.

Slowly, quietly, I opened the door, and we stepped through.

Geoffrey Sunshine stood in front of his desk, facing away from the door, his pants pooled around his ankles so that his pimply butt was staring straight at us. He was playing hide the salami with a woman draped facedown across his glass-topped wooden desk, each thrust causing a banging on the table. The woman's skirt was pulled over her head, her panties were around her knees, her butt was plump and pale. The sight of him pounding away from behind her was like watching some bizarre exhibition at a carnival freak show. *Step right up, ladies and gentlemen, and watch the amazing rabid ferret as it mounts and violates an oversize honeydew melon.* Gad. It was more nauseating than the King Farouk cigar.

"For the sake of all that's decent in the world," I said, "and for the sake of my stomach, stop."

At the sound of my voice, Geoffrey Sunshine spun out and faced us. Double gad.

"Dear Lord," said Beth. "Pull up your pants."

"Get out of here," he snarled while, thankfully, complying with Beth's demand.

"I don't think so, Jerry," I said.

The woman on the desk raised herself on her elbows and turned her face toward us. Rosy-cheeked, wide-eyed, lipstick-smeared, satisfyingly bored. "Can I get up now, Mr. Sunshine?"

"Call the police, Bridget, we have intruders."

Bridget didn't look first to the phone, she looked to the desk, to a spot on the glass that had been cleared of paper. Sunshine followed her gaze, widened his eyes, and then reached over and pushed a file to cover the empty desk space.

Not much of mystery there, hey.

"Go ahead, Bridget," I said. "First, why don't you pull up your panties?"

Bridget, unembarrassed, slid off the desk, pulled up her lingerie, smoothed down her skirt, stood. She was a big, good-looking woman, with a waitress's dress and a milkmaid's face. Even in her flats, she towered over the restaurateur.

"Now you can call the police," I said. "And be sure to tell them to bring their narcotics test kit so they can take samples from the desktop."

"I don't know what you're talking about," lied Sunshine.

"Just like you didn't know that Velma Wykowski married Samuel Takahashi, the guy who bailed your restaurant out of bankruptcy just a few months ago."

"Should I call the police, Mr. Sunshine?" said Bridget, looking down at him for some direction.

Sunshine glanced at the desk and then at us, thought about it a moment, and shook his head.

Just then the bodyguard appeared in the doorway, his fists balled for action, a napkin still tucked into his neck. His lunch had evidently been interrupted by the news of our appearance, and he was none too happy about it. He charged into the office and grabbed me by my neck. It seemed to fit rather too comfortably in his fist. Then he lifted.

I grappled at his wrist and said something devastatingly witty, but only a cricket's chirp came out of my constricted throat. I struggled to breathe and failed.

"Nice of you to show up, Sean," said Sunshine.

I gestured at my throat.

"I'll toss this riffraff out back, boss," said Sean.

I gestured ever more wildly.

"It's a little late for that, don't you think? Mr. Carl is seeming to have some trouble breathing. Is that right, Victor?"

I waved my arms like a madman.

"Let Mr. Carl down," said Sunshine, "and then you and Bridget can leave us."

"It won't be no problem taking care of them, boss."

"No, I suppose not, but still. We'll discuss where you were later, but now do as I say."

Sean dropped me to my knees. I coughed my throat clear, sucked down great, noisy gulps of air.

"What about what we talked about, Mr. Sunshine?" said Bridget, a hopeful expression on her pretty face.

"Let's schedule another meeting," he said.

Her hope dissolved into annoyance. "Another meeting? It isn't my fault we were interrupted. For heaven's sake, Mr. Sunshine, I was just asking for a change of shift."

40

"So what of it?" said Geoffrey Sunshine, sitting now behind his desk, having regained some of his oily composure. He rubbed his hand across his wavy black hair, making sure each strand was glued in place. "Takahashi made a good investment."

"But you told us you didn't know who Velma Wykowski had married," said Beth. "That was a lie."

"Sit down, please," said Sunshine, gesturing to the chairs in front of his desk.

"That's okay," she said. "Really."

Beth and I were standing as far away from that desk as the room dimensions would allow.

"Why did you lie?" I said.

"I didn't think it was important."

"Important enough. See, Jerry, Takahashi only bailed out your sorry ass because his wife asked him to. And why would Velma do something like that for someone like you unless she wanted something in return? And to be honest, knowing you as I do, the only thing anyone could ever want from you is silence."

"Maybe she was being sweet to an old friend."

"A lot of adjectives come to mind when thinking about Velma Takahashi, but sweet is not one of them."

"What do you want, Victor? Let's get this over with. I have a business to run."

"Not for long, from the look of the produce you're getting or from the noise Takahashi is making."

He started. "What's he saying?"

"Let's answer my questions first. You told us about the famous Wykowski sisters before they met François. I want to know what happened when they came back."

"How do you know they did?"

"Because it's the only thing that makes sense, the only thing she would be worried about, what with the terms of her prenup."

"Why should I tell you?"

"I could say do it for old times' sake, but all our old times were rotten. I could say do it for François, but when was the last time you did anything for anyone other than yourself? So let's put it this way: Spill, or I'm going right back to Samuel Takahashi and tell him everything I know. How in the past you pimped out his wife to a prospective chef. How in the present you are running the restaurant into the ground while using his investment capital to buy coke and screw waitresses. And how the whole point of his investment in the first place was so that his wife could keep lying to him."

"He'd shut me down."

"Yes he would, but that wouldn't be the worst of it."

"What do you mean?"

"He's a scary man, Takahashi. Have you ever met him?"

"No. Just a lawyer."

"Well, I have, and let me tell you. He's no ordinary tycoon. He's connected, connected to people you never want to meet. You ever hear of Yakuza?"

"Japanese gangs? Don't be silly. He's not . . ."

"Oh, yes, he is."

Sunshine paled.

"Are you aware of the tradition of *yubitsume*?" I said.

"No."

"*Yubitsume*. It is a form of penance. In the world of the Yakuza, when you mess up, you cut off one of your fingers and send it to the boss as an apology, hoping he won't kill you and your children and your children's children for what you did. Hold up your hand."

He did as I instructed.

"That one," I said.

"Victor, you wouldn't go to him. You wouldn't do that to an old friend, would you?"

"Not only would I do it, Jerry, old pal, I'd enjoy it. And get this—he'd pay me in the process."

He rubbed his hand back and forth across the edge of his desk as he thought it through and then stopped the rubbing, opened his palm, looked at it. It's funny the things you grow attached to in this life. Like fingers.

"Let's have it," I said.

"It's no big deal anyway," he said.

"Go ahead," said Beth.

"Really. I don't know why Velma was so adamant I keep quiet. It was nothing."

"Go ahead."

He hesitated a bit, fiddled with a flower in a vase on his desk, pushed a file to the side, rubbed his finger on the desk's surface and then on his gums. "It was after the separation," he said. "Velma was only trying to cheer Leesa up."

"And how did she do that?" said Beth.

"The return of the famous Wykowski sisters. Velma brought her back to the club, they hung out at the bar, and it was just like old times. Or a semblance thereof. At the start Leesa wasn't into it, she was still in love with François, still devastated by the breakup, concerned about her daughter. But Velma tried hard, always telling her to snap out of it, to live a little. And the three of us would come down here and party, and that seemed to loosen her up a bit. But not too much. With Velma it was like she was right back in the old days, she was into it. Like she was all too ready to fling off the constrictions of her marriage. Drinking too fast, flirting with the men at the bar, letting it go too far. But Leesa, you could tell, it wasn't the same. Something had gone out of her. At least until Clem."

"Clem?"

"A bad boy. Clem. You know the type, Victor. Like the greasers who roamed the halls in high school. Leather jacket, mussed hair, half-shaven beard, a bad boy who looked like a bad boy. And there was that danger in his eye that's like catnip to a certain type of woman. So one night he shows up, and Velma just pounces. Next thing you know, they're in the corner, making a spectacle of themselves before they're roaring off together on his motorcycle, leaving Leesa alone and looking more forlorn than ever."

"And his name was Clem?" said Beth. "What was his last name?"

"Who the hell knows? He was just Clem."

"Where was he from?"

"Arizona or something. Guys like that are never from any-place specific, just someplace far away."

"What did he do?"

"He played, is what he did. Or fought. And the scars only made the women want him more."

"So Clem was with Velma. Is that what she wanted to hide from her husband? That's the big secret? She had an affair."

"Of course. With that much money on the line, wouldn't you want to keep it quiet? But that wasn't all of it. After a while of playing around with Clem, she got a little bored, like she always did. And she was still feeling sorry for her friend. Still trying to cheer her up. So Velma did with Clem what she did with François. She gave him to Leesa."

I tilted my head at that, leaned forward, felt a shiver roll down my spine. "What do you mean?" I said.

"She gave him to her," said Sunshine. "Like a gift. First it was Velma and Clem. And then it was Leesa and Clem. And Clem was into it."

"How do you know this?" I said.

"He told me the whole damn story and laughed about it. Right here, while we were doing lines together. Clem, that crazy son of a bitch. He loved it. Clem, Jesus. But by then, as with all guys like him, his charm was starting to be less charming. And you started noticing things. Like his breath and his temper."

"So what happened?"

"Leesa wanted it to stop. She wanted out. But Clem wouldn't let her go. 'I leave,' he said one night, spilling a bottle of beer with the slap of his hand on the bar. 'No one leaves me.' On another night there was a blowup at the club, an argument while Clem and Leesa and Velma were all together. Clem pushed Leesa away. She fell over a table and banged up her shoulder. She ran out. Velma ran after her. Clem stayed at the bar, getting drunk, muttering darkly to himself. That was the last time I saw Leesa. She was murdered only a few weeks later."

"And this Clem creep?"

"Gone."

"You tell the police this?" I said.

"Nah. No one ever came asking. And Velma came back to the club one night and begged me, begged me not to say anything. She couldn't let her husband know, she said. So I agreed. What with the eyewitness I heard about and the picture in Leesa's grip, I figured like everyone else it was

François who killed her anyway. No reason to ruin the reputation of a dead girl."

"And the investment?"

"That came later."

"When?"

"Just before you got François that new trial. Velma came to
me, said someone might come around asking questions. She
asked, she begged me to keep my mouth shut. I told her I was
having financial troubles. She said she would get me some
cash flow for the club if I would just keep quiet. So I agreed."

"And you'll testify to all of this?"

"I'm not going to lie on the stand, Victor. How do you think
I'd do in jail?"

"A rat like you, Sonenshein. I think you'd do fine."

Outside, in the alleyway behind Marrakech, Beth hugged me
hard, kissed me on the neck, and then spun away and did a
little pirouette.

"What are you so happy about?" I said.

"Sunshine. What he said. We know who killed Leesa."

"Do we?"

"Sure we do. It was that guy. Clem. He did it."

"I don't know that he did anything. I don't even know who
the hell he is."

"Do we need all the details in order to make him a suspect?"

"An actual name would help, but no. The story is
enough."

"And isn't this Clem the one thing we've been missing, another suspect?"

"Yes."

"Well, then we have him, Victor. We have him." She did
another spin, a little pirouette like I had never seen from her.

"Where did you learn that?"

"Five years of ballet as a little girl. We have a real chance now. We're going to win."

"Don't be so sure."

"Oh, Victor. You always slight yourself. You're a genius. I knew we could count on you. That stuff about the Japanese gangsters."

"The Yakuza."

"Is it true? Is Takahashi a Japanese gangster who will demand a finger for Sunshine's mistakes?"

"I would doubt it," I said. "He went to Stanford."

She laughed, spun back to me, and hugged me again. "I have to go. I have to tell François. François will love the Yakuza story. It was brilliant, Victor. Purely brilliant."

"Yeah," I said. "It was, wasn't it?" And I guessed right then that it must have been, because slipping under Sunshine's oily sheen of composure and getting him to spill had seemed so easy, so damn easy it was scary.

CHAPTER 41

The far-too-bright beige waiting room, the magazines laid out in perfect rows, the overhead fluorescent lights, the incessant Muzak, the hall of fame of perfect smiles, the perky young woman behind the desk, with her daunting cheerfulness, her gleaming teeth. Just being there gave me the skives, and I wasn't even scheduled to be in the chair that day.

"Hello, Mr. Carl," said Deirdre, the receptionist. "It's so good to see you this afternoon, but I wasn't aware you had an appointment."

"I came to check on Daniel Rose. I'm a friend of the family."

"Daniel is in with the doctor right now."

"No screams of agony yet?"

"We never hear anything out here," she said without a hint of irony. "The door is soundproof."

"Why do I find that weirdly upsetting?"

"I don't know, Mr. Carl. Daniel's mother is sitting over there if you want to speak to her."

"Thank you," I said

Julia Rose, dressed in jeans and a T-shirt, was sitting motionless in the corner, legs crossed, arms crossed, head tilted as if deep in thought. It showed just how little I understood about her that I had no idea what she might be thinking, or whether she was thinking anything at all. Heretofore I had seen her as someone whom we needed to get to do this for her son or that for her son, an obstacle to the proper care and feeding of my young client. I had thought of her as the problem without much considering that she might have problems of her own.

I sat down beside her. "How are you doing, Julia?"

Without looking up at me, she said, "I'm trying not to cry."

"He's a brave kid. He'll come through it fine."

"I know. I'm not worried about him in there."

"Then what is it?"

She turned her pretty face to me, the skin beneath her eyes dark with worry. "Do you care? Really?"

Before I blurted out the yes, I thought about it for a moment. Did I care about her, or did I just want her to get on with it, to do the right thing so that Daniel could wind up with half a chance in this world and I could get back to the petty concerns of my own petty life? She wasn't my client, my responsibility, so did I care? Really?

"Yes," I said finally, surprising myself. "Strangely enough, I do."

"I know I'm not the best mother in the world. I try, I do, Mr. Carl, but I've never had enough to do all I wanted to do for my boy. And I've never known enough neither. But I love him. I do."

"That might be true, Julia. But sometimes love alone isn't enough."

"I know that, but I'm trying. Except sometimes there are things too big to handle. They're just there and they grow worse and there's nothing you can do. My life has been like that since I was in grade school. I just knew it wasn't right, but there was nothing I could do about it except go along and take it. And everything happened for the worst, just like I was sure it all would."

"It's okay, Julia," I said, putting an arm around her shoulder. She was crying now, crying softly, I could feel her sobs in my arm and chest, and I sensed it wouldn't be okay. But what the hell was I supposed to do about that? "We'll get through all of this."

"No, it's not like that, Mr. Carl." She pushed herself away from me, wiped her nose with the front and back of her hand. "Daniel's teeth. I knew they was a problem. First they was perfect and white, and then they started turning black. But what was I going to do about it? When was there anything bad I could do something about? So I didn't want to tell anyone or show anyone. But every time I looked at his teeth, it broke me up. And embarrassed me, too. Which was why I wouldn't take Daniel to the doctor. I knew the looks I'd get, the lectures. I been lectured all my life about everything I ever done wrong. But never about the wrong that was done to me. And them teeth turning black, it wasn't my fault, it was just the way his teeth was. Like the way the world is. And because of that, I figured there was nothing I could do about it. But now . . ."

"They're going to be fine. Dr. Pfeffer is going to fix them."

"I know," she said. "I know. It's like this hole in my heart has been filled. Thank you so much, Mr. Carl. Thank you for caring about Daniel. Thank you for finding Dr. Pfeffer. He must be like a saint."

"Just like," I said.

"I am so relieved. He's going to be fine, my little Daniel. Perfect again. Something worked out after all. That's why I'm crying. That's why."

"Okay."

"It gives me hope, you know?"

"That's nice to hear. I'm really glad. But, Julia. There is something I have to ask you."

"Anything, Mr. Carl."

"I want to show you something."

I took out a piece of paper, a signed document with an official stamp at the end and handed it to her. She looked at it, turned it over to see if there was anything on the flip side, turned it back, started to read it.

"What's this?"

"It's an order, Julia, from the judge. It appoints me to be the lawyer not just for Daniel but also for Daniel's sister, Tanya."

A stillness descended after I said the name, as if a barrier had been broken and there was nothing but silence on the other side. I didn't know what would happen then, whether I'd lose her right there, lose her for good. I didn't know if she'd refuse to say a word and then take Daniel, with his newly fixed teeth, and disappear. I didn't know, and Tanya's fate seemed to tremble in the balance.

"Tanya is Daniel's half sister," Julia said after a long pause.

It was a start. And I don't think she would have answered me the day before. She would have run. But she said that Daniel's getting his teeth fixed had given her hope, and maybe that slight glimmer of hope was what prompted her to answer. Because maybe, along with the hope born out of the new possibilities for Daniel's teeth, she suddenly found some hope for the missing girl, too.

"How old is she?" I said.

"She'll be seven next month."

"I need to see her, to meet with her. She's my client now. So, Julia, I need to know. Where is Tanya?"

"I don't know."

"How do you not know?"

"Now you're going to lecture me."

"No lectures, okay. I promise."

"I've tried to be a good mother. I tried so hard. I just did what I thought was best for both my children."

"Julia, try to answer my question. What happened to Tanya?"

"I gave her away."

"To whom?"

"A lady in my old neighborhood. A fortune-teller name of Anna."

"Why did you give Tanya to her?"

"She said she could take care of her. She said she knew a place for her."

"No, Julia. Why did you give Tanya away?"

"Because Randy told me to. He didn't really like her much, and he said it would be better for all of us, Daniel especially, if she was with some other family."

"I don't understand."

"He didn't like having a little black girl following us around. She had a different father than Daniel, and he didn't like having to explain to his friends why she was with us. He's trying to move us to a better part of the city, but he said she wouldn't like it over there."

"Is that what he said?"

"What's wrong?"

"You need to tell me where this Anna lives."

"I don't know exactly."

"Tell me what you know," I said.

After she gave me a vague description of where Anna might be, she said, "What are you going to do, Mr. Carl?"

"I'm going to find her. I'm going to make sure she's okay."

"And maybe you'll help her like you're helping Daniel?"

"Sure."

"Randy said it would be better for both of them. Randy said it was the right thing to do."

"Okay, Julia. Thank you for your help."

"Stop looking at me like that, Mr. Carl. I'm doing the best I can."

"I know you are."

Just then the soundproof door opened and Daniel came out, his eyes red, his fists balled, followed by a smiling Dr. Bob in his green scrubs, his mask down around his neck. Daniel looked around, panicky for a moment, then saw us and ran over to his mother, jumping on her lap, burying his face in her neck.

"It's all right, baby," she said, patting his back. "It's okay, sweetie. Mommy's here."

Daniel pushed himself away from her. His face was trembling, as if he were about to break into tearful howling, but that's not what he did.

What he did was smile. And the caps on his teeth glistened in the bright fluorescent light.

Dr. Bob was still at the reception counter after Julia and Daniel left the office. He had given Julia printed instructions on caring for the caps, arranged a follow-up appointment, and sent them on their way. Now he was annotating the file.

"Daniel's teeth look great," I said to him.

"I got to him in the nick of time. A little more damage and there would have been nothing I could have done to save some of them."

"He seemed pretty happy. He actually smiled. Thank you."

"It's good to do good, isn't it, Victor?"

"I suppose," I said, and then I turned to face the door where Julia and Daniel had just left. "Although sometimes it feels like hell."

"The best things in life are never easy," he said as he gave the file to the receptionist. "You're going out with Carol again tonight, aren't you?"

"Yes, actually," I said.

Bob winked. "Have fun," he said.

CHAPTER
42

   I am in the middle of sex with Carol Kingsly. Umm, yes, right smack in the middle. I didn't realize that business was such an aphrodisiac, but when Carol saw me seal the deal with Takahashi, she decided it was time to seal the deal herself. And is it good? you ask. Well, tell me, is it ever really bad? Let's just say it ain't no root canal, baby. But this is something I've never before experienced. This, this is an out-of-body experience.

   So I am out of my body, sitting in a chair in the corner of Carol Kingsly's Laura Ashley bedroom, watching myself and Carol Kingsly do our thing on her Laura Ashley sheets. It looks a little silly from over here, a lot like two awkward swimmers working on their butterfly strokes in a sea of tiny pastel flowers. And the sounds we're making. Really now, kids, get a grip.

   But I'll say this for her, my God, she is good-looking. Her pretty face, her silken hair, her body, which, I must tell you, is miraculous, as lean and lithe as the latest diet craze can make it, honed and toned by hours in the gym, as flexible as a soft pretzel through her yoga, yet still abundant where raw abundance is most appreciated. And it's the real thing, let me tell you, yes, yes it is, or at least I think it is. And truthfully, between you and me—nudge, nudge—who the hell cares?

   I am the dog, aren't I? What hot-blooded heterosexual

man or homosexual woman would not want to trade places with me right now? Not a one, that's who. And look at that move I just put on. The referee is awarding me two points for a reversal. I'm the man, I'm the king, step aside, Elvis. Quite the dog. So tell me, what the hell am I doing watching from the chair as the main event plays out on the bed?

"Put your hand there," she says in a soft purr. "Move your leg there. Yes, a little more. Ummm, good. Now move your elbow."

Are we having sex here, or are we playing Twister?

Look at me up there, perched atop her, working hard to follow her instructions. Her expression is suffused with the sensual pleasures of the flesh, mine is diffused with the burdens of a piano mover. And frankly, I have to admit that from this vantage I look a bit ridiculous. My skin is pale, my muscles flaccid. And is that my butt or two skinny white Chihuahuas wrestling over a bone? But the *pièce de résistance* of my ridiculousness, the thing that truly embarrasses me about the whole *mise-en-scène*, is that I'm wearing the tie.

Yes, the damn tie.

It was her idea. We were rolling around, trying to rev up the *moteur de passion,* but there was something missing. Maybe my French wasn't good enough, or maybe it was that I was trying to speak French in the first place, but somehow it wasn't quite working. And then she made the suggestion. Who was I to say *non?* And she reacted with such gratifying enthusiasm to the very act of my tying it; she curled to every twist, moaned to every swish, stretched to her full naked length as I tightened the knot. Finally, when I crawled again atop her, she grabbed the yellow silk and pulled me close, and as we kissed, she tightened the tie until my throat constricted and I loudly gagged.

And away we went.

And was I into it? Hell yes. Well, just look at her. Who wouldn't be? I kissed her jaw, her shoulder, her breast. One hand was rubbing her hip, the other gripping her thigh. You know, I've done this before. My fingers were tapping out mystical rhythms on her skin, I was riffing like a jazz master, I was into it. But when I tried to loosen my tie just a bit so I could, like, breathe, she stopped me. And when I caressed her shoulder, she pushed my hand to her breast. And when I bent down to kiss the ridge of her hip, she pushed my head to her belly.

"Try this," she said. "Yes, harder. No, not too hard. Just like that. Faster. Slower. Shift over. Watch your knee."

I was into it, yes I was, really into it, and then my arm started to get tired from this one repetitive movement that she seemed to like, and when I stopped, she said, "Don't stop," and when I slowed down, she said, "Keep going," and my arm started cramping, and next thing I knew, I was in the chair, watching. And let me tell you, all you Internet-porn jockeys riding your mice like the joystick of an F-16, watching is nowhere near as good.

But there is one advantage to being in the chair; you have time to think. In the middle of the *Sturm und Drang,* your mind switches onto autopilot, but in the chair you can ponder the great questions of the day. Like, if French is the language of having sex and German is the language of watching sex, does that explain that last thousand years of European history? Or, if that's not deep enough, then why is someone who looks like Carol Kingsly at this very moment having sex with someone who looks like me? And what was that wink Dr. Bob threw at me all about? Did he know I was going to get lucky before I did?

Things are just going too fast, things seem just too peculiar. Dr. Bob had pulled my tooth, he was building me a bridge, and now he is getting me laid. On the whole, pretty damn good service, but still. And does any of this have any relation to the murder trial of François Dubé? I have a new suspect, a new theory, I am ready to try the sucker without a single reference to dentistry, yet still Dr. Bob is working mightily to curry my favor. All his little stories, his repeatedly saying that he just wanted to help, his gratis treatment of Daniel Rose, and now his setting me up in a relationship with Carol Kingsly that was almost fulfilling and had certainly turned sexual, all of it seems part of some message. And that message seems somehow connected to François. But how? Why? What is he trying to tell me?

Uh-oh, something is happening on the bed. Ah, yes, it's unmistakable. Look at the way her legs are stretching out, her toes are curling. Look at the way her jaw has tightened up. And my own face, I'm working so hard it's a wonder my heart doesn't give out right there. Things are coming to the proverbial head. But wait. She's grabbing at my tie. The thin piece with one hand. The knot with the other. I'm working so hard there's nothing I can do about it. And she has this twisted little smile. And suddenly she jerks the knot tight.

Aaaaack.

I'm back.

"That was so nice," she said after, stroking the yellow silk, now wrapped loosely about my neck.

"It was, wasn't it."

"This is going so well."

"It is, isn't it."

"Dr. Pfeffer will be thrilled."

"Can't we keep him out of it?"

"Oh, no, Victor, I couldn't do that. I tell him everything. He's my dentist. Did Mr. Takahashi hire you yet?"

"He tried, but I had to turn him down."

She hit me, hard.

"Ouch."

"It wasn't easy for me to get you that job."

"I had no choice," I said. "I had a conflict. The guy he wanted me to send into bankruptcy court is a witness in my murder case."

"And you couldn't finesse it."

"No."

"If you want to succeed in business, Victor, you need to become a little more unscrupulous."

"I lose any more scruples, I'll end up in the Senate."

"I told him you were the best lawyer in the city."

"You told your client a lie?"

"That's what I do. Public relations."

"Maybe I should put you on retainer."

"I'll write you up a proposal in the morning."

"I'm kidding."

"I'm not. I don't kid about business. You know what we should do next?"

"No, what?"

"Something I've been wanting to do with you from the first moment I saw you."

"Throw me on the ground and suck on my neck?"

"No, don't be silly. I want to help you pick out a new pair of shoes."

CHAPTER
43

Tommy's High Ball, midday.

I stepped inside from the bright sun, squinted into the smoky, neon-tinged dusk, made my way to the bar. It was busy for that time of day. Two men were shooting darts, a card game was going on, Motown was playing softly. A couple of old-timers were talking baseball at the bar. I wasn't thirsty, but I ordered a beer. I wasn't hungry, but I grabbed a handful of peanuts and rattled them in my fist. Wearing a suit as I was, I didn't exactly blend, but it didn't take long for interest in my presence to subside.

"Is Tommy around?" I said to the barkeep with the white hair when I ordered a refill. He was way tall and way thin, and his frame was curved like a question mark, as if from a lifetime of trying to avoid hitting his head on low-hanging fixtures.

"Tommy who?" he said.

"Tommy from Tommy's High Ball."

"Mister, that Tommy's been dead for twenty years."

"Then why don't you change the sign outside?"

"They call me Whitey."

"I guess that explains it. Rumor is, a man who might be interested in finding a chess game could do worse than coming here."

His eyebrows rose. "You any good?"

"Not really."

"Then you're out of your league."

"Still, it might be fun, don't you think?"

"No, no fun at all, unless you think sitting in the dunk tank at the fair is fun. You bring any money?"

"Some."

"That might be enough." He lifted his head to call over my shoulder. "Hey, Pork Chop, you got time to teach this fellow a lesson?"

I turned around. Alone in the booth closest to the door, a chessboard with its pieces arrayed in front of him, a thick green paperback in his hand, sat Horace T. Grant.

"I don't got time for fools," said Horace T. Grant, staring at the board. "Tell him the grade school down the block has got a chess club first Tuesday of every month. That might be more his level."

"He says he got some money," said the bartender.

"With that suit? He don't have enough."

"But the tie is nice," I said. "Don't you think?"

"How much?" said Horace.

"Let's say five a game?"

"Get your skinny ass over here to my office," said Horace T. Grant. "And make sure you bring me a cold one, too. Whipping white boys sure builds a thirst."

I bought the beer, slid into the booth, watched as Horace set up the board for a game. A few men ambled over to watch.

"What's the book?" I said.

"Alekhine."

"God bless you."

"Here's an idea. Why don't you keep your mouth closed so we don't learn just how stupid you really be?" A chuckle from the onlookers. "I'll let you move first, seeing as you'll need every advantage you can take."

"You know, I've played before," I said.

"I suppose you probably screwed before, too, don't mean you know what you doing."

The men watching laughed out loud.

"Go ahead," he said.

I surveyed the board, nodded a bit, pushed the pawn in front of my knight two spaces.

"You might as well give me that five right now," said Horace with a chuckle.

"I made one move."

"One was enough," he said, and then proceeded to beat me bloodless in just a few short minutes. The men around him cackled as his queen sliced through my defenses with alarming savagery and checkmated my king.

"Again?" I said as I held out the five.

Horace shrugged, snapped up the bill, set up the board. The men who had been watching shook their heads at my stupidity and dispersed. My chess had been so ugly they couldn't bear to stand through another game.

"Go ahead, boy," said Horace. "Make your move."

I reached into my jacket pocket, took out a folded document, dropped it on the board.

I watched carefully as Horace T. Grant read the order appointing me as counsel to Tanya Rose, a minor, location unknown. There was something in his face, something soft where I had never seen softness in him, something trembling just beneath the surface.

"I need your help," I said.

44

It could have taken me weeks to find the exact location of the fortune-teller named Anna that Julia Rose had told me about. I would have called some cops I knew in the district, I would have checked out the Yellow Pages under "Tellers, Fortune," I would have gone door-to-door in the general vicinity asking the question, and let me tell you, going door-to-door as a stranger in a strange neighborhood asking about someone who's a stranger to you and a neighbor to them is not the most pleasant or efficient way to maintain your teeth. It could have taken me weeks to find her, if I found her at all.

I gave Horace T. Grant my phone, and he had the exact address in ten minutes.

"She's in that there house," barked Horace.

I had followed his directions, had parked where he told me to park. Now we sat in my car across the street from a sagging brick row house with a long stoop. "The old lady's got herself the entire first floor."

"Does she know we're coming?" I said.

"Don't be a dumb cluck. Of course she does. She's a fortune-teller."

"I meant, do you think any of the people you talked to might have tipped her as to what we were after?"

"I didn't tell none of them what we wanted with her. Just

said I had a fortune that needed telling. You think the girl's in there?"

"I don't know," I said, "but if the old lady knew we were looking for her, I'm pretty sure she would have packed her off somewhere before we showed up. You get any more information about this Anna other than her age?"

"Just that she's got deep connections in the spirit world."

"Why don't I find that comforting?"

"Because," said Horace, "you don't believe in anything beyond your own infinite ignorance."

"And you, I can tell, are much more at one with the great mysteries of the universe."

"I like to think I have a spiritual dimension to my nature. I'm a churchgoing Baptist, if you need to know. Besides being good for the soul, it helps keep me regular. And let me tell you this, boy, you been on this earth as long as I have, you learn there ain't nothing much more important in life than keeping regular."

"Thank you for that advice."

"No charge for it neither. But this Anna, she's nothing but a charlatan. The only fortune worth telling is that we're all going to die, and I don't need no witch to tell me that."

"Let's go," I said. "And, Horace, let me do the talking."

"Oh, I intend to. Nothing more entertaining than watching a young fool trip all over his own damn self."

We stepped slowly up the cracked cement stairs and then across the bending floorboards of the porch. Beside her door was a clay medallion of a cherub's face. The cherub was smiling, but its expression was more doleful than glad, and its eyes were blazing with some awful certainty. It was disconcerting seeing it sitting there staring, as if it were looking into my soul and not liking what it found. Hell, I didn't blame it, but still. I looked away as I pressed the doorbell. I didn't hear anything inside, so I banged lightly on the door.

I was about to bang harder when it slowly opened just a crack.

"What you want?" said a whispery voice from inside.

"We're looking for Anna," I said.

"What you want with Madam Anna?"

"We just have some questions," I said.

"You the two men she expecting?"

I looked at Horace.

"What two men?" he said.

"A young one and an old one."

"I suppose, then," said Horace, "that would be us."

The door opened wider. A thin old woman with wild, straggly hair and one milky eye stepped forward into the light. "Tell me your names."

"I'm Victor Carl," I said. "He's Horace."

"Come on in, then, Victor Carl. And you, too, Horace," she said, stepping aside. "You got any cell phones, you better turn them off now. Madam don't like radio waves slipping into her home. They interfere with her readings."

I took out my phone, pressed the off button until the light went dead, and followed her inside.

We were swallowed by the gloom of the apartment's parlor. Pushed to the walls were a pair of shaggy couches, a passel of old chairs, a high and heavy breakfront. A hooked rug lay like a beaten corpse in the middle of the floor. And all of it was covered by a thick layer of dust and the twining scents of must and incense. It was a room for meetings of unnameable associations, for bizarre sacrificial rites involving roosters and snakes. I looked around for any sign of a child's presence, dolls or toys or small shoes; there was none. But if this Anna had actually been expecting us, then maybe Horace had slipped up in his inquiries and she knew what we wanted. It wouldn't be a trick to clean the place of the girl's presence for our visit.

"Wait," said the woman, standing now at the far side of the room. We waited as she slipped through a doorway. A moment later she came back out, leaving the door open for us. "Have a seat, and Madam Anna will be with you shortly."

She watched us carefully with her one good eye as we stepped through the opening, and then she closed the door behind us.

The room we found ourselves in was small and dark, devoid of windows, with two doors. The walls were painted a glossy maroon and covered with strange symbols painted in yellow: swirls and stars and staring eyes. Set in the middle of the room, surrounded by four chairs, was a round table painted a pale blue, with the same yellow symbols. The flames of three thick candles, each placed in the center of a yellow star on the table, provided the only light. A stick of incense smoldered, the air thick with mystery.

I looked at Horace T. Grant in the flickering candlelight, tilted my head, widened my eyes. "I see dead people."

"Shut your mouth, boy. This place gives me the creeps enough without you adding the horror of your sense of humor."

We both pulled out chairs and sat and waited. And waited. I checked my watch. I sneezed at the incense. I tapped my foot. Horace, sitting next to me, was literally twiddling his thumbs.

"How do you do that?" I said.

"It takes talent and coordination," he said, "which means you can count yourself out."

I was about to get up and go looking for her when the far door opened and a woman stepped inside. She was wearing a shimmering green robe, her eyes were closed and her feet were bare, and she was chanting softly in some language that sounded like it was long dead. I swiveled my head and looked at the door we had come in, then turned back to the chanter. It was the same straggly-haired woman who had greeted us at the front door. Madam Anna, I presumed.

"You couldn't have just come in with us?" I said.

"I was preparing for our session," she said as she sat down across from us at the table, "and it helps for me to get a sense of my visitors." She spoke now with a slight accent that I couldn't quite place, as if she had been born somewhere in the ocean between Haiti and West Philly. "Now, you said you have questions."

"That's right," I said.

"Of course. We all have questions. And I know what it is you are seeking."

"You do?"

"You have lost someone. Someone you care about very much. And you've come to me to find this person."

"How do you know?"

"It is my business to know. Just as I knew that you were coming. Take off your shoes, please."

"Our shoes?"

"Oh, yes. It is very important. Our reception from the other world comes through every part of our bodies, including our feet."

"You want us to take our pants off, too?" said Horace.

"Just the shoes." As I untied my wingtips, she said, "I will also need an offering of good faith."

"What kind of offering?"

"Something to show that your heart is pure, your intentions honorable, your search sincere."

"Let me guess," I said. "How much?"

"Two hundred dollars for our first contact."

"You must be confused," I said.

"But it is you with the questions, so which of us is confused? The offering is not a gift to me, it is a gift to the spirit world in which we will be looking for answers. It is not easy to enter the world of the dead. But before we can discuss the offering, we have business to finish." She turned her milky eye to the old man beside me, lowered her voice into a schoolmarmish snap. "Horace, you haven't yet taken off your shoes."

"I don't take off my shoes for no one," he said. "I didn't take them off in Japan, I didn't take them off in Korea, I didn't take them off in my Aunt Sally's house with all them stupid white carpets, and I'm not taking them off here."

"You must humble yourself, old man."

"I'm too old to be humble and not old enough to be called old by the likes of you."

"Madam Anna," I said, "I think you have the wrong idea about us."

"You're not lost souls?"

"Well, maybe you're right about that part."

"And you don't want to communicate with the dead?"

"Who wouldn't, actually? But that's not why we came to you. We're looking for a missing girl."

"And you want me to ask the spirits to help the search. It is not what I normally do, but it can be arranged. Though the offering will of course be higher."

"We're not here to ask the spirits, you half-blind witch," said Horace. "We're here to ask your sorry ass."

I put my hand on Horace's biceps to calm him down, squeezed hard to remind him that I was to do the talking, was surprised at the thinness of his arm.

"What my friend means is that we are looking for a missing girl and we hope that you can help us. Her name is Tanya, Tanya Rose."

She didn't move after I said the name, didn't so much as twitch. She stared at me with her one good eye as if trying to banish me with only her gaze. Then she closed her eyes and started her chanting once again. It was strangely beauti-

ful, her chant, strangely haunting, but she could sing all she
wanted, we weren't going anywhere.

After finishing, she opened her eyes and saw, with a flash
of disappointment, that we were still at the table. "Who are
you to her?" she said.

"I'm her lawyer," I said.

"How does such a girl have a lawyer?"

"A judge appointed me to find her, to make sure she is all
right."

"I can't help you."

"You mind if I look around?"

"You don't believe me?"

"No, frankly, ma'am, I don't."

"She's not here, I promise you that."

"But you know where she is."

"What would you do if you found her, Victor Carl? Would
you send her back to the mother that gave her away? Would
you send her back to that man who lives with her mother?
Would you feel she is safe, her with him?"

"She's my client. I'll do whatever is in her best interests.
And I have the law behind me."

"Where was your law when the mother was trying to toss
her aside?"

"You took her, didn't you?"

"I did what I could for her."

"And if she's not here, you gave her away. Again. But I'd
bet it wasn't free. I'd bet there was one of your offerings involved. How much did you sell her for?"

"This session is over," she said, blowing out one candle.
The room darkened.

"What have you sold her into?" I said. "What terrors is
she feeling now? Tell me where she is, Madam Anna, or I'll
bring the police with me next time I come."

"You want to bring the police here? That's a laugh. I've

been calling them for months. The prostitutes are working this corner every night now, and they do nothing. The cars come by honking, they park in front of my house. Every morning I sweep up the condoms. Tell them to come. Please." She blew out another candle, the room darkened further. Only one candle now burned, its faint flicker reflecting on all our faces before dying at the room's edges.

"Maybe when they come, they'll check your license," I said. "I'm sure you have a business-privilege license as required by law. And this house, I'm sure, is zoned for commercial use."

"Oh, yes, that is the work of your law. Shut me down, the scourge of the neighborhood. Forget the whores, forget the drugs, the gangsters. Good day, Victor Carl."

She was about to blow out the last candle when Horace said, "We care about her, too."

Madam Anna held her breath, raised the gaze from her one good eye to Horace. I turned my head, too, because there was a note of tender softness in his voice.

"The way her eyes squint when she laughs," said Horace. "The way she skips instead of walks. The cool feel of her hand when she's holding yours. The way she looks up at you with a face full of trust. You care about her, I see it in you. And we do, too. A girl like that, with a mother like that, she needs all the help she can get in this world."

"What do you want?" said Madam Anna.

"We just want to know where she is," I said. "And that she's okay."

"Leave your card," said Madam Anna.

I took a card from my jacket, tossed it on the table. While it was still spinning on the wood, she blew out the last candle.

The room plunged into darkness, nothing to be seen but the faintly glowing tip of the incense stick. I stood up quickly, went to grab hold of her, grabbed only air, and howled out in pain.

"What happened?" barked Horace from the darkness.

"I stubbed my toe."

"What kind of fool takes off his shoes whenever any old lady says so?"

I took out my phone, flipped it open, turned it on, used the faint light from the display to check out the room. Madam Anna was gone, and so was my card.

With the cell-phone light, I found my shoes, slipped them on, moved around the table, and opened the door that the fortune-teller had come through. There was a hallway and a bedroom and a kitchen and a bathroom, but no sign of the old woman and no sign of the presence of Tanya Rose either. I took the liberty of searching the rest of the apartment. Nothing. Madam Anna was gone, and Tanya, if she had ever lived there, lived there no longer.

"What's next?" said Horace T. Grant on our way out of the apartment.

"I don't know."

"You better figure out something, boy."

"Yes, I better. That was quite the speech in there, Horace."

"A bunch of horse crap tied in a pretty knot."

"I don't think so."

"Think whatever the hell you want."

As we stepped out the door, two men stood on the porch. One was older, bent, wearing a black mourning suit. The other was far younger, a teenager almost, holding on to the old man's arm.

Horace stared at the two men for a long moment and then held the door open. "Go right on in, gentlemen," he said. "She's expecting you."

With my search for Tanya Rose stymied by Madam Anna's milky-white eye, I turned my attention back to the François Dubé case. Which explains why I was sitting next to Beth in my car in the salubrious environs of the Peaceful Valley Memorial Park.

"There's something almost cheerful about a cemetery on a shining day, isn't there?" I said. "The bright grass, the gleaming stones."

"I find it morbid," said Beth.

"Or maybe I just enjoy the peace and serenity, as if a manifestation of the promised sweet kiss of death."

She leaned back, looked at me. "The sweet kiss of death?"

"Wouldn't it be nice to just be finished with all the striving, the hopes, the jarring needs, the raging disappointments? Wouldn't it be nice to just be done with it all and to fall into the arms of that final, gentle sleep?"

"You don't have to die for that, Victor, just retire to Boca."

"I can't eat dinner at four."

"I think you like cemeteries because it's the one place in the world where you're surrounded by people with less promising futures than your own."

"That must be it. You've been cheery lately."

"Have I?"

"Oh, yes. Smiling at your desk, dancing in alleyways."

"Maybe anyone who doesn't look forward to the sweet kiss of death seems cheery to you."

"No. It's something else. You're glowing."

"As promised by that infomercial for this year's revolutionary new skin-care treatment."

"Is that it? Did you make that call to change your life?"

"No. I still haven't used up last year's revolutionary new skin-care treatment. Where is she?"

"She should be here soon."

"You couldn't have just called her?"

"Where's the impact in that? Our intrepid investigator, Phil Skink, left us a schedule of her regular visits around the town. Today it's the Peaceful Valley Memorial Park before she heads to her upscale nail salon."

"And you don't think it's rude to intercept her here?"

"Perfectly appropriate, if you ask me."

"How's Carol?"

"Fine."

"I agree, mighty fine. But how are things with her?"

"Progressing."

"You don't sound so excited."

"She's rather assertive."

"And that's a problem how?"

"I don't know, Beth. I sort of like to dress myself in the morning. Wait, over there. Is that a hearse or a limo?"

"A limo."

"Bingo," I said.

The long black car eased to a stop at Row U. The driver hopped out, opened the back door, and out slid Velma Taka-hashi. She was dressed for the part of the grieving friend with a terrible secret: white scarf around the hair, dark glasses over the eyes, deep red lipstick on her puffy lips, a single white rose in her hand. She walked slowly down the row and then stopped at a granite marker and stared for a moment before kneeling in front of it. We gave her some minutes to perform her ministrations, smoothing the grass, tossing off the seedpods from the maple overhead, we gave her some minutes to wallow in her guilt before we stepped out of the car.

Her head rose at the sound of our doors closing. She aimed her dark, round glasses our way, stared for a few seconds, and then turned back to the gravestone as if she had been waiting for us all along.

We walked slowly toward Velma until we were standing behind her. In front of us was a marker that spread across three sites. CULLEN. And carved over the site to the right, where Velma knelt, was the name LEESA SARA, and beneath that the words BELOVED DAUGHTER AND MOTHER. Her parents had scrubbed her married name and wifely status from Leesa's gravestone, and you couldn't really blame them.

"We need to talk," I said.

"Uh-oh," she said without turning around or rising at the sound of my voice. "Does that mean we're breaking up?"

"Something like that. We need to talk about Clem."

"What is there to talk about?" she said. "He is nothing, a figment of a bad dream from a different life."

"But you think he might have killed Leesa."

"Since when does what I think matter? I think people mourning their friends at a cemetery should be left in peace, and yet here you are."

"What is Clem's full name?"

"Clem."

"Where is he now, do you know?"

"He's nowhere. He's a phantom. He appeared as if by magic, did his damage, and now he's gone."

"We're going to need you to testify about him. About how

you met him, how you gave him to Leesa, how they fought, how after she was brutally murdered, he disappeared. We're going to need you to tell the jury everything."

"You know I can't do that."

"Why the hell not?" said Beth with a snap of anger in her voice. "What kind of witch will pay for François's defense but not tell the truth to save him?"

Velma Takahashi turned toward Beth and stared at her through the dark glasses. "He's quite charming, isn't he?" she said, a spider's bite in her voice. "So much the gallant. But maybe, dear one, he's not as gallant as he seems."

"He needs your help," said Beth.

"Why does he need mine when he already has yours?"

I didn't like the tone of Velma's voice, the way the two women had squared off. I didn't like any of this. She was playing with us, was Velma Takahashi, tossing us about like balls of catnip placed here for her amusement. But I knew how to shut off the game. I reached into my jacket pocket, pulled out a legal document stapled on a blue backing, dropped it onto Leesa Dubé's grave, right in front of the still-kneeling Velma Takahashi.

"You've been served," I said.

"What is this?" she said, scooping up the subpoena and rising angrily to her feet. "What the hell are you doing?"

"The trial starts next week," I said.

"You know that my situation is delicate."

"Funny thing, Velma, I don't care about your prenup. If you don't show up when I tell you, I'll have a bench warrant issued. And then I'll have you arrested. A picture of you in the paper with your hands cuffed behind your back will be just what your husband wants to see."

"You must leave me out of it."

"Can't," I said.

"Don't do this, Victor." She took a step forward, reached

a hand to my chest, let her expression turn dewy and moist. "Please."

"It's done," I said.

"Victor?"

"This Grace Kelly, Kim Novak thing you have going on is very becoming, really. That scarf, nice touch. But I have to say I like you better in your tennis outfit."

Her moist expression turned bitter in the blink of an eye. "Don't forget your place, you dickless wonder," she said.

I laughed, which only made her angrier. She threw the subpoena at my chest. As the paper slid to the ground, I laughed harder.

"You thought by controlling the money you controlled the story," I said, "but I don't work like that."

"Make me testify and you won't get another cent."

"I'll find a way to get paid," I said. "Maybe your husband will cover the bill in gratitude for proving your infidelity. And if he won't—screw it. I'll finish the case pro bono just to make you squirm."

"You're an insignificant worm."

"Yes I am," I said cheerfully, "on a useless piece of rock hurtling through a universe devoid of rhyme or reason. And yet you're still going to testify."

She stood before me for another moment, swaying as if she had taken a shot, and then stormed off toward the limo.

I kneeled down, picked up the subpoena. "You forgot something, Velma."

She didn't slow her pace. "Screw yourself."

"Show up, or I'll put you in jail."

She stopped, turned around. "You have no idea what you are getting into."

"You're exactly right. I move through life in a blissful state of ignorance. It's the only way people like you and me can live with ourselves. See you in court."

She turned away again, headed in a trot toward the limo.

"Oh, and Velma, when you come," I called out after her, "the scarf thing would work wonderfully on the stand."

We watched as she dived into the open limo door, watched as the driver pulled immediately away, watched the dust kick up as the limo made its exit from the Peaceful Valley Memorial Park. I had enjoyed the whole scene immensely, and yet something troubled me.

"Do you feel," I said, "like we've just been in the middle of something staged for the adoring crowd?"

"She seemed angry enough," said Beth.

"That's exactly it. Angry enough. She comes to the cemetery to drop a flower at her best friend's grave, we show up asking about Clem, a man who might have killed said friend, and suddenly the scene erupts. But it's exactly everything you would expect from such a scene. First she acts all imperious, then she tries to seduce me, then she challenges my manhood, then she cuts off our fees, and then she's rushing off as if she's late for a manicure."

"As usual you're looking too hard," said Beth. "She doesn't want to testify. We're a threat to everything she's worked for."

"Of course we are," I said. "But still, even with all she said, it seemed the only time there was real venom in her voice was when she went after you."

I looked at Beth, her gaze nervously danced away. "She was out of line," said Beth.

"Was she?"

"Well, maybe not on the dickless wonder thing, but on everything else."

I laughed and then stopped laughing. Beth and I were staring one at the other. There was something in her face just then, was it fear, maybe? Fear of what? Of what she was feeling, of what she was risking, of everything going all to hell? After a moment she turned away, looked down at Leesa Dubé's grave.

"We need to find him," she said, a note of desperation in her voice. "There's no telling what Velma will say in court, and we can't trust Sunshine. We need to find Clem."

"We're doing what we can."

"I know, but it's not enough."

"You're in deep, aren't you?"

"It's not like you think."

"Then what is it like?"

She didn't answer.

"I don't trust him," I said.

"You don't have to."

"You want the lecture?"

"No."

"Okay," I said. "But it can't come to anything."

"I don't want anything except to help him every way I can."

"We're lawyers, Beth. We have rules."

"Is this the lecture?"

"Maybe. I don't know. But, Beth, something isn't right here, and that son of a bitch, I'm telling you, is in the middle of it."

46

I was in the tar pit, reviewing once again the transcript of Seamus Dent's testimony at the first François Dubé trial, when Whitney Robinson III strolled into the room. I startled when I saw him. It was as if I had conjured him with my thoughts, because the whole time I was examining the transcript, I had actually been thinking about Whit, and this is what I had been thinking: Why the hell hadn't he ripped poor Seamus Dent a second asshole on the stand? Whitney had been gentle, almost kind to the kid. But as I examined the testimony, I could see the flaws in Seamus's statement, the avenues wide open for attack. I didn't yet know if Seamus had been telling the truth or not, but I sure could have placed doubt in the jury's mind, and so could the Whitney Robinson I had seen in court over the years. So why, in this trial, had Whit given Seamus Dent a pass? And it was not the first fairly grievous error I had caught in Whit's performance at the trial.

"Whit," I said, standing quickly and dropping the transcript as if I had been caught at something. "How nice of you to visit."

"I was in the neighborhood, old boy," he said. "Thought I'd see how you're getting along. Your secretary remembered me and sent me on back. I hope you don't mind."

"No, not at all. It's great to see you."

"You look busy." He glanced around at the piles of paper scattered across the table and the floor, stacked on the chairs. "Think you have enough material to work with?"

"Just about."

"I remember trying murder cases with a file thinner than a comic book. I guess the times have passed me by."

"Never," I said.

I cleared off a chair, bade him to sit. His whole body shook with effort as he lowered himself onto the seat. He took out a handkerchief and wiped his forehead. He was wearing his normal costume, argyle socks, tan pants, blue blazer, red bow tie, but his expression showed more age and worry than I remembered in him. It made me think of the strange comment that ended our meeting at his house at the start of the case: *You can't imagine the price.* What price? I wondered. And how had he paid it?

"I thought I'd come by to see if I could help your preparations," he said. "To see if you had any questions about the first trial that I could answer for you. Anything I can do to help, I'd be delighted."

I glanced down at the transcript and then up at the old man and his aged, worried eyes. It seemed just then that the way he sat, the way he hunched over with the weariness of age, answered all my questions about the prior trial. "No, Whit. Everything seems pretty clear."

"I'm more than willing to talk about the case, Victor. To see if I can add anything to your efforts."

"I appreciate that, but we seem to have it under control."

"Good. Grand. How are your teeth getting along? Last time I saw you, at the hearing, your whole face was swollen."

I rubbed my tongue over the temporary crowns and the healing gap where my cracked tooth had been. "Actually, my teeth are doing quite well. I took your advice about Dr. Pfeffer."

"Yes, I know. He called to thank me for the referral."

"He hasn't been the most gentle of doctors, and there has been some pain involved, great spasms of pain, actually, but it almost seems like he knows what he's doing."

"Oh, he does, I assure you."

"What do you know about him?"

"Dr. Pfeffer? Interesting character. He talks a bit much while he's in your mouth, but he's quite good. I met him quite by chance at the time of François's first trial. My teeth were in sorry shape when he took control, but they are much improved, I am glad to say. Nothing like a good ear of corn on a summer's eve, yes, Victor? And I've found he can be rather helpful in many other ways, too."

"How so?"

"Well, he seems to know everybody and enjoys making connections. He likes to feel at the center of things, I suppose, but the connections can be quite valuable all the same. He helped my wife and me with our daughter's care. In fact, the nurse we have now, who has been a lifesaver, was referred to us by Dr. Pfeffer."

The nurse with the pale face and black eyes who had been staring out the window of his house as we spoke in the back, that nurse. How strange was that?

"You should let him help you any way he can if you have the chance," said Whit. "I sense he's a bit of a sad case, actually, a lonely man who likes to do good."

"I don't know how lonely," I said. "Not with Tilda to keep him company."

"Oh, you don't think . . ." He paused for thought and then burst out into laughter. "Oh, my, you might be right. But what an odd couple. She must give him quite the workout." More laughter. "I'd bet she could twist him into a pretzel. But, Victor, enough gossip. Old men talk about what others are doing because we can't do it ourselves any longer. But a young man like you—"

"Not so young."

"Bosh. So about the trial, did you find anything new to argue? Have you a theory of the murder that might sway the jury?"

"As a matter of fact," I said, nodding, "we've stumbled onto something. Remember when you said your biggest problem at the first trial was that you had no suspects? Well, we found one."

"Really?" His eyes brightened with interest, he leaned forward. "Who?"

"Someone not mentioned in the first trial at all," I said. "A man named Clem." And then I told him of what we had learned, about Leesa's good friend Velma, about their attempts to relive their wild youth, about the man with the motorcycle whom Velma took on as a lover and then passed on to Leesa, about the fights, the intimations of violence, and the way Clem had up and disappeared suddenly after the murder. I watched closely as I told him everything. I worried that he might act defensive, might wonder how he had missed such a suspect, might think I was accusing him of failing at his prior representation of my client, but the only expression I could see on his face was relief.

"That's extraordinary, Victor. Do you have evidence for all of this?"

"Absolutely."

"Simply extraordinary. And the prosecution, Ms. Dalton, does she know about Clem?"

"Not that I know of," I said with a smile.

"Marvelous." He clapped his hands and laughed. "I am so proud of you, boy. You have taken the case and made it your own. I thought I might be able to help, but I can see that I am not needed at all."

"Well, there is one thing," I said.

"Pray tell."

"François says the landlord sold off all his possessions while he was in jail, but I think there was stuff missing even before the murder. Any idea what might have happened to it?"

Whit pursed his lips, thought about it. "No, no idea. Is it important?"

"I don't know, that's the point. I'm just curious."

"Curiosity. Very good," said Whit. "That's always the key to being a good lawyer."

"Or a dead cat. Can I ask you something else?"

"Of course, anything."

"This is a bit awkward."

"Go ahead, my boy."

"François. Is he . . . how should I put this?" I glanced around, stood, walked over to close the conference-room door. When I sat back down, I leaned close and spoke softly. "In your experience with François Dubé, have you found him to be a creep?"

"A creep?"

"Is that too loose a term?"

"No, I think I understand. Why do you ask?"

"My partner."

"Ms. Derringer."

"I think maybe she's . . . I don't know for sure, but . . ."

"You think she's become emotionally involved with your client?"

"In some way, yes."

"That's bad, Victor. Very bad."

"I know."

"No, you don't. How serious is it?"

"I think damn serious."

"François has a certain power. My wife felt it when she

met him. She was in her seventies, way past menopause and already ill, and still she felt it. She said it was something in his eyes. The way he looked at her. Maybe it was his French sincerity, maybe it is that little flaw of gold. But you have reason to be worried."

"Why?"

"Between the idea and the reality, between the motion and the act, falls the Shadow."

"Whit?"

"It's from a poem by Eliot, called 'The Hollow Men.' François Dubé can be a charmer, but there is something hollow inside him."

"Whit, she's my partner, she's my best friend."

"Between the conception and the creation, between the emotion and the response, falls the Shadow."

"What shadow?"

"There are things I cannot tell you, Victor, you understand. My relationship with François remains as protected as yours. But these things, if you knew of them, in the context of which now we speak, would disturb you greatly. And these are not just stories I am talking about."

"I don't understand."

"There may be evidence."

"What kind of evidence?"

"Physical evidence. I never saw it, mind you, but in the course of my representation, I came to learn of its existence. And the whole of the trial, I was terrified that it would somehow show up. I knew that its presence before the jury would be devastating."

"Where was it?"

"I don't know."

"What happened to it?"

"Whether it has been destroyed or hidden, I have no idea. But under any circumstance, you cannot let this evidence be exposed to the jury. At the same time, Victor, and I tell you this as a friend, you have good reason to be worried about Ms. Derringer."

"Whit, you need to tell me more."

"Between the desire and the spasm, between the potency and the existence, between the essence and the descent, falls the Shadow."

"Whit, what are you trying to say?"

"I'm answering your question as best I can, within the bounds of my duty. You asked me if François was a creep. And what I'm saying is that you can't imagine the half of it."

47

I know how to open a bottle of wine—twist the corkscrew until the cork disintegrates, pour through a strainer. And I know how to open a new CD in its theft-proof package—fire up the chain saw. But the right way for a defense attorney to open up a murder trial, now, that's always a bit of a puzzle.

Some parts are simple. When the judge calls your name, you stand and button your jacket, step toward the jury. You smile at the fourteen of them, twelve jurors and two alternates, as if they were your bestest, bestest friends, even though all the time you're thinking, How did we end up with these bozos? And then you begin.

"Ladies and gentlemen, my name is Victor Carl. My partner's name is Beth Derringer. And today we stand before you with the awesome responsibility of defending our client, François Dubé, against the charge of murdering his wife."

Now you have to describe the crime scene. You have to talk about Leesa Dubé sprawled on the floor of her bedroom, lying in a pool of her own blood, her neck torn apart by a bullet fired at close range. You even let your voice choke when you talk about the blood soaking her beautiful auburn hair. You can't minimize the murder, you can't dismiss it or avoid it—she's dead, baby, ain't no use denying that fact—so instead you embrace it. Don't ever let the pros-

ecution possess the murder, snatch it from them and make it
your own.

Then, and this is important, then you have to step over to
your client. You have already put him in a suit, a nonyellow
tie, you've had him don a pair of studious-looking glasses.
Now you have him stand and face the jury while you put
your arm around his shoulders. The prosecutor has already
stuck his finger in your client's face and called him a murderer, you have to do him one better. You've just barely held
on as you described the crime, now you stand with your arm
around the man the Commonwealth has accused of commit-
ting it. You don't have to say a thing, the jury understands.
How could you embrace this man unless you were sure he
was innocent. How indeed?

Because it is the job, ladies and gentlemen. If he smelled
like a dog dipped in shit, I'd stand just as close. But you
don't say that. Instead you wait there silently, letting the
image sink in, before you start the usual tap dance.

"I want to introduce you to François Dubé, a loving father
and a loving husband. He is a chef, he owned his own restaurant, he is an artist with artichokes and duck, with butter and
lobster and vanilla beans, with the very sustenance of our
lives. But most of all, this is a man who loved Leesa Dubé.
She was his wife, had been his lover and best friend, was the
mother of his beloved daughter. He loved her with all his
soul. He loves her still."

Now you have your client sit back down again. You don't
want the jury to look too closely, after all, you don't want the
jury to see his scarred hands, the insolence in his eyes, you
don't want the jury to feel the same way you feel about him.
So you sit him down and slowly walk back to the front of the
jury box.

"Was the marriage perfect? Whose is? Certainly not the
marriage of the Dubés. Yes, they were having troubles, we

won't deny that. They were young, and François worked crazy hours in his restaurant, and the pressures of a young child in the household often take a toll on newlyweds. And unfortunately, yes, there was infidelity, and yes, they had separated, and yes, they had decided on a divorce. But, you see, they had decided, and they were working it out, and they were both parents to the same beautiful little girl, and they were making accommodations one to the other. This happens every day, everywhere, to half of all marriages in this great country."

You look over to François and say, "It is a reason for sadness and regret, absolutely." And now you turn back, raise your voice just enough to show your indignation. "But, ladies and gentlemen," you say as you slap the rail for emphasis, "this is not a motive for murder."

Step back now. Take a moment to compose yourself, a little dramatic pause to let the bite of righteous anger settle upon the courtroom. As you calm yourself, you rest your hand on the railing and lean on your straightened arm. This last bit is quite important, as you want to look completely at ease when you begin to mention, however obliquely, the prosecution's evidence. The prosecutor has stood before this same jury and listed the great gouts of evidence she has against your client. You'd like to ignore it, let it disappear, but you can't.

"Ms. Dalton spoke about the evidence collected by Detective Torricelli." You step over to the prosecution table and stand right in front of him as you continue. "She told of all the things he so conveniently found after he determined that my client was the primary suspect. And you shake your head at such convenience, because it never happens like that in your own lives, only in books or movies, pieces of fiction created by quite imaginative folk." As you make your point, you give the detective a smile, which is in stark contrast to the ugly sneer he gives you back. "But let me tell you, ladies and gentlemen, what you won't be seeing during this trial. No one will testify that he saw this crime happen. There will be no video or photographs submitted showing the murder. No one will testify that he saw my client anywhere near the scene of the crime at the time of the crime. None of those fancy forensics tests you see on television will prove that François Dubé was in any way involved in this terrible murder that shattered his family and separated for all time his daughter from her mother."

It's time to pop a jab at the prosecution. "Ms. Dalton told you that the evidence in the case is wholly circumstantial. And we all know, ladies and gentlemen, what circumstantial means. It means that no one really knows what the heck happened, we're all just guessing, and when anyone tells you otherwise, she is lying."

This is when the prosecutor hops up and objects. It's fun to see her jump, like a frog poked with a stick. Hop, hop. And her objection is a good thing, even when the judge sustains it, because it allows you to shrug, and smile a little half smile, and act as if you and the jury are all in on a little secret that the prosecution is trying to hide.

"Ms. Dalton told you that direct evidence is when you go outside and see for yourself that it's raining, but unfortunately for her, she doesn't have any of that type of evidence in this case. No one saw the murder of Leesa Dubé. And Ms. Dalton also told you that circumstantial evidence is when you see someone come in the front door and his hair and clothes are soaked, and from that you can infer that it's raining. But the problem with circumstantial evidence is that the inferences drawn are only as sharp as the person drawing them. Now, we know that Ms. Dalton is a very sharp lawyer, otherwise why would she be pulling down the big bucks at the district attorney's office and driving a Chevette?"

This time, as the jury chuckles, you glance back at the

prosecutor, so the whole jury follows your gaze. The prosecutor will be doing a slow burn. You wait, patiently, until her
obligation to the truth forces her to her feet and she says,
through clenched teeth, "Objection, Judge. Mr. Carl knows
full well I drive a Civic."

Then you turn back to the jury, raise an eyebrow, watch as
they all crack up at that. "A Civic," you say, raising your
hands high in the air. "I stand corrected. But even a lawyer
as sharp as Ms. Dalton, tooling around town in her Civic,
ladies and gentlemen, can see someone walk through her
front door all sopping wet and assume that it is raining outside, when really she simply forgot to turn off her sprinkler."

Bada-bing.

A fun little gag, sure, but all of this is routine, all of this
any legal hack could pull off without breaking a sweat. But
what to do now, there's the puzzle.

Do you play it safe and do the old Reasonable Doubt
Shuffle, a sort of jazzy dance in which you raise your arms
and shake your legs and repeat those two words over and
again, as if the jury had never heard them before? It is the
safe opening, the no-opening opening, which leaves you free
to create your theory of the case on the fly. But with no story
of your own to tell at the outset, you're playing defense the
whole trial, and by the time you figure something out, the
jury might have already made up its mind.

Or do you go right out and tell the jury your story from
the get-go? If the story is convincing enough, and the evidence doesn't contradict it, then the jury will do your work
for you. On the downside, it's like one of those cigars Curly
Howard used to smoke—one contradictory piece of evidence and it can all blow up in your face.

What to do? What to do? Do you play it safe? Or do you
take the gamble? Oh, what the hell. It's only François's neck
on the line.

"Now, Ms. Dalton told you about François's affairs, as if that was some big revelation. Yes, François had affairs. We admit it. He was a hound dog, even in his marriage. Nothing to be proud of, certainly. But now I need to tell you the other side of the equation. I'm not here to cast aspersions, the Dubés were separated, this is not a matter of blaming the victim, this is just the truth. Leesa Dubé, lonely after the separation from her husband, found solace of her own with another man. You will hear testimony about that, and about the nature of their relationship, and about the violence that was lurking within it.

"Why did Ms. Dalton not tell you this? I don't know. Maybe she didn't think it important enough to mention to you in her opening. Maybe she's a little too eager to discount anything that doesn't fit neatly within her theory. Or maybe so quick was the rush to judgment against François Dubé that she and Detective Torricelli never took the time to even learn of this man who had entered Leesa Dubé's life. But he existed, and you will hear all about him, and it is far more likely that he, rather than the loving husband, committed this horrible crime.

"So this is what I beg of you, ladies and gentlemen. Listen carefully to all the evidence, and as you do, ask yourself who is the more likely culprit, Leesa's husband, the father of her child, or the violent stranger who swept into her life shortly before her murder and swept out of it just as quickly. And when this is over, and you've heard everything, I'm going to come back to you and ask you to return the only verdict you possibly can, a verdict that finds François Dubé not guilty of the murder of his wife."

Mia Dalton was livid at my argument.

You could tell by her easy grin as she came up to me after

the jury had been dismissed for the day, by her insouciant pose, by the hand calmly resting in her skirt pocket. Dalton didn't grin unless she was angry, she was one of those lawyers who snarled at good news and smiled at trouble. At least I hoped so, because if Mia Dalton wasn't livid after my opening, then I had done something seriously wrong.

"You going to bring it into the courtroom?" said Dalton. "Give it a number, lay a foundation to introduce it into evidence?"

"Bring in what?" I said.

"My Civic."

"Liked that, did you?"

"It's always fun when opposing counsel claims I'm too stupid to figure out the truth of a case because of the car I drive."

"I wasn't blaming the car. It's not the car's fault."

"Why don't you tell us the name of the deceased's lover who you claimed murdered her?"

"Not quite yet."

"If he's a murderer, shouldn't we take him off the street as a matter of public safety?"

"You've waited this long to get the right guy, I suppose a few more days won't matter."

"I suppose not," said Dalton. "It's never good practice to make a promise to the jury you won't be able to fulfill."

"Watch me."

"Oh, I will, Victor, believe you me." She winked. "And I'll enjoy it, too."

I didn't like that wink. There was something in it that gave me a chill. Probably the usual Mia Dalton intimidation, but still, as I watched her walk out the courtroom door, I suspected she wasn't as livid as I had hoped.

CHAPTER
48

Mia Dalton wasn't a rock star in court. She didn't hold the jury spellbound in her fist, didn't shoot off pyrotechnics in the middle of the trial, didn't croon out like a crooner her sad, sweet ballad of blood and murder. More stonemason than Rolling Stone, she left the fireworks to the defense attorneys trying to bring down the house as she slowly and carefully laid her bricks of evidence. And that is precisely what made her such a devastating prosecutor. In the confines of the courtroom, never underestimate the riveting brilliance of sheer competence.

"She was a lovely girl, bright and lively, full of love, she was," said Mrs. Cullen.

"And do you remember when she met the defendant?" asked Dalton.

"Oh, yes, I do, of course I do. She was head over heels. So happy she was, my little girl. So full of life and love."

I could have stood and objected at that point. I could have yelled out "Hearsay" and the judge would have sustained my objection, and the love that Leesa Dubé told her mother she felt for my client could have been erased from the record, but what kind of idiot would do something like that? So I sat on my hands, and I let Mrs. Cullen have her say. Yes, Leesa was in love with François, yes, their wedding was storybook, yes, they were both excited about the baby, yes, everything was going so well. But of course François worked late hours at the restaurant, and of course there were the inevitable problems with money, and yes, of course, Leesa did feel abandoned and depressed after the baby came and François was less and less in evidence at their apartment.

"And then," said Mrs. Cullen, "she found out about the affairs."

"What was her reaction when she found out?"

"What do you think? She was devastated."

Of course she was.

"And what did she do when she found out?"

"What do you think? She kicked the slime right out of the house and filed for divorce."

Of course she did.

"Objection to the epithet," I chirped.

"Sustained," said the judge.

"Please try not to label the defendant a slime, Mrs. Cullen," said Mia Dalton.

"I'll try," she said, "but it will be no easy task, Ms. Dalton, because he's a slime if ever there was one."

Of course he is.

Every murder trial has two questions: How and Why. When the answer to How is strong, when five people and a video camera catch the defendant take out a gun and pop the deceased, who the hell cares about the Why? But when the How is based on a mess of circumstantial evidence, as in the François Dubé case, suddenly the Why becomes powerfully important. Which explains why Dalton, ever the artisan, was holding the How for later and leading her case with Why.

After Mrs. Cullen testified about the deteriorating relationship between her daughter and her son-in-law, after she testified about the acrimonious divorce proceedings and the fights over Amber, after Mrs. Cullen was able to vent all the bile from her spleen, Dalton turned to me and said, "Your witness."

There was so much I was ready to ask Mrs. Cullen, about her strained relations with her daughter, about how her daughter would never have confided in her about a lover, especially a bad boy like Clem, about her utter ignorance of what actually happened on the night of her daughter's death. There was so much ammunition. I stood up, stared at Mrs. Cullen, and leaned forward as if readying to unleash the furious fusillade of my cross-examination.

"I am so sorry for your loss, Mrs. Cullen," I said finally. "No questions for this witness."

I have learned from our first president that sometimes retreat is the most aggressive strategy. She was the grieving mother, she had taken on the burden of the young granddaughter, she could do my client no good up there on the stand. Get her off, as quickly as possible, and move on, that was my plan. And as a side benefit, there was a little message to the twelve and two alternates who mattered. *I am not going to ask her any questions*, I was telling the jury, *because nothing that she said is of any import to the meat of the case. Nothing she can say makes it more likely that my client killed his wife.*

As Mrs. Cullen climbed down from the stand and made her way out of the courtroom, Dalton stood and said, "Prosecution calls Darcy DeAngelo."

Of course it does.

She looked quite tasty as she walked down the aisle, Darcy DeAngelo, one of the women who'd had an affair with François. She was a sturdy woman, with her hands tightly clasped and a thin, pretty face, and she was dressed for court, a modest skirt, low pumps, her hair pinned up. She made quite the tasteful impression, though probably not the one Dalton would have liked. If Mia Dalton had dressed her, she would have worn a black bustier and high-heeled shoes with straps that climbed her thigh, she would have had long, clawlike nails and makeup smeared bright, and she would have looked like she had just come in off a late-night shift on South Street. But no such luck for Dalton, although it might have been a nice sight to see.

As Darcy DeAngelo was sworn in, I took a quick look at the audience in the courtroom. A high-profile murder case always draws a nice crowd, and this was no exception: a few reporters, an artist trying to get my jawline right, the usual gang of time wasters finding their entertainment in the criminal courts. And then a more interested crew: the Cullens and their entourage; Detective Torricelli, sitting alongside Mia Dalton at the prosecution table; and my old friend Whitney Robinson III, keeping tabs on everything.

It wasn't much of a story, Darcy DeAngelo's story of the affair. She worked under François in the kitchen, that she would end up under François in the bedroom was only to be expected. Commercial kitchens are like the bathhouses of the culinary set, bubbling pots of stock, prep guys with big knives, Wellfleet oysters, duck confit, earthy black truffles, demi-glace, *oui, oui*. Late nights, after the crowd had gone home and the doors had been locked, sitting at the zinc bar François had imported from France, drinking champagne at cost, feeling the exhausted exuberance of two comrades who had just survived another night of the gastronomic wars. And she didn't say it on the stand, but I could bet it was atop that very same bar that their affair was consummated. I have it on good authority that champagne and zinc are the two primary ingredients of Viagra.

"Mr. Carl," said the judge after Dalton had led Darcy DeAngelo through the recitation of her affair with my client. "Do you have any questions?"

I did, actually, and I must admit that during most of her
direct, I had been playing them out in my mind. *"Do you
like Mexican food, Ms. DeAngelo?" "Yes, actually, I do, Mr.
Carl." "I know this place on Thirteenth Street, supposed to
be excellent." "I've heard that it is." "Do you think, Ms.
DeAngelo, you can join me for dinner there on Saturday
night?" "Oh, I think I can, Mr. Carl." "Call me Victor."
"Okay, Victor. And please, call me—"*

"Mr. Carl," said the judge impatiently. "Do you have any
questions for this witness?"

I stood, buttoned my jacket, looked at the pleasing figure
of Darcy DeAngelo on the stand. The affair was a problem,
absolutely, but I couldn't deny its existence, and the witness,
in her direct, had made it seem almost banal. Banal adultery
was good, banal adultery is not an incentive for murder, simply an incentive for more and better adultery. There was one
moment that had caused a tremor, when she testified that
François had told her, "I'll never let Leesa take my daughter
from me, never." Not good, absolutely, but in it came, over
my useless objection, and there wasn't much I could do with
it. I could ask her if she ever saw violence in François, I
could ask her if he was a tender lover and a tender man, I
could try to use François's adulterous lover as a character
witness, but that seemed a little unseemly, didn't it?

"No questions for this witness, Your Honor."

"All right, Ms. DeAngelo, you are excused," said the
judge. "And I assume, Mr. Carl, at some point in these proceedings you're going to ask a question or two."

"I haven't needed to yet, Judge, but I'm guessing that
eventually Ms. Dalton will come up with something in this
trial that's actually relevant to the murder."

"I'm sure she will. Next witness, Ms. Dalton."

"The prosecution calls Arthur Gullicksen to the stand."

This was trouble, totally expected, but trouble still. Arthur

Gullicksen was an out-and-out shark, with three rows of
pointy teeth and a shiny gray suit. Normally these are traits
I greatly admire and do my best to emulate, but Dalton
wasn't calling Gullicksen to the stand to show off his bite.

Beth stood up as soon as Dalton stated the name. "Can we
approach, Judge?" she said.

"Will this take a while, Ms. Derringer?"

"I suspect it will," she said.

"Let's have a recess, then. Fifteen minutes. Lawyers in
my chambers."

"Mr. Gullicksen, the prosecution's next intended witness,"
said Beth when all the lawyers, along with the clerk and the
court reporter, had been wedged uncomfortably into the
judge's chambers, "was Leesa Dubé's divorce attorney."

"And your point is?" said the judge.

"In light of that unique relationship," said Beth, "we believe it necessary to limit the bounds of his testimony."

"Yes, yes, of course," said the judge. "Mr. Gullicksen will
not be able to testify about his privileged communications
with the deceased. It would all be hearsay anyway. Is that
satisfactory, Ms. Derringer?"

"As a start, yes, Judge. But we'd also like to limit any testimony that can be seen as the fruits of those privileged and
hearsay communications."

"Meaning what?"

"Meaning, we would like the prosecution to be barred
from asking Mr. Gullicksen about the pleadings in the divorce case, as they would necessarily be based on statements
you have already barred."

"Interesting. Ms. Dalton?"

"The pleadings are public records, Judge," said Dalton
calmly, "and we intend to introduce them not to show the

truth of the allegations within but as proof of their very existence and of their effect on the defendant's state of mind."

"But, Your Honor," said Beth, "some of these allegations are so inflammatory as to be unduly prejudicial to our client."

"What exactly are we talking about here, Counselor?"

"There was an allegation of harassment, of infidelity, of failure to pay child support, all of which had not yet been litigated at the time of the murder, and so no legal determination had yet been made."

"I see," said the judge.

"And there was also a rather spurious allegation of physical abuse of both Mrs. Dubé and the couple's daughter, lodged by Leesa Dubé against her husband, along with a request for a restraining order."

"Yes, I do see."

"Your Honor, there was never any evidence presented in the divorce proceedings to support these allegations. They are entirely unsubstantiated, unduly prejudicial, and based solely on the hearsay statements of the deceased. Their introduction would unfairly inflame the jury and irrevocably taint these proceedings against our client." Beth reached into her briefcase, pulled out numerous copies of a thick memorandum. "There are cases that support our position, and I have briefed the issue."

"Anything in this jurisdiction on point?"

"Not directly, Judge, but there is a case from Alaska that is startlingly similar."

"Which would be useful if we were trying this case in Nome. Ms. Dalton?"

"I understand Ms. Derringer's anger. These are hurtful accusations that would upset anyone, especially if untrue. Which is the whole point here, Judge. Mr. Carl, in his opening, seemed to indicate that the Dubé divorce was amicable, which is absolutely false. This was a brutal, no-holds-barred fight for money and custody, with the direst accusations being thrown about."

"And you believe the nature of the proceedings is an important part of the defendant's motive?"

"A crucial part, Judge."

"What will Mr. Gullicksen be testifying to?"

"The allegations in the divorce case coming from both sides and his observations of Mr. Dubé's reaction to his wife's accusations."

"He wasn't pleased, I take it."

"No, sir, he was not. In fact, threats were made."

"This is why I stay away from family court, criminal trials are so much more civil. And what would you have Mr. Gullicksen limited to testifying about, Ms. Derringer?"

"The weather?" said Beth.

"Okay," said Judge Armstrong. "I've heard enough. I will read your memorandum, Ms. Derringer, because I so enjoy your writing, but I can tell you all now, I am inclined to give Ms. Dalton a free hand here. I, too, took note of Mr. Carl's characterization of the divorce proceedings in his opening. He said the Dubés were working it out. The jury has the right to see exactly how. I will instruct the jury not to consider the truth of the accusations, only their effect on the defendant, but that's as far as I will go."

A few minutes later, as we waited in the courtroom for the judge to finish reading Beth's memorandum before he could dismiss it outright and rule against us, Beth was still fretting over Gullicksen's testimony.

"Calm down," I told her. "It will be all right."

"He's going to kill us," she said. "I don't care how the judge instructs the jury, once they hear the claim of spousal and child abuse, the jury will never look at François the same again."

"How about you? Do you see him differently?"

"I know it's a lie."

"How do you know?"

"I just know," she said, steely voiced.

"Then maybe the jury will be able to tell it's a lie, too."

"The judge is getting it wrong," she said, "flat wrong."

"That's what judges do, but we'll be okay. Maybe we can turn this whole thing to our advantage, build some sympathy for François."

"How?"

"I've been doing some research. That year, four of Gullicksen's other clients made the same claim of physical abuse by their spouses. It was a standard ploy in his practice before he was sanctioned for it by the bar association."

"You have the proof?"

"The pleadings are in my bag, along with the sanction. The language in each case is startlingly similar."

"Why didn't you tell the judge?"

"And spoil the surprise? No, this cross-examination should be fun, me going after Gullicksen, shark to shark."

"You think you'll draw blood?"

"Oh, I hope so, but it doesn't really matter. This is all just the preliminary fencing. None of this really matters."

"Then what does?"

"Sonenshein," I said. "Everything depends on little Jerry Sonenshein. You want to worry about something, worry about him."

CHAPTER

49

Horace T. Grant stood on the corner in front of Tommy's High Ball, his chin up, his creased face creased with concern. It was not a good look for Horace. His natural expression was one of repugnance, disdain, his features were generally etched with a sweet scorn for the general stupidity of the world. I watched him a moment as he worriedly fingered his bow tie. I almost felt something for him then, some sort of empathic pity, before I beeped the horn and he saw my face in the window and his normal derisive expression returned.

"You get lost, boy? Seems like I been standing here since Truman was president."

"The judge held us longer than I expected."

"Did you tell him I was waiting? Did you tell him his inconsiderate lethargy was seriously inconveniencing an upstanding member of the community? I'm an old man, I don't got time to waste."

"Probably less than you think. I'll tell him next time."

"You do that. Remind him he works for us, not the other way around." He bent his ancient frame to fit into my car. "Now, where we going? You found us a shaman this time, or a conjure man, or any other of your garden-variety frauds and tricksters intending to feed us smoke and mirrors and tell us squat?"

"We're going back to Madam Anna."

"That old scarecrow? Why we going to waste any more time with her? I'd just as soon stick a hot poker in my ear as listen to her screech again about my shoes or that there spirit world she's in touch with."

"She called me," I said. "We set up a meeting."

Horace T. Grant leaned back, stared at me for a long moment. "How'd you get that one-eyed witch to call you?"

"It was funny, actually. Out of the blue, an L&I inspector paid our Madam Anna a visit. Would you believe she didn't have a business-privilege license after all?"

"Shocking," said Horace T. Grant.

"The inspector, in the course of his writing out the violation notice, mentioned my name. It turned out that I successfully defended this same inspector in a DUI case just last year. Funny how that works, isn't it? When she called, I said I would tell her how to take care of the violation notice, so long as I learned what I needed to learn about the girl."

"I must then say, I am sorry."

"For what?"

"For calling you a less-than-useless piece of seagull doo."

"Apology accepted."

"See, I can admit when I am wrong. Takes a big man to do that, but here I am. You still a piece of seagull doo, and you still pretty much useless. But not less than that, no, sir, not less than that at all."

It wasn't long before we were back in that maroon room in Madam Anna's apartment, candles burning on that pale blue table, the yellow symbols dancing around us as if alive. We were waiting again, that seemed to be Madame Anna's method of operation, make the stiffs wait so long that when she finally does appear, it seems like a deliverance from on high. Horace's black porkpie hat sat in front of him on the table.

"How's this?" I said, showing Horace my thumb-twiddling technique. "I think I have it down."

Horace took a look, raised his gaze to the ceiling. "Lord, save us from amateurs."

Just then the far door opened, and Madam Anna, in her shimmering green robe, entered the room, accompanied by a skinny man in a plain black suit, white shirt, narrow black tie. The man had long arms, yet still the sleeves of his jacket reached his knuckles. He looked, the man, with his long arms and hunched shoulders, as if he had just come from burying the dead. The two sat across from us and stared for a moment. We let them.

"I have something for you," Madam Anna said finally. She reached into one of the sleeves of her gown, pulled out a piece of paper, handed it to me.

I hoped it was an address. No such luck. Instead it was a notice of violation made out to Madam Anna by the Licenses and Inspection Department of the City of Philadelphia. I looked at it and shrugged as I tossed it onto the table.

"They want five thousand dollars in fines and fees," she said. "You will take care of that."

"Tell me where Tanya Rose is."

"I don't know where she is," she said. "But I brought the Reverend Wilkerson to talk to you. He's a man of the cloth, so I assume you will trust what he says."

"I appreciate the reverend's being here. We can all use the help of the Lord in our endeavors. But I'm not here to pray, I'm here to find a little girl. An address is all I need."

"We understand the seriousness of your mission, Mr. Carl," said the Reverend Wilkerson. He had a beautiful, deep voice and a warm smile, both of which seemed out of place in his small, hunched frame. He sat with his hands clasped in front of him, and he fixed me with his eyes as he spoke, as if they had some unearthly power. "And our hearts are touched by your concern for such a young and vulnerable member of our community. That is why I have come. I am here to assure you that she is in the best of hands and there is nothing for you to fear."

"So why am I suddenly more afraid for her than I was before?"

"I can't imagine," he said, still smiling.

"Who are you to the girl?"

"She is among my flock."

"I suppose, then, you are exactly the man I should be speaking to." I took a copy of the order appointing me to be Tanya Rose's counsel and placed it in front of the reverend. "I have been named by the Court of Common Pleas as counsel to the young girl we're talking about. I need to see her, and I need to see her right away."

"That's not possible."

"And why is that?"

"Because she is now happy and healthy with her new family. Everything is going wonderfully. Your appearance would disturb her delicate equilibrium."

"Me? I'm a sweetheart. Aren't I a sweetheart, Horace?"

"He's a sweetheart, all right," Horace said with a grump in his voice.

"See? I wouldn't disturb a fly."

Reverend Wilkerson glanced at Madam Anna. "Some would beg to differ," he said. "And the family she is now with is frightened of what you might do. Frightened that you might take away their child."

"First, she is not their child. Second, I don't have the power to do anything on my own, everything I do is within the bounds of the law. And third, anyone who is keeping me from seeing my client is indubitably not working in her best interests."

"Indubitably, Mr. Carl?"

"Quite," I said. "Let's start at the beginning here, Reverend. How did you get involved with Tanya?"

"Madam Anna and I have known each other for some years. She understands my deep concern for the children of the community. When she mentioned to me that she was aware of a girl who needed a home, I told her I would make sure she was taken care of."

"Any money change hands?"

"Is that important?"

"I suppose that means yes."

"There may have been expenses we reimbursed."

"And you investigate these homes carefully, Reverend? You do home visits, background checks, follow-ups to make sure she is being properly taken care of? An outreach program with ongoing support and evaluation?"

"I do what I need to do, the good Lord does the rest."

"So let me get this straight. Tanya's mother simply gave the girl to Madam Anna. Then Madam Anna sold the girl to you. And you gave her away, or sold her to the highest bidder, hoping that providence would keep the girl safe, is that it?"

"What are you really doing here, Mr. Carl? What's your angle in all this?"

"I'm here pro bono."

"Who the hell's Bono?"

"U2?"

"Me what?"

I sighed loudly. "This girl is my client. I'm just doing my job."

"But how did she just happen to become your client? That order drop out of the sky into your hand?"

"Something like that," I said, although, truth be told, it wasn't something like that at all.

"Have you ever considered, Mr. Carl," said the reverend, "that we are just trying to help that girl?"

"You're trying to help, I'm trying to help, everyone seems to be trying to help, but things keep getting worse, don't they?"

"You won't leave this be, will you?"

"No, I will not."

"So we are at an impasse."

"Not for long," I said, standing. "You do know, both of you, that baby selling is against the law. Expect the police to show up at your door, Reverend."

"I have the protection of the First Amendment."

"That's what they said at Waco."

"I know you," said Horace to Reverend Wilkerson. "I recognize your voice. You drive that hearse through the city, the one with the fake coffin and the body sticking up out of it, the one preaching out against drugs and violence."

"That is I," said the reverend.

"Driving around with that ugly thing on top your car, quoting Scripture out a bullhorn, making all kinds of racket when we're just trying to sleep. What do you think you're going to accomplish?"

"I'm trying to save our community."

"How about saving my sleep? You get my age, it don't come so easy. And then, just as I'm sinking into slumber, you drive along and blast me sky-high with your preaching."

"Maybe you need saving, too, old man."

"And you got that run-down hotel on Fifty-first that you turned into some sort of shelter and meeting place, the Hotel Latimore, it is, where you take care of all kinds of families don't got no homes for themselves."

"I do what I can."

"Yeah, I know you, all right," said Horace. "We got enough folks making things worse, so I appreciate those fighting to make things better. But you should appreciate what this boy's fighting to do, too. He's not from us, is ignorant of our ways, among many other things, but that don't mean he don't care. He had a choice, he could have walked away from this girl who he's never in the life of him ever met. Others would have, said it was too hard, thrown up their hands. But he didn't. Now he got himself in the middle of a mess, legally responsible for a girl he can't find, standing up to a man with a bullhorn. It takes a heap of stupidity to do all that. It's not up to you to shut him out."

"I have my responsibilities," said the reverend.

"So does he."

"I am sorry," he said. "I've done all I can."

"That's not good enough," I said. "I am scared for my client, and I am not in the mood to be patient. I tried to do this the polite way, Reverend, but that's over. Let's go, Horace."

Horace pushed himself to standing, propped his hat on his head. "Quite a boy, ain't he?"

"A real firebrand," said Wilkerson.

"I taught him everything he knows," said Horace.

"Oh, Mr. Carl," said Madam Anna before we could leave. "We had a deal. What about this paper from the city? What about the fines?"

"You want my help, is that it? My expert legal opinion?" I stepped to the table, picked up the notice, scanned it quickly. "This shouldn't be a problem."

"What should I do?" she said.

"Pay it."

CHAPTER

50

"**There it is**," said Horace. "It used to be a place in the old days, used to be something special. 'Where you staying?' we'd ask our cousins visiting from down south. They chests would swell with pride, and they'd say, 'The Hotel Latimore.' "

Horace was nodding toward a dilapidated four-story building, made of brick, wedged between a linoleum outlet on one side and a Chinese restaurant on the other. There were people milling outside, some going in, some going out, some just sitting on the porch and spitting. Parked in front was a large white van with a dummy in a suit on top, sitting up as if it had bolted right out of the coffin in which it had been laid to rest. An old neon sign swung above the building's door, hissing as it blinked on and off: HOTEL LATIMORE.

"From what I been told," Horace said, "his office is on the first floor. And there's an old ballroom on the top where he has his meetings."

"Who's that guy standing by the steps?" I said.

"He's big, isn't he?"

"Big isn't the word. Monumental, epic, and massive come to mind."

"Never seen him before."

"With his size, that black leather jacket, and the way he's

standing there, looking around like he owns the place, I'd make him for some sort of muscle."

"What would they be needing with muscle at the Hotel Latimore?"

"Good question, but a guy that size, I'm not going to tap him on the shoulder and ask."

"Does that mean you're not going in?"

"I thought we'd sit here and stake out the place, maybe catch Tanya coming in or out."

"And how would you recognize her, you fool? You got a picture?"

"No, I've got something better."

"What?"

"You. We'll stay right here, keep an eye out while we're keeping out of the big guy's way."

"I didn't know I was sitting next to a coward. Ugly, I knew. Dumb as a post, I knew. A taste in clothes would kill a mongoose, I knew."

"What about the tie?"

"The tie, I like. What happened, you pull it out of a box of Cracker Jack?"

"It's silk, baby."

"Then it must have been a gift, because you being cheap as a two-bit whore, I knew. But I didn't mark you as a coward."

"Well, now you know that, too."

"Keep hold of that tie. Yellow suits you."

"Wait a second," I said as a big red car slid to a stop right behind the van. "Wasn't that car parked outside Madam Anna's?"

We had driven to the Hotel Latimore right after our meeting with the good reverend in the fortune teller's fortune-telling room. We had parked well down the road, in what I thought to be prime surveillance position. I had hoped we could get a jump on the situation before Reverend Wilkerson put out the word that Horace and I were personae non gratae, but that plan now seemed to have gone awry. The reverend himself stepped out of the red car, looked around, stopped his pan in the direction of my car, peered a little closer. He put his hand on the big guy's shoulder and had a few words, pointing in our direction. I was coming to the conclusion that my surveillance technique, to be frank, sucked.

"You think he's talking about us?" I said.

"You maybe. He's got no beef with me."

"Don't slight yourself, Horace."

"Go ahead, try to push this all off on Horace T. Grant, you yellow-tie coward. But that dog won't hunt. Any idiot can see I'm just along for the ride."

"You know, Horace," I said, "except for that you are a hundred years older than me and a foot shorter than me and black, except for all that, we could be twins."

"I dress better."

"That you do. Here they come."

"Shouldn't we drive away?"

"That would denote weakness."

"Nothing wrong with denoting. I'm all for denoting. But if we're not driving away, shouldn't we maybe lock the doors?"

"I tried that once before, and it didn't work out so well. Come on, let's step on out and face the music."

We both climbed out from the car and leaned against the hood in as close to a posture of nonchalance as we could muster while Reverend Wilkerson, with his graveyard hunch, crossed the street toward us. The man mountain in the leather coat stayed slightly behind the reverend as they approached, and he looked away from us, first down one side of the street and then down the other, not an ounce of concern on his face. As far as he could tell, we weren't trouble, we weren't even potential trouble, we were gnats on the wall.

"I expected you'd pay us a visit, Mr. Carl," said Reverend Wilkerson with his usual broad smile, "but I didn't think you'd move with such alacrity."

"Horace was telling me about the good work you do here, Reverend. I was hoping you could give me a tour of your facilities."

"That won't be possible. We don't allow uninvited visitors, and you most surely are that. No one likes a snoop, especially Rex. Isn't that right, Rex?"

The big man, while still looking away, scrunched up his face and grimaced, showing a row of twisted teeth. "That's right, Mr. Reverend, sir," he said in a rich bass.

"And of course the remark comparing what we do here to Waco was rather frightening, seeing as that situation ended in fire and death. Did you mean that as a threat, Mr. Carl?"

"Not at all," I said. "I merely used it as an example of how small misunderstandings between people of goodwill can sometimes spiral out of control."

"But we don't have a misunderstanding. You think you are doing good, but you are only a well-intentioned fool bound to leave behind nothing but pain and misfortune as you skip from one little project to the next."

Ouch, I thought.

"I don't want to have to clean up your mess," said Wilkerson. "I've cleaned up enough in my time. Rex, take a good look at this man."

"Don't forget my friend," I said, indicating Horace with my thumb.

"Right you are." The reverend smiled at me. "Rex, I want you to take a look at these two men. They are not welcome here, not welcome in the hotel, not welcome anywhere near our work."

Rex turned his attention to us for a moment, as if burning

our visages into his distracted brain, and then looked away again. "Got it, Mr. Reverend, sir."

"You better be off now, gentlemen."

"We'll be off when we are good and ready to be off," said Horace, "and not one minute before."

"What's your name again, old man?"

"Horace T. Grant. My friends call me Pork Chop."

"What does he call you?" said the reverend, indicating me.

"He calls me whatever he damn well likes."

"So tell me, Pork Chop, what are you doing, going around town carrying his load like a caddie? Don't you have any pride in yourself? You need the work so bad, come work with us."

"There's no shortage of pride in me, you smiling fraud, and I'd sooner pluck my eyebrows than work for you. And you might be drawing the wrong conclusion about who here is caddying for who. All we want to do is find that girl, and the more you stand in our way, the more suspicious we get."

"You two better scoot," said the reverend, "before an accident occurs."

"Not till we're good and ready. This is a public street."

Wilkerson leaned forward, broadened his smile. "See, Pork Chop, that's where you're wrong. It's not public, not public at all. Keep them company, Rex, until they leave us be."

With that, Wilkerson spun around and headed back to the hotel, leaving Rex to stand close to us while not looking at us. Even without saying anything, he was quite a presence, his breaths were heavy, his body gave off heat. Finally, while still looking away, he dropped a meaty hand on my shoulder.

"Time to go," he said, his voice deep as a Texas well.

"We're looking for a small girl," I said softly when Wilkerson was far enough away not to hear. "She'd be about seven. Her name is Tanya."

Rex looked behind him, looked to the side. "Tanya?"

"That's right, Tanya Rose."

"What you want with Tanya?"

"Believe it or not," I said, "I'm her lawyer. I just want to find her, talk to her, make sure she's okay. Is she here, in the hotel?"

"Not anymore."

"Where is she?"

Rex shrugged, looked down, kicked at the street.

"Who would know where she is?"

"The reverend."

"Who else?"

"Miss Elise, maybe."

"Where's this Miss Elise?"

"In the hotel."

"Can I get in to talk to her?"

"No."

"Can I talk to her without it getting back to the reverend?"

"Hardly."

"It's like that between them, is it?"

"Time to go."

"I need to talk to Miss Elise."

"No you don't," said Rex, pressing down now with his hand. "You need to leave."

"We're not leaving till we're good and ready," said Horace.

Rex squeezed my shoulder.

"I don't take orders from a fraud like that, I don't care what he says," said Horace. "We're not moving an inch, not an inch, until we're damn good and ready."

Rex squeezed harder.

"We're ready," I said in a wounded screech as my knees buckled in pain. "We are so ready."

Rex stayed right where he was, not watching me as I clawed my way back to my feet, not watching us as we jumped like thieves into the car, not watching us as we drove away. It was as if he was afraid to stare straight at us, afraid that we'd see something soft in his eyes.

"She was there," said Horace.

"Yes, she was."

"That boy knew her."

"And he liked her, too."

"She's a likable young girl."

"But still he wouldn't talk to us."

"He was afraid of something, afraid of Wilkerson. What do you think is going on?"

"I have no idea," I said, "and that's what frightens me."

"So what are you going to do now?"

"I don't know."

"You better come up with something quick."

"Yes, I better. But to tell you the truth, Horace, I think this whole situation has gone beyond my meager talents. I think it's time we call upon a higher authority."

"The police?"

"I don't know if that would get us what we need. If she really is in trouble, and the police do show up asking all kinds of questions, I'm afraid of what these people might do to her to keep themselves off the hook."

"What then? That judge?"

"No, higher."

"The mayor? You know our skunk of a mayor?"

"Higher."

"Who then? Who's higher than a judge, who's more powerful than the mayor? Who you got in your pocket that's going to help?"

"My dentist," I said.

CHAPTER

51 Fingerprints and blood.

Dalton's slow but steady presentation of evidence against François Dubé continued, day by day. After Gullicksen testified about the bitterness of the divorce proceedings and the allegations of child abuse, allegations that caused the jury to squint with disapproval despite the judge's instructions and my stirring cross-examination, Dalton called a uniformed officer to the stand, the first cop to arrive at the crime scene. There had been no word from Leesa Dubé for a number of hours, he said. She hadn't shown up to collect her daughter from her parents' house in the morning as planned, he said. She hadn't shown up for work. She couldn't be reached by telephone. The police had been called and directed to the scene. The door had been locked, it was forced open. A scene of horror.

The photographs were passed around the jury box, hand to hand, mouths tightening at the posture of the body, at the spill of the blood. Leesa Dubé in her bloody T-shirt, her right arm twisted beneath her lifeless body, the blood splattered across her face and forming a pool around her head in the shape of a lopsided heart. The jurors sneaked glances at François as they examined the photographs. His mouth was twisted as if he had eaten an overcooked steak au poivre.

And then Dalton began with the meat of her case, fingerprints and blood.

The Crime Scene Search officers testified as to how they had processed the crime scene, as to where they had found the fingerprints they'd lifted, as to where they had found the blood. And then they testified as to their search of François's apartment the day after the murder, pursuant to a request by Detective Torricelli, and what they had found there.

"Officer Robbins," said Dalton, "did any latent prints you found in Leesa Dubé's apartment match any of the inked impressions given to you by the detectives?"

"Yes, ma'am. We found matches to two individuals."

"Go ahead."

"We found a number of prints matching those of the victim and four others, two found on a wall switch, one on a door, and one on a table, that matched up with the prints of the defendant, François Dubé."

"Did you find any other prints that matched those of the defendant?"

"Yes. There were two latent prints found on the cartridges loaded into the revolver found at the defendant's apartment."

"The revolver that was introduced as People's Exhibit Six?"

"That's right, the gun found in Mr. Dubé's apartment that was determined to be the murder weapon."

A nice dramatic moment for Dalton, but not so hard to deal with. Before the divorce, François had lived in that apartment, before the divorce, the room would have been filthy with François's fingerprints, as would the gun, which he had purchased and loaded and given to his wife.

"Now, Officer Robbins," I said as I stood before the technician, "the prints you discussed with Ms. Dalton, coming from the wall switch and the door and the table, were latent prints, were they not?"

"That is correct."

"There were no visible prints at the crime scene that you were asked to test, is that correct?"

"That's right."

"A visible print would be a print that was made, let's say, after the murderer had accidentally gotten the blood of the victim on his fingers and then touched something, so that the print was visible without special techniques."

"Right."

"But even with so much blood, there were no bloody fingerprints at the crime scene that matched the defendant. All you had to work with were latent prints."

"That's right."

"Are you able, Officer Robbins, with any of your fancy tests or superscientific instruments, to determine the age of a latent print?"

"No, sir."

"The prints on the wall switch, for example, could have been there a week, a month, maybe longer?"

"That's right. Latent prints have been known to survive, in certain conditions, for years."

"For years," I repeated, and then repeated again. "For years. Fascinating."

"Of course, they are usually removed with cleaning."

"I suppose they would be," I said, nodding, as if the officer's interjection was thoroughly welcome. "And we all know, Officer Robbins, how often we all scrub our light switches clean. Scrub, scrub, scrub. Did you find any latent prints at the crime scene or on the outside of the murder weapon that you weren't able to match up?"

"There were no prints on the outside of the gun. It had apparently been wiped clean, possibly by the shirt that was wrapped around it when it was found."

"Wiped clean and then left at the defendant's apartment until it was conveniently discovered by Detective Torricelli?"

"Yes, sir. But there were numerous prints at the crime scene we could not identify."

"They could have been the prints of anyone, isn't that right?"

"That's right."

"A friend, a lover, the real murderer, or maybe all three in one?"

"We couldn't match them up."

I looked at the jury, raised an eyebrow. I work on that in the mirror at home, the one raised eyebrow. It should be a course of its own in law school. You sort of have to relax one half of your face, contract the muscles on the other, all while keeping a sweetly sardonic expression. You do it wrong, you look like you just ate bad jalapeño. You do it right, it denotes skepticism, it denotes shared knowledge, it was as good as shouting to the jury. I raised my eyebrow, they thought of my opening and of Leesa Dubé's as-yet-unnamed lover.

Not bad, but that was just the fingerprints.

The more difficult evidence to explain away was the blood. There was blood everywhere at the crime scene, on the victim, on the floor, on the walls, gouts and gouts of blood, but that wasn't the blood that concerned us. No, the blood that concerned us was found in François Dubé's apartment after he was arrested and a search was conducted by Detective Torricelli.

"All right, let's talk first about the shirt," I said during my cross-examination. "This white shirt that happened to be discovered by Detective Torricelli, the one balled up in the corner of the defendant's closet, wrapped around the gun. You examined this shirt yourself, did you, Officer?"

"Yes, I did."

"And you found the blood smeared on the front?"

"That's correct."

"And this blood you determined to be the blood of the victim?"

"Correct."

"And so we are to assume that this shirt, this white shirt, the most popular color for criminals about to pursue a criminal act, was worn during the murder."

"I don't know what you are to assume. I just testified as to what I found on the shirt."

"You testified you found a single smear, with a repetitive transfer pattern created, as you testified, by the balling up of the shirt."

"That's right."

"Now I'd like to show you photographs from the crime scene. This photograph, People's Exhibit Twelve, for example, showing a close-up of the victim's face. What do you see on her cheek?"

"Something dark. The photograph is in black and white, but it appears to be blood."

"Is it a smear of blood?"

"No, sir. It appears to be a series of droplets."

"And this picture here, People's Exhibit Fifteen. What do you see on the wall?"

"Blood."

"Droplets of blood in a specific pattern, isn't that right?"

"Yes, sir."

"And this one here, People's Exhibit Nine, a pattern of droplets on the floor?"

"That's what it shows."

"Now, droplet patterns are very valuable in investigating a crime scene, aren't they?"

"They can be."

"In fact, you are trained to examine these patterns of

droplets to determine direction of travel or the location of the blood source, isn't that right?"

"Yes, we are."

"So what did the pattern of droplets on this shirt tell you, based on your training?"

"There was no pattern of droplets on the shirt."

"No pattern, then, just the droplets?"

"There were no droplets. Only the smear."

"But from these photographs it seems what happened was pretty clear. The victim was shot, and blood started flying all over the place. Droplets hitting everywhere."

"Not everywhere."

"Hitting the walls, the floor, the victim, everywhere we can examine with the camera. But in this maelstrom of blood, we're to believe not a single speck landed on the white shirt the defendant was wearing while he went about the process of murdering his wife? Because, based on your testimony, there were no spots, no splatters, not a single droplet."

"That's what I found, yes."

"Scotchgarding just gets better and better, don't you think?"

"Objection."

"Sustained. Move on, Mr. Carl."

"Sure, Your Honor, maybe we'll move on to the boot. The victim's blood was found on the sole of one of the defendant's boots, is that right, Officer?"

"Yes."

"And you were directed to the boot by the ever-vigilant Detective Torricelli, isn't that right?"

"Yes, sir."

"And you don't know for certain how the blood got there, do you?"

"No, sir."

"But let's say that Ms. Dalton is correct in her supposi-
tion. Let's say that the boot was worn at the time of the murder, that the wearer of the boot had accidentally stepped in
the victim's blood, and then the boot was worn back to the
defendant's apartment. Let's say that."

"Okay."

"Then what would we expect to find?"

"Blood on the boot."

"Yes, of course, which is precisely what you found. But
what else would we expect to find, Officer?"

"I suppose you're going to tell us."

"Footprints. I'm talking about the murderer's footprints,
marked in blood. Did you find such footprints?"

"There were footwear impressions in blood found at the
crime scene."

"And how were they discovered?"

"Some were apparent. Others, more faint, were developed
using a solution of leucocrystal violet. After being sprayed
with the solution, even faint bloodstains become visible.
Then photographs can be made."

"You make it sound like there were a lot of footprints."

"There were more than we would have liked. When the
responding officer entered the scene, he immediately went
to the victim to check out her condition. Others came in with
him. There was a significant amount of traffic before the
crime scene was secured."

"And all these footprints showed up?"

"Many did."

"Were you able to identify all the footprints you found?"

"Some of them we were. We compare the markings of the
shoe soles much like we compare fingerprints. Imperfec-
tions in the treads, scuffs on the soles, holes and such often
show up and allow us to make positive identifications. We
could positively identify the shoe prints of the first respond-

ing police officer and the landlord. Others we were not able to identify."

"You were not able to positively identify, for example, any of the footprints as matching the defendant's boot?"

"Not to a reasonable certainty, no."

"But there were bloody shoe prints you found that you were not able to positively identify, isn't that correct?"

"Yes, sir."

"No idea whose shoe they could be?"

"No, sir."

"The murderer, perhaps?"

"I couldn't say, sir."

"Of course you couldn't. And in the defendant's apartment, while executing the search warrant, did you search for any bloody footprints?"

"We made an examination."

"With that fluid stuff, leuco something?"

"Leucocrystal violet, yes."

"What did you find?"

"Nothing."

"No bloody footprints."

"No."

"Even though there was blood on the boot."

"That's correct. Of course, the floor could have been cleaned before our tests."

"Yes, it could have. It would have made perfect sense, wouldn't it have, for the defendant, racked with a guilty conscience and fear of getting caught, to clean the floor of all evidence while leaving blood on the bottom of his boot, and to wipe the murder weapon clean of prints while leaving it wrapped inside a bloody shirt on the floor of his closet. One last question. The blood on the boot, was it a droplet of blood?"

"No."

"A series of droplets?"

"No."

"How did you describe it in your report?"

"Let me check. Yes, here. I said it was a smear on the arch of the sole."

"A smear on the boot discovered by Detective Torricelli. A smear on the shirt discovered by Detective Torricelli." I turned to face the good detective sitting red-faced at the prosecution table. "A smear in court."

"Objection."

"Mr. Carl," said the judge with a bite of anger in his voice.

I spread my arms out wide, put on my most innocent expression. "What?" I said.

And then I raised an eyebrow.

CHAPTER

52

Lucky me, I was back in the chair, my temporary crowns pried off, the permanent metal covers of my bridge being fitted and fixed by Dr. Bob. No Novocain for this procedure, just pressing and pulling, bending and scraping, the excruciating squeal of metal against raw nerve.

"So let me get this straight," said Dr. Pfeffer as he adjusted the light and peered into my mouth, his expression hidden by his mask. "Daniel's sister, Tanya, is missing. This Reverend Wilkerson knows where she is but won't say. This Miss Elise also knows where she is, but Miss Elise is somehow hooked up with the reverend. And someone named Rex, who is as big as a house, guards the entrance to the Hotel Latimore, where all the answers are to be found."

"Ahaouih," I said.

"Interesting. This whole thing sounds faintly Tolkienish. Maybe what you need is a Hobbit. Open wider. It's still not quite a perfect fit. A few more adjustments."

He reached in, did something painful, nodded as if the way my eyes scrunched and hands balled was only to be expected.

"What are you going to do?" he asked.

"Iohwohw."

"A difficult dilemma. But I think what you're attempting is most valuable. This little girl could be in dire trouble, and you could be the only one looking out for her."

"Ahihehahly," I said.

"And, Victor, this I can tell you with utter certainty: You must never underestimate the effect of childhood trauma. You would think we can escape it, but we never do. It often explains everything. Open wider. Yes, another tweak is needed."

He reached in again, the back of my neck constricted in pain.

"Let me tell you a story. Very instructive. There was a doctor who lived in New Jersey. A medical doctor." Dr. Bob sniffed in disparagement. "For what that's worth. A young man with the whole of the world in his grasp, a lovely wife, a beautiful daughter, an honorific of which, to be honest, we are all overly proud."

Dr. Bob reached for another set of pliers. He adjusted the light, shook his head as if in pity for the young intern whose story he was relating, snapped the teeth of the pliers twice before reaching them into my mouth.

"One day our doctor was driving home after picking up his young daughter from school. Suddenly an orange Gremlin turned without stopping at a stop sign and forced the doctor out of his lane, spraying the doctor's Pontiac with pebbles in the process. Remember the Gremlin, a beastly little car? If it had been a Cadillac, our doctor might have let it go, but a Gremlin? Doctors don't get cut off by Gremlins. Hold still. Yes, looking much better. So our young doctor followed the Gremlin, angrily bleating his horn. He caught up to it at another stop sign, jabbed his finger at the other driver, ordered the car to the side of the road."

Dr. Bob peered closely at my mouth for a moment, let out a perplexed "Hmm," and readjusted the light. He took one of his pointy metal thingers and scraped at the gum line of my lower front teeth. "I'm not sure I like that?"

"Wha?"

"Do you floss?"

"Uhie."

"Well, sometimes is apparently not enough. I don't have the time this afternoon, but next visit you'll need a full cleaning. Much would be made in the press about the driver of the Gremlin, about his suspended license, his prior drug convictions, and, as was the case in those days, his race. But if you read carefully the news reports, you can see that just then, in a strange neighborhood, on the side of the road, with this stranger coming at him, bellowing in that harsh, professional voice, the other driver was simply scared. Scared enough to pull a gun out of his waistband and fire into the good doctor's chest."

"Oohieah."

"Yes indeed. Now, as a criminal lawyer, Victor, you must know that most murders are accidents of blind happenstance. Afterward, no matter how much investigation occurs or brainpower is used, no one can really figure out why the murder victim lies sprawled on the ground. Nobody intended it, everyone wishes it would be otherwise, including the killer, but there's nothing to be done. Another absurd event in an absurd world. But the pure contingency of it all doesn't lessen the murder's impact, does it?"

"Iowuherah."

"Think of the doctor, his glorious grip on the world loosed in an instant. Think of the driver of the Gremlin, destined to die in jail. And think of the daughter, sitting in the back seat of the car, lap belt tight, watching her father slam on his brakes, curse, charge after the Gremlin. Watching helplessly through the windshield as her father yells, and then backs away, and then clutches his chest and spins around and collapses to the ground. Think of her, the daughter, and the scars she undoubtedly carries from a bullet that cut not her flesh. Think of how that brutal event still curses her life, affects her behavioral patterns in ways she doesn't even recognize today."

"Iaheeah."

"Of course you can. What I'm saying here, Victor, is if you can save this young girl, this sister of Daniel, from any such pain, if you can help her minimize the traumas of an already traumatic childhood, then that is a cause worth fighting for."

"Ighahee."

"Perfect. Let me take off the metal framework so I can send it back to the laboratory to have the porcelain put on. One more visit and we'll be done, Victor. It will be nice to have that hole finally filled, won't it?"

"Ahouhie."

"Tilda."

Another magically quick appearance. "Yes, Doctor."

"Owheoooah?" I said.

"I'm just about finished here," said Dr. Bob. "Prepare the cement so I can reattach Victor's temporary crown."

"With pleasure, Doctor."

"Isn't it nice to see Tilda so enthusiastic about her work? Somehow your very presence encourages her so. What do you think it is, Victor?"

"Ehaeal?"

Dr. Bob laughed.

I was standing at the reception desk, waiting for Deirdre to return from the back room after maxing out my credit card, while Dr. Bob made his notations on my file. I absently took in the photographs in Dr. Pfeffer's smile hall of fame on the wall.

"When this is over," I said, "are you going to take a picture of my mouth for your wall?"

He looked up from the file, gave me an appraising stare before turning to face the array of photographs. "No," he said.

"What would it require?"

"Massive reconstruction," he said, turning his attention back to the file.

"You know, some of those smiles look awfully familiar."

"I would hope so. You're sleeping with one of them."

"Excuse me?"

"We'll call you to set up your next appointment. Sometimes the laboratory takes longer than we expect. Remember that you'll be having a thorough cleaning, too. I can see you wince. Don't worry, Victor, the procedure is relatively painless."

"Relative to what?"

"That's always the question, isn't it?"

"What about Tanya?"

Dr. Bob put down his pen. "What about her?"

"I need to find her."

"I suppose you do."

"I could use some help."

"Are you asking? Think a moment, Victor. Are you asking? Because a favor like this is not easily repaid."

"What do you have in mind?"

"One never knows in advance, does one? But I like to be of assistance when I can, and sometime in the future, you might be of assistance to me."

"Sort of like paying it forward."

"Sort of, but without the swelling music and the tears."

I thought for a moment. I felt like I was getting myself into something I didn't quite understand, but I needed the help. Tanya needed the help. "Okay. Yes. I'll repay you if I'm able."

"All right, then. We have a deal. I'll see if the Hotel Latimore takes reservations." He chuckled as he folded the file, slapped it on the desk, and headed back toward the examination rooms.

I watched him go and then turned again to the wall of smiles. Healthy gums, shiny teeth, a certain arrogant joie de vivre. That one there, I figured, must be Carol Kingsly. Or maybe that one there, because I have to tell you, more than one looked awfully familiar. But it wasn't only the strangeness of the smiles on the doctor's wall that was preying on my mind, smiles hung like trophy heads in a hunting lodge. There was something else that puzzled me. I had come to the conclusion that Dr. Bob wasn't one for idle chatter. All his stories had a purpose. And so what the hell was the purpose, I wondered, of the strange story of the doctor and his daughter and that little orange Gremlin?

I figured it out eventually, yes I did, even a dumb cluck finds the acorn now and then. And I figured it out, perversely, while staring at photographs of the dead body of Leesa Dubé.

53

Dr. Peasley was a tall, lugubrious man with pale skin and a very brown toupee. I sometimes think we develop our personalities by modeling behaviors from the people we come into contact with most often, which goes far, I think, to explain the testimonial style of the coroner. By the time he spelled his name and listed his qualifications, snores were being heard from the back of the courtroom.

Nothing like a slow monotone, with frequent inexplicable pauses, to keep things humming.

I had already read the report, I knew how Leesa Dubé had died, and Beth was responsible for objecting when necessary and for the cross-examination, and so as Dr. Peasley droned on and eyelids all over the courtroom started drooping, I let my mind wander. And where it wandered to was Dr. Bob.

For some reason I felt squirrelly about what the dentist had said while adjusting my new bridge. Why had he emphasized over and again the contingent nature of most murders? Why had he warned me so vociferously never to underestimate the effect of childhood trauma on the adult psyche? And most troubling of all, what the heck had that story of the doctor and the Gremlin and the girl in the back seat been all about?

Think of her, the daughter, and the scars she undoubtedly

carries from a bullet that cut not her flesh, had said Dr. Bob. *Think of how that brutal event still curses her life, affects her behavioral patterns in ways she doesn't even recognize today.*

How would the curse play out? I wondered. As Dalton passed to the jury certain photos from the autopsy and Dr. Peasley, in his slow, deep voice, explained how a gunshot at close range had torn apart Leesa Dubé's neck and caused her to bleed to death, I considered the possibilities. Had she become a violent psychopath, the girl in the back seat of the Pontiac? Had she become a manic-depressive? A gun enthusiast? A peacenik? A taxi driver? What?

And why would the dentist be telling me the story if there wasn't something I could do to help relieve her pain? Who could she be? I wondered. Was it Carol Kingsly, with whom he had set me up? Was it Julia Rose, the mother of both his patient Daniel and the girl of whose perilous fate I had just informed him? Or was it Dr. Bob himself, Dr. Bob before the sex change? That one I liked, that one I thought about for a while, let the possibilities simmer in my mind.

And then it came to me in a shiver. It came to me with the force of undiscovered truth, as if I had been born with the knowledge, as Plato believed, and was just waiting for Dr. Bob to act as my Socrates and pull the blindfold from my eyes. It came to me as Dalton reached the climax of her examination of Dr. Peasley.

"Now, Dr. Peasley, you put the time of death at approximately midnight, isn't that right?"

"Yes," said Dr. Peasley, in his slow, deep voice. "That is right."

"And you saw her how much later?"

"She was brought to me at approximately noon the next day. So it was approximately twelve hours later."

"And what condition was the body in then?"

"When a person dies," said Peasley slowly, slowly, "the body goes through a number of specific stages of deterioration. At the very moment of death, the heart stops, the muscles relax, the bladder and bowels release. Depending on the environment, the body will begin to lose approximately one and a half degrees Fahrenheit each hour. This loss of temperature is referred to as algor mortis."

"What happens after thirty minutes?"

"Under normal conditions, after thirty minutes blood begins to pool in the lower portions of the body, which is referred to as livor mortis. The skin turns purple and waxy. The hands and feet turn blue. The eyes begin to sink into the skull."

"And after four hours?"

"At four hours, the pooling of the blood and the purpling of the skin continue. And rigor mortis begins to set in."

"What exactly is rigor mortis, Doctor?"

"Rigor mortis is a rigidity of the body that occurs after death. It is effected by chemical changes in the muscle tissue and causes the joints to become so stiff it is almost impossible to move them without breaking the bone. This starts after about four hours, becomes full at twelve hours. After that, the body gradually returns to a limp state."

François was listening to this testimony with a sense of bland detachment on his face, which didn't surprise me. Testimony on the texture of dead muscle was no mystery to a four-star chef whose signature dish involved a rack of ribs, I figured, even if the dead muscle being testified to was that of his wife. But Beth's emotionless reaction, as she sat between François and me at the defense table, was somewhat puzzling. She had a yellow legal pad before her, a line drawn down the middle of the page, and she bit her lip with concentration as she listened to the doleful responses of Dr. Peasley and took notes on the testimony in preparation for her cross. From her expression, the witness could have been talking about real estate valuations or a stock deal that went south, not describing the condition of a murder victim laid on his autopsy table or the stages of deterioration of the human body after death.

"Now, when you examined the body at the morgue," said Mia Dalton to the coroner, "you determined that she had been dead for about twelve hours."

"That's right. I determined the time of death first by analyzing the algor mortis. I did this by taking the temperature of the liver, which was just over eighty degrees, and doing the calculation. I also examined the extent of livor mortis, or the pooling of the blood, which was extensive, and determining the state of rigor mortis, which at the time was full."

"Which meant what, Dr. Peasley?"

"All her muscles and joints were completely stiff."

"At that time did you try to move any of her joints?"

"Yes, I did. Her right arm was bent beneath her, as you can tell in the photographs from the crime scene. In order to examine her hand, I had to move the arm. It was quite difficult."

I leaned over and looked at Beth's notes. Algor mortis—80 degrees. Livor mortis, pooling of the blood. Rigor mortis, completely stiff. "How about mortis and pestle?" I said softly.

"What?" she whispered back.

"If you're going to include all the mortises in your notes, you shouldn't forget the good old mortis and pestle."

"That's mortar and pestle," she said without looking away from the witness.

"Or my grade-school friend Freddie Mortis."

"Happy boy?"

"No, actually, a bit depressed. Obsessed with death, for some reason. I suppose we know why this Dr. Peasley went to med school."

"Be quiet."

"To fight the scourge of insomnia."

"Shhhh. I need to get ready for my cross."

"What are you going to ask him?"

"If he'll share his Valium with me," said Beth.

"Were you able to see the deceased's hand?" said Dalton after glancing our way with irritation. I smiled back.

"Eventually, yes," said Dr. Peasley.

"What state was it in?"

"It was blue and clenched."

"Did you have cause to open her hand?"

"Yes. As part of the autopsy, it was important to examine her hands and fingers for any possible wounds, also to determine if there was any tissue matter under the nails, which we could analyze. Unfortunately, there was not."

"Can you describe opening the hand?"

"It was difficult. It was clenched tight."

"Could that have been the result of rigor mortis?"

"No. A hand won't clench as a result of rigor mortis, it will just stiffen. Her hand was already clenched when rigor mortis began to set in."

Beth jotted down this little nugget on her notepad. I stared at her profile for a moment, sturdy and sincere, her forehead attractively creased in concentration. It was the familiar profile of my best friend, yet somehow different than I had ever seen it before. And then François leaned forward, so that in my viewpoint his handsome features were now side by side with Beth's. The girl in the back seat of the Pontiac would have seen her father ripped from her youth in the most violent way. For the rest of her life, she'd be pining for him. And perhaps looking for a substitute. An older man, maybe. Or a doctor. Or a man with a streak of anger in him. Or maybe a man similarly separated from his child, his daughter. Maybe a man who looked to that girl in the back seat, now grown, as his only hope for salvation.

"And what did you find when you tried to open her hand?" said Dalton to the witness.

"As slowly as I could, I pried open her fingers. I was working carefully so as not to break any bones. And that is when I saw it."

"Saw what?"

"The thing that she had been clenching."

"Did you recover it?"

"Yes."

"What state was it in?"

"It was creased, there was some blood, but it was still recognizable."

"I want to show you what is marked as People's Exhibit Twenty-one. Do you recognize that exhibit?"

"Yes. It is the object I found in the deceased's hand. It has my initials on the back."

"And what is it, exactly?"

"It is a photograph," he said, and then he pointed his long, bony finger at François. "Of him. What I found clenched in the murder victim's hand was a photograph of the defendant, François Dubé."

There were gasps in the courtroom. Dalton had cleverly not mentioned the photograph in her opening and it was a surprise to the jury and some of the spectators, and so there were gasps. And at that very moment, along with the jury, I gasped, too.

But not at the photograph.

And that was not the last of the surprises for me at that trial. Let me tell you, the hits just kept on coming.

CHAPTER

54

Mia Dalton stood at the lectern and gave me a sly smile. It wasn't overt, and because the prosecution always sits closest to the jury box, and because she was turned from the jurors when she gave it, it wasn't discernible by the twelve and two alternates who really mattered, but there it was, clear as the sun on a clear, sunny day.

Son of a bitch.

"Please state your name for the record," she said to the witness.

"Geoffrey Sunshine," said Geoffrey Sunshine, who proceeded to spell his name as if we all were second-graders who needed the help.

"Is that your real name?"

"That's my business name. My real name is Gerald Sonenshein. But it doesn't have quite the same sparkle."

Little Jerry Sonenshein, being called as a prosecution witness. This was bad, very, very bad. I had of course objected. "He is nowhere on the prosecution's witness list," I had loudly proclaimed, with a tone of righteous indignation. But when Dalton pointed out that Sonenshein was on my witness list, along with a few dozen other names put on there just to confuse the apparently unconfused Dalton, the judge simply shook his head and denied my objection. For some reason Dalton thought Sonenshein was a witness who could help her case, which was problematic for me, since I had thought this witness was the very heart of my defense.

One of us was wrong.

"And your job, Mr. Sonenshein?" said Mia Dalton.

"I own a supper club," he said. "Marrakech. It's pretty well known in the city."

"Did Leesa Dubé ever go to your restaurant?"

"Oh, yes, of course. Before her marriage, I'm talking about now. She was a regular. The downstairs is the restaurant proper. Upstairs we have a club. She wasn't much of an eater, but she was upstairs at the club all the time before she married him." He pointed at François. "She would go there with her friend, Velma Wykowski."

"And how do you know she was a customer?"

"Hey, two girls that pretty and that easy who hang out at your club, you get to know them fairly well."

And then, in response to Dalton's careful and measured questions, little Jerry Sonenshein detailed the exploits of the famous Wykowski sisters. It was everything he had told us in that first meeting in the smoking room at his upstairs club. I would have objected, would have stood up and pounded the table and raised every ground I could have manufactured to keep it out, and my objections would have been upheld, too, except it was the very testimony I had intended to elicit when I called him to the stand. So I looked at François, who seemed strangely worried, and at Beth, who shrugged with puzzlement, and let it go on, and so it did. The whole before-marriage scene, the famous Wykowski sisters, the coming of François into their lives.

"And you were aware, Mr. Sonenshein, when Leesa Dubé married the defendant."

"Of course."

"Did she ever come to your club after the marriage?"

"Once or twice with François."

"Ever alone or with friends?"

"No."

"Were you aware when they were separated?"

"François had his own restaurant then. In this business we all gossip about one another, so yes, I heard."

"Did Leesa ever come into your club after the separation?"

"No."

Like a slap.

"Never met any man at your club after the separation?"

"Not that I ever knew of, no."

Like a crisp slap about my head.

"Did you ever tell anyone any different?"

"Yes. I told—"

"Objection," I said, none too calmly.

"Grounds, Mr. Carl?" said the judge.

Because he's lying, Judge. Because he's crapping in my hat out of high-school spite. Because Dalton is playing dirty. Because the whole thing is pissing me off. Because I feel like I've been slapped. This is what I wanted to say, but a trial is run on the rules of evidence, and none of those extraordinarily valid reasons fit within the rules. So instead I sort of croaked out some boilerplate nonsense about relevance and hearsay and such.

"Your Honor," said Dalton, with the calm of a woman who had figured this all out the night before, as opposed to yours truly, who was winging it badly, "Mr. Carl, in his opening, introduced the possibility of Leesa's having met another man. Mr. Carl claimed that this man is the true murderer, and he has continued implying such in his examinations. We are entitled, in our case in chief, to refute the proposition that Mrs. Dubé was ever involved with another man during her separation. Mr. Sonenshein is testifying that Leesa Dubé didn't meet any such man at his club, the place where she had gallivanted as a single woman and where she had met the defendant. Mr. Sonenshein made a statement inconsistent to his current testimony. In the interest of full disclosure, and so that the jury won't think we are hiding something, we are allowed, by the rules of evidence, to let him testify about that prior inconsistent statement."

"I think she is allowed that, Mr. Carl. Objection overruled."

"But, Judge," I stammered.

"Overruled.

"Exception."

"Noted. Now sit down, Mr. Carl, so Ms. Dalton can finish this."

I sat. Dalton slipped me that sly smile once more, and then she continued.

"Did you ever tell anyone, Mr. Sonenshein," said Dalton, "that Leesa Dubé actually did meet a man at your club after her separation, some violent motorcycle rider named Clem?"

"Yes, I did."

"Whom did you tell?"

"Mr. Carl and Ms. Derringer over at the defense table."

"And was what you told them the truth?"

"No. It was a lie."

"There is no Clem?"

"No."

"He's completely make-believe?"

"Like Mickey Mouse, without the ears."

"Why would you do that? Why would you lie to Mr. Carl and Ms. Derringer?"

"Other than for the fun of it?" said Sonenshein. "I did it as a favor for a friend of Leesa's."

"What friend?"

"Velma. That Velma Wykowski I mentioned before, who is married and now called Velma Takahashi."

"She asked you to lie."

"Yes."

"And so you did."

"Right."

"But you're not lying now."

"Now I'm under oath."

"One more thing, Mr. Sonenshein," said Dalton. "You are currently under criminal investigation by our office, is that right?"

"So I've been told."

"For fraud and embezzlement and tax evasion, all involving your restaurant, is that right?"

"I'm not admitting to anything, but that's what I've been told."

"And the purchase of certain illegal narcotics."

"So you guys say."

"And you volunteered this information why?"

"I hope it helps resolve my situation."

"Any promises from our office?"

"None, even though I tried to get them. But I'm a hopeful guy, and so I'm hoping."

"Hoping what, Mr. Sonenshein?"

"That the truth will keep me free."

"No further questions," said Dalton. "I pass the witness."

She passed the witness, sort of like a soldier passing a live grenade. *Hold this a minute, will you, pal?* François looked sick at the end of the table. Beth was furious. I leaned over and asked her what she thought.

"He's lying," she said. "He's full of crap and he's lying. Lying through his teeth."

"What do you think I should do?"

"You have no choice," she said. "Go after the bastard. Screw him to the wall. You sure have enough to work with."

And she was right about that. There was the lying, the criminal investigation, the currying of favor with the prosecution, his general all-purpose sleaziness. It wouldn't be hard to split his festering carcass on the stand. I had the material, I had the wherewithal, and believe you me, there was nothing I wanted more. I had been waiting for this opportunity since high school. Destroying him would be as easy as stomping on a roach, and twice as much fun. I stood and stepped to the lectern and stepped back and stepped forward again. I was like a shark getting ready to attack. My blood was up, chum was in the water, an old high-school chum. I was ready.

But there was something in Dalton's smile, something in the unconcern with which Sonenshein sat in the witness stand, something about what the bartender at his club had said, something about a flower in a vase.

I shook my head and tried to dismiss it all. He was there, on the stand, with a bull's-eye on his chest. Impossible to resist. I leaned forward, pointed my finger, opened my mouth and . . .

And it came to me again. The image of a single flower in a narrow vase.

I couldn't place it, the image. I turned my head, looked again at Dalton. She was watching me with more than her usual interest, she was watching me as if I were some sort of specious jewel that she was trying to appraise. And I remembered the wink she gave me after my closing, the wink that had sent chills down my spine.

"Mr. Carl?" said Judge Armstrong. "We're waiting."

I nodded, leaned forward on the lectern, tapped it once, twice, turned once more to look at Dalton and then at Beth, her face twisted in anticipation, and at François, his own face creased with worry. They were waiting for me. They

were all waiting for me, waiting for me to rush forward and
tear this bastard apart.

"Mr. Carl?" said the judge.

"Your Honor," I said, biting my cheek in frustration all the
while, "the defense has no questions for this witness."

55

I was in my car, driving and stewing, accompanied by the raging of my anger. I had been lied to, I had been used and abused, I had been manipulated like a monkey. It had all been a fabrication, the whole violent affair between a dead woman and a mysterious motorcycle maniac named Clem, a figment of one person's twisted imagination.

And I had bought it.

That's what got to me the worst, not that I had been lied to—I'm a lawyer, everybody lies to me; lying to the lawyers is the true national pastime, as American as baseball and cheating on your wife—but that I hadn't sussed out the lie. And it's not like there weren't enough clues. The overly dramatic visits to the grave site by Velma Takahashi. The way I forced the story of Clem out of that bastard Sonenshein with my way-too-clever threat of Japanese gangsters. The manner of Velma Takahashi, going through the motions during our confrontation about the mystery man. And what had she said of him? *He is nothing. He's nowhere. He's a phantom.*

Sometimes I almost think I'm clever, and then reality spits a glob of humiliation in my face.

I realized it all while staring at Jerry Sonenshein on the witness stand. And still I thought of going after him, of showing him to be a liar and continuing with the Clem de-

fense. The believable lie is often the best approach in court.
Where would lawyers be if all we had to work with was the
truth? But the strange image that kept coming back to me,
the image of the flower in the vase, convinced me otherwise. Even one question to that bastard would have been
one question too many. So I declined our cross-
examination. And as the spectators let out a collective gasp,
I stormed out of the courtroom without another word, leaving it for Beth to clean up the mess.

And now I was in my car, driving and stewing. Stewing
and driving. But I wasn't just driving hither and thither,
without a plan. I knew where I was headed. It was a Thursday afternoon, and I was going to the manicurist.

The joint was posh, with a long maroon awning fronting
the entrance, with blue and gray velvet curtains and fresh
flowers artfully arranged in the waiting room, with a marble
floor and a woman sitting behind the appointment desk so
pale and so cold she might as well have been made of porcelain. Her face cracked a little when she saw me charge
through the front door.

"Helloo," she said. "Do we have an appointment?"

"No," I said as I moved right past her. "We don't."

"Sir, you have to—"

"I can't wait," I said, showing her the back of my hand,
wiggling my fingers. "It's a cuticle emergency."

She recoiled in horror at the sight of my nails, which gave
me enough time to slip through the doorway and into the
salon proper. There were a series of workstations on either
side of a hallway, each curtained off for privacy. I moved
through the salon with an abiding sense of purpose, flicking
open the curtains to check who was being worked on, elicit-
ing a series of shrieks as I made my way toward the rear.
And then I found her, swathed in a thick white robe, a towel

around her head, leaning back in a lounge chair, being fussed over, literally, hand and foot.

"Why did you do it?" I said.

"Have you come for a pedicure, Victor?" said Velma Takahashi as the two slim woman working on her nails turned their faces toward me. "Minh here has such a deft touch. It is so relaxing."

"Why did you do it?"

"Do what? Choose this color polish? I thought it matched my eyes. You don't think it matches my eyes?"

Just then the receptionist came up from behind me, holding a nail file like a knife. "I tried to stop him, Mrs. Takahashi," she said.

Seeing the situation, one of the seated women grabbed a pair of scissors and held it high, as if she were about to stab me in the kneecap.

"It's okay, dears," said Velma to the women. "He works for me, though I do think after this I'm going to have to let him go." The receptionist retreated, the manicurists went back to work.

"Why did you set up François?" I said, still standing before her as the women filed and painted and buffed.

"I would never set up François."

"But it sure seems like it. I've been trying to figure it out, and I can't. Do you hate him so much you were trying to torture him further, providing him false hope and then manipulating his defense attorney into relying on a premise so easily shown to be false?"

"Tell me what happened, Victor."

"Your buddy Sunshine spilled it all to the D.A. The way you convinced him to tell his cock-and-bull story about Clem and Leesa, the way he duped me into believing it."

Her mouth twitched and then regained its normal artificial poutiness. "He's a pathetic liar."

"Yes, he is," I said. "But this time he's telling the truth. And now François is screwed, and I've been played for the fool."

"Your natural position. I guess you won't anymore be needing me to testify."

"Why, Velma? That's what I want to know."

"Have you ever regretted anything in your life, Victor?"

"Only everything."

"So you know the way it seeps through your bones like an acid. Drip, drip, drip."

"But what is it you regret? A life wasted in the pursuit of someone else's money?"

"Is that a waste?"

"The series of surgeries that turned you into a Kewpie doll?"

"I thought you liked the result."

"Or do you regret killing Leesa Dubé?"

"Oh, Victor, you've come unhinged."

"Have I? You say you didn't try to set up François, so maybe you were actually trying to help him and botched it. But then the question is why? Why help that slimy son of a bitch? The answer might be in the visits to the grave site, the guilt in your eyes. Why would you concoct this lie except to make some amends? Did you kill her, Velma?"

"Why would I kill my best friend?"

"Maybe she knew more than she should have. Maybe she knew enough to prove adultery to your husband and ruin your marriage, not to mention your bank account. All those years with Takahashi wasted if he could enforce the adultery provisions of the prenup. So Leesa had to go, and to keep attention away from you, you framed the husband. You sneaked into his apartment after the deed, dropped the gun in his shirt, smeared some blood on his boot. A perfect frame."

"You're being silly."

"Am I? Or am I so dead-on it's scary?"

"It's scary, all right. The thing is, Victor, your motive is empty. I've never cheated on my husband."

"I'm supposed to believe that?"

"No, of course not. Why would you? It's only the truth." She pulled her hands away from the manicurist. "I'm sorry, but I have to go. I have a meeting."

"To figure out another lie to tell?"

"One mustn't become bitter, Victor. Life is full of wonderful surprises, so long as you aren't looking too hard for them. Like love, when you thought you were incapable. I still have some time here. Why don't you take over the rest of my appointment? Your hands could use some work, and I don't even want to imagine your feet."

"That's okay," I said.

"No, really, Victor. Take advantage." She lifted her feet off the pads, slipped them into a set of slippers, stood up from the chair, waved her hands in the air in an effort to dry the polish. "Minh is the best in the city."

"I'll pass."

"You don't think much of me, do you, Victor?"

"No, actually."

"Well, I might agree with you. But quick, choose: love or money?"

"Both."

"And so you have neither. I wasn't satisfied with that option."

"I don't see you going for the daily double," I said.

"You're not looking hard enough." Velma pursed her lips at me as if to air-kiss. "We're all just trying to get by, Victor. Doing the best to get what we want. Is that so bad?"

"When someone else pays the price."

"Oh, Victor. Someone is always paying the price. Win a case, and someone else loses. Marry a man, and someone else is heartbroken. Become a saint, and someone else's beatification is delayed. I didn't invent the world, I'm just a little girl doing my best."

And then she was off, out of the curtained cubicle down toward the dressing room, leaving me alone with the two manicurists. I was about to run after her, but what was the point? So I just stood there for a moment and tried to gather my thoughts.

Then one of the women motioned me to the chair.

I shook my head, but she took hold of the fabric of my suit and gently tugged. Next thing I knew, I was sitting in the chair as Minh slowly untied my shoe.

56

I was strangely serene when I returned to the office that afternoon. And for some reason I had the bizarre notion to go out and buy a pair of sandals. But Beth, waiting for me in the conference room, wasn't so calm.

"Are you trying to sabotage this case?" she said. "Because from what I saw today, it looks like you are tossing our client to the wolves."

"It was all a lie," I said as I pulled out a chair and sat down. In front of me on the conference table was the photograph of Leesa Dubé, taken before her murder. She was pretty, she was smiling, she was alive. I had stared at that photograph enough over the last few weeks that it had become oddly familiar, like an old friend. And still, after all this, I didn't know what had really happened to her. All I knew now was that the killer of this lovely woman wasn't some motorcycle maniac. "The whole story about Clem and Leesa was a lie."

"How do you know? Maybe Sunshine is lying now. Maybe to get his little deal, he took the stand and said just what Mia Dalton wanted him to say."

"She wouldn't put on a lie."

"But she put on a liar, because if Sunshine was telling the truth today, then he lied to us."

"Yes, he did."

"So you didn't think it was valuable to point that out to the jury?"

"Dalton already did that for us. We can argue it at closing."

"Oh, that will be effective. Why don't we save time and let her put on our entire case? Tell me truthfully, Victor. Is this some misguided attempt to save the poor damsel in distress?"

"Is that what you are?"

"You're no white knight, and I don't need your help."

"Beth—"

"Or are you just jealous? Is that it?"

"Maybe I am, a little."

"You're a bastard."

"But that's not why I did what I did."

"So then tell me why, Victor, because I don't understand. How can you be so sure which was the lie and which was the truth? And if you are certain, why didn't you cross-examine the lying bastard anyway? Any first-year law student could have destroyed Sunshine's credibility up there. Afterward, we could still have put Velma on the stand to tell her story about Clem. It would have been a she-said-versus-he-said, and he would be a proven liar. It would have been reasonable doubt."

"It would have been a disaster," I said.

"What makes you so certain we couldn't pull it off?"

"Because there's a tape."

"A tape?"

"Of Velma asking him to lie, a tape in which she details the story she wants him to tell and he agrees to tell it."

"Oh," she said. "A tape."

"Yeah."

"Extrinsic evidence of a prior consistent statement."

"Right."

"That wouldn't have been so good, would it?"

"No."

"Then maybe I was a little out of line."

"Just a touch."

Beth might have been angry and confused, but she was always a terrific lawyer and saw the issue right away. If there was indeed a tape of Velma convincing Sonenshein to lie, the rules of evidence prohibited Mia Dalton from playing it during her direct examination. But if in my cross-examination I tried to show that Sonenshein was lying on the stand, suddenly Dalton could play the tape to disprove my point. It's a bit complicated and legalistic, but suffice it to say that Dalton expected that I would attack her witness, opening the door for her to play the tape for the jury. It was a trap I had barely slipped out of.

"Are you sure?" she said.

"Sure enough. It was in the way Sonenshein sat on the stand, smugly confident. It was in the way Dalton stared at me, almost like she was hoping I wouldn't fall for it. And because it was little Jerry Sonenshein, the AV geek up there. Remember how the bartender at his club said that he was always taping the help, to see if they were stealing? Real James Bond stuff, he said. And remember how wherever we ran into him there was a little flower in a vase that he was always fiddling with, both in the cigar lounge and in his downstairs office? He was taping us, and if he was taping us, he was taping her."

"That means we can't use Velma either."

"Right." Because Dalton would simply play the tape to refute her story.

"So now we have nothing. We're in the middle of a murder trial without a strategy, without a theory, without a suspect."

"But we've got each other."

"Oh, God," she said as she put a hand over her face. "It's hopeless." And then, with her hand still over her face, she began to cry. It wasn't loud, it wasn't maudlin, it was mostly just a few shakes of her shoulders, but it was enough to tear at my heart. I looked again at the picture of Leesa Dubé, who had once loved François, and then at the woman with apparently the same affliction, crying a few feet away. It was a plague.

"Tell me about your father," I said quietly.

She wiped her eyes with the back of her hand, shook her head as if she were shaking a rattle, squinted at me. "What?"

"I asked about your father."

"I heard you," she said, giving a quick rub to her nose. "What does he have to do with anything? He lives in Cherry Hill, he's getting a hip transplant, he plays golf."

"Really?"

"I guess it's more like he plays at golf. But you've met him. He's been to the office."

"That's right. Of course."

"So?"

"Is he your real father?"

"Victor?"

"I'm just curious."

"He's been the only father I've ever known. He married my mother when I was six."

"So he's your stepfather. What happened to your real father?"

"He died. Victor?"

"How?"

"He just did. Victor, stop."

"You never told me what happened to your real father."

"That's right, I never did."

"Do you want to now?"

"No, I don't. Victor, what are we going to do about François?"

"I don't know." I picked up the photograph of Leesa

Dubé, showed it to Beth. "She looks awfully familiar, doesn't she?"

"A woman that pretty, I don't think you'd forget."

"No, I don't think I would."

"And I must admit she had marvelous teeth. All right, I'm going to go talk to our client before they ship him out for the night."

"Okay."

"Are you going to come up with something? Anything?"

"I hope so," I said, though what I really meant was, *I doubt it.*

She stood up wearily, made to leave the room, and then stopped. "By the way," she said, "someone mailed back that key you lost."

"I didn't lose a key."

"You must have. It came for you, in an envelope, with no note." She pointed to a manila envelope addressed to me, with no postage and no return address.

"Hand-delivered?" I said.

She shrugged.

I emptied the envelope into my hand. A single bronze key with the number 27 stamped on it and the word E-ZEE.

"It's not mine," I said. "It must be a mistake."

"Then toss it," she said before leaving the room.

I turned the key over in my hand, back and forth, trying to figure what it might be, and failing. The hell with it, I thought as I slipped it into my pocket. I had other things to concern me just then.

I had felt a strange hope for a moment, a hope that I'd been wrong when I imagined the little girl in the back of the Pontiac to be Beth. Yes, I knew her father, a charming man with a slight limp and a penchant for bad jokes. No, Beth was not the type to be haunted by her past. And yes, she would have told me the truth of it long before. We were best friends. There were no secrets between us. But of course I had secrets I'd never told her. And, it appeared, she had secrets of her own.

So it was just as I had imagined. I had mentioned my concerns about Beth to Whitney Robinson. Whit must have told Dr. Bob. Dr. Bob must have burrowed like a mole into Beth's past to see what he could find. And then, in my next appointment, Dr. Bob had maneuvered his one-sided conversation to spill the horrific events of that past to me. The whole chain of events made me feel like I had fallen into a pit of sludge.

What a strange man he was, Dr. Bob. Dentist to François's first defense attorney. Dentist to the troubled boy who testified to seeing François at the crime scene. Dentist now to François's second defense attorney. He seemed in the middle of everything. Well, almost everything.

I picked up the picture of Leesa Dubé. Turned it one way, turned it the other. What was it Beth had said? *And I must admit she had marvelous teeth.* And they were, weren't they? Like a pretentious movie director, I used my fingers to frame the photograph so that only her smile was visible.

Holy molars, Batman.

Now I knew why the picture seemed so familiar. I had seen that smile before, every time I stepped into Dr. Bob's office. It was on the wall, part of the smile hall of fame. Dr. Bob was Leesa Dubé's dentist, too. Did that explain anything? Who the hell knew? But I was going to find out.

I picked up the phone, placed a call to his office, got the great man himself on the phone.

"Hey, Doc," I said, "you want to go out for a beer?"

CHAPTER

57

The shoreline of Chicago is one of the great sights to behold from behind the window of a passenger jet. The smooth surface of the great lake seems to glisten with endless promise, and then, there in the distance, at the very edge of the water, rises a fabulous assortment of idiosyncratic towers, all shapes and sizes and colors, all shining majestically in the sun. You feel, while still over the expanse of Lake Michigan, that you are soaring toward Oz.

Which I found somewhat appropriate, because just then I was flying into Chicago to discover the man behind the curtain.

You must never underestimate the effect of childhood trauma, had said Dr. Bob. *It often explains everything. Look in the past, and the present becomes clear.* He was talking about Tanya Rose, and I believe he was trying to explain, in his roundabout way, what was actually going on with Beth. But as a species we are relentlessly self-referential. If Dr. Bob was giving me advice on finding the root of Beth's character, maybe he was inadvertently giving me advice on finding the root of his own. After our meeting in the bar, with the bizarre fistfight and the blood on the floor, I figured it was time to peek into my dentist's childhood.

But where had that childhood even been?

To his patients, Dr. Pfeffer's boyhood home seemed to be

as mysterious as the rest of his life. Carol had listed the possibilities with a sense of wonder: Albuquerque, Seattle, Burma. Burma? Is there even a Burma anymore? I decided to forget about the rumors and think it through on my own. It wasn't as if Dr. Bob hadn't given me enough clues. There was the fishing he did as a boy, yellow perch, he'd said, using fathead minnows as bait. There was the way he referred to soda as pop and the way he said he was used to cold weather. All this indicated that he spent his formative years somewhere in the upper Midwest. But what narrowed it down for me, I suppose, more than anything, was his antipathy for the New York Mets.

Now, I could relate to his loathing. I grew up a Phillies fan, and we feel about the Mets the way Pakistan feels about India; the nuclear option is never off the table. But I know they don't feel the same way in Albuquerque or Seattle or Rangoon. In those far-off places, the Mets are just another bad baseball team with ugly uniforms. But that's not all they were to Dr. Bob.

Our plane headed north along the coast of Lake Michigan before leaning to the left and slipping inland, toward O'Hare. Even though the seat-belt sign was on, I climbed to the other side of the plane, to a vacant window seat. From there I could see the coastline as it fled north, as if trying to outrun the fancy apartment buildings that ran along its length into the suburbs. I was looking for something specific, trying to follow the converging lines of the avenues as they made their way toward a singular shrine. And then I spotted it, smaller than I imagined, stuck smack in the middle of its urban neighborhood, without the seas of parking lots that ring most of its kind. A dark boomerang of a building surrounding a wedge of jade.

Wrigley Field.

The ballpark was why I had come to Chicago. *One per-*

son's miracle, Dr. Bob had said, *is another person's disaster.* What did that mean, or the strange invocation of a name that seemed still to haunt him? *And don't get me started,* he had said, *on Don Young.* Who the heck was Don Young?

The story is sad and all too familiar. It is 1969, in the heat of summer, and the Chicago Cubs are solidly ensconced in first place. This is a great Cub team, managed by Leo the Lip, with Ernie Banks, Ferguson Jenkins, sweet-swinging Billy Williams, Hall of Famers all, and the legendary Ron Santo, who should be in there with them. On a July night, the Cubs arrive at Shea Stadium, ready to put away the fading Mets. The Cubbies are up three to one in the ninth, when the Met second baseman hits an easy liner to center field. Inexplicably, the Chicago center fielder, a raw rookie, breaks back, allowing the ball to fall in front of him for a double. One out later, the mighty Donn Clendenon hits a shot deep to center. The rookie gets a jump on it and snags it just as he hits the wall, but the blow knocks the ball loose. Another double. Jones and Kranepool do the rest, knocking in three, giving the Mets the game. The next night, Tom Seaver pitches a one-hitter. The Cubs are reeling, the Mets, the eventual World Series champion "Miracle Mets," are rising, the season has turned.

And the rookie center fielder's name? Well, of course it was.

And who else would remember it but a native, a kid who was living and dying with his hometown team the way only hometown kids can? Once that was figured out, it wasn't so hard to narrow the location down even further. *I could hear the groaning from my backyard,* he had said. Which explained why, after I arrived, I rented a car and headed down the parking lot that was I-90, looking for the exit that would take me to the part of Chicago on the North Side known, for obvious reasons, as Wrigleyville.

There weren't that many Pfeffers listed in Chicago. The

one who lived in Wrigleyville had moved there three years before, after living for years in New Jersey. Of the others, there were a few who knew a Bob Pfeffer here or there of the approximate right age, but none that matched closely enough the description of my dentist.

"Does Dr. Bob have relatives that you know of?" I had asked Carol Kingsly after my Pfeffer search came up blank.

"He never mentioned any," she said. "How does that fit?"

"It's a little tight."

"That's good. Tight is good."

"It's not very comfortable."

"Honey, it's a shoe. Try wearing these for a day." She exhibited her shapely leg, showing off a red patent leather pump with a narrow spike. I got her point. It wasn't so much that her shoes were uncomfortable, rather that if I wanted to take them off her feet again with my teeth, it was time I changed my footwear.

"But there are no laces," I said.

"Isn't that wonderful? Buckles are fabulous."

"I feel like Buster Brown." I looked at the salesclerk who had shaken his head with such despair at my thick-soled black wingtips. "What is this again?"

"It's a Compton," he said, "from Crockett & Jones."

"Weren't they the cops on *Miami Vice*?"

He sniffed. "It's a British manufacturer, sir."

"How much?"

"Four hundred forty dollars, and a steal at that."

"I suppose it is, for Mr. Crockett. Do you have anything else, maybe something on sale?"

"Daffy's is just down the street."

"Then how about something just a little less buckle-ish, maybe."

"I understand," he said. "I'll check the synthetic leathers."

"You sure do know how to impress the help," said Carol after the clerk left to return the Comptons to the back room.

"What is a Pfeffer anyway?" I said. "It sounds like a smoker's cough. Pfeffer. Pfeffer."

"I think it's German."

"For what, pain?"

"Don't be silly. *Pfeffer* is German for pepper."

Driving around Chicago is a little like looking for drinks in Salt Lake City, you pretty much need to be a local to get where you want to go. And it didn't help that I had the usual rental-car sense of dislocation; how could I find the right street if I couldn't even find my turn signal? But I had a map and a plan. I left the highway at Belmont, followed Belmont down to Clark, and then Clark up until I eventually arrived at the marker I was looking for. The Cubbies were out of town, so traffic was light and the corner of Addison and Clark was empty except for the massive white structure with its great red sign. WRIGLEY FIELD / HOME OF / CHICAGO CUBS. As if we didn't know. I looked at the map, and from there it was a breeze. Up a bit, over a bit, just about three blocks west of third base, and there it was.

It was an old shambling two-story house on a block of old shambling houses, with only narrow walkways between them. But this house was smaller, darker, meaner than the rest. Some of the homes had been freshly painted, some had lovely lawns, new windows, a nice car parked out front, but not this one. It was owned by a Virgil Pepper. It had been owned by Virgil Pepper for forty years. Three Peppers were listed at the address: Virgil, James, and Fran.

The door was opened by Fran. "What do you want?" she said. She was short and heavy, wearing the sort of well-worn housedress that indicated she wasn't planning to go out that day. Based on the state of her hair, the paleness of her face, the way she squinted into the sunlight, she wasn't planning to go out tomorrow either.

"I called," I said. "My name is Victor Carl."

"You're that lawyer fellow, right?"

"That's right," I said.

"What is it you wanted to talk about again?"

"I wanted to talk about your brother," I said. "Your brother Bob."

CHAPTER

58

"**We thought he** was dead," said Jim Pepper, leaning back on his recliner, wincing as he shifted his position.

"We hoped he wasn't," said Fran.

"Of course we hoped he wasn't," snapped Jim. "What kind of fool wants his little brother dead?"

"I was just saying," said Fran.

Fran sat on a sagging, mud-colored couch. I was sitting stiffly on a stiff fold-up chair. Both Jim and Fran spoke with a slightly southern accent, more a West Virginia twang than the flat prairie accent of Chicago.

"When was the last time you saw your brother?" I said.

"Let's see, now," said Jim, talking over the television that remained on, a daytime drama with perfect teeth and concerned faces. "He was seventeen, I think. A real hippie-dippie, hair down to his ass, into the drugs and the causes."

"Bobby was a hippie?"

"Sure. Grapes. Something about grapes, I remember, and a Mexican feller he was all up in arms about. Times was tough around here, what with our mother gone and our father away and our father's sister trying to take care of us. She was a bitter old witch, less than useless, with a mouth on her." Jim raised his chin to the ceiling, raised his voice to a shout. "Did you hear that? Less than useless."

There was a bang from upstairs, as if a wall had been slammed in response.

"No one ever accused Bobby of being quiet," continued Jim calmly. "One day the two of them, they got into a fight, and things was said. That night he just took his guitar and left. This was like 1975 or so."

"It was 1978," said Fran.

"Something," said Jim, shooting his sister an impatient glare. "We got a couple cards, something from Albuquerque, but then nothing."

"You would expect that he'd keep in touch," said Fran. "Visit for Christmas or the anniversary, but no."

"We thought he was dead," said Jim.

"Why wouldn't he come back to say hello?" said Fran. "Tell us he's alive, at least? Daddy would have liked to hear from him."

"When did your father die?" I said.

"He ain't dead," said Jim with a snort. "He's upstairs." Jim raised his voice again. "Nothing but a useless bag of bones anymore."

An angry grunt came from above, and then another, more plaintive.

"Hold your horses," shouted out Fran. "We got a guest."

Another grunt, and then a bang.

"You want some tea, mister?" she said, smiling sweetly.

"That would be nice," I said. "Thank you."

"Bobby just disappeared off the face of the earth," said Fran, without making any effort to rise up and boil some water. "No letters, no calls. But that was always like him, so concerned for the world, without no care for his own family. Couldn't he at least a done something to let us know he was still alive?"

I shook my head in agreement, even as I wondered that he had stayed as long as he had.

However dark and forbidding the Pepper house was outside, the inside was worse. Greasy wallpaper, collapsing furniture, lights dim, shades drawn. Jim was puffy and pale, about fifty-five years old but already a physical wreck, wincing in his chair, fiddling with his cigarette. Wearing sweatpants, a flannel shirt, dingy socks, he lay stiffly on his recliner as if he had been screwed in place. When he died, forget a coffin, just set the chair on full recline and lower them both into the hole. His sister leaned back on the couch, her bare, venous legs crossed so that one pilling slipper was hoisted in the air, bouncing back and forth to some twitchy rhythm. And everything smelled of smoke and cabbage, of mice urine and green beans, of the browning scent of decay and death.

"What is it exactly you're doing here again?" said Jim.

"Your brother is involved in a very delicate mission," I said, somewhat truthfully.

"What kind of mission?" said Jim.

"Oh, I can't disclose anything more. You both understand, I'm sure, what with the current climate."

"He's into something, isn't he?" said Jim. "Bobby was always into something. He liked to play with knives, poking and prodding. Does he still do that?"

"In his way, yes," I said. "But in order to allow him to handle the sensitive matters which I've already described, we are required to do a customary background check. It's quite usual. I just wanted to come to his boyhood home and find out if his childhood was normal."

"Normal?" said Jim. "What the hell's that?"

"You know, baseball, birthday parties, that sort of thing."

"There's never been nothing normal here," said Jim.

"But Bobby did like baseball, Jim, you remember," said Fran. "In the afternoons he used to sit in the backyard listening to the games on his transistor radio. He said, with the play-by-play and the cheers from the ballpark, it was like sitting in the bleachers."

"I ain't cared much for baseball," said Jim, "not since they kicked away the pennant that year."

"Don Young," I said, nodding.

"Don't get me started on Don Young," he said.

"What we're especially curious about," I said, "is whether or not there were any childhood traumas that might affect Bobby's performance on his mission."

Jim squinted at me for a moment before looking at his sister, who gazed back with tenderness.

Just then another grunt from upstairs.

"You feed him yet?" said Jim softly.

"He spit up most of the oatmeal," said Fran, "but enough stayed in to keep him till supper."

"What are you giving him for supper?"

"Oatmeal."

Jim laughed. He didn't look so much like his brother, but they had the same laugh. Fran, on the other hand, was Dr. Bob in drag.

"You said you wanted some tea?" Fran said to me.

"That's right, ma'am," I said.

"How do you take it?"

"Just a little sugar."

"That's nice," she said, remaining solidly on the couch, her raised slipper still twitching back and forth. "I like a little sugar, too."

"So you want to know about childhood traumas?" said Jim, taking out another cigarette, lighting it with his Bic. "Well, let me tell you, mister. You come to the right place."

It was the father, Virgil, at the center of the story. With his own father and mother and spinster sister, he had come up to Chitown from the hills of Appalachia as part of a famous migration north from coal country. There was a whole community in a part of the city called Uptown, mostly poor and struggling, but Virgil didn't come up north to live the same life he had fled. He found a good job, ventured out into the city, met a pretty Polish girl on the elevated line one afternoon. Her name was Magda, Maggie, and she fell for his tricky accent and rawboned good looks. When he popped the question a month later, she was only too thrilled to get out of the stifling atmosphere of her father's house with her seven brothers. Virgil's factory job paid enough so that eventually he could buy a house south of Uptown, just a few blocks from the baseball field, and he and Maggie started a family. First Jim, then Franny, and finally, almost as an afterthought, little Bobby.

"It's like the American Dream made real," I said.

"Maybe," said Fran, "except Daddy never was the dreamy type."

He was a hard man, he worked hard, drank hard, was hard on his family. If the children misbehaved, they got the back of his hand. If they spilled their milk, they got the back of his hand. If they breathed wrong after he had been drinking, they got worse than that. And he was harder on Maggie.

"It wasn't really his fault," said Fran. "He was just born in a different place. He didn't know no better. He used to tell us that was the way his daddy treated his mommy, too."

"But his mommy lived till she was eighty-nine," said Jim.

"True," said Fran. "Got to give her that."

It might have been easier if Maggie just took it, like Jim and Franny took it, but that wasn't her way. She had a temper, too, and she liked her drink, too, and as she got older, she turned more than sturdy. Sometimes they would go at it for hours, the fight ranging over the whole of the house, pots flying, vases, invective screamed in two languages. In the middle of it all, the children would hide in the darkness of a closet, peeking out the crack of a barely opened door, helpless as their world imploded in on itself. Jim had learned that if he got in the middle, he would get hell, not just from his father but from his mother also, so he kept out of it, and he kept the others out of it, too.

"It wasn't so hard keeping Franny in that closet," said Jim, "but Bobby, he was a troublemaker."

Little Bobby was more like his mother. He wouldn't simply accept getting hit by his father as would Jim and Franny. Instead he would reflexively strike back whenever his father smacked him, and even though his blows had no real effect, they only made his father hit back harder. He was the youngest, but of the three children, he was the most battered. And when the three were hiding in the closet, with the cage match going on throughout the house, he was the one who wanted to run out and defend his mama.

"The little fool was small for his age," said Jim. "An eight-year-old midget thinking he was going to stop them two. You know, when they got like that, they weren't aware of nothing but each other. They would of killed him, he tried to get in the middle. So I held him back best I could. Sometimes he struggled so much I had to tie a rope around him to keep him from running out and doing something stupid."

"How long did this go on?" I said.

"Until it stopped," said Jim.

A groan from upstairs, a banging on the wall.

"Shut up, you," yelled Franny. "I'll change your pan when I'm good and ready. Didn't I tell you we got a guest?"

"He still can be demanding," said Jim cheerfully. "But he ain't forty no more."

"Wouldn't matter much even if he was," said Fran, "the way half his body don't work and he lost his speech."

"Thank God for that," said Jim.

"Why did it stop, the fighting?" I said.

"He killed her, that's why," said Jim. "Stuck a knife in her neck."

"Sad," said Fran. "It was Bobby who found her."

Came home from fishing. To find his mother. Dead. On the floor. He was ten. This was just after the Cubs collapse in '69, the last baseball season any of them cared about. He rode his bike home from the lake, pulled up to the porch, left it there as he pushed open the front door. And saw the blood.

"Daddy got out after twenty years," said Fran. "Parole, on account of his condition. We was still here, still in the house. He moved right back in, thought it would be the same. But it wasn't."

A groan, a bang, and then a thump as if a sack of sand had landed on the floor.

"Sometimes he thrashes about so much," said Fran, "he falls right out of his bed."

"You going to go haul him back up?" said Jim.

"I will eventually. But first I'd like some tea. Would you like some tea, mister?"

"No, thank you," I said. "I'm really not thirsty, and I do have to be going."

"You got what you needed?" said Jim.

"Pretty much," I said, standing.

"Our Bobby passed the test?"

"Oh, yes."

A groan from upstairs, a single fist pounding the floor.

"You'll tell Bobby to visit, won't you?" said Fran.

"Sure I will."

"We'd love to see him. And I'm certain he'd like to see his daddy. It's been a long time since he's seen his daddy."

"You tell him we think of Mama every day," said Jim.

"I will."

When I got to the doorway, I stopped and turned around.

There they sat, brother and sister, watching the actors pretend to have lives on the television. I thought of their mother,
dead and bloody on the floor, and I flashed on a photograph
that had become all too familiar, a photograph of another
woman lying dead and bloody on another floor.

"Can I ask one more question?" I said.

"Go ahead," said Jim.

"Where was she when Bobby found her?"

"Upstairs," said Jim, "in the bedroom."

"On the same floor where Daddy's lying now," said Fran.

"There was blood all over everything," said Jim. "The
couch, the rug"—he indicated toward the parlor couch and
rug as if they were the very same—"and then there was a
trail of blood up the stairs. Bobby followed it up, followed it
into the bedroom. That's where he found her, sprawled dead
on the floor. The knife was in her neck up to the hilt."

"It wasn't no mystery who done it," said Fran. "They
found blood on his clothes and his shoes. Daddy even admitted it. Almost like he was proud of it. She had it coming,
he said."

"But still, what Bobby found in her hand was pretty damn
interesting," said Jim. "Like she had climbed up them stairs
just to fetch it."

"A photograph of her husband," I said.

"That's right," said Jim. "How'd you know that?"

Just then there was a groan from upstairs and a strange
swishy sound.

"Oh, my," said Fran. "Daddy wet the floor again."

59

In the interstices of the American landscape, we have built our cathedrals. Upon useless wedges of real estate they sprawl, upon the trash-strewn boundaries between one exurb and the next, upon land fit neither for human nor for beast. Squat, rectangular, with cinder-block wall and steel door, the monuments of our age have risen to embrace the very stuff of the American dream. And what is that exactly? Why, stuff itself.

E-Zee Self Store sat just off a highway near the town of Exton, Pennsylvania. I stood before the red corrugated-steel door of unit 27 as the hiss and vroom of highway traffic rose and fell behind me. Weeds to the left of me, desolation to the right, here I was, officially nowhere. Exton. But behind the red steel door, I believed, might be a message from a murderer.

It was on the plane home from Chicago, with the stink of the Pepper household still in my nose and the certainty in my gut that Dr. Bob had killed Leesa Dubé, that I realized the message might exist. I was sitting back in the seat, arms folded, trying to figure it all out, the whole horrid story, when I felt this jabbing in my chest. I ignored it as best I could as I struggled to come up with an explanation for why Dr. Bob would murder Leesa Dubé. Had she betrayed him in some way? Had she rejected him somehow? Had she failed to floss?

None of it made much sense, except that he had done it. It wasn't François, it wasn't Velma, it wasn't the mythical Clem, it was Bob. The similarities were too similar to be a coincidence, two murders that somehow involved Bobby Pepper, the picture of the murderous husband gripped in the murdered wife's hand. It was his way to deflect blame, almost a reflexive action. How do you frame the husband for a murder you committed? Reach into your past, pull out a trick. Yes, Dr. Bob had killed Leesa Dubé, but why?

Blaming the murder on the dead woman's dentist, without a motive, wasn't going to help François, it was just going to make us all look desperate and pathetic. I needed a why. I sat back in my seat and crossed my arms and let the question rattle about my brain. Even as I felt something jab into my chest, I ignored the pain and tried to think it through.

There was an image I couldn't shake, hadn't been able to shake since I left that sad Chicago house, and I let it overwhelm me for a moment. The three Pepper children hiding in the closet as the fights between father and mother rage. And little Bobby Pepper, peering out the crack of the door, wanting to step in and stop it, wanting to save his mother from the brutality of his father, wanting to do something. Yet stopped, stopped by his older brother, tied up to stop him, helpless within the closet, watching his life tear itself apart. *I like to help,* he often said, and suddenly you could understand why. But what did that have to do with Leesa? Was she stopping him somehow? Was she threatening to tell about something? What? Why had he killed her? It again all came down to the why. Sitting in that plane, I thought it through, and I came up with, and I came up with . . .

Nothing. Not a damn thing. Except for the point that was jabbing into my chest. I uncrossed my arms, reached into my jacket pocket, pulled out a thin piece of metal.

The key that had been sent to me as if I had lost it, except

it had never been mine. I held it in my hand and turned it
over and again. The bronze caught a shard of sunlight from
the window and threw it straight into my eye. I had mentioned to Whit that I was worried about Beth, and next thing
you know Dr. Bob was telling me all about Beth's painful
past. I had mentioned to Whit that I was wondering about
François's missing stuff, and lo and behold, as soon as my
Clem defense crumbles, like a message from on high comes
a key. I held it out in front of me and looked at it closely, as
if maybe it had an answer for everything. And surprise, surprise, maybe it did.

E-ZEE.

With that key in my hand, I leaned down and unlocked
the padlock of E-Zee Self Store unit 27. I pulled up the door
and stepped inside and switched on the light and closed the
door behind me and found myself smack in the middle of a
puzzle.

The space was about the size of a two-car garage, with
cinder-block walls and a cement floor. Stuff was massed in
dusty piles, all kinds of stuff, cartons, couches, a brass
lamp with its pleated shade askew, spotted mattresses
along with their box springs, pots and pans, strange masks,
big copper bowls, a computer, a headboard, leaning towers
of books, a large ceramic Dalmatian. But it wasn't the
amount of the junk in the piles that surprised—indeed, the
amount was just what I expected, create a space for junk in
America and America will fill it—but it was the way the
piles were formed. Everything was jammed up against the
walls, stacked high in teetering heaps that reached almost
to the ceiling, so that in the middle of the unit was created
a clearing.

And in that clearing, like a tableau of the ordinary in an
avant-garde museum, was situated a La-Z-Boy chair and a
six-pack of beer and a television and a VCR, the latter two

connected to an extension cord that ran up to the light fixture in the ceiling.

Now, this was most peculiar. All of the contents of the
unit, including the chair and television and beer, were covered in the same layer of dust, so nothing had been moved
or touched in years. But why was this chair here, this television and VCR, the beer? Someone with a key had pushed
everything to the walls and set up the television for viewing.
Who? When? For whose viewing? And for viewing what?
And even if it was clearly set up this way long before I first
met François Dubé, why did I feel as if it had all been set up
for me?

See what I mean about the puzzle?

In the cleared area were two boxes, one cardboard and
one wooden. I opened the cardboard box first and immediately recoiled. I knew now what Mrs. Cullen meant when
she talked about toys. Harnesses and cuffs, rings and elec-
trical devices with long dangling cords, a hodgepodge of
bizarrely shaped phallic toys made of metal, plastic, sili-
cone, leather, all well worn, all enough to make me sick to
my stomach. So tell me this, is there anything more disgusting than someone else's used sexual devices?

I quickly closed it up and kicked it aside, then I stooped
down to the wooden box, which sat beside the VCR. I lifted
off the top. A box of videotapes, about twenty in all. I went
through them, one by one. *Fantasia*? *Sillyville*? *Magical
Musical Mansion*? Yes, tapes to keep the daughter happy
when she came for a visit. Park her in front of the telly, press
play, watch her pupils dilate.

But there were other videos, with less childlike names.
*Sodomania 36. Aim to Please. Sluts with Nuts 5. Succubus.
Oh My Gush 7.* And the ever-popular *Bad Mama Jama*. Nice.
Let's just hope he never intended to show his daughter *Snow
White* and by accident slipped in *Nubian Nurse Orgy* instead.

And then there were a series of videocassettes without preprinted labels or covers, cassettes with French words scrawled across white labels, some of the labels badly stained with spots of something that looked like coffee. At least I hoped it was coffee. Yuck. Home movies of birthday parties and the like or something a little less innocent, though no less staged? I remembered the inventory found in the apartment at the time of François's arrest, the video camera with tripod and lights but no videos. Now here they were, waiting for me.

I turned on the television, powered up the VCR, slipped in one of the self-labeled tapes. While I was waiting to see what was what, I sat down in the chair, pulled a beer from out of the cardboard six-pack holder, blew away the dust, twisted off the cap, took a whiff.

Skunk city. Ugh.

I twisted the cap back on, replaced it, leaned back in the La-Z-Boy, rested my shoes on the conveniently risen footrest.

Static, then the swelling music and HBO logo indicating the showing of a feature presentation, then a blank screen for a moment, before a fixed shot of a bedroom appeared on the screen. I had never seen the bedroom before, but I recognized it right off, what with the same brass lamp with pleated shade, the same headboard, the same ceramic Dalmatian that stood in the piles pushed to the walls. François's bedroom. No clap from the clapper, no shout of "Quiet on the set and . . . action," but it wasn't needed, was it? First there's nothing but the bedroom, then an entrance from stage left.

Gad.

Beth was waiting for me at the bar of Chaucer's, a bottle of Bud in front of her.

I had called her from the seat of the La-Z-Boy and asked her to meet me here, and now I slipped in beside her and ordered another beer for her and a Sea Breeze for me.

When the bartender spotted me, he gave me a look. "No trouble tonight, right?"

"No trouble," I said.

"It was bad enough cleaning up the blood from the last time you were here. Who was that creep anyway?"

"My dentist."

"Really? Is he any good? Because I've been having this trouble with my . . ."

As the bartender described his dental issues, pulling down his lower lip to show a jumble of stained Chiclets, Beth stared at me as if I had grown a second head.

"Have you ever noticed the teeth in this city?" I said after the bartender, mercifully, had cut off his demonstration and left to get our drinks. "It's like we're living in England."

"How was your trip?" she said.

"Instructive."

"Anything I should know?"

"Just that our client didn't do it."

"I already knew that," she said, and then she realized what I might have said. "You found proof in Chicago?"

"I found a strange coincidence that might be seen as proof," I said, "if I can figure out one more thing."

"What?"

"Why would my dentist murder Leesa Dubé?"

I told her about my trip to the Peppers', about what I had discovered, about the coincidence of the photograph clutched in the dead woman's hand. Beth gave me a hug when I was finished, like I had discovered a cure for cancer.

In the midst of her celebrations, the bartender brought our drinks. I lifted my glass. "Cheers," I said.

We clinked, we drank, I drank fast. I felt suddenly better and gestured for another. Anything to get the sight of that video screen out of my head.

Beth suddenly grew pensive. "Is the coincidence enough?" she said.

"No, but it's a start. We still have to figure out the why. But there's something else I wanted to talk to you about. Whitney Robinson dropped in to see me the other day and he said something that troubled me."

"I know Whit's your friend, Victor, but I don't trust him. He's a little too tweedy, don't you think?"

"Never trust a man in tweeds, is that it?"

"Yes, actually. A hard-and-fast rule that has held me in good stead over the years. And bow ties trouble me, too."

"What about George Will?"

"Proves the point on both counts. But there's something else about Whit, at least as it relates to François. He seems— how do I put this?—a little too interested."

She might have been right, but just then I didn't care. "During Whit's visit," I barreled on, "he told me something intriguing about François that I thought I ought to pass along."

"I'm not sure I want to hear it."

"He said that François, for all his charming surface, is hollow inside."

"He doesn't know him."

"Maybe not. But he said there existed some physical evidence to prove his point. Our client lied about his stuff. It wasn't all gone. It was in a storage locker. And this afternoon I found it."

"Oh, I bet you did."

"Beth, you need to listen—"

"No, I don't, Victor. I don't need to listen to anything that Whitney Robinson has to say about François. Or you either, for that matter. You said you wouldn't give me a lecture."

"Maybe I care for you too much to stay quiet."

"Well, try, Victor. Tell me, how's your friend Carol?"

"She's fine," I said.

"I love the enthusiasm in your voice whenever you mention her name."

"She's beautiful, well dressed, well mannered, and she doesn't have cats. In short, she's everything I've ever wanted in a woman."

"But still, something's not right."

"We're not talking about my love life now."

"Maybe we should. You think you have the right to lecture me, you with your never-ending line of women, whom you complain about even as you sleep with them, women like your Carol. I might be confused, but at least I feel something. You should try it sometime."

"And what is it exactly that you're feeling?"

She took a swig of her beer, thought about it a bit. "Do you know that fizzy sensation you get when you first fall in love, like your brain is floating in champagne?"

"Yeah."

"Well, it's not like that. It's not romantic. It's something different, deeper in a way. It's as if the reason I went to law school was to someday help François."

"Beth."

"As if everything in my life has been leading me to him. I don't understand it, and I'm not going to act on it now, because I'm a lawyer and he's our client and he needs us in a different way, but I'm not going to stop feeling it. And, Victor, there's nothing you can do about it."

"You sure about that?" I reached down into my briefcase, pulled out one of the videocassettes with French scrawled across the stained label, slid it across the bar until it was in front of her.

She looked down at it for a moment, then shook her head. "I don't want it," she said.

"You know what I discovered today? I discovered that you can learn a lot about a man from the pornography he creates. And I'm talking about more than the size of his cock. I'm talking about the cruelty, the pent-up violence, the way the world exists solely to satisfy his depraved needs."

"Go to hell."

"You ought to take a gander. This one has quite the cast."

"People change. He's not the same person he was before. He's been in prison now for three years. He hasn't seen his daughter in three years. That does something to a man. It has to."

"One viewing."

She shoved it back at me. "Put it away, Victor. Burn it if you want. I don't need it."

"Later you might," I said.

"Remember years ago, right after your cross-examination of Councilman Moore in the Concannon case, when you told me it was never going to happen between us?"

"I remember."

"That was your choice."

"I know."

"So from now on, butt out."

"This has worked out quite nicely, don't you think?" I said. "A pleasant drink with a friend."

She drained her beer, slapped the bottle on the bar, dropped off her stool. "You'll cover these," she said, waving her finger at the empty bottles.

I raised my glass in assent.

"Thanks," she said. "Don't worry about me, Victor. Worry about figuring out why your dentist killed Leesa Dubé so we can get François out of jail."

"That's what I'm not getting paid anymore to do."

She stood beside me for a moment and then reached over and tapped the tape. "This doesn't change anything for you, does it? You're not going to suddenly take a dive at the trial to protect me, are you?"

I took a long swallow. It was tempting, letting François rot, yes it was. But I had few enough lodestars to cling to in my life, and my obligation to my clients was about the only one I could trust utterly.

"No," I said. "Once you have me on your side I'm like a leech. I might suck out all the blood I can, sure, but I'm hell to get rid of."

"Good," she said. "You may be an asshole, Victor, but you're a hell of a lawyer."

Then she leaned down and kissed me on my head before leaving the bar. I didn't turn to watch her go. Instead I snatched down the rest of my drink and ordered another.

I was just bringing the newly filled glass to my lips when I felt a tap on my shoulder. I swiveled around. Beth was standing there, her head tilted to the side.

"Just out of curiosity . . ."

I laughed, she joined in, and for a moment it almost felt all right between us.

When she left for good, I tried to think it through again. I was failing to make some obvious step. That night with Bob in this very bar seemed to hold an answer for me. What had he said after all the violence and the blood? *Whom did you help today?* Yes, right, as if I were the hapless, selfish failure, all of which I admit to, and he was the saint. And then something else. *Accidents happen, Victor, remember that. Sometimes even the best of intentions go awry.* That's right. And he said something similar earlier, when I was in the chair. *Most murders are accidents of blind happenstance,* had said Dr. Bob. *Another absurd event in an absurd world.* But even Camus knew that the absurdity of the universe could only explain so much. Even if the murder itself was an accident, why was Dr. Bob in Leesa Dubé's apartment on the night of the murder? What was their connection, other than doctor-patient? What was going on? Why?

In frustration I tapped the black plastic of the videotape with my fingertips. Then I stopped the tapping and looked at the vile thing in front of me. I lifted it up and examined it closely. The black plastic, the French scrawled on the white label, the stains that spotted the paper. The spots. The stains.

And suddenly, strangely, the thing grew hot in my hands.

61

Defense attorneys like weakness. We are always on the prowl for some small flaw we can relentlessly attack, a crack to pound and pry until the whole facade of personality crumbles into dust. That's why we're such fun at parties. But Detective Torricelli, lunkhead though he might be, was a surprisingly uninviting target. Not that there weren't flaws. The man was as ugly as a pig's foot and had the surly manner of the guy who cleans your sewers. But though he might not have been a stellar detective in the street, he had learned to play one on the stand.

Dalton had called Torricelli to go through his entire work on the case as a review for the jury. But he wasn't only there for backup, he was also there to add a little kicker at the end, because it was Torricelli who had performed the initial interrogation of François Dubé.

"Did you inform the defendant of his constitutional rights?" said Mia Dalton.

"Sure I did," replied Torricelli from the stand. "And he signed a form that said his rights had been read to him and that he had understood them."

"I'd like to show you People's Exhibit Forty-eight. Do you recognize that exhibit, Detective?"

"Yeah, that's the form that the defendant signed while he was with me."

"I move People's Exhibit Forty-eight into evidence."

"Any objection, Mr. Carl?" said the judge.

"Only to the detective's sport coat," I said, "not to the form."

"You don't like plaid?" said the judge.

"I haven't seen a plaid that blue, Your Honor, since my prom tux."

Torricelli turned his baleful glare upon me as the jury laughed. I was hoping they'd laugh long enough to miss the rest of his testimony. No such luck.

The statement François gave to Torricelli was very similar to the story François gave me. He had worked late the night before. He was exhausted the night of the murder. He had left the restaurant early and gone home alone to get some sleep. It was a no-alibi alibi, it couldn't be directly disputed, but because there was no corroboration, it didn't do much good either. If you believed François, you thought he was asleep in his bed at the time of the murder; if you thought him a lying, murderous son of a dog, then he had no alibi. Torricelli shook his noggin enough during his recitation of the statement to let the jury know exactly on which side of that line he stood.

"Did the defendant say anything to you about the pending divorce from his wife during his interrogation?" said Dalton.

"He told me it wasn't going smoothly," said Torricelli.

"Did he mention that he had been accused of physical abuse?"

"No, he did not."

"Did he mention anything about his daughter?"

"He said that she was what they had been fighting over, more than the money. He said that his wife was seeking full custody and intended to move away. And then he said something I thought a little strange, considering the circumstances."

"Objection," I said.

"No editorializing, Detective," said the judge. "Just answer the questions."

"What did the defendant, François Dubé, say, Detective?"

"He said, and I wrote this down exactly, because it seemed of interest. He said"—and then the detective recited in monotone—"'I could never let her take my daughter away, don't you see? She is my life, she is everything to me. Take my daughter and you might as well kill me dead.' And then he looked at me and said, 'And I know that Leesa felt the same way.'"

"Did you ask him what he meant by that?"

"I did, yes. He simply shrugged and looked away. That was the end of the interview."

"What do you mean, that was the end? You had no more questions?"

"No, ma'am. I had more questions. But after that he refused to give me any more answers. He said he wanted a lawyer. Mr. Robinson was hired to represent him," said Torricelli, nodding at Whitney Robinson in his customary seat in the front row behind our table. "After Mr. Robinson came on board, there were no more interviews."

"Thank you, Detective," said Dalton, heading back to her seat. "I pass the witness."

"I didn't know he was being graded," I said, to some titters, as I rose, pulled my jacket straight, buttoned it over my yellow tie.

I stood at the podium for a moment, thought about what I was going to do, what I was getting myself into. Torricelli stared at me, at first with wariness and then with a slight smile as he saw my hesitation and mistook it for fear of his undoubted gifts on the stand. But it wasn't Torricelli I was afraid of just then.

I felt a cold wind flit across the back of my neck. I spun

around. A reporter, out for a smoke, had slipped back inside, letting in a draft. He started at my sudden movement, as if he had been caught at something. My gaze slipped over to Whitney Robinson, who stared at me with his forehead creased in concern, as if somehow he could read my exact dilemma.

"Mr. Carl," said the judge.

I turned around again. "Yes, sir."

"Do you have questions for this witness?"

I thought about it for a moment more, slipped my tongue into the gap that still existed in my teeth, pressed its tip into the hole in my gum. I felt a clip of pain just then, and somehow that decided it. I pounded the podium lightly.

"Oh, yes," I said.

CHAPTER

62 "**Detective Torricelli,**" I began, "you were the lead investigator on the Leesa Dubé murder, isn't that right?"

"I took the lead on this case, yeah," he said from the stand. "It was my ups when the call came in."

"And as part of your investigation, you spoke to Mrs. Dubé's friends and family, isn't that right?"

"When we are investigating a murder, we try to learn as much about the victim as we can."

"How did you find the names of all these people you interviewed?"

"We spoke to the victim's family, and they gave us names of friends. The friends gave us more names. That's how it's done."

"You didn't use a little black book?"

"During our initial and subsequent searches of the victim's apartment, we couldn't locate an address book or a PDA. Without that, we were forced to build a chain of contacts from our interviews."

"Was that unusual, not finding an address book or a PDA?"

"Not really, though in this case it was a little surprising. Mrs. Dubé seemed to be a very organized woman."

"Could the address book have been stolen during the time of the murder?"

"There was no other evidence of a robbery. It's unlikely that a robber would leave the jewels and cash and yet take the address book."

"Unless the murderer's name was in the book and he wanted to remain nameless. Now, Detective, without the address book, were you able to talk to Leesa Dubé's doctors?"

"We found some names and made some calls, sure, but such inquiries are often not effective, and these calls were similarly not helpful. There is the matter of doctor-patient confidentiality, which often makes getting information difficult, and the prior doctor visits can happen months, sometimes years, before the crime. In specific cases, where the medical status of the victim becomes more relevant, we have ways to get more specific help."

"Was this one of those cases?"

"No. The report of the medical examiner gave us no indication of a medical problem. We did find the name of the victim's gynecologist, and we asked if she had noticed anything unusual going on with the victim in the year or so before her murder. The answer she gave, without violating doctor-patient privilege, was no."

"What other doctors did you call?"

"The pediatrician for her daughter. Mrs. Cullen, the victim's mother, had the pediatrician's name. Again, there was nothing noted by the doctor which might have had an impact on the investigation."

"None of the abuse invented by Mr. Gullicksen for the divorce pleadings?"

"Objection to the term invented," said Mia Dalton.

"I'll rephrase. Did the child's doctor see any signs of abuse?"

"There was nothing noted by the pediatrician, no."

I turned, smiled at François like an uncle who had just received comforting news. These are the things you resort to in a murder case. "Did you contact any other doctors in the course of your investigation, Detective?"

"Not that I recall."

"What about the victim's psychiatrist?"

"Objection," said Dalton. "Assumes a fact not in evidence."

"Sustained."

"Were you aware, Detective, if the deceased was seeing a psychiatrist?"

"No."

"A dermatologist?"

"No."

"A chiropractor?"

"No."

"A dentist?"

"No."

"You weren't aware whether or not the victim had a dentist?"

"I assume she did, but it wasn't of much interest to us. There was no question as to identity, for which dental records might have been of use. There was no damage to the victim's teeth in the attack. The M.E.'s report noted that the victim's teeth were in excellent shape. There was no reason to talk to her dentist."

"Except that Leesa Dubé's dentist might have been one of the names in the missing book."

"Is that a question, Counselor?" said Torricelli.

"Not really, but this is: There was quite a lot of Leesa Dubé's blood spilled on the floor at the time of her murder, isn't that correct?"

"Yeah. So?"

"Is it possible to determine if all of the blood that bled out of the deceased was accounted for on the floor, or if some was missing?"

"No."

"So some might have been taken, collected for some purpose by the killer, isn't that right?"

"Technically, yes."

"Only technically?"

"Well, if such was the case, we would expect to see some indication of the collection process. Everything leaves a mark."

"Let me show you this photograph of the crime scene, People's Exhibit Ten, which shows the apartment floor covered in blood. I want you to look at the bottom-left corner of the photograph. Do you see a pattern there, Detective?"

"Not really."

"You don't see a swirl in the blood?"

"I don't know, maybe."

"Maybe a swirl, is that it? Maybe a swirl caused by a small towel, used to wipe up some blood, for some later purpose?"

"I can't tell from this photograph."

"Maybe to be stored in a plastic bag, to be used later to wipe some of the blood off on a shirt or on the sole of a boot?"

"Am I supposed to answer that?"

"Where was the photograph in Mrs. Dubé's hand taken from?"

"I don't know."

"Your theory is that she was shot in the neck and in her death throes grabbed the photograph of her husband to show it was he who killed her, isn't that right?"

"I'm just testifying as to what I found."

"The woman was mortally wounded in the neck, was bleeding badly, and you believe she grabbed hold of a photograph. My question is, examining the blood at the crime scene as you did, the position of her body, the layout of the room, could you tell us from where she took the photograph?"

"Not precisely."

"Isn't it just as likely that the photograph was put into her hand?"

"She was gripping it pretty tightly."

"But right after her death, her muscles would have gone slack, that's what the coroner testified to. Isn't it possible that the photograph was put into her lifeless hand and then the fingers pressed over it to frame the husband?"

"It seems far-fetched."

"And then the blood was taken, as that swirl shows, to be placed in the husband's apartment."

"You're going off into the ozone there, Counselor."

"And maybe this was all done by someone familiar with the victim's personal situation, as well as familiar with the properties and consistencies of blood. Maybe by someone like a dentist?"

"What is it with you and dentists?" said Torricelli.

"It's called dentophobia. Fear of men with hairy forearms wielding drills and picks in your mouth. I cheerfully admit to my own case of it. And based on your smile, you might have a touch of it yourself. Tell us, Detective, do you ever talk to the dentist while he's cleaning your teeth?"

"Maybe."

"Ever tell him how goes the family as he's digging away into your gums?"

"Mostly I just scream."

"So, Detective, let me ask you again. Do you have any idea of the name of Leesa Dubé's dentist?"

"No."

"Don't you think you ought to find out?"

"Our investigation is complete."

"Obviously not."

Just then I heard a rustle from behind me, something I'd been expecting for a while.

Whitney Robinson III was standing up, trying to slide past the other spectators on his bench as he made his way to the exit. The expression on his face when he saw me catch him in his egress was horrifying, as if my few questions about blood and dentists had somehow rent the entire fabric of his life. Then, finally, he was out into the aisle, turning to the door, stalking out of the courtroom. At his first opportunity, he would make a call.

And I knew damn well whom he would be calling.

Torricelli waylaid us before Beth and I could leave the courtroom. The jury had been dismissed, the judge was off the bench, François had been taken away by the bailiff, and I wanted nothing more than to get the hell out of there, too, but Torricelli had other ideas. He was not a man easily gotten around, especially when he stood in the aisle between you and the door.

"Detective," I said. "I hope I wasn't out of line with that crack about the sport coat."

"My wife says worse."

"And yet you persist."

"Old habits. Nice bit of vaudeville today."

"I do my best."

"You want to give me the handle of the dentist?"

"Not yet."

He snorted. "Figures. I thought I'd seen it all from you, Carl, but then you go and blame the murder of that woman on a noble professional."

"I tried to pick a suspect the jury would despise even more than a lawyer."

"Pretty low, even for you."

"You think that was low," I said, "hold on to your hat."

"I was expecting you to mug me about planting the evidence I found. I was geared for a grilling."

"Sorry to disappoint you."

"I know what my reputation is. I'm too fat to be smart, I'm too surly to be truthful, I'm a lifelong cop so I must be on the wrong side of the line."

"You don't have to convince me."

"That's right, I don't. But no matter how slipshod you run your business, I give a damn about mine. I don't like to get things wrong. It alters the balance of things, you understand?"

"You talking karma, Detective?"

"Call it what you want. But I go out of my way not to slap the right beef on the wrong tuna."

"Why am I suddenly hungry for surf and turf?"

"You have the wrong man this time, Detective," said Beth.

"I don't believe we do," said Torricelli. "But if you think so, tell me the skinny I need to get it straight. Give me a name."

"That would spoil the surprise."

Another snort. "Dalton told me to go out and earn my paycheck. I'll have the name by morning."

"You want to know something?" I said after Torricelli had headed out the door and we were left alone in the courtroom. "I might have underestimated that man."

"Is that possible?" said Beth.

"It's scary to think so, isn't it?"

"Do you think it was too soon to bring up the whole dentist thing?"

"The jury liked it."

"But, Victor, Torricelli will probably discover your dentist's name. And if he wasn't in town that day, or he has an alibi, or we can't figure out a motive, all of which is quite possible, then it's game over."

"I know."

"So?"

"We don't have much choice, do we? After the Sonenshein debacle, we have to take a risk. And this is it."

"But—"

"Beth, look at me."

She turned to face me, her pretty, worried eyes focused on my own.

"Do you trust me?" I said.

Her gaze rose to the ceiling. "Why does that question always scare me?"

"Look at me."

She did.

"I don't like him," I said, "and I don't like how you feel about him, and I wish we never took the damn case. But a woman is dead, a little girl has lost her mother, her father is my client and he's fighting for his life. All of that I take as seriously as anything in this world. So whatever happens in this courtroom the next few days, you have to trust me that I'm trying to do the right thing."

"Is it going to be wild?"

"Yes."

"But you really do believe François, don't you?"

"I don't believe a word out of his pouty little French mouth, but he didn't kill his wife."

"Okay. Good. Then let's do it. Let's you and I nail that dentist to the wall."

"If he doesn't nail us first."

It started with a phone call in the middle of the night.

No one calls in the middle of the night to invite you to a party or set up a dinner date, not unless her wireless plan is seriously deficient. No, a phone call in the middle of the night is the heart-stopping herald of tragedy, of calamity, of nightmare become real. So when my phone rang in the middle of the night, yanking me out of a fitful sleep, between the time I realized what was going on and the time I was able to pick up the handset, the horrifying possibilities tortured me. My apartment building was on fire. My father had died. My mother was calling from Arizona to say hello.

"What is it?" I said, on the verge of panic.

No response.

"Hello. Who is there?"

No response.

"Mom?"

Nothing.

After a few more moments of silence, I hung up. Wrong number, I figured, but even so, it wasn't easy to get back to sleep. The call had jacked my heart rate, the scenarios of calamity were still flitting through my brain. Where my sleep had been fitful before, it became impossible now. I tossed and turned and stared at the shaft of streetlight that painted my ceiling.

It felt as if I had just fallen back into slumber when the phone rang once more. I jerked awake, noticed that it was light out, grabbed at the handset.

"What?" I said.

"Dude, about the car."

"What car?"

"The red Caddie ragtop. Is that price firm?"

"What price?"

"It says here twelve hundred. I was wondering if there's any wiggle room."

"No," I said. "No wiggle room, and no car. You must have the wrong number."

"You sure?"

"Quite." I hung up and looked at my clock. It was seven in the morning, I had barely slept, and I was due in court at ten that day. I tried to shake my brain awake when the phone rang again.

"What?"

"Dude, about the car."

"Didn't we have this conversation already? What number are you trying to reach?"

He told me.

"That's my number, but there's no car," I said. "Really there isn't. It must be a misprint. Please, don't call again."

I was getting out of the shower, toweling off, when the damn thing rang again. Still dripping, I bolted into the bedroom and picked it up.

"Yo," came a slow, deep voice. "I'm calling about the convertible."

I left a new message on my answering machine—"There is no car"—and slipped on my suit and tie. I stopped in the diner for a coffee, large, before heading on. I had just reached Twenty-first Street, and the caffeine had just started opening my eyes, when my cell phone rang.

"Victor Carl here," I said.

"Hello, yes. Thank you for answering." It was a woman's voice, very proper. "I understand you have a litter of Labradoodles you are trying to sell."

Sometimes, I admit, I can be a little dense, but suddenly I knew who had rung my phone in the middle of the night.

My office, when I arrived, was a madhouse. There were a score of applicants for the open paralegal position, with a base salary of $45,000, plus benefits, plus bonuses, all of which would have made it a pretty sweet gig, except that there was no open paralegal position at our office, and $45,000, plus benefits, plus bonuses, was more than Beth and I were pulling down as lawyers. The group of job seekers was standing in front of my secretary, Ellie, pointing their fingers at the large advertisement in the classifieds.

"I don't care what it says printed there," she was telling them, "there is no job. It's a mistake. Go home."

When she saw me, she raised her hands in exasperation.

I slipped to the front of the crowd, leaned over, said softly, "Sorry about this. Any messages?"

"You have seven offers for the Jimmy Page–autographed guitar."

"Jimmy Page? From Led Zeppelin?"

"I didn't know you had a Jimmy Page–autographed guitar."

"Neither did I." I looked around at the crowd. "I'll be in my office. I need to make a call. Just thank them for coming and tell them all that the job's been filled. It will be easier."

"What's going on, Mr. Carl?"

"Someone's having a little fun with me."

"With all this, I'm going to need a raise," she said.

"Sorry," I said. "After we pay the paralegal, there won't be enough money left for paper clips, let alone a raise."

I closed the door to my office, sat down at my desk, drained the coffee, watched the lights of my office lines twinkling. So Bob was playing games, calling me in the middle of the night, placing false advertisements in the newspaper to tie up all my phones. He'd have to do better than that, I figured, but still, it was annoying, and I didn't have any doubt as to how he'd found out about my questions to Torricelli the day before. When a line cleared, I quickly snatched up the phone and dialed.

Whitney Robinson III laughed when I told him what had gone on that morning.

"You didn't think he'd be happy, did you?" said Whit.

"No," I said.

"Or that he wouldn't find out."

"No, not that either."

"So there you go, my boy. What else could you have expected? It was a mistake to bring him into it. You are endangering his work."

"Dentistry?"

"More like a ministry."

"Whit, I don't have a choice here."

"We all have choices."

"And you chose to act as a spy."

He chuckled at my accusation. "I like to think I'm performing a service to both of you. Think of me as a conduit. I'm very fond of you, Victor, you know that. And he is a remarkable man, truly an extraordinary man."

"He's a dentist."

"Oh, my boy, he is more than that. He is a sterling example to the rest of us. We all wander through the world spotting poor souls in trouble, and what we do is cluck our tongues in sympathy as we go on our way. But he stops, takes their hands in his, does something to help. I can't tell you the number of people he's helped in so many ways, large and small. And you are one of them, Victor, don't forget. He's helped you plenty already, and those young children you are so interested in. And he can help you more."

"Sounds like a bribe."

"If it does, then you still don't understand. There is nothing venal here. He sees a woman in trouble, becomes involved in her life, and acts toward her as if she were his responsibility. You aren't yet a father, Victor, but let me tell you from personal experience, a father will stop at nothing to save his child. Nothing. Remember that. But the extraordinary thing about this man is that he feels that same way toward total strangers. He sees a way he can help and he strikes out after it."

"Like some sort of Lone Ranger riding the range, trying to lend a hand."

"And succeeding, my boy. Succeeding."

"Like he succeeded with Lisa Dubé?"

"He did what he could."

"He killed her, Whit."

"Oh, no, he did not. You're being silly now. His whole life is about helping others. He's not a murderer. He's a lifesaver, if anything."

"He killed her."

"Stop it, now. You are upset, you haven't thought this through. Listen to me, my boy. I know you don't trust me as you used to. I understand that. Divided loyalties. But if ever you did trust what I said, then trust this: He didn't kill that woman."

"Who did?"

"It doesn't matter anymore."

"Even if I believed you, Whit, I still have an obligation to my client."

"Save your client without bringing him into it."

"But the only way I can see to save my client is to use him to at least create reasonable doubt."

"Think about it, Victor. Examine all your options. You are endangering more than you know. Not just him, but his mission, too, and that he can't allow. He can be a wonderful friend, as he has shown, but he can also be a most dangerous foe."

"I don't know about that. A few false ads, a few late-night calls. I can handle it."

"Oh, Victor, my boy. Don't underestimate him. Our mutual friend is just clearing his throat."

64

I liked the image, Mia Dalton swaying on a hammock in a soft breeze, eyes closed, an umbrella drink in her hand and a rumba playing softly on the radio.

"The prosecution rests," she said.

"I could use a little rest myself," I mumbled to Beth.

"Did you say something, Mr. Carl?" said the judge.

Why did I feel like I was back in fifth grade? "No, sir."

"Do you have witnesses to present?"

"Yes, we do."

"Let's have the jury take a break while we go over some legal matters, and then you can begin your case."

"All rise," shouted the bailiff. We all rose. The key for a defense attorney as jurors file out of the courtroom is to maintain your air of benign confidence until the door closes behind them. Then all bets are off, and you can sink back into your seat with a despondent expression of utter defeat.

Beth made the usual motions to dismiss, raised the usual arguments, accepted stoically the usual denials.

"Anything else I can reject?" said the judge.

"My credit card was refused last week," said Beth, "so I suppose that's about it."

"Fine," said the judge. "Twenty minutes, folks," and we rose once again when he made his way off the bench.

"That went well," said Beth.

"About as well as could be expected," I said as I stood at the table. "Dalton's case was pretty thorough."

"Are we ready for our defense?"

"I think so," I said, but just as I said it, Beth's eyes grew large and I felt a lurking presence behind me. I winced even before I turned around.

Torricelli.

"His name's Pfeffer," said Torricelli. "Robert Pfeffer."

"How'd you find him?"

"One of the victim's friends told us. A Mrs. Winterhurst. Turns out she was the one who recommended him to Leesa in the first place. So after we got the name, we swung by his office. Nice little guy. And he seems to know what he's doing. I had a dental question that he answered quite thoroughly."

"You make an appointment?"

"As a matter of fact. He seems quite competent, and I heard he has gentle hands. Of course, it turns out he also has an alibi for the night of the murder."

"Of course he does," I said. "You check it out?"

"It holds," he said. "He was with someone the entire night."

"Dr. Bob, that dog," I said, shaking my head. "Who would have figured? You mind telling me whom he was with?"

"Confidentiality prohibits it, but let's just say he had his hands full."

"Got you." Tilda. Oof.

"So that's that, right?" said Torricelli.

"I suppose."

"And we can forgo all the dental crap in this trial?"

"I don't think so."

"Carl, you know what you are? Vexing. You are one vexing son of a bitch."

"Thank you, Detective. Can I make one suggestion?"

"Go ahead."

"Before you sit in Dr. Pfeffer's chair, you might want to check out his diploma. There's a little smudge where his name is. Turns out he wasn't born a Pfeffer. Before you let him reach into your mouth, I suggest you find out why he changed his name."

I might beweep a bit too much my outcast state, but there are admitted joys in this job. Chief among them is cashing a retainer check. I also like cross-examining fools, reading deposition transcripts—that's a little sick, I know, but there it is—and instructing my secretary to hold all calls. I especially like the way people recoil when I tell them I'm a lawyer. Try it sometime at a party or on the street, tell someone you're a lawyer and watch as they dance away. It almost makes me want to sign up to work for the IRS. And it was a joy just then, let me tell you, when I told Detective Torricelli that his new dentist, Dr. Pfeffer, had doctored his diploma and changed his name for some unknown reason, and then watched as Torricelli's eyes boggled and he nervously rubbed his tongue across his teeth.

"Call your first witness, Mr. Carl," said the judge.

"Your Honor, the defense calls Arthur Gullicksen."

Arthur Gullicksen approached the stand wearing an expensive gray suit, black loafers with tassels, and a fine head of gray hair sleeked neatly back. In fact, *sleek* was exactly the word for him, his trim figure, his polished nails and sharp teeth, the way his face came to a razor's edge at the front. You might remember the name Gullicksen, he was Leesa Dubé's divorce attorney, whom we had tried to keep off the stand during the prosecution's case. Now he was our first witness. Funny how things change. To see Gullicksen in the flesh was to open once again the eternal debate of nature versus nurture. Are lawyers that look like Gullicksen attracted to matrimonial law, or is it the job itself that turns them into such repulsive specimens?

As Gullicksen sat on the witness stand, he pulled out his cuffs, smoothed his jacket sleeves, adjusted his tie so it sat neatly between the points of his collar. His yellow tie. The very same tie I now was wearing. Would the humiliation over my neckwear never cease?

"Thank you for coming back, Mr. Gullicksen. I have only a few questions. You testified before that you were Mrs. Dubé's divorce attorney, is that right?"

"That's correct," he said while examining his manicure.

"How was it going?"

"Excuse me?"

"The case. From the pleadings you put into evidence in your prior testimony, it is apparent that you and Mrs. Dubé were fighting for custody of the daughter, you were fighting for a lion's share of the matrimonial assets, including a piece of François Dubé's restaurant, and you were fighting for a substantial amount in child support and alimony."

"We were only seeking what she was entitled to."

"Fine, we're not going to dispute any of that here. But what I want to know, Mr. Gullicksen, is how was your case proceeding? Did it look like you were going to be successful on all those requests?"

"It is hard to say."

"Try, Mr. Gullicksen. Let's take the child-custody issue. You alleged physical abuse of Mrs. Dubé and Amber Dubé at the hands of the defendant. What kind of evidence did you have for that?"

"Leesa Dubé was prepared to testify."

"But you had no other witness, did you?"

"Leesa had told her friends of the abuse."

"That was hearsay, and so not admissible. And the pediatrician, as we've heard already from Detective Torricelli, saw no indications of abuse. Did you have any other witnesses or admissible evidence on the abuse issue?"

"Not at that point, but I was looking for others."

"Now, in his responsive pleadings, Mr. Dubé alleged that his wife was addicted to painkillers, often dumped her daughter at her mother's house while she went on unexplained trips out of town, and was in many ways an unfit mother, isn't that right?"

"Those were his allegations."

"Did he have witnesses to back up those allegations?"

"He claimed he did."

"You depose them?"

"Some of them, yes."

"How'd the depositions go?"

"There were avenues to discredit the testimony."

"I've been a lawyer long enough to interpret that. The testimony was pretty strong, wasn't it?"

"It had some strength to it, yes."

"Mr. Gullicksen, in your opinion was there a chance that Leesa would lose custody?"

"Objection as to relevance of the witness's opinion," said Mia Dalton.

"Mr. Carl? Is this whole line of questioning relevant?"

"Yes, Your Honor. I ask for some leeway here. I am not attempting to try the divorce case in this courtroom. But I do think it extremely relevant what Leesa Dubé's lawyer thought of the case and what Mrs. Dubé thought of her chances in turn. Her fear of losing her child is at the heart of our defense."

"Go ahead, then, but be careful."

"Thank you, Your Honor. Mr. Gullicksen, was there a chance that Leesa would lose custody?"

"Yes."

"A pretty good chance?"

"A more-than-negligible chance."

"And as per the ethical requirements of the Bar Association, you relayed that to your client?"

"I did."

"How did she take it?"

"I can't disclose anything she told me."

"Of course not, but you can tell us her state of mind. How did she take the very real possibility of losing custody of her daughter, Amber, to the defendant?"

"Not well."

"How about the money stuff? How was that looking?"

"There was going to be some alimony, absolutely. I was convinced we could get a significant amount of Mr. Dubé's income, but, unfortunately, that income was limited. Child support depended on the custody issue, so that, too, was in doubt. And our investigation showed that there was really no equity in the restaurant, due to the financial structure of the business. So there was a chance that Leesa might have ended up with very little."

"And you told her that, too?"

"Of course."

"How'd she take that?"

Gullicksen smoothed back his hair. "Divorce is a very difficult time for all the parties."

"She was upset?"

"You could say that."

"Distraught at the possibilities?"

"If you choose to be dramatic about it, yes."

"What would have helped, Mr. Gullicksen? How could she have improved the outlook of her case?"

"A divorce case is like every other type of trial. The quality of the lawyers is important, that's why I get paid, but by and large it depends on the evidence."

"So what she needed was more and better evidence, is that right?"

"Yes."

"And you told that to Mrs. Dubé?"

"Yes, I did."

"Did you tell her what kind of evidence might be most helpful?"

"I told her evidence that cast doubt on her husband's ability to care for the child would be most valuable."

"Evidence of drug use?"

"Absolutely."

"Evidence of multiple sex partners?"

"Yes, of course."

"Evidence of bizarre sexual perversions?"

He smiled and bared his teeth as if he were being offered a plump swimmer's leg. "Such evidence is always helpful in these cases."

"Did you suggest to Mrs. Dubé that she hire an investigator to see if such evidence existed?"

"I did, but she claimed she didn't have sufficient funds after paying my retainer."

"How much did you get up front, by the way?"

"Objection," said Dalton.

"What's the purpose of that question, Mr. Carl?" said the judge.

"Professional curiosity. I might be in the wrong branch of the business."

"Objection sustained."

"Thank you, Judge," I said. "And thank you, Mr. Gullicksen. I have no further questions."

65

I don't know why I awoke when I did. There was a stillness in the air, and maybe that was it. I lived in the city, and in the early summer I kept my bedroom window open to the breeze, so I was serenaded to sleep each evening by the rise and fall of traffic, the distant horns, the laughter of passersby on my street having a better life than was I. But when I awoke that night, there was only the quiet. Maybe I was like the London man who was startled out of his slumber when Big Ben failed to chime.

Or maybe I was waiting for him. If so, he didn't disappoint.

I was lying with my eyes open, letting the pieces of my consciousness fall together and adhere to one another, when the phone rang. My nerves reflexively jangled at the sound.

"Hello," I said quickly.

No answer, and suddenly I knew who it was.

"It's you, I suppose," I said, without any desperation this time. In fact, if anything, my voice was downright hearty.

I heard nothing but the slight rasp of a breath.

"I figured you'd call again," I said. "You don't have anything to say? That's okay. But please, don't hang up. I have a special message especially for you."

I waited a moment. The line stayed open.

"But before I relay the message"—was that a sigh I heard

from the other end of the line?—"I wanted to tell you that there's nothing personal in what I am doing. I like you, actually, against my better judgment maybe, but I do. And I sort of admire you, too. Those false classified ads were pretty funny. Annoying, yes, and you ruined my secretary's day, what with all the people showing up for the paralegal job, but still, it was a pretty good gag. And the worst of it was those damn Labradoodles. My cell phone never stopped ringing. I turned it off to escape the desperate yapping of the callers, and whenever I turned it back on, there were, like, twenty new messages, all asking about Labradoodles. I still don't know what the hell a Labradoodle is, it sounds like a kind of processed breakfast meat, but the demand, I can tell you, is insatiable.

"And I liked how you arranged to have those porno magazines scattered around my office with my name on the fake subscription labels. Cute. My secretary was not happy about that, first realizing what you had done and then searching high and low to see if she got them all. I'll have you know I've taken them home with me, and I have spent hours scouring the evidence and I am still puzzled. *Bottoms Up,* I can understand, *Jugs,* sure, but *Lesbian Grannies*? Really? No wonder I'm having trouble sleeping. I can barely wait to see what you have in store for me next.

"But it isn't the cleverness I most admire about you, or the wherewithal to inconvenience my life so. It's the sense of obligation you have, the sense of mission. You like to help, you always say, but it's more than that, isn't it? More like an obsession. And I think I understand where it came from. But you have to understand, I have my own obligations. And my main obligation, right now, is to my client. Frankly, I don't like François any more than I suppose you do, but still, he's my client. That means something, at least to me. I have to do what I can to help him, and from where I'm sitting, to do that I have bring you into it all.

"You still there?"

I listened. Just the raspy breath, but it was enough.

"It's sort of nice to be the one talking for a change, almost as if I have my hands in your mouth."

I laughed a little, but he didn't, not at all.

"I don't understand everything that happened the night Leesa Dubé died. Who did what to whom and where? It's all a muddle. But I know for sure that you were somehow involved. And I believe that I might be able to convince the jury of that, too. And if I do, there's a chance François could be acquitted. Whether that is a good thing or a bad thing is not for me to say. I tried once to play judge and jury, and it didn't work out too well. What I learned is that I don't know enough. To be frank, I barely know enough to get myself dressed in the morning, and Carol Kingsly will tell you I don't do a very good job at that. But all I can be certain about in this world is that I have this job to do and I'm going to do it, and no amount of harassing phone calls or false subscriptions to porno magazines can change that.

"I just wanted you to know. Nothing personal.

"Okay, I guess it's time for the message. I was in Chicago a few days ago, right by the ballpark. A little house about three blocks west of third base. That's right. Your house, your boyhood home. You're not the only one who can dig into the past. I had a nice little talk with Jim and Franny. Your brother and sister were so happy to hear about you. They hadn't heard from you in so long they thought you had died. There were almost tears when I told them how well you were doing. Almost. And believe it or not, your father was with them. Good news. He's out of jail. But I think he had a stroke, and frankly, I don't think he's being treated so well, not that he deserves much better. I thought you should know. But the message I have is from your brother and sister. They said your dad would like to see you, and they would like to see you, too. They want you to visit. They want you to come home."

I waited awhile for some sort of reaction, but there was nothing, just the rasp of breath. And then a click.

Good.

I hung up, laid my head on the cool of my pillow, felt my lids grow heavy. That worked out pretty well, I thought. Tonight it would be his turn to lose his sleep.

66

Tommy's High Ball, early afternoon on a day court was in recess. I stepped into the cool of the bar, waved at the barkeep with his shock of white hair. He nodded and gestured me over to the booth next to the door, where Horace T. Grant sat with another old man, a chessboard between them, the pieces scattered like weary soldiers across the black and white squares.

Horace looked up when I stepped on over, grimaced as if experiencing a shooting pain in his hip.

"You here for another whipping?" he said.

"No, sir," I said. "The scars of our last meeting haven't yet healed."

"I wouldn't think so." He turned his attention back to the board. "You going to move that knight, Simpson, or you going to stare at that miserable position of yours for the rest of this beautiful afternoon?"

"I got possibilities," said the man across from Horace.

"Maybe," said Horace, "but they're all bad."

"I got possibilities, I say," said Simpson, "all kinds of possibilities. And I don't need you sitting across from me and being so high and mighty. I've taken you down before."

"You did what?" said Horace, the tone of his voice rising with incredulity. "When?"

"That time, remember, with the pawn and the queen. A brilliant combination, if I do say so myself."

"I must have been too drunk to remember," said Horace, "and I haven't been that drunk since Wilson Goode dropped a bomb on my neighborhood and scared me sober."

"I didn't say it was recent."

"No, you didn't," said Horace. "Now, move before my bones turn to dust."

"Too late," I said.

Simpson laughed at that, covering his mouth with long, bony fingers. Horace just shook his head.

"What you want?" he said finally.

"I can't stay, I have a meeting upstairs." Horace raised his eyebrows with interest. "I just wanted to tell you that I'm working on setting up the match I told you about. I haven't heard yet."

"All right," he said.

"But I'm hopeful it will come soon."

"You know where I'll be."

"Yes, I do."

"That it?"

"Yes, it is."

"Good, then maybe you can leave us be. You hovering there all fat and goofy like a piñata makes it hard to concentrate on anything other than banging your head with a baseball bat, not that I need much concentration to beat this fool."

"Take this," said Simpson, moving his knight with a flourish.

"Don't mind if I do," said Horace, smacking down the horse with a bishop from the corner.

"Damn," said Simpson.

Isabel Chandler was upstairs in the apartment with Julia and Daniel Rose. The place was a jumble of cardboard boxes and black plastic garbage bags stuffed full.

"We're moving," said Julia, beaming. Daniel sat in her lap in shorts and a clean, long-sleeved T-shirt, his head pressed tightly into her neck. "Randy found us a place in Mayfair, like he had been trying to. It's closer to his job, and there's a room for Daniel. The school there is supposed to be really good."

"That's great," I said, wondering why Daniel was hiding from me.

"Julia has been showing up at most of her parenting classes," said Isabel, her file open on her lap. "I've told her that we expect her attendance to improve, and she promises it will. And Daniel's teeth are doing really well."

"Smile for me, Daniel," I said.

Daniel lifted his face from his mother's chest and, with sad eyes, bared his new teeth for just an instant, before burying his head back into his mother's neck.

"You're moving when, exactly?" said Isabel.

"Next week," said Julia. "The new apartment is already empty. Randy's been spending nights fixing it up for us, using paint the landlord supplied. Powder blue."

"Nice," I said.

"Why don't we set up an appointment with one of our pediatricians in the area," said Isabel, "so the doctor can get a jump start on monitoring Daniel's progress."

"Do we have to? Can't we get settled first?"

"I think we should set it up now. How's Daniel's health been?"

"He's been gaining weight," said Julia. "He's eating more. It must be his teeth. That doctor, Dr. Pfeffer, he did such a wonderful job."

"He's a helpful guy," I said. "Make sure you follow his instructions."

"We are. Randy is being especially attentive. Everything is going so well."

"I'm happy for you, Julia. I really am. Do you mind if I take Daniel for a walk down to the park while you finish up?"

"We're pretty much done, aren't we, Miss Chandler?"

"I think so."

"Why don't we all go?" said Julia. "Daniel could use some fresh air, and so could I."

"Grand," I said.

We made an odd group walking down the street toward the park. Isabel and myself in our suits, Julia in jeans and a T-shirt knotted at her side, Daniel holding tightly to her thigh. It seemed evident from the clothing and the group dynamic that Isabel and I were representatives of the state, there to monitor and judge the singular relationship between mother and son. Frankly, I didn't like the role. Who was in worse shape to judge the mother-son relationship than I? It had taken me years to get up the courage to reestablish a relationship with my own mother, and still, the possibility of her calling in the middle of the night left me gasping. And who was I to judge anyone's relationship with a child, when all I really knew about children was that they sometimes messed up my suits? But there I was, and it seemed that Julia had finally gotten serious about doing what was required to properly take care of her son. Was I deluding myself to think that maybe my mere presence on the scene, looking out for Daniel's interests, was having a positive effect? It almost made me feel . . . What was the word I was going for? I couldn't grab hold of the exact word, but all of it made me feel . . . something.

Damn, maybe this pro bono stuff didn't blow after all.

At the park the three adults sat on a bench and talked about Julia's plans for her son as Daniel wandered aimlessly around the equipment. At one point he started climbing on the jungle gym, bracing himself with his knees, reaching up to a higher bar with his left hand. And then he stopped and carefully climbed down again.

"I'm going to have a little talk with Daniel," I said.

He was standing by the seesaw, gripping the handle in front of one of the seats, pushing it up and down.

"How's it going, Daniel?"

"Okay," he said without looking at me.

"Are you excited about moving?"

"I don't know."

"You don't sound excited."

"I like it here."

"It will be nice there, too."

"What if she can't find us?"

"Who?"

"You know."

"Tanya?"

"How is she?"

"I don't know, I haven't found her yet, but I'm still looking, and I'm getting closer. I'm going to find her. And I'll know where you'll be, Daniel. I'll bring her to you."

He turned his head and stared at me. "No."

"What's wrong?"

"He doesn't like her."

"I know. I'll be careful. But what about you, Daniel? Does he like you?"

"I don't know."

He turned away from me again, ambled over to the slide, rubbed his left hand on the shiny metal. I looked over at Isabel and Julia on the bench. Isabel was on her cell phone, her file open on her lap. Julia was staring at Daniel with a troublesome worry on her face. She stood up and started walking toward us. I stepped over to Daniel and situated myself so that the boy was shielded from his mother.

"What happened to your arm?" I said.

He drew his right arm close to his body. "Nothing."

"Let me see it, Daniel. Please let me."

"Nothing."

I stooped down, gently took hold of his wrist, pulled his arm until it was straight out from his body. He winced.

"Did you hurt it playing?"

"No."

"Did you fall off something?"

"No."

"I'm going to roll up your sleeve, okay?"

"No."

"Yes, I am," I said, and then I did, and in that moment something shifted inside me.

"He burned it on my cigarette," said Julia, standing now right behind me as I continued to stare at Daniel's arm.

"I didn't know you smoked, Julia," I said, still stooping before Daniel, still holding his wrist, brushing the hair from his forehead so I didn't have to look anymore at the arm.

"Sometimes I do."

"I know Randy smokes."

"It was an accident."

"I don't understand you. I'm sorry, I've tried to understand, but I just don't. First you give away Tanya, and now this. It doesn't even matter that they are your children, I don't have any of my own, so I won't even try to figure out how that must feel. But it is enough for me that they are children and they needed someone, and what they had was you. They needed you to protect them, and you turned away."

"It was an accident, I tell you."

"There are three burns healed to varying degrees. This last one is an open sore. All three are just the size of a lit cigarette tip. This was not an accident."

"We're going home now," said Julia.

"No," I said. "No, you're not."

"Come on, Daniel," she said. She reached out for her son. Daniel looked at me and didn't move.

"What's wrong?" said Isabel, coming up to us now, still clutching her file, cell phone open in her other hand.

"Call the police," I told her. "We need a patrol car and a detective from the Special Victims Unit here right away. And we need to find some safe place for Daniel to stay."

67

I was late for my date with Carol Kingsly. What with the police and the paperwork, the arrest warrant sworn out for Randy Fleer. What with returning to Julia's apartment and packing up Daniel's clothes in a spare black garbage bag and driving him to Social Services, where Isabel worked the phones to find him a foster home. What with going along with Isabel as she drove Daniel to the house of a nice, smiling couple, parents of two older children, who had volunteered to take a foster child on an emergency basis and had already been interviewed and examined and prequalified. What with all that, I was late, yes, I was late. But I didn't think it was anything to cry about.

Obviously I was wrong. Because there was Carol Kingsly, at our table in a crowded little restaurant called Rembrandt's, a place not far from the great blackened hulk of Eastern State Penitentiary, with a half-drained glass of white wine in front of her, and she was crying.

"What's going on?" I said as I sat. "I'm not that late, am I?"

She just waved away my question and tried to compose herself. She wasn't doing a whole sobbing-out-loud thing, which would have been really uncomfortable. It was more a soft, contained cry, like her cat had died or something. Except Carol Kingsly didn't have cats.

"Carol?" I said. "Are you okay?"

She gained control, expertly wiped her eyes with her fingertips, leaving her mascara intact. "No," she said, shaking her head.

"What happened?"

"I received some really bad news. I'm not okay."

A bolt of terror slashed through me. She had some sort of disease, I could tell. She had cancer. I was sure of it. I had a vision of Carol Kingsly in her hospital bed, her limbs withered, her head shaved, looking up at me with sunken eyes. Gad. Looking up at me with the expectation that I would care for her. Me. Somehow now she was my responsibility? We had only been going out for a couple of weeks, I didn't even like her all that much, and still I was on the hook? What were the rules on that? And with whom could I lodge my appeal? I had the almost uncontrollable urge to excuse myself, to stand up, step outside, and run like the wind. When it's fight or flight, my first impulse is always to gallop the hell out of there. But this time I gripped the edge of the table, pressed myself back into my seat, tried to not show my terror.

"What is it?" I said. "Something serious?"

"Very."

"Tell me. What?"

"Remember I told you about my yoga instructor, Miranda? Who recommended I start going to Dr. Pfeffer?"

"Your yoga instructor?"

"She's very concerned about me. She said I looked out of sorts, and after class, she gave me a private reading. What she found was terrible."

"Your yoga instructor?"

"Yes. Victor, the quality of my chi has turned. The energies of the five elements are not interacting within me in a positive way. Everything's feeding upon itself. Water extinguishes fire, fire melts metal, metal cuts wood, wood controls earth, and earth absorbs water. Do you see?"

"No, I don't."

"My life is out of balance. Do you know feng shui?"

"All that mumbo jumbo about where to place the couch?"

"It's not mumbo jumbo, Victor, and it's about more than interior design, though the interior-design part of it is really lovely. But it's also about keeping a balance in every part of your life."

"And your life is out of balance?"

"So she says. I have to make a change, or the destructive energy is going to cause serious damage to all my chakras."

"Okay," I said. "That's okay, Carol. Stay calm. It's not a disaster. We'll make some changes. What is the problem? Is it your job?"

"No."

"Your apartment?"

She shook her head.

"Do you need a new car? An upgraded wardrobe?"

"Do you think I need an upgraded wardrobe?"

"Well, you always say there's not much a new pair of shoes can't cure."

"It's not my shoes, Victor."

"Then what is it?" I said, like a dope.

She sat and stared at me for a moment, and tears again began to fill her eyes.

"Oh," I said.

"Yeah," she said.

"Does this mean now? Right away? Can we at least have dinner?"

"I'm sorry, Victor. I'm so sorry. But I felt that things weren't exactly perfect with us, even from the start. And you must have, too. There was always this distance between us. I tried, I thought maybe time might help. But now Miranda tells me that I don't have so much time. I'm sorry."

"So am I," I said, and surprisingly, I was.

I had never given Carol a real chance, and that was a crime, because if I sensed anything about her, it was that she had a true and yearning heart. Maybe she was too pretty for me, too well dressed, too obvious in her attempts to find answers where there are no real questions. Or maybe she was too damn connected with Dr. Bob. But whatever it was, I had never really made the effort to see her clearly. She had seemed to me like a finished product, picking a man the way she picked a blouse, trying to find something that matched her sense of style, but I think I was wrong in that judgment. She was no different from the rest of us, searching for something solid to hold on to in this world. I don't know if I could have been that for her, or she for me, but I had blown any possibility of our finding out.

She downed the rest of her wine, wiped a tear from her cheek with a knuckle, gathered her things, clutched her bag to her chest as she stood. I stood, too. It seemed the polite thing to do.

"Good-bye, Victor," she said.

"Good luck with your . . . whatever."

"My chi."

"That's it."

"Thank you," she said before she started walking off.

"Carol." She stopped and turned. "I've got something I want you to have."

I reached up to my collar, loosened the knot of my yellow tie, untied it, held it out to her.

"Victor, that's yours."

"It's not really my color. Keep it as a memento. Or give it to your friend Nick. He could use a neckwear upgrade. Take it. Please."

She looked at me for a moment and then took the tie. She closed her eyes as she rubbed the silk against her cheek. Tears welled, and I wouldn't have been surprised had I heard the sweep of violins.

"We'll always have Strawbridge's," I said.

Damn, I thought as I watched her walk out of the restaurant and out of my life, she sure is pretty.

And then something caught my attention at the bar on the other side of the restaurant. It was an old man, tall and dapper, staring at me through the bar's entranceway.

Whit.

He stood there and stared until he was sure I had seen him, before following Carol out the door. I suppose he figured he didn't have to stay, that just his presence left enough of a message. This wasn't simply the inevitable ending of a tepid affair, though it was certainly all of that. This was also another shot across my bow. Dr. Bob, my dentist, had told his patient, Miranda, the yoga instructor, to instruct Carol Kingsly, my sort-of-fulfilling sexual relationship, to give me the boot. And Whit, my old friend Whit, had shown up just so I got the full impact of the message.

The D.D.S. giveth, the D.D.S. taketh away, blessed be the name of the D.D.S.

I sat back down at my table and was thinking it through, the breakup, the warning, the sacrifice of my tie, the increasing amount of pressure being brought to bear, when the waitress appeared at the table.

"There's only one of you now?" she said.

"Afraid so."

"So what will it be?"

I looked up at her. She was pretty cute actually, short orange hair, black lipstick, a stud in her nose. She looked like she might be fun. I know she was only a waitress, and men are helplessly attracted to waitresses, it is something in our jeans, but still, it was a pretty good sign. I guess it hadn't taken me too long to get over Carol.

"Let me have a hamburger," I said, "and burn it."

They have damn good hamburgers at Rembrandt's, and I suppose, after being pushed around once again by Dr. Bob, I was in the mood for charred red meat.

CHAPTER

68

    A professor in law school used to tell us that we, as lawyers, were like gods of creation in the courtroom. Nothing existed unless we chose to show its existence. We picked the evidence, we picked the witnesses, we framed the questions, we created the universe of the trial. The next day in court, I was one angry deity, ready to shift that universe on its very axis, and I felt, strangely, up to the task.

I was feeling more myself than I had for weeks. I was bursting with energy, my mood was brighter, I had a little bounce in my step. What was the cause of my newfound confidence? Let's put it this way: Popeye needs his spinach, Queeg needs his strawberries, Sauron needs his ring. And me, I suppose I need my red polyester tie. With my old friend rescued from the bottom of the sock drawer and back around my neck, I was ready to rumble. And my tag team partner that day was our criminalistics expert, Dr. Anton Grammatikos.

You want your expert witness to be tall and gray and well spoken, or maybe short and energetic and familiar to the jurors from the O. J. Simpson trial, or at least someone who doesn't look like he's ready to sell you a used car at a steep discount. Which is why Anton was available at a moment's notice and a pauper's price. But the thing about Anton Grammatikos, despite the underwhelming impression he made on the witness stand, was that he really knew his stuff.

"Your Honor," I said after I had exhaustively questioned Anton on his credentials, which, despite his checkered sport coat, unshaven face, and truck driver's manner, were quite impressive, "I move to qualify Dr. Grammatikos as an expert in the forensic sciences."

"Any objection, Ms. Dalton?" said the judge.

"Could I ask just a few questions on his qualifications, Judge?"

"Go ahead."

Mia Dalton winked at me as she stood up. "Dr. Grammatikos," she said, "I understand you have written a book on the forensic sciences, isn't that right?"

"Yeah, that's right," he said. "It's like one of those educational books, you know, like *Golf for Idiots* and *Piano for Dummies*."

"And your book is in one of those series, Doctor?"

"Nah. When I pitched them, they said they wanted someone a little more famous, like that Dr. Lee guy, who doesn't really know as much as he thinks, believe me. So instead I decided to start my own series. Well, you know, the idiot thing and the dummy thing had all been copyrighted, so I had to come up with something new, something fresh."

"So what is the title of your book, Dr. Grammatikos?"

"Forensic Science for Mental Midgets."

Dalton turned to the jury and watched as they laughed. I told myself they were laughing with my expert and not at my expert, although my expert wasn't laughing.

"How is it selling, Doctor?" said Dalton.

"Not so good."

"Any idea why?"

"I don't know. Maybe it's not quite the right title for Harvard."

"I wouldn't think so," said Dalton.

"But you should read it, Counselor," said Anton, leaning forward, nodding his head sagely. "It's right up your alley."

Mia Dalton's jaw tightened as the jury laughed again.

"No objection," said Dalton.

"Dr. Grammatikos is hereby qualified as an expert in the forensic sciences," said the judge. "Go ahead, Mr. Carl."

"I want to ask you now, Doctor, about the E-Zee Self Store just outside Exton, Pennsylvania. Are you aware of that facility?"

"Now I am, sure."

"How did you become aware of it?"

"You gave me a call, asked me to examine one of the units there, number twenty-seven."

"Did you ever learn who had rented that unit?"

"Yeah, I did. I examined the records at the self-store office."

"And whose unit was it, Dr. Grammatikos?"

"It turned out to be rented by the defendant sitting over there, François Dubé. He rented it out about the time he and his late wife separated, but before the murder. According to the books, he paid for five years of storage in advance."

Every head in the courtroom swiveled to stare at François, who looked up at me with a quizzical expression. I gave him a look that said it was going to get worse before it got better.

Slowly, carefully, I took Anton into the storage locker, let him describe the strange scene, with the lounge chair, the television and VCR, the box of videos, the six-pack of beer. He had taken photographs of the locker, and after a long bit of legal wrangling, I was able to introduce those into evidence. He testified, based on the amount of dust, the state of insects trapped beneath the recliner, the self-store records, that the locker had been set up in this weird way at least two years before he examined it but after the date François Dubé was first arrested.

"Now, Doctor, it's important to know if this was indeed set up after François was in jail, because he has not been out since his arrest. Are you sure about your analysis?"

Anton shrugged. "I been doing this for a while, Counselor. I even wrote that book. Besides, I had something a little more concrete as to date."

"What was that?"

"The beer bottles had dates printed on them based on the day and date they were brewed. That batch was brewed two months after the defendant's arrest."

"Thank you, Doctor," I said. "Now, you mentioned a box of videos, is that right?"

"Sure, there was a box. You can see it in a couple of the pictures."

"What kind of videos were in the box?"

"It was a rather eclectic selection. There were two types of commercial videos. There were some kids' videos, about five or six, and then a number of commercial pornographic tapes. You want me to give you the titles?"

"Sure, go ahead."

"Aim to Please, Succubus, Oh My Gush 7—"

"Is this necessary, Mr. Carl?" said the judge.

"Not really, sir, I just get a kick out of the titles."

"Then that's enough."

"Fine. Now, Doctor, were there any noncommercial videos?"

"Yes. There was the defendant's wedding video, they made a beautiful couple, and one family video, with shots of the defendant and his wife and his very young daughter. And then there were three homemade videos of, how should I put it, a more prurient nature."

"Sex videos?"

"There you go."

"Who was in them?"

"The defendant and a number of other persons I couldn't identify. Along with some objects and masks that were also in the storage locker."

"I want to show you some videocassettes," I said as I brought three cassettes, each in its own plastic bag, to the witness. "Do you recognize these?"

"These are the sex videos I was talking about. I recognize the labels with the spots, and I put a tape on each of them with my initials."

"Now, after you took the photographs and examined the videos, did you examine the storage unit for fingerprints?"

"That's what you told me to do."

"Did you find any?"

"Sure. The place was thick with prints."

"Even after all those years?"

"A place like that, a storage locker with little air circulation, almost zero foot traffic, and a layer of dust over everything, is a perfect place for the maintenance of prints. There's no limit to how long they could stay in such an environment."

"Were you able to match up any of the prints you found?"

"Sure I was. Some of the prints, I am sorry to say, were yours. You got to be more careful, Victor. In fact, I found two of your prints on the one opened bottle of beer."

"Sorry about that."

"I also found prints on certain of the stored objects that matched the defendant and the victim. This was not unexpected, since some of the stuff in the locker apparently came directly from the apartment they shared."

"Were there any prints that you were not able to identify?"

"Absolutely. There were a number of prints that I couldn't account for. This was to be expected also, especially since the guy in the self-store office had records that movers were used to transfer the stuff from the defendant's apartment to the unit."

"Were you able to match up any of those unidentified prints?"

"One."

"Go ahead."

"You provided me police records that showed certain unidentified prints found at the scene of Mrs. Dubé's murder. One of the prints found on the light switch at the crime scene matched up with a print found in the storage unit. It appears to be a right index finger."

"How confident are you in the match?"

"Very confident. I found twelve matching ridge characteristics in the two prints. I'd like more, but I found no dissimilarities, so it looks pretty solid. I also found the same print on one of the homemade porno videos."

"Any idea who belongs to the print?"

"None."

"But based on your testimony, some unidentified person was in the locker, held the video at some point, and was also at the crime scene."

"That's right."

"The murderer, perhaps?"

"Objection," said Dalton.

"Sustained," said the judge. "This is not argument, Counselor."

"I am so sorry, Judge," I said, staring at the jury, who could tell I was not sorry at all. A few of the jurors had dazed expressions on their faces, as if nothing was getting through one way or the other, but some were looking at Anton with creases of concentration spreading across their foreheads. They saw the possibilities, and they would tell the others. This case all along had begged for another suspect. I had in-

tended to use Sonenshein to create one for me, until that
blew up in my face. Now I was using a fingerprint to do it.
Whose fingerprint? Who else's? Dr. Bob, come on down.

"Now, back to the videos," I said. "I notice that these labels are spotted and stained."

"That's correct."

"Were you able to identify the stains on these labels?"

"Sure."

"What were they?"

"Blood," said Anton Grammatikos. "Human blood."

I let the murmur in the courtroom rise and swell and re-
cede again, like an ocean wave, before I continued.

"Whose blood was on the label?" I said.

"I took a small sample from each of the labels and came
up with a DNA signature. Then I matched that signature
with the police forensic reports for this case. I've concluded
that the blood on these labels is the blood of Leesa Dubé."

I looked at the jury. Puzzled expressions all around. Mia
Dalton had the same puzzled expression. She seemed to
want to jump up and object, but she couldn't quite find
something to object to. It was fun to watch her search and
fail.

"Could you make any conclusion, Dr. Grammatikos, as to
whether these tapes, found in the locker, were at the crime
scene at the time of the murder?"

"After analyzing the photographs of the pattern of blood
on the floor and the walls of the crime scene, and then comparing the blood patterns on the labels, the best I can say is
that it is quite possible that the videos were at the apartment
at the time of the murder."

"Your Honor," I said, "I'd ask that these videos be placed
into evidence, and then I ask that we be permitted to play
these videos, in their entirety, to the jury."

I said it calmly, matter-of-factly, I didn't put any undue

emphasis on the words, so it was rather interesting the reaction my simple statement received. As I expected, François jumped up in protest, shouting *"Non, mon Dieu, non,"* which I think is French for "My lawyer is screwing me up the ass." Beth jumped up and stared at me as if I were an idiot. There was quite the commotion all through the courtroom, tittering from the jury and spectators alike. Only Mia Dalton surprised me by not joining the melee. She sat calmly, deep in thought, as the judge cut through the commotion with his gavel and his high-pitched voice and said, none too kindly:

"In my chambers, now."

CHAPTER

69

"I won't let this happen, Mr. Carl," said Judge Armstrong. "You will not turn my courtroom into a pornographic emporium."

"Without the magazines or the twenty-five-cent peep-show booths," I said, "it would hardly qualify as an emporium, Judge."

"What possible purpose could be served by playing those tapes?"

"That's a good question, Your Honor," said Beth. "I'm curious myself."

"Those videos," I said, "not just their existence but the images captured on the magnetic tapes, are central to our defense. They are the reason that Leesa Dubé is dead, they are the reason my client is on trial for her killing."

"Go ahead, Mr. Carl," said the judge. "Explain how playing those tapes is crucial to proving your theory of the case, and you better dazzle."

"It's not enough for the jury simply to know that these tapes exist. They have to see them, Judge, they have to feel the revulsion that I felt when I first saw them and that the killer felt, too. The person who killed Leesa Dubé was trying to help her in her divorce case. Mr. Gullicksen had told Leesa she was in danger of losing her child. He testified that evidence such as these tapes would have helped her cause.

She told someone of her problem, and this someone simply tried to help. First he broke into the defendant's storage locker to find the tapes and then broke into Leesa's apartment to give them to her. He thought he was giving her back her daughter. But something went wrong. Leesa must have awoken, must have been frightened by the stranger in her apartment. She grabbed her gun, confronted the burglar. A struggle in the darkness ensued, ending with the gun firing and a bullet piercing Leesa Dubé's neck from close range. It was an accident, it was against all the intruder's intentions, but accidents happen, and Leesa Dubé still was dead. After it was over, while she lay dead on the floor, blood all over the room, the killer took a photograph of the defendant and put it into her hand to frame my client. And then broke into my client's apartment to plant the blood and the gun."

"That's your theory?" said the judge.

"That's it."

"That's about the most ridiculous thing I've ever heard."

"But it's more than just a theory," I said. "It's what actually happened."

"And why would the killer frame your client?"

"To protect himself," I said, "and also to protect the daughter. When you see the tapes, you'll understand. Some of the actors are quite possibly underage. They provide not only the motive for the killer's being in the apartment but also for the frame-up after the killing."

"It all seems far-fetched, Mr. Carl. I don't know how you're going to prove it up or get a jury to buy it."

"We have a plan," I said.

"I suppose you do. I'll have to preview these tapes before I decide, of course, but my inclination is that they have no business being played in my courtroom. Ms. Dalton, you have been unusually quiet in this debate. What is your position?"

"I have no objection, Judge."

"Excuse me?"

"If these tapes are as Mr. Carl describes, and I'm willing to believe they are, pending my own review, then I have no objection to their being played. As a matter of fact, they only serve to strengthen the Commonwealth's case."

"How so, Ms. Dalton?" said the judge.

"Dr. Grammatikos testified that the tapes were in the victim's apartment at the time of her death. We'll accept that opinion. These tapes were surely something the victim intended to use in the divorce proceedings. If the defendant was aware that his wife had found the tapes, he would have immediately gone to retrieve them. He would never let his wife use them against him in the custody fight. So he went to find the tapes, fought with his wife, killed her, took the tapes, and put them in his private storage locker, still covered with blood. The tapes strengthen our case immeasurably."

Just then I felt a sharp pain in my shin. I looked down. Beth had kicked me, she had kicked me hard, but she needn't have bothered. I understood exactly what was happening, and all of it was bad. The judge was exactly right. As I explained my new theory of the case, it sounded far-fetched, even to me. And I knew Dr. Bob. How would it sound to the jury? Not so good, I realized. And Dalton was exactly right, too. The tapes did help her case, they provided a specific motive driving François Dubé to have killed his wife. I thought I was being clever, but as always when I thought I was being clever, I was too clever by half.

"If Mr. Carl doesn't put the tapes into evidence and play them for the jury," said Mia Dalton, "I will."

"All right," said the judge, shaking his head, not just at the argument but also at the state of the modern world. "Let me review the tapes in camera, and I'll decide. I'm not happy, but if both sides want these tapes played, then I suppose I'll go along."

On the way out of the judge's chambers, Beth said to me, "Do you have any idea what you are doing?"

, "I thought I did," I said, "but now I'm not so sure."

"Why doesn't that statement inspire me with confidence?" she said.

The next morning the courtroom was closed to the public and the press, though I noticed that a number of court clerks had wiled their way into the viewing. A cart with a television monitor and VCR stood in front of the witness stand. The first tape was inserted, the play button was pushed. There might as well have been popcorn.

All it needed was some cheesy organ music to accompany the embarrassment of moaning and groaning that came from the television's tinny speakers.

Having seen and heard it all before, I didn't have to look carefully at the videos again, thank goodness, so I spent my time calculating their effect on the courtroom inhabitants. The jury watched the dark, murky images on the screen with the general arc of emotions elicited by pornography in the uninitiated: first horror, then transfixion, then boredom. And then, as the tapes ground forward, it was horror again. I caught them taking quick glances at François, all trying very hard to hide their disgust even as their pinched mouths betrayed them. The judge was also scanning the jurors' faces, to gauge their reactions and determine if he had made a mistake in allowing the tapes to be played. Dalton and Torricelli sat at the prosecution table with arms crossed, putting on a little show of shock and dismay. So alike were their postures and expressions, they must have practiced the pose together the afternoon before.

But the more interesting show, at least to me, was happening at the defense table. François was leaning back in his chair, watching raptly as he debased himself on the video screen. At first he mimed embarrassment and dismay, but that didn't last long. After the opening moments, when the courtroom had made it through the initial graphic images and settled into the viewing, François's expression changed. The false appearance of humiliation turned into a sly smirk. He couldn't help himself. Even though the afternoon before he had loudly castigated me in his smarmy Gallic accent, claiming that I was crucifying him on the cross of America's Puritanism, now, as his sexual fantasies played across the video screen, he couldn't help but gloat, and his expression betrayed his thoughts. *You're all jealous*, he was thinking, *you would all take my place in an instant had you the guts and imagination.*

And this was interesting. Sometimes he subtly mouthed a moan along with the video. It was as if he couldn't help himself, like a schoolgirl listening to her favorite song on the radio, singing to herself without even knowing she was moving her lips.

I'd had the son of a bitch pegged right from the first, didn't I?

But even more interesting, for me, was watching Beth's reaction. And even though I tried not to admit it to myself then, I can admit to myself now that, to me, she was the most crucial viewer in the courtroom. I might have been able to make my argument and relay my theory with just a basic description of the tapes by Anton Grammatikos, who would have relished describing their contents more fully to the jury. Yes, I thought that seeing it would make my theory more believable to the jury, and yes, the showing increased the impact of what I would tell them in my closing, and so yes, the showing of the tapes was more than justifiable as legal strategy. Still, I also knew that showing them in the courtroom could turn at least some of the jurors against my client. Yet I was willing to take that risk, because I hoped it would turn Beth against him at the same time.

But what I saw in her face was less than comforting. There was sadness in her eyes, and pity, too. There was embarrassment in her cheeks and tension in the way her fingers twisted as her hands lay folded together atop her yellow legal pad, all of which was as I had expected. And more than anything else, in the squint of her eye and the way her mouth curled down at the edges, there was disgust, which I had expected, too. But the disgust wasn't aimed at the videos, no, nor at our client sitting just to her left. Instead I saw her disgust plain only when she turned her head to stare at me.

And I deserved every bit of it.

CHAPTER 70

I worked late at the office that night. I had hoped Beth would come back after court so I could explain myself, but what was there to explain? She had told me her feelings toward François were not romantic, yet I hadn't believed her. She had refused to see the tape when I had offered it, so I jammed it down her throat in court, even if it meant risking our client's case. I was playing the paternal role, even though I wasn't her father. I would damn well help her whether she liked it or not.

He was rubbing off on me, was Dr. Bob. And as I realized it, a chill rode up my spine. Next thing you knew, I'd have this strange desire to drill Beth's molars.

As I waited vainly for Beth, I prepared for the rest of the trial. First I called Mrs. Winterhurst, who had recommended Dr. Bob to Leesa. I remembered that during one of my emergency visits, the doctor had to run out and treat Mrs. Winterhurst in the other room, she was the woman with the complaining manner and the fancy clothes. Yes, she told me over the phone, of course she would testify. She said it would be so exciting, and she had just the outfit. I was sure she did.

Then I was on the phone to Chicago, speaking first to Franny Pepper, then checking the flights from O'Hare, and then trying to find the right nurse to take care of Virgil Pepper while she flew in to testify. I doubted whether Jim could even get out of the lounge chair, better yet climb the stairs to take care of the brutal old man. So I called a couple nursing homes, I asked the administrators if any of their nurses moonlighted, I requested someone with strong hands and a nasty temper. You'd be surprised how many candidates I found.

When all was put in place, I typed up a subpoena for Dr. Bob. Tomorrow court was in recess, the judge had a conference, so I'd have time enough to pay a visit on my dentist, though hell if I'd ever let him touch my teeth again, despite the gap that still remained unfilled.

So it was late by the time I shut off the office lights, locked the office door, stepped out into the warm, humid night. I was exhausted and hungry, and the Phillies were in San Francisco for a late-starting game, which meant I'd fall asleep on the couch by the third inning, which sounded just right. On the way home, I bought a six-pack of beer and a take-out cheese steak—yes, we actually do eat those things—grabbed my mail from the entranceway of my building, and headed up the stairs to my apartment.

I opened the door, stepped inside, and stopped cold.

There was something familiar and terrifying in the air. And something else, too.

I had left the place a mess, yes, I admit it, but not this big a mess. Clothes were strewn, the cushions of the couch were slashed, the dining table was overturned, chairs were scattered, framed posters were flung about, my cheap china was shattered, and, worst of all, the television was crumpled on the floor, its screen smashed. No baseball for me. My first thought was whether my homeowner's insurance would cover it all, and my second thought was that I didn't have any homeowner's insurance. Before I could conjure a third thought, something grabbed me around the neck and killed my breath.

My back was pressed against a wall, wide and surprisingly soft. I was lifted into the air. My throat was constricted in on itself. I am using the passive tense here on purpose, because frankly, in the first few instants I was paralyzed into passivity by shock.

When I finally realized what was happening, I grappled helplessly at the thick arm around my throat. I slid my hands down the shaft of the arm, hoping I could find my attacker's hand and maybe bend a finger back to force him to let go of me. I felt a thin layer of latex over an unmovable mass of gristle and bone. So much for that.

The finger gambit having failed miserably, I took my next-best option, and as my lungs started screaming for oxygen, I flailed about like a madman. I might have looked like some bad Elvis impersonator dancing to "Jailhouse Rock" on a bed of hot coals during an epileptic fit, but it wasn't all about styling.

My heel hit a shin, my knuckle landed on something soft in the middle of a face, my elbow banged a rib. The monster holding me started hopping, loosened its grip, and let out a quick exhale along with a deep grunt.

Next thing I knew, I was facefirst on the floor. I started struggling to my feet, but something hard and heavy slammed into the small of my back and I was pancaked again onto the floor. The whole of my front was in pain, and it seemed to center on a sharp jut in my cheek.

I lifted my head away from the pain and something smacked it hard so that my nose smashed against the floor.

"This is your last chance, bucko," came a sharp Germanic whisper.

Something grabbed my ear and twisted it so hard I screamed.

The weight on my back disappeared. I again jerked my head up to escape the pain in the cheek. I tried to turn around to see who was there, and something inside my face slipped. I stopped moving, reached a hand gingerly to my cheek. It came away slick, as if my cheek was covered with a viscous oil. But it wasn't oil.

I lifted myself slowly to my hands and knees, sat down on the floor, reached again to my cheek. Something was sticking out, some shard. I took hold and pulled, and after an initial tug of resistance out it came, with a little slurp. A wedge of glass, slightly curved. I wasn't the first person skewered by television, but all in all I would have preferred it be on *60 Minutes*.

I thought about climbing to my feet, staggering down the steps, seeing if I could spot my attacker, but as the nausea started blossoming like a beastly flower in my gut, I thought better of it. And I already knew, didn't I?

Tilda. It rhymes with Brunhilda. The fat lady had sung.

71 **I entered Dr. Pfeffer's** waiting room with great wariness. I almost expected Tilda to be guarding the entrance with a baseball bat and a sign saying NO TWO-BIT LAWYERS ALLOWED, but everything was as it was before. The walls were still beige, pretty Deirdre behind the desk was still smiling. The same bright lights, same jaunty Muzak, same oppressive sense of cheer.

And I, apparently, was still more than welcome.

"Oh, Mr. Carl, we're so glad you've come for a visit. Is that a new tie? And what's that on your cheek? I hope it's nothing serious."

"Just a little too much television," I said, not mentioning the hours spent in the emergency room, the needles of Novocain, the fourteen stitches.

"I don't see you down as having an appointment today. Are we mistaken?"

"No, Deirdre, your book is right. I thought I'd drop in for a friendly little chat with the doctor. Is he in?"

"Dr. Pfeffer is seeing another patient right now, but he'll certainly be glad to see you. You're one of his favorites."

"Tell me about it."

"I think one of the examination rooms is available. If you want, Mr. Carl, you can wait for the doctor in Examination Room B. As a rule we don't let visitors in the operational part of the office, but I'm sure that's a rule we can bend for you."

I looked at the closed door that led to the hallway that led to the examination rooms and the examination chairs and the picks and the drills and the . . . I looked at the door and I shuddered.

"No, thank you," I said. "To tell you the truth, you couldn't drag me back there with a chain and a backhoe."

She smiled, unsure of what to say to that. "Then please take a seat. I'm sure the doctor will be out shortly."

I sat in a beige chair, picked up an old magazine, tried to calm my nerves. It was unsettling enough to be there in the first place—it was the waiting room to a dentist's office, after all—but it was doubly so since this dentist seemed to be after more than the usual amount of my blood. He wanted me to leave him out of the Dubé case, and the pressure was accelerating at an alarming rate. It had to stop, somehow, and that was the purpose of my visit. I could back off, sure, but as much as I had decided to do just that the night before, as the doctor was tying up the stitches in my cheek, one after the other after the other, I'm not built that way. I don't have much of a spine, it's a wonder I can stand up in the morning, but push me like he had been pushing me and whatever is actually there stiffens with doggedness. So I figured the way to get it over with was to get it over with, to drop the damn subpoena on his lap and end the suspense.

The door to the examination room opened. I jumped to my feet. Tilda stood in the doorway, bent stiffly to the right, her left eye swollen shut. She stared at me with malice in her one open eye before she moved to the side and Dr. Bob and his patient, a lovely young woman, brushed past her to the desk.

Dr. Bob stopped suddenly when he saw me, his face startled for a moment before recovering into a smile. "Victor, hello. What an unexpected pleasure."

He squinted at the bandage on my cheek, as if he were actually surprised to see it, then turned to take in Tilda's sorry condition.

"Have you two been seeing each other behind my back?" he said, his voice wide with amusement.

I waited as he spoke to his patient while writing a note in her file. She looked nervously at the bandage on my cheek before leaving. When the door closed, I stepped over to the reception desk with the subpoena in my hand.

"I have something for you, Doctor," I said, and then, quick as that, I served him. I felt suddenly lighter, as if, instead of a few official pages backed with blue cardboard, I had shed a couple barbells and a curling iron.

He looked the subpoena over briefly, shrugged. "I'll see if I'm available on that date," he said flatly. "But on to something far more worthwhile." His face abruptly brightened, his voice turned hearty and cheerful. "I seem to remember I wanted to give you a thorough cleaning before I installed your new bridge. Well, I have good news. A hole has opened in my schedule. I have time to do the cleaning right now. Come on back."

"I don't think so," I said.

"Oh, don't be worried, Victor, this is the easiest part of the process. Sometimes I have Tilda do the cleanings, she's very thorough, as you can imagine, but you I'll take care of myself."

I glanced over at the now open doorway, from where Tilda glared. "I'm not going back there."

"Of course you are," he said. "I noticed your gums are quite spongy. A cleaning will do wonders. Your smile will shine, I promise you."

"I'll find someone else to do it, and to fill the hole, too."

"But that's such a waste. Your bridge will be here any day. Oh, don't be such a chicken boy. Cluck, cluck, cluck. We're both professionals, are we not? If we are to trust anything in each other, we at least must trust that. Can I have Victor's file, please, Deirdre?"

I watched nervously as Deirdre left the front office to retrieve the file, leaving me alone with Dr. Bob and Tilda, who continued to stare with one eye swollen shut and the other eye evil.

"Come on back, now," said Dr. Bob as he headed past Tilda and through the door. "This won't take much time. And while I'm scraping the tartar and buffing the enamel, I have some interesting news to tell you. That address you were looking for? I found it."

"The key for me was Rex," said Dr. Bob as he slipped his metal pick between my tooth and gum and scraped and scraped and scraped.

"You remember Rex, of course, the rather large man with the unfortunate teeth stationed outside the Hotel Latimore. Loosen your lower lip, please. Don't fight me here, Victor. I need to get beneath the gum line. Whoever taught you to floss should be shot. Once I figured that Rex was my key to entering the Hotel Latimore, it was only a matter of finding a way to reach him. Lucky me, I have rarely seen a man more in need of a dentist."

Frankly, I was having a hard time concentrating on Dr. Bob's story. I was having a hard time not bolting out of the examination chair and running for my life. But Dr. Bob had an address and a story to tell, and I needed both, not to mention that my teeth could always use a good cleaning. So I decided to gut it out, even though my nerves were so hyperalert that every time the metal of his pick touched tooth or gum, I jumped. But, surprisingly, Dr. Bob was being uncharacteristically gentle. In fact, the most pain I was experiencing was the cramping in my hands as I gripped tight the arms of the chair.

"I must say he was a better patient than you, Victor. A higher tolerance for pain, or maybe he simply doesn't know me as well as you do. Well, Rex led me to a young woman named Claire, who worked in the office with the formidable Miss Elise, the Reverend Wilkerson's unlikely-looking paramour. I first tried with Miss Elise and got nowhere. Such a dried-up old spinster, immune to all my charms, imagine that. But Claire was something different. Very beautiful, idealistic, a truly spiritual young woman. I think Rex has a thing for her. Wouldn't it be nice if I could get those two together? I think I'll make that my next mission. Why don't you spit?"

Spit, splot, splat.

"It was Claire who finally located for me the address. A rather simple operation in the end. Only had to break a few minor laws. But it wasn't the address I found most interesting in the whole affair. It was Rex.

"We seem to be a little jumpy today. Why is that? You know, you're going to have to come in more frequently, Victor, if we are to avoid such problems in the future. Considering the state of your teeth and gums, you should come in every three months. As we always say at the A.D.A. convention, the two things you can never have too much of are anal sex and dental care.

"Okay, I think we're finished with the bottoms. Open wide, and we'll attack your uppers. What kind of toothbrush do you use? Maybe you need something new. It helps if you don't use the same brush two years running."

Pick, scrape, jab, scrape, pick pick pick.

"I'm always on the lookout for new talent, a pure soul with the heart, the muscle, the determination to make a difference in the world. I could point you to a woman in Baltimore, to a couple in Albuquerque, to a man in Mexico City who can move mountains. All of us, all we want to do is to help. And I think Rex might be another. He is very much a raw talent, he so lacks confidence in anything except his size, but his heart is pure, and he's much sharper than he lets on. I think he'll be a fine recruit, if I only have the time to properly work with him. But in this business one never knows when the time will run out.

"Oh, I'm sorry, I maybe dug a little too deep. From your reaction it looks like I hit a nerve. Hold on a second, and let me get some suction in there."

Awhoosh-ashiga-awhoosh-ashiga-ashiga-ashiga-awhoosh.

"My, you are quite the bleeder, aren't you?" said Dr. Bob as he went back to picking and scraping. "I once considered recruiting you, too, Victor. Your wisecracking, hard-bitten cover is so obviously a false front. I hoped inside wasn't simply the usual dark recess of selfish indifference. But no, I've discovered something remarkable in you, something I had hoped to work with. Look at the way you are helping that boy, Daniel, and your crusade on behalf of his half sister. And even your work for that horrid waste of humanity, Mr. Frog, the short-order chef. Yes, you have so much potential, and your empathy would have been your greatest strength. Yet, as so often happens, there is a flaw.

"Well, now, I think I'm finished." He stuck a mirror in my mouth, whipped it around. "Yes, all done. That wasn't too bad, was it?"

Shockingly, it wasn't. Except for the minor incident when he drew blood while he was talking obliquely about the subpoena, the whole cleaning was relatively pain-free, relative to kidney surgery, maybe, but still.

"Time to polish," he said cheerily.

As the round brush whirred across my teeth, Dr. Bob continued. "Some recruits never make the final leap. It all becomes too personal. I look at your face, and I look at Tilda's eye, and I feel that I have failed her. She is a wonderful woman, strong and fearless, and surprisingly agile in bed, but her impulses are all wrong. It is always better to be Loki than Thor. Now, hold on, I'm almost finished. Yes. Done. A fine job, if I do say so myself. Rinse carefully and spit."

Splish, splosh, splish, splosh—splat.

"Is that it?" I said hopefully.

"Not yet. Tilda," he called out. The wounded Valkyrie appeared. "Mr. Carl needs his fluoride. What flavor do you take, Victor? Chocolate, piña colada, or mint?"

I eyed the huge woman standing the doorway and my nerves crashed in on themselves. "Let's say we skip the fluoride," I said in a girlish squeal.

"Nonsense," said Dr. Bob. "Piña colada, why don't we say? That would go so well with those Sea Breezes you favor. Take over for me, Tilda, won't you? I'll be back in a flash."

He disappeared, leaving me at the mercy of his hygienist. I looked up at the fearsome, swollen face. "Open wide, *ja*," she said as she reached for my mouth. "And no crying this time, bucko."

I was still shaking from the ordeal of the fluoride when Dr. Bob stepped back into the room. His mask was on, his little blue cap, his hands were held out from his body like a surgeon, fingers up, palms toward his chest, rubber gloves already in place.

"I think that's it, Victor," he said. "We're done here. I have another patient waiting, so I can't dally and chat."

"Thank you," I said.

"Deirdre will let you know when the new bridge comes in so we can snap it on. That won't take but a moment. Then you and I, we'll be finished. I now have to request that you take back your silly subpoena. It is difficult for me to ask this of you, believe me, but I have no choice. And we did have a deal."

"Did you kill her?"

"No," he said with a flat sincerity. "She was a patient, just like you. I only wanted to help her."

"Either way, you need to testify."

"So you won't withdraw the subpoena?"

"There is nothing I can do."

"I'm sorry to hear that, but it is as I supposed."

"You said there was a flaw in me. What did you mean?"

"We're seeing it play out right now, aren't we? A certain stubborn belief in the status quo and the rote laws of men. A certain feigned helplessness in the face of a mutable world. You say there is nothing you can do? I say there is nothing you can't achieve, as long as you are willing to pay the price. I suppose I'll see you at least once more to install the bridge, and we'll talk all about it then."

As he turned to leave, I said, "What about the address?"

"Check your shirt pocket."

I did, and there it was, written neatly on a small scrap of paper.

"Why do you do that?" I said.

"Some tricks never grow old," he said before he disappeared, and maybe he was right.

72

I didn't stop at the office, I didn't stop at Tommy's High Ball to pick up Horace, I didn't stop at Social Services to get ahold of Isabel, I didn't stop anywhere. I left Dr. Bob's office and jumped in my car, checked the map, and then drove straight west, out to the address Dr. Bob had left in my shirt pocket.

And I drove fast.

I had no real idea of what I'd find when I got there, other than a girl who had been deserted by her mother and failed by everyone she had ever come in contact with, but I expected the worst. Philadelphia might be the City of Brotherly Love, but it's also the city of Erica Pratt, who was brutally kidnapped and who escaped her captors by chewing through the duct tape binding her body, the city of Gary Heidnik, who kept a torture and sex-slave chamber in the basement of his Philly home and who fed his victims the flesh of those he had murdered.

Was my imagination running amok? You bet, and when it came to a child within the ambit of my responsibility, I wouldn't have it any other way.

The street turned out to be just a stone's throw from Cobbs Creek, Philadelphia's best municipal golf course, in a section of the city called Overbrook Hills. I drove past a WATCH CHILDREN sign, turned right, passed by the address and spied nothing unusual. I drove through the alley behind the house, past the front again, and then parked halfway down the block and across the street so I could keep my eye on the front door.

Once again I was surveilling. You'd think I would have learned.

It was a neighborhood of row houses, great lengths of identical brick homes lining either side of streets laid out in a rectangular grid. These houses were newer and smaller than the usual Philly row house, without the grand architectural details or great stone porches found in the older sections of West and North Philadelphia, just flat brick fronts, with the occasional pediment above aluminum screen doors. The lawns were narrow and scruffy, about half were fenced in.

As I stared at the house, I tried to conjure again the horrors of possibility, but it was harder now that I saw the street. There were children's toys all over the place, plastic cars, large plastic play sets, a blow-up pool within the confines of a fence. And people were out and about, youngsters moving together in groups, teenagers, kids zipping by on their bicycles. An old man sat out on a lawn chair, sucking on a cigar in the shade of a green plastic awning. A woman was sweeping.

I sat back, scrunched down in my seat, and waited.

I wanted to see someone go in or out of the house; I wanted to get a sense of what I was dealing with. I had my cell phone, and if anything scared me enough I was ready to dial 911 and call out the SWAT team, but I thought I'd better get a grip on things before I did.

The door remained closed, the windows were dark, nothing was happening.

You stare at something long enough, your mind slips into a meditative fog, which is what must have happened, because I didn't notice until too late the car that slowly slid beside me.

"Is there a problem?"

I startled at the sound, turned to see a cop car blocking my exit, the uniformed driver looking me up and down, wondering, I was sure, what a stranger in an old car and a cheap suit with a bandage on his face was doing in this neighborhood.

"I'm fine, Officer, thank you," I said.

"Anything I can help you with?"

"Nothing right now, thank you."

"Can I ask you what you're doing here?"

"You can ask, sure," I said.

We stared at each other for a moment, and then a moment longer, before he figured out the gag.

"Step out of the vehicle, please," he said.

I guess he wasn't amused.

The name on his shirt was Washington, and he told me that his dispatcher had received a number of calls about the presence of a strange car on the street. After checking my license and registration, and wincing at the Bar Association card I keep in my wallet, he listened patiently as I explained what I was doing there. I showed him the notice of appointment from the judge, I gestured toward the quiet house on the quiet street that matched the address I had been given.

"Why don't we just go up and ask them?" he said.

I started to say something about Erica Pratt or Gary Heidnick, but within the aura of Officer Washington's calm, I realized I was being an idiot.

"Sure," I said, and we did.

The woman who answered the door was plump and pretty. She rubbed her hands nervously together when she saw the uniformed cop and the guy next to the cop in a suit.

"Yes?" she said. "Can I help you?"

"Good day, ma'am," said Officer Washington. "This man's name is Victor Carl." The woman reacted to the name as if it was Beelzebub. "He has a court order that appoints him the lawyer for a girl named Tanya Rose. He's trying to locate her and believes she could be here. Do you have any idea where this Tanya Rose might be?"

"How did you get this address?" said the woman.

"I just want to find her," I said, trying to flash a comforting smile and, based on her reaction, failing miserably. "I just want to make sure she's all right."

"I need to make a call," said the woman.

"Is she here?" I said.

"I need to make a call before I let you do anything. I have rights. You just can't come barging in."

"Ma'am," said the officer. "Based on the order, he has a right to see the girl if she's here."

I heard a light tread bouncing down the stairs. I stepped past the woman into the dark parlor of the little house. I didn't notice the ragged furniture or the wall hangings, the old shaggy rug, the spicy scent coming from the kitchen, I didn't notice anything except the small set of white sneakers jumping down the stairs, the thin bare legs, the denim jumper, the little girl with pigtails and wide eyes who was holding on to a brown stuffed unicorn.

She stopped when she saw me staring at her. "Mama," she said, "what's going on?"

"Is your name Tanya?" I said.

She didn't answer. Instead she backed away, back up the stairs, frightened. I was wrong, Dr. Bob had blown it, she wasn't the right girl, this woman she called Mama was her mother. I didn't know what else to do except keep on talking.

"My name is Victor Carl. I'm a lawyer. If you're Tanya, I've been appointed to help you in any way I can."

The girl tilted her head as if I were an idiot telling a nonsensical story in a language of my own devising. I thought about turning around, apologizing to the woman and to Officer Washington, of ducking out of there and avoiding any more humiliation, but then I thought of three more words to say.

"Daniel sent me," I told her.

Her smile blew a hole in my heart.

And here's the thing that surprised me and mystified me and cheered me all at the same time: Tanya was okay, Tanya was in good hands. The Reverend Wilkerson, against all my suppositions and, I have to admit, all my prejudices, the Reverend Wilkerson had done his best by the girl.

The woman's name was Mrs. Hanson, and she was sweet and nervous and scared to death of me. "Are you going to take my Tanya away?" she said.

"I don't know," I told her, and I didn't.

So we sat in her living room and we talked, Mrs. Hanson and Officer Washington and myself. Tanya went back up to her room to play, sneaking down every now and then to listen before running back up again. Mrs. Hanson called her husband home from his work, and while we waited for him, she made us tea and she told us about her family, about her older son, Charles, who attended Central High, the premier magnet school in the Philadelphia school system. And she told us that when she heard from the good reverend of this girl who needed a family, she and her husband talked about it and prayed about it and decided there was nothing they could do but open their door to her. They would make the effort, suffer through the inconvenience, give this poor girl the benefit of a home, whatever the burden. What they didn't expect was that they would fall, all three of the Hansons, so much in love with the little girl.

After a while Officer Washington raised his eyebrows,

and I nodded that it was all right, and we both thanked him for his time. After he left, Mr. Hanson showed up, a short, energetic man in blue work shirt and pants, and the three of us talked some more. They told about the friends Tanya had made, they told me about their trip to King's Dominion.

"The Elvis karaoke bar in the Northeast?" I said.

"No," said Mr. Hanson. "The amusement park in Virginia."

"Ah, yes," I said. "Of course."

The furniture was aged, the paintings on the wall were the kind you buy in warehouses, the television was a decade old, one wall was covered with the style of block mirrors they used to advertise on UHF channels twenty years ago. Not rich, maybe not even middle class, but they were a family, the warmth was palpable, and my scalp didn't itch inside their house, which was a good indication that the abject dysfunction that had marred my childhood didn't have a hold here.

When I asked if I could speak to Tanya alone, they looked at each other nervously and then led me up to her room.

She was on her bed, surrounded by a sea of small stuffed animals. It appeared that she was putting on a play of some sort, but when she saw me standing in the doorway, she stopped, lowered her hands.

I stooped down so our eyes were roughly level, not that she was looking at me, and I told her who I was, why I was there. I could see she was listening, the way she smiled when I mentioned Daniel, the way her mouth tightened when I mentioned her mother, but she didn't respond at all until I asked her if there was a place nearby to get some ice cream.

"A couple blocks away," she said.

"You want to go?"

"Okay."

Mrs. Hanson wasn't happy that I was taking Tanya for a

walk, but her husband calmed her down and gave me directions. He also, I noticed, followed us from a distance, which I didn't mind at all. We walked quietly together, Tanya and I, turning left and then right, ending up at a small drugstore with a large white freezer in the corner. She picked the prepackaged ice cream cone with the chocolate and nuts on top, I took the Chipwich. We found a curb on a quiet street on the way back to sit while we finished off the treats.

"Do you like it here?" I said.

She nodded.

"You called Mrs. Hanson Mama. Why did you do that?"

"She likes it."

"Do you like her?"

"Yes."

"Why?"

"She's nice. She fusses over me and buys me stuffed animals. Did you see how many I have?"

"Yes, I did. Wow. It's like a zoo in there."

"I'm going to fill it up until I can't hardly walk into the room. Then I'm going to jump right on top of the pile and sleep there every night."

I glanced up the street. He was sitting on a hydrant about a hundred yards away, just keeping an eye on things. I gave a little wave, and he waved back. "Do you like Mr. Hanson?" I said.

"He's nice, too."

"And Charles?"

"Yeah, though he's not home much. He's really smart. He's, like, a brain."

"Do you think about your mother ever?"

"Yeah."

"Do you miss her?"

"Yeah."

"Do you want to go back and live with her?"

"I don't know. I like it with the Hansons. Is Randy still there?"

"Not right now. You don't like Randy?"

"He didn't like me. Always yelling, smacking me. Can I have another cone?"

"I don't think so."

"Just asking. How's Daniel?"

"He's all right," I said. "I think he's okay now. We fixed his teeth."

"They sure needed fixing. I miss him. Can you go to my mommy's place and tell him I miss him?"

"He's not with your mother right now."

Her eyes widened.

"Randy was hurting him, and your mother didn't stop him. So Randy was arrested and Daniel's now with another family."

"I want to see him."

"I'll see what I can do."

"Are you really here to help me?"

"That's right. Believe it or not, I work for you."

"I don't have any money to pay you."

"That's all right," I said. "Why should you be different from any of my other clients?"

"What happened to your face?"

"My television bit me."

"I guess that's why they don't let me watch too much."

"Does that make you sad?"

"Not really. There's a nice school here. I can walk to it and it's a pretty color outside and the kids I play with in the neighborhood, they go there, too, and will walk with me. Sam, he has a little pool and we swim together when it gets hot."

"So what do you want me to do for you?"

"I don't want to leave. I like the school."

"Okay."

"But I miss Daniel."

"Okay."

"Maybe he can go to the school, too."

"He's still a little young for school."

"Yeah. Can I have another cone now?"

"No," I said.

I left her with the Hansons. I thought about it, thought about the options, and the responsibility of the thing scared the hell out of me, but sometimes I think the braver thing is to do nothing, and Tanya deserved my bravery, so I left her there. I gave Mrs. Hanson Isabel Chandler's name and phone number. I told her to call, to set up an interview with Social Services, to do what she had to do to become a certified foster home so her custody of Tanya could be made official. But until then I wouldn't do anything to remove Tanya from her home.

"I was so worried when the reverend told us you were asking around about Tanya," said Mrs. Hanson. "I was having nightmares about you."

"I seem to have that effect on people."

"She's such a wonderful girl. She's already part of the family. I told the reverend I was terrified you were going to take her from us."

"I was terrified, too," I said.

Sometimes I almost start to believe that the human race, contrary to all reason and against all odds, has a chance after all.

What do Broadway musicals and murder trials have in common? Leggy blondes with short skirts and high-heeled tap shoes? Only in my dreams, which might say more about my subconscious than I am comfortable with. No, they both need to end with the big finish, and I'm not talking about some glandular case named Paavo. I would have put on a big production number if they let me, but François Dubé's fate was playing out not on the Broadway stage but in a court of law, where the performers wear suits and intone Latin and are required to follow the rules of evidence. Nothing puts a crimp in the old song and dance like the rules of evidence, believe me, but I still had my big finish planned. Mrs. Winterhurst to link the victim to Dr. Bob, Franny Pepper to link Dr. Bob to the circumstance of the photograph in Leesa Dubé's cold, dead hand, and finally, Dr. Bob himself, to lie on the stand and then wither under the onslaught of my brilliant cross-examination.

I was so confident of the power of my big finish that I was barely paying attention in court. Beth had taken charge of the timeline of François's alibi. It wasn't much of an alibi, to be truthful, but every little bit helped. So Beth was putting on testimony of François's whereabouts through the whole of the evening of his wife's murder, placing him in the kitchen till the restaurant closed, at the zinc bar for an hour or so after, finally walking off into the night exhausted and ready for sleep. The jurors were ready for sleep, too, by the look of them, and I could relate. In fact, I was just about to zonk off myself when Torricelli waved his fingers at me.

I snapped awake. What the heck was that? It was as if he were saying "Toodle-oo," which was strange, because Torricelli was not a toodle-oo kind of fellow.

The mystery of the little finger wave was solved at the lunch recess. As the courtroom cleared, Torricelli came over and placed his big old hand on my shoulder.

"How's it hanging, Carl?"

I looked at his hand, looked back at Torricelli's ugly mug. "Fine?"

"What happened to your face?"

"My television bit it."

"No matter how inviting the porn, Victor, you still can't jump through the screen and join the action."

"Have you been drinking, Detective? Because some people when they drink become overly friendly."

"Not me," he said cheerfully. "When I drink, I turn into a mean son of a bitch."

"So it has no effect."

He laughed, which was more than disconcerting. Torricelli was in way too good a mood.

"What are you so merry about?" I said.

"I've been having this problem with my tooth. I couldn't figure what it was, but suddenly it's taken care of."

"You don't say."

"It was a simple thing, a cavity hidden from the normal probes. An X-ray caught it. My tooth has now been drilled and filled, and I am feeling fine."

"Sounds like you found yourself a dentist."

"Yes I did. Nice guy, too. Maybe you know him."

"Maybe I do."

"Think of it, Victor. I come to him just to ask a few questions about a murder, and I come out with a whole new outlook on the world."

"He has that way about him, doesn't he? Did he explain away the name change?"

"He said it wasn't the right image for a dentist to be named after a soda pop, which makes some sense, doesn't it?"

"And you bought it?"

"Why not? And after he fixed me up, he gave me a little parting gift."

"A lollipop?"

"His fingerprints."

"You don't say," I said, though he just had.

"Quite voluntarily, I might add. I made the suggestion, and he ripped his rubber gloves right off and offered me his hands."

"He is obliging, isn't he?"

"You want to know the results of our comparisons?"

"Your smile pretty much says it all," I said as a sickening slick of despair rose in my gut.

"They didn't match," said Torricelli, enjoying this way too much to stop. "The latent we found at the crime scene, the one that your expert identified as matching the one he found at the storage locker and then on the tape, didn't come from Dr. Pfeffer."

"I'll have my expert check the results."

"Do that, but he'll come to the same conclusion. First, he's got an alibi. Then the fingerprints don't match. It sort of puts a hole in your theory that the dentist did it."

I twisted my lips and tried not to throw up.

"I hope I didn't ruin your lunch," said Torricelli.

But he had, hadn't he? The little treat of information he'd passed on had sent my stomach spinning. It was the kind of news that hurts the most, the news that you've been both dreading and expecting all along.

You might remember I had pocketed Dr. Bob's whiskey glass during our strange night at the bar. But that glass still lay in its plastic bag, the prints still latent, still waiting to be spirited into being with chemicals and powders and then memorialized forever on contact sheets. I had never sent the glass to Anton Grammatikos to be tested.

Why had I never sent it? Because there were two possible answers, either Dr. Bob's prints matched the unknown print from the tape and the crime scene or they didn't, and my defense could survive only one of those answers. Better an uncertainty you can argue to the jury than a certainty that renders your defense a nullity. But now Detective Torricelli, proving himself to be quite the detective after all, had just done the rendering.

With my appetite having fled, I thought it through over the lunch hour and kept at it as Beth continued laying out the timeline in court. My whole theory depended on the killing being an accident. Dr. Bob had been trying to help Leesa Dubé. Dr. Bob had been bringing the tape to Leesa to help in her divorce case. Something had gone wrong, and Leesa had ended up dead, and Dr. Bob had framed François before squirreling the tape back to François's storage locker, still covered as it was with Leesa's blood. The picture found in Leesa's hand, much as a picture had been found in the hand of Dr. Bob's mother, was the crowning piece of evidence. In fact, I even believed that Dr. Bob had set up the storage area just as it was so that if anyone came snooping, like, say, me, he would sit in the chair and be horrified at the tapes and know that the frame had been the right thing to do.

But now it seemed that Dr. Bob was not the person who had taken the tape from the crime scene.

Who could it have been? The district attorney's answer

was damn convincing. Who would the tape hurt the most? François. Where was the tape with the victim's blood found? In François's storage locker. Who had the motive? François. It was all so clean, made so much sense, except why would François keep that tape after that? Why had it not been burned, shattered, destroyed irrevocably? Why had it been left lying around for someone to find? Because he was arrested too soon? Because he didn't have time to destroy it? Time to return it to the locker but not destroy it?

None of it made sense if Dr. Bob hadn't done the crime. But if Dr. Bob hadn't done the crime, who had?

Strangely, at that moment I thought of Rex, the man mountain with the soft gaze who had confronted me outside the Hotel Latimore. Something Dr. Bob had said about Rex struck a chord. *I'm always on the lookout for new talent,* had said Dr. Bob, *a pure soul with the heart, the muscle, the determination to make a difference in the world.*

Rex had entered the story far too late to be involved, but maybe it was one of Dr. Bob's other recruits who had done it, maybe someone whom Dr. Bob had found and trained, someone who had done Dr. Bob's bidding and then left to go out on his own and who had now gone deep underground. But who could it be? And how would I find him? And how could I use him to save my client?

It was the phrase "deep underground" rattling through my thoughts that finally clued me in to the entire truth. When it came to me, it was as if a window shade had been lifted and the sun was streaming through. When the light hit my face, I stood up suddenly.

Beth was in the middle of framing a question. She stopped midsentence and looked at me. The courtroom stilled, all heads turned in my direction.

"Is there anything you want to say, Counselor?" said Judge Armstrong.

"Just that I have to go, Judge," I said. "Right this instant."

"Something you ate, Mr. Carl?"

Before the laughter died, I was out the courtroom door. Where was I headed?

To find me a two-bit whore.

Detective Gleason was nothing if not a professional. It was in the way he could spot the prostitutes from even a great distance. "Look for the shoes," he advised me. It was in the way he walked on the street with total assurance while I sat in the car, the way he approached the claques with a smile and a wave, the way he spoke softly to the women one at a time, the way he asked his questions, laughed at their wisecracks, listened to their answers with nodding unconcern, the way he slipped them the bills when he was through talking.

And he did all this, projected all this authority, without a badge, being as he was still confined to desk duty. But for him this wasn't business, this was personal.

I had found his Elvisine figure at the auto squad's front desk, sitting there glumly, answering phones, handing out paperwork to the saps who had lost their cars. When he looked up and saw me, it's safe to say he didn't flash a smile of welcome.

"I need your help," I said.

"Your car missing?"

"No."

Detective Gleason shook his head. "No crying in the chapel, boy. We've helped each other enough. I helped you get a new trial for your sleazeball client, and you helped get me permanently deskbound."

"Yeah, sorry about that. Want me to talk to the commissioner?"

"You really want to bury me, don't you? What happened to your face?"

"My television bit me."

"So even your TV hates you."

"That's me, Mr. Popularity."

He let out a long breath. "What are you looking for, Carl?"

"The truth," I said, "about Seamus Dent."

His eyes squinted at the name.

"I think I know what he was doing in that crack house when he was killed," I said, "and I think I know who drove him to it."

"Okay, so?"

"You want to help me prove it?"

"Not especially. I'm moving on. And it's hard to dig out facts from behind a desk."

"You're not allowed on the street officially. Don't do this as a cop, do this as a guy who wants to find out what really happened to a kid he helped."

"And why should I care anymore?"

"Because you tried to make a difference in that boy's life and you want to find out why it went all wrong and who might be responsible."

"Some things just don't work out."

"No, this was more. There was someone who pushed Seamus in the direction he took, someone who set him on the path that led to his death."

"And you think you know who?"

"Oh, yes."

"Baby, what do you want me to do?"

"I want you to help me prove it."

"How?"

"There's a girl."

"Isn't there always?"

"Not like this one, a sad mess of a girl who is looking for the surest path to oblivion. Drugs, violence, complete and total self-degradation."

"You think she's on the street?"

"Can you think of a better place to find what she's looking for? Her name's Kylie, and I think she's the reason Seamus is dead. If anyone knows what really happened to Seamus, it's Kylie."

"So why do you need me?"

"You were in vice before homicide. You know the street better than I ever will. I need you to help me find her."

Gleason leaned back in his chair, stroked his sideburns. "You're going to get me fried again, aren't you?"

"That's not my intent."

"For those who really screw the rest of us, it never is," he said. "I get off at four."

"That's great. You won't regret it."

"I do already."

I looked around at the auto squad's lobby, the empty space with its plastic chairs. "Can I wait for you here?"

"No," he said.

I drove my car down a dark, narrow street in an old, abandoned part of the city, a festering urban sore just east of the Schuylkill River, within a stone's throw of the refineries and porn shops that line the expressway. Whatever light had been left in the day when we started our search had fled west, so we were now cruising in shadows, only a few scattered shards of asphalt illuminated by the dim streetlights. This wasn't a high-priced locale for selling your body, this wasn't even Wal-Mart, this was a place for discontinued lines and damaged goods, this was streetwalker hell.

"My God," I said. "Who would come here for a hooker?"

"That's not the question," said Gleason, "because they'll always come. Set up in a cemetery, open a coffin, and watch the line form. The question is, who has fallen so hard that she has to sell herself here?"

"Kylie."

"From what I could gather, she's pretty much hit bottom. A bad drug jones, a pimp who kicked her out when she couldn't make enough to keep herself above the Mendoza line, a body riddled with shakes and sores."

"Last-chance corner, is that it?"

"This is where they end up when their last chance fails."

"Where do they go from here?"

"The morgue."

"Seems that's what Kylie wants."

"Hold on," said Gleason. "What's that over there?"

There was a shadow leaning against a wall not far from a lamppost. I pulled the car into the dim circle created by the streetlight. The shadow pushed itself off the wall, strolled over, looked fore and aft before bending down so that its arms leaned on the doorframe and its face loomed close to mine in the window, a hard, tired face, dark eyes, pale lips, a red welt on the cheek.

"You boys looking for a party?"

"What's your name, honey?" said Gleason, leaning over from the passenger seat.

"Do it matter?"

"We got to call you something."

"How about Jenny?" She smiled, and her teeth were like the neighborhood in which she worked, a few crumbling structures teetering over vast vacant lots. "You want to party with Jenny? I got tricks."

"I'm sure you do, sweetheart," said Gleason, "but we're not looking for a Jenny. We're looking for a Kylie."

The woman lifted her head up, glanced down the street. "Who are you?"

"We're here on business," said Gleason.

"What the hell you think I'm doing here? That don't mean we can't party together. I got a place right back here, you want. I'll make you happy"—she slapped her butt—"if you're man enough to handle this."

"We need to ask Kylie some questions," said Gleason. "You mind if we take your competition off the street for a bit?"

She snorted. "That skinny bitch ain't no competition."

"Where is she, Jenny?"

"Is she in trouble?"

"Nah," said Gleason. "Just some questions."

"Too bad. Trouble would be a step in the right direction for her. Try a few blocks up on the right, in that warehouse where she does her stuff. You find her, you tell that princess with her little white ass that Jenny says fuck you."

"It's nice to see such camaraderie among the working folk," said Gleason as Jenny backed away and blended again into the shadows.

I drove to the warehouse and pulled right behind an old two-tone Chevy parked at the curb. The warehouse was a crumbling brick building, its windows and door boarded with gray plywood. The thin wood over one of the low windows was smashed, darkness streamed out like some vile smoke from the opening.

Gleason cut the engine and we waited quietly.

A few moments later, a shadow slipped furtively out from the gap in the window, over to the Chevy, around the front. It glanced our way as it opened the door, slid into the front seat. The engine of the old beater roared through a failing muffler as it drove off.

"I suppose it's our turn," said Gleason.

"We're going in there?" I said.

"Don't worry," said Gleason, reaching into the glove compartment of his car. "I got my little friend."

I was disappointed when he pulled out a heavy blue flashlight.

"No gun?"

"I'm still on desk duty," he said.

Out of the car, I followed him across the wide sidewalk to the shattered window. Gleason slipped over the sill and through the narrow opening. I hesitated for a moment and then followed, landing unsteadily on my feet on the other side. It was pitch-black in the building, fetid and dank, it smelled of urine and wet cement, of rats with damp fur, of sweat and cinder and old sad stories turned to ash.

Gleason turned on his flashlight, illuminated the piles of garbage, the twisted beams, the crumbling plaster walls, a sleeping bag in the corner quivering with life. And then, all the way to the left, a mattress, and on the mattress a young woman, all in rags, sitting with her arms wrapped around her legs, her chin on her knees, her eyes staring straight up at the light, a sneer of defiance on her lips.

"Turn it off," said the woman in a lifeless monotone. Her face was round, and it had been pretty once, you could tell, but not anymore. Her hair was greasy, her eyes red and watery, her cheeks sunken, her lips scabbed, her skin mottled with blood and filth.

"Are you Kylie?" said Gleason.

"I'm nobody," said the woman.

"Then you're our girl," I said.

"Turn off the light, assholes," said Kylie, raising a hand to ward off the beam.

"We want to talk to you," said Gleason.

"It costs extra to talk."

"How about if we only talk?"

"That you can't afford."

"Are you hungry, Kylie?" I said. "Do you want to get something to eat?"

"I don't eat anymore."

"Are you thirsty?"

"No."

"I am," came a voice from the sleeping bag. "I'll drink anything, don't matter what, so long it's got a proof on it."

"Shut up," said Gleason.

"I didn't mean nothing," said the sleeping bag, "but I could always use a drink."

"Just shut up."

"Whatever you got, give to Al," said Kylie. "You don't need to liquor me up, I'm not that type of girl. Just shut off that light and do whatever you want."

"We want to talk," I said. "We want to hear a story."

"Buy a book."

"A story about Seamus Dent," I said.

"Seamus? Jesus. What about Seamus?"

"We want to know why he died."

"That's easy," she said. "Because he cared."

"About what?"

"Everything."

"What about you? What do you care about?"

"Nothing."

"Not even Seamus?"

"Turn off the light."

"If we turn it off, will you tell us?"

"If you turn it off, I won't claw your eyes out."

Al, in the sleeping bag, laughed.

"Name a price," said Gleason.

"Now you talking," said Al. "How much you talking about?"

"What does it matter anymore, what happened to Seamus?" said Kylie.

"It matters to the man here," I said, indicating Gleason, "who did what he could to clean up Seamus when he found him wasted and lost in a drug house. And it matters to my client, who's on trial for his life for something I think Seamus might have done. And it matters to Wayne, who still feels betrayed by Seamus because Seamus saved Wayne's life and then apparently gave his up for nothing."

"Wayne? You've spoken to Wayne?"

"That's right."

"Jesus. Wayne. You're hitting the trifecta. How's he doing?"

"All right, actually. Seamus took him to Father Kenneth back in your old parish, and Father Kenneth helped him clean himself up. Wayne works at the church now."

"He always had a pious streak in him."

"He's getting his life together."

"Good for him," said Kylie.

"Let's talk some more about the money," said Al.

"What are you, her agent?" said Gleason.

"Just a businessman trying to do some business."

"And a hell of a successful businessman at that, I can tell," said Gleason, waving his flashlight about the decrepit space.

"Turn out the light," said Kylie. "I can't talk when I can still see myself."

"Will you tell us the story if we turn it out?"

"I don't know it all," she said. "I don't know exactly what he did before, but he said it was bad."

"Tell us what you do know."

"He said he didn't mean it, that it was an accident, that he was only trying to help her, not kill her. And that afterward he tried to make it right but the lawyer wouldn't let him."

"Is that why he got the trench coat?"

"He said the trench coat was like a cape the superheroes used to wear in the comic books. He decided that was what he was going to be, a superhero. That was how he was going to make it right."

"For the accident, for killing that woman."

"Yeah."

"Is that why he fell back into drugs? Because of the guilt? Is that why he ended up in that crack house where he was murdered?"

"He was clean at the end," said Kylie. "He didn't come to the house for drugs. He came for me."

"Damn cowboy," said Gleason.

"If we turn out the light," I said to her, "will you tell us the whole story?"

"I don't know it all."

"As much as you know."

"Will you leave me alone after?" she said.

"If that's what you want."

"And the money," said Al. "Don't forget the money."

"We won't," I said. "We'll take care of both of you. All right, turn out the light."

Gleason flashed the beam around to see if anyone was behind us, and then he clicked off the flashlight. Darkness fell over the clammy space like a fetid blanket. Something scurried in the corner, something wet fell from an overhead rafter, something in the distance moaned. We stood in the uneasy quiet of collapse and decay and waited, and waited some more.

And then Kylie began to talk.

It was early morning when finally we left that dank, stinking warehouse. Gleason and I had stood for a long time in the darkness, listening as Kylie told us her story, emotions overflowing in all of us, even Kylie, I could tell, despite the dead monotone of her voice. And when, at the end, Gleason turned the flashlight back on, the filth on her face had become streaked by her tears. Now, in the car again, we could see the first stirrings of dawn in the eastern sky as I drove us out of the rotting neighborhood. I drove east until I hit the expressway and then west to 676, east to 95, north again to the Aramingo Avenue exit and on to Fishtown.

They were waiting for us at the church, standing by the side entrance. Father Kenneth was leaning against the wall, hands in his pockets, the light from the fixture over the door falling like a blessing on his head and shoulders. Wayne was slapping at his arms as he walked back and forth along the street, back and forth, pacing as nervously as an expectant father in the maternity ward, waiting to hear if he would be embracing that morning a boy or a girl.

It was a girl.

CHAPTER
75

I hadn't slept yet when I banged loudly on the great wooden door. It was light out but still early enough that a gentle tap or a warning phone call might have been polite. But having heard what I heard from Kylie that very night, I wasn't in the mood just then to be polite. So I banged. Loudly. And I banged again.

It took longer than I would have thought for the door to be answered, and what I encountered was not what I expected. Yes, it was Whit, my old mentor Whitney Robinson III, on whose front door I had been banging, but he was not dressed in his usual fastidious style, no handkerchief in his jacket pocket, no jacket to be precise, nor even a shirt. It was T-shirt and pajama pants, bare feet, unshaven jaw, gray hair mussed tragically, eyes haunted, pale lips trembling at the sight of me.

The last bit of which I could understand, being as I represented, in a way, the ghost of Whit's past.

"Not a good time, I'm afraid, my boy," he said.

"It will have to do."

"Ah, the determined young man out to get to the bottom of it once and for all. I didn't think you had it in you, Victor, and I must say I'm disappointed. Self-righteousness might be a pleasant enough vice for its holder, but it can be so wearying for those on the other side of its wrath."

"What did he give you, Whit? What did he do for you that impelled you to ignore Seamus Dent's confession and ensure François's conviction?"

"He played God."

"That seems to be his thing."

"What happened to your face?"

"The dental hygienist."

Whit's eyes widened. "Quite a woman, that Tilda. I suppose you'll be coming in whether I invite you or not."

"You suppose right."

"Then all I can do is welcome you again to my humble home. Come inside, there's someone I want you to meet."

As I followed him into the large stone house, I noticed how stooped and thin he was, how much the years had pressed their weight upon him. Without his upper-crust uniform, he appeared more fragile than I had ever imagined, less the highly polished product of the top tier of the American caste system and more the doddering old man, clutching feebly to whatever straw he could grab hold of in this life. I had admired him for years, and then feared him in the latter part of this case, but now, unaccountably, I felt sorry for him.

He led me through the faded hallway and then to the right, through the dining room that, even with its great oaken table and heavy crystal chandelier, felt like it had been abandoned years before. Whatever joyous occasions had been celebrated in that room, whatever festive dinners had been thrown or gracious toasts offered, were well in the past. This room was now just a passageway that led to another room at its far end, a room that in its heartbreak had clearly become the center of the house.

Guarding the entrance was the white-faced nurse whom I had seen through the window my last visit. Tall and gaunt, like a withered stalk of corn, she stared with an admixture of fear and disgust, her thin mouth twitching at the sight of me.

"Leave us some time alone, will you, Miss MacDhub-shith."

"The poor girl, she needs her rest," said the nurse in a strong burr.

"Of course she does," said Whit. "Take your break. I'll stay with her."

The woman gave me a final glare before stalking off. Toward a telephone, I presumed, to squeal on the two of us to you-know-who. When she left, Whit passed through the doorway, and I followed.

I found myself in an old sitting room, wood-lined, with bookshelves and fine stained-glass windows. It was a room that should have held red leather chairs and calfskin-bound volumes of Dickens and Thackeray, Tocqueville and Maupassant. The fireplace should have been roaring, the port decanted, a game of whist going on in the corner. And at one point I'm sure all of that had happened here, but not now and not, I could tell, for years. Now it had been turned into a shrine for the living dead.

"This is my daughter, Annabelle," said Whit, gesturing to the hospital bed set into the middle of the room and the woman who lay uneasily upon it. He sat down in the chair placed by the bed, leaned over to his daughter, gently laid the back of his hand on her cheek.

She was seemingly young and pretty, her hair cut short, her skin shiny, her hands waxy and smooth with long, tapered nails. Her pale blue eyes were open and darting about the room as if she were trying to take it all in, but it became clear, after only a moment, that she was taking in nothing. And her body shook and contracted in on itself to some strange, unnatural rhythm. The only things that kept her on the bed were straps binding her arms to the bed frame.

"My youngest child," said Whit. He leaned forward and kissed her quivering forehead. "My little princess. It came out of nowhere. She was skiing, in Colorado. A heart attack and then a stroke that acted together to deprive her brain of oxygen for far too long. She was left in an appalling condition."

"I'm so sorry, Whit. How long has she been like this?"

"Five years," he said. "Five impossible years. At first she was in a minimally conscious state. She had some real awareness of what was going on, sometimes you could tell she was even trying to speak. It was heartbreaking. It looked as if she was inside this shell, trying to break out. But then, at least, there was still hope."

"What kind of hope?"

"An experimental procedure that showed much promise, something called neural modulation. Electrodes are implanted deep into the brain, and then a battery is placed in the chest, much like a pacemaker for the heart. The deep-brain stimulation had been shown to have real effects in changing the very structure of the brain, in allowing the parts still healthy to take a more prominent role, so long as it was applied very quickly after the damaging event. If it worked, she'd be back, my daughter, my sweet, sweet little girl. Back to us. But there was a problem. The FDA had approved a very small case study, with very rigid parameters. The doctors said that Annabelle didn't qualify. The precipitating event had happened too long ago."

"Was there any way around the requirement?"

"None that I could see. I pushed every button I could, but to no avail. I was distraught. And then Seamus Dent showed up in my office. This was just before the trial. I knew he was a witness against François. I was shocked to see him. But he told me he had something to say."

"What did he tell you, Whit?"

"A strange, fabulous tale of a dentist who had this wonderful ability to help people in need."

"Pfeffer."

"Yes. He told me how Dr. Pfeffer had worked on his teeth and in the process how he was recruited by this doctor to help in his causes. And one night Dr. Pfeffer had given him the mission to help Leesa Dubé. There was a key and a videotape. His job was to enter her apartment, leave the tape in the VCR, program it to start playing in the morning, and quietly leave. She was supposed to be dead asleep, it was supposed to be so easy. But the woman awoke and was so frightened at the intrusion that she came at him with a gun. And he reacted badly. There was a struggle, there was a shot, and the bullet went through her neck. He said it was a hurricane of blood. He ran away and called Dr. Pfeffer, who said he'd take care of it, and he did."

"And when he told you this, Whit, what did you do?"

"I went to see the mysterious Dr. Pfeffer. I wanted to confront him, to learn the truth. But in the course of our conversation, the doctor mentioned that he knew of my daughter's condition and that he could help. He said he had contacts, he said he had a way to get her in the study. He told me he would take care of it, and he did. She was the last patient admitted. Dr. Pfeffer gave her a chance at life."

"And for that you ignored Seamus's confession."

"I did what I had to do. I convinced the boy his statement wouldn't do any good, that no one would believe him. He would get in trouble, yes, but my client wouldn't have been helped. The best thing, I told him, the only way to keep himself out of trouble, was to repeat in court what he had already told the police."

"So you betrayed your client."

"You have no children, Victor, so you might not understand the great fear that comes upon you at the moment of birth. There is the love, yes, such a sweet, thrilling emotion, but there is the fear, too. The fear that somehow you will fail them. It never leaves you, the awesome and terrifying responsibility you hold for their welfare. Would you have done anything differently if it had been your daughter lying there?"

"I don't know."

"Who did she have but me? My whole life I had fought for my clients. This time I sided with my child."

"And how did it turn out, Whit?"

"You can see for yourself. The procedure didn't work. Her condition deteriorated, her muscles are in constant, irregular spasm. It is all I can do to care for her. It isn't easy, it killed my wife, the strain, and it has drained me completely. But Dr. Pfeffer continues to help. He found me the nurse, he keeps the doctors on their toes, he convinced the insurance company to allow me to care for my princess in my home."

"Maybe it would have been better if you had left it alone."

"She deserved a chance."

"So did the person whose admittance to the study your daughter edged out."

"I did what I had to do."

"He's an amateur at it."

"At what?"

"Playing God," I said. "You'll testify for François."

"That's out of the question."

"I don't think so." I pulled out a small, minicassette recorder. "They make them so small now, quite ingenious."

"What Seamus told me is hearsay. It is not admissible."

"Seamus's statement was against his penal interest."

"You need circumstantial evidence of the statement's trustworthiness."

"I've got it."

"Where?"

"From our dentist's past."

"I see you've done your homework. It's almost a pity that he won't let you present it all to the jury."

"He'll try to stop me."

"And he'll succeed. He's very clever."

"Not clever enough. And the proof is, sadly, right here in this room. Tell me, Whit: You gave up everything you worked for your entire life, every ounce of meaning in your career, for a chance that failed. Would you do it again?"

"Every day, forever and again."

"Now who's the hollow man?" I said. "I'll see you in court."

When I left the room, he was still leaning over the bed, brushing again his hand against his daughter's cheek, oblivious to anything other than her trembling body, her lifeless, roaming eyes.

I made my way through the pale, sad dining room to the center hallway, where she was waiting for me. Of course she was. Nurse MacDhubshith, standing before the front door, her hands behind her back. Dr. Bob's first line of defense.

"I'll be having the tape recorder now, Mr. Carl," she said.

"Didn't your mother teach you it's impolite to eavesdrop?"

"We built an intercom into the room so I can monitor her wherever I be. Sometimes there is much distress."

"I'll bet."

"That tape, then."

"I don't think so," I said.

"You didn't believe we'd let you bring it all crashing down, did you?"

"We all do what we must."

"That we do," she said as she took her right hand from behind her back. She was gripping the handle of an absurdly large cleaver.

"Tell me this, Nurse MacDhubshith. What did he do for you?"

"He fixed me overbite and saved me brother's life."

"And for that you'd hack me to death?"

"Don't be daft. I'm not out to kill you, Mr. Carl. The knife is only to slice you a bit, maybe cut off an ear." She smiled as she took her left hand from behind her back. "And this is to stop you from leaving with the tape."

In her left hand was a syringe, an old Gothic appliance with round metal loops for her fingers and a long metal needle dripping with some vile fluid.

She took a step toward me, the needle outstretched.

I faked left, went right, pushed her aside as I tried to rush by her toward the door.

The cleaver swung through the air with a flash of light. I jumped back. The blade just missed my stomach, piercing my jacket before burying itself in the wood-paneled wall.

I fought to pull away, but my jacket was pinned to the wall. I tried to spin out of the jacket, but I failed.

Nurse MacDhubshith came at me with the syringe.

I lifted my leg and kicked her away, hard.

As she sprawled on the floor with a shriek and a groan, I grabbed the handle of the cleaver and levered it back and forth until it released from the wall and freed my jacket

I tossed the cleaver to the floor, lunged for the door, when something grabbed hold of me. I tried to shake her off, I tried to push her away, the nurse was so thin it should have been nothing to get her off my back. But it wasn't nothing, and it wasn't the nurse.

"Be a good boy now, bucko," said Tilda's heavy German accent, "and take your medicine, *ja*."

Next thing I knew, there was a pinching in my neck and something cold slipped through my collarbone, racing down and across my chest, into my very heart.

I flailed out with my arm and caught Tilda with my elbow in the same spot I had slammed her before. The force of it freed me for a moment. I took a step toward the door, then a stagger. The room shifted on its axis. The floor slid noisily beneath my foot as I lost my balance. I looked down. My foot had slipped on a flat piece of metal. I bent over, grabbed the metal blade by the handle, tried to stand up straight. The room shifted again.

I reached for the doorknob and missed, smacking my head on the wood. I recovered, reached again, felt the cool brass in my overheated hand. I turned the knob, pulled the door toward me, staggered back.

"Hello, Victor," said Dr. Bob, standing now in the entranceway. "So nice to see you again. Put that down. We have no need for violence."

The cleaver fell from my hand and slammed point first into the wooden floor. I staggered back, lurched forward, fell to my knees.

"I'm so glad to be able to catch you," said Dr. Bob, stepping forward and grabbing hold of my arm to keep me upright as my head lolled to the side. "What do you say to one more session in the chair, Victor, for old times' sake?"

CHAPTER

76

I awoke from a dream I can no longer remember, in a musty, damp darkness that was spinning around like a carnival ride. There was some sort of chair, it was tilted back weirdly, and I was in it. I tried to move my arms, my legs, my neck, but everything was frozen. I tried to open my mouth and failed, which was pretty much a first. The darkness was spinning, spinning about me. I fought to stay awake, but nothing in the world seemed as sweet as closing my eyes and drifting back into my dream, a dream as pliable and sweet as saltwater taffy, stretching and pulling until it wrapped me completely in its pale, sticky arms.

I dreamed that I awoke and a bright light was shining on my face. My mouth was propped open with a piece of rubber jammed between my teeth. A dentist, in mask and cap, his face blanked out by the light shining behind him, had his hands in my mouth. They say you can't feel pain in your dreams, but that is a lie, because this dream hurt like hell.

I heard voices. I must still have been dreaming, because the voices became part of a fabulous panoply of shapes and colors. I was in a magical world where flowers blossomed and sprites flitted and shiny white teeth with straw boaters danced on their roots, swinging toothbrushes like vaudeville canes while singing bright songs of oral hygiene. Two women strode onto the scene, beautiful, beautiful women, all in white. One spoke with a Scottish burr, one spoke with a German accent, so sexy for all its harshness, and both of these beautiful women were speaking about me. What I felt for these two women in white was as real as anything I had ever felt before in my life. What I felt was love, sweet and painful and true as the dancing teeth before me.

There was someone knocking at the door. Knocking and knocking. Answer it, I tried to call out, but it emerged as a muffled grunt, because again I couldn't open my mouth. Knocking. Knocking. And then I realized the knocking wasn't on a door, it was on my skull. I opened my eyes, and there was Dr. Bob, lightly knock knock knocking on my forehead.

"Hello, Victor. Are you ready to come out and play?"

I started to the surface of my consciousness, and for a moment everything was clear: the light, the darkness behind it, the damp of a basement, the chair in which I was somehow bound. And of course Dr. Bob, smiling paternalistically as he watched while I slowly started to drift back down to the lower depths.

Dr. Bob knuckled my head once more.

"It's so good to see you finally awake," he said. "How are you feeling? Quite rested, I should think."

I grunted something and ran my tongue across my teeth. The gap was still there, but my two temporary crowns were now gone, and in their places were the nubby posts, sticking up forlornly from the base of each tooth. I felt somehow denuded.

"A dentist walks into a bar," said Dr. Bob. "Stop me if you've heard this one. He walks into a bar and meets this girl. When he tells her he's a dentist, she's suddenly all over him. 'What's so great about dentists?' he asks. And she says, 'They're the only men who tell me, "Spit, don't swallow." ' Ha ha ha."

I tried to struggle out of the chair but failed. My head was somehow stuck in a position that made it impossible to see my arms or legs, but I could feel some give in the binding, so it wasn't my muscles that didn't work, which was a relief. Whatever the bastards had injected into my neck hadn't paralyzed me.

"Wait, there's more," said Dr. Bob. "So the dentist, he takes this girl home, and after they're done, she says, 'You must be a very good dentist.' 'How do you know?' he says. And she says"—he paused for effect—" 'Because I didn't feel a thing.' Ha ha ha."

I struggled once again against the binding, groaned loudly.

"I don't blame you," he said. "Dentist jokes are the lamest things in the world. Maybe because there really is nothing funny about poor oral hygiene. How about this one? A dentist says to a sexy woman patient, 'Will you have sex with me for a million dollars?' She says, 'Sure.' He says, 'How about for a buck thirty-nine?' She says, 'Certainly not. What do you take me for?' And the dentist says, 'We already established what you are, madam. Now we're just negotiating the price.' Ha ha ha."

He pulled back a bit, put his fist to his chin in thought, considered me like he was a grade-school teacher determining what to do with a recalcitrant pupil.

"You're still not laughing, Victor. Maybe it's because you're gagged. Or is it because it hits a little too close to home? Hmm? Is that it? But isn't it better to be up-front about these things, especially when all my subtle hints and warnings have had no effect?"

He showed me the tiny tape recorder I had hidden in my jacket pocket. He switched it on for a moment. Out came Whit's voice, slightly muffled but still clear enough. *"She was supposed to be dead asleep, it was supposed to be so easy. But the woman awoke and was so frightened at the intrusion that she came at him with a gun. And he reacted badly. There was a struggle, there was a shot, and the bullet—"* Dr. Bob snapped off the tape player.

"So, Victor, tell the dentist your price. What? You want to say something but you can't? Maybe it's the duct tape over your mouth. How about we do this?"

He reached for my mouth, quickly pulled something off with a searing *rrrrrrrrippp.*

"Aaaargh," was the best I could manage.

"Much better," said Dr. Bob. "I do love a good negotiation. So, Victor, let's—how do you people say it? *Hondel*? You first. What will it cost to buy the tape and stop you from bringing me into this mess?"

"Where am I?"

"Mr. Robinson's basement. He has this wonderful vintage barber's chair, which is where you're sitting now. I can pump you up or down, just like in the office."

"I can't move."

"Isn't duct tape wonderful? I used two whole rolls to tape you to the chair. That's enough to affix a Buick to the wall."

I struggled some more, felt the tape give a bit again, but failed to gain anything close to freedom. "What did you put in me?"

"Oh, nothing serious. Something I use for my more squeamish patients. FDA-approved, very mild. Nurse MacDhubshith might have been a mite overly enthusiastic in the dosage"—he shook his head in disappointment—"but still nothing to worry about. So, we were talking about price."

"A trip to California, like you gave Mrs. Dent?"

"If that's what you want."

"I like it here," I said. "No price. I'm for sale, always, but not to you."

"Oh, come on, man, don't be obtuse. Who can give you more than I? Do you want Carol Kingsly back? Have you been pining for her smile? Or maybe you'd like a position on Mr. Takahashi's legal staff? Quite a lucrative position, I might add. No more nickel-and-dime cases for you, Victor. Think of it, zipping around the world on the corporate jet, staying at the best hotels, growing fat on expense-account meals. You could use a few pounds, I daresay, especially after this little ordeal. Are you hungry?"

"I want to throw up."

"I suppose, then, food right now wouldn't be the best inducement. I know what you'd like. One of my patients is the wife of the hiring partner at Talbott, Kittredge and Chase. Quite the white-shoe firm, Victor. They have an opening for a trial lawyer in their criminal-defense department. You'd be perfect. Think of it. A little staid, maybe, but a very prestigious outfit, and your clients would be all the best people."

"I have a client."

"Of course you do. But he's a witless scumbag who abused his family, cheated on his wife, abandoned his child, dived deep into debauchery, and now is playing games with your partner's emotional life. What do you owe a creature like that?"

"The best I have. Let me out."

"Oh, I can't do that. Consider all my endeavors, all those souls I'm in the process of helping."

"There are a lot of people in prison you can help, too."

"I'm not a criminal."

"Then what are you?"

"I'm someone who won't sit back and let people's lives fall apart without doing what I can. I am an optimistic man of action. A fighter of dental disease and the malaise of life. Looking for a love connection? I'll make it. Your boyfriend stalking you? I'll keep him away. Is a young girl missing? I'll find her." He paused for a moment, looked at the tape player in his hand. "Is your father abusing you? I'll make sure he doesn't have the opportunity anymore."

"You're referring to François Dubé. That was why you sent Seamus in to deliver the tape."

"He was so eager. It was such an easy mission. Put the tape in the VCR, set the timer to start when Leesa woke up. And there it would be, proof of his debauchery and her avenue to win custody playing right there on her television screen."

"But she ended up dead."

"An accident of blind happenstance. It was nobody's fault. Things happen."

"The death might have been an accident, but not the frame-up."

"He would have gotten custody. He would have had complete dominion over his daughter. What happened in the apartment was a tragic accident, yes. But I couldn't allow that man to get his clutches on that poor girl. You, more than anyone, know the harm that a parent can inflict on a child."

"You're beautiful."

"Thank you."

"Why don't you join the army and save the world?"

"I do the same work, I just do it my own way."

"Unfettered by the law, by any oversight, by a system of checks and balances."

"I can be trusted."

"And you decided François's fate based on what? The bitter ravings of a separated wife spewed out while you drilled her teeth?"

"The family dentist always knows."

"You might be wrong."

"Believe me when I tell you this, Victor: I'm not."

"You're still the little boy in the closet, aren't you? Held back by his siblings as he helplessly watches his father beat his mother."

"I was that boy. Powerless and afraid. I'm not him anymore."

"But the results are the same, aren't they? You stayed in the closet, and your mother ended up bloodied and dead on the floor. You tried to help, and Leesa Dubé ended up bloodied and dead on the floor. It's the law of unintended consequences: No matter our good intentions, the unintended consequences of our acts will predominate."

"So what are we to do, Victor? Nothing?"

"Maybe just our jobs. You fix teeth, I'll represent clients, and in the end we'll see how it all shakes out."

"A world where everyone disclaims responsibility because caring is not in the job description."

"A world where everyone minds his own damn business."

"But you don't want that anymore, do you? Really?"

I pressed my tongue into the gap in my mouth, thought of Daniel Rose's scarred arm. I said, "Let's ask Leesa Dubé what she thinks."

"Yours is not a world in which I choose to live."

"Maybe you should adjust your medication."

"So what are we to do with you, Victor?"

"Give me a ride home and a parting gift of the home version of your game?"

"I hardly think so," said Dr. Bob, before turning out the light and rising from his seat. As he walked off, his shoes sounded harshly on the basement floor.

*   *   *

I don't know how long I lay there, taped to the chair in the darkness. It seemed like hours, longer. But once I ended up at the Ice Capades and that seemed like weeks, so my conception of time is quite elastic. I screamed for a bit, but that just ripped up my throat without doing any good. I struggled again to get free of the duct tape, and I did manage to free my head, but when I looked down, my whole body was covered with silver. There was no getting out of that. Still, I tried. I even imagined myself the Incredible Hulk as I fought to break free, but if I turned green, it was from nausea alone, and I stayed just as trapped.

I fought to calm myself. At first I tried meditating, wiping my mind of all thoughts, and I was pretty successful, clearing my brain of all thoughts save one. But the one that stuck was that I was at the mercy of a certifiably insane dentist whose stock and trade was blood and pain. Or was it pain and blood? One or the other. Neither of much comfort, and together a terribly ineffective mantra. So much for meditating.

Then I tried to figure out why I hadn't just gone along with the bastard. I was in trouble, I should have agreed with whatever he said and then run like hell.

But then what? To betray him would have given him an excuse to destroy me. Which was a strange thing to think, because why would he need an excuse? What excuse had he needed to drug me into a stupor and drag me to the basement and bind me with duct tape and pry off my crowns?

But there was something in the thought, wasn't there? And when I finally realized what it was, it calmed me considerably. I remembered the way he looked at Tilda after he noticed the gash on my cheek, as if he hadn't been the one to send her. I remembered the way he criticized her for being more Thor, the Norse god of thunder, and less Loki, the trickster god of mischief. And I remembered the way he shook his head when he mentioned that Nurse MacDhub-shith had been a bit too enthusiastic in the amount of drug she administered. It was as if there were lines he wouldn't allow himself to cross. And I knew why, too.

Nothing is more delusional than the benign beatings of the human heart.

I must have fallen asleep again in the chair, because I dreamed the footsteps before I actually heard them. I tried to keep my eyes closed as I fell out of sleep. I wanted as long as possible to gather the loose beads of my consciousness. So with my eyes closed, I listened. One pair, three pairs—no, four pairs of footsteps. The whole shooting match had come to say good-bye.

"Wake up, bucko," said Tilda as the lids over my eyes turned red with light. "The time has come to take care of you for good, *ja*."

The chair jerked upward, my eyes jerked open. Dr. Bob and his hygienist stood before me. Behind them stood the strange pair of Whitney Robinson III and the pale Nurse MacDhubshith.

"Any new thoughts?" said Dr. Bob. "Have you reconsidered my offers? One call and you'd be atop the hiring list at Talbott, Kittredge and Chase."

"Once that was all I ever wanted."

"Then take it, my boy," said Whit. "You'd do wonderfully there. Shake all the bluebloods up."

"I can't."

"That is a shame," said Dr. Bob.

"Except, you want to know something?" I said. "I'm

trussed like a turkey, I've been shot full of dope, my caps are gone, and I'm totally at your mercy. But the strange thing is, I'm not afraid of you."

"The brave hero, is that it?"

"No, Whit will tell you. I'm an abject coward. But in the end I know you won't hurt me."

"How are you so sure?"

"Because you see yourself as a caped crusader, as a moral exemplar in a compromised world. You won't hurt me, Doctor, because you believe, in the deepest part of your sadly confused soul, that you are good."

"You had such potential," he said, shaking his head. "Nurse."

Nurse MacDhubshith stepped forward with a pair of scissors in one hand and a syringe in the other. She cut open my shirt and pulled from her pocket a small cloth reeking of alcohol. The nurse rubbed my shoulder with the cloth before jamming in the needle. A cold slid up my arm, and I immediately felt the dizziness again.

"One question," I said as it started to overcome me. "Why the hell didn't you just mail the tape to her?"

"It wouldn't have had the same effect as her finding it, quite by chance, playing on her television," he said.

"Always the trickster."

"Do you believe in God, Victor?"

Growing drowsier by the second, I mumbled, "I'm . . . I'm not sure."

"Well, maybe it's time to figure it out," said Dr. Bob from farther away. "Find me when you do, and we'll talk again. There's so much good you could accomplish. Open his mouth, Tilda."

Tilda grabbed my jaw with one of her huge hands. She squeezed at the edges, and my mouth split as easily as the seam of a rotten melon. Before I knew what was happening, a piece of rubber was jammed between my teeth, keeping my jaw wide open.

"*Adieu, mon ami. Adieu,*" said Dr. Bob from so far away it was as if he were already across the ocean. "That's French. I figured it was time to learn another language."

77

I had too many teeth.

I lay spread-eagled and naked on my bed, my head throb-
ing, the skin of my arms and face raw. I was groggy enough
ot to know the time or the day or where I was going to
row up—though I was going to throw up. I wasn't even
rtain if I was alive or dead. But of one thing I was sure: I
ad too many teeth.

The teeth on the bottom row of my jaw were pressing
adly one against the other so that they had to be bursting
rward out of my mouth like the rushing torrent of a
wollen river upon the breaking of a dam. He had reached
to my mouth with his tools and techniques and turned me
to a grotesque. He had made of me a monster, a sideshow
eak. *Come one, come all, step right up and see for yourself
e horror of our age, the beast from which sickened eyes
nnot turn away: the inimitable, the indescribable, the in-
edible lawyer with too many teeth.*

Slowly, fighting the terror, I checked the lower jaw with
y tongue. Startlingly, everything seemed to be in order,
erything seemed even and neat, except for one thing that
lt strange. What was that? And then I realized the gap in
y teeth was no more.

Dr. Bob had put in my bridge.

I opened my eyes. Sun was streaming through my win-

dow, showing my bedroom still trashed from Tilda's earlie
visit. My digital clock said it was 1:30 P.M. And something
metal was sticking out of the pillow, right next to where my
head had been.

I sat up in terror. What the hell was that? Oh, yes, of
course.

It was a metal dentist's pick, jabbed into the foam, pin
ning in place a piece of paper. I pulled the paper over the
pick. *Care and Cleaning of Your New Dental Bridge.* Ever
as I was reading it, trying to figure out what it really meant
the nausea overcame me, and I rushed to the bathroom. No
much came out—I don't know when was the last time I had
eaten—but it was still rough enough to strip the enamel of
my new prosthetic tooth.

"Welcome to my world," I said aloud to the bridge.

Showered and shaved, my new tooth brushed along with
all the others, I checked my messages. I got a sense of how
long I'd been away from the number flashing at me: 17
Beth, Ellie, Beth, Beth, Torricelli, Dalton, Beth, Gleason, a
reporter, Judge Armstrong's clerk, Franny Pepper, Beth
Beth . . . And the messages were all the same: "Where the
hell are you?"

"How long have I been away?" I said to Beth after the
histrionics were over and we could get down to business.

"This is the third day you've been missing."

"Jesus, no wonder I had nothing in my gut when I puked
What's going on in the trial?"

"The judge put us in recess until you got back. He said
next time you showed up in court, you'd better bring either
a damn good story or your toothbrush."

"I have a story," I said. "But I'll take my toothbrush all th
same. Never underestimate the value of good oral hygiene
Beth. That's the lesson I'm holding on to from all this. I
Franny Pepper in town?"

"I put her up at the Sheraton."

"Nice."

"Are you going to tell me what happened?"

"Later," I said.

"Is it interesting, at least?"

"Interesting as hell. Now, this is what I need you to do. Tell the judge I'm back, that I'm prepared to finish up the trial starting tomorrow morning. First we need Mrs. Winterhurst ready to testify how she recommended Dr. Pfeffer to Leesa Dubé and how Leesa became his patient. Then I need Whitney Robinson in court. He'll be home with his daughter. Drop a subpoena on him, I need him tomorrow. I wish I still had a statement he made on tape, that would make his testimony certain, but I can badger the truth out of him without it. Then have Franny Pepper ready to go after that."

"Did you find something?"

"Yes, I did."

"Is it good?"

"Good enough."

"What do I tell François?"

That stopped me for a moment. It all seemed so clear just an instant ago: I was still alive, my teeth were fixed, I had the trial in my hand. And then I remembered who my client was and what Bob had said about him. I didn't know if I could trust what Bob had told me, but when I thought back on everything, I realized that in all our dealings, he had never lied to me. He had embarrassed me, made my life a living hell, kidnapped me and pumped me full of drugs and performed unauthorized dental surgery, sure, but he had never lied to me. Which meant that my doubts about François remained profound. There was the young daughter waiting for him. What about her?

"Victor," said Beth. "What do I tell François?"

"I have to go," I said. "Just make sure to get everything done."

"While I'm doing all this, what are you going to do?"

"Me, I'm going live the dream and put a dentist behind bars."

When I hung up with her, I called Torricelli.

I was eating a falafel I bought off a cart on Sixteenth Street. This was the first thing I had eaten in three days and it wasn't sitting well in my empty stomach—fried chickpeas I should have known—but still I was so ravenous I couldn't stop chomping. My face was buried deep in the pita when Torricelli suddenly appeared.

"That's a sight I'd like to forget," said Torricelli.

I lifted my head and smiled, the white tahini sauce smeared on my cheeks.

"It's dripping on your tie," he said.

I looked down, a white splatter on the red. "So it is. Fortunately, I'm no longer wearing the yellow silk number." I took my napkin and wiped the splatter clean away. "This baby is made out of a special Teflon-coated polymer. The dry cleaner who sold it to me said it wasn't just stainproof, it was bulletproof, too."

"Handy. You know, Carl, when you didn't show up in court, I was strangely worried about you."

"You don't say."

"You're like a toe fungus; you've grown on me."

"Thank you, I think. And remind me never to see you in sandals. Do you have what we need?"

"Pattycake, baby."

"Then let's do it." I moved to toss the rest of my sandwich into a nearby trash can, thought better of it, and took another bite.

Side by side we walked into the Medical Arts Building, rode the elevator to Dr. Bob's floor, walked past the sign with his name on it and into the now familiar beige waiting room. A few patients were idly turning the pages of old magazines as they restrained their natural terror. I gazed around once more for old times' sake, soaked in the Muzak, the sterile cheerfulness.

"Oh, Mr. Carl," said Deirdre, the pretty and pert receptionist. "It is so nice to see you again. And it is good to see you, too, Detective Torricelli. I don't think either of you has an appointment today. But, Mr. Carl, I'm so glad you came in, because I have something for—"

"Is the doctor in?" I said, interrupting her.

"He's seeing a patient now. But if you wait—"

"We'll just pay a quick visit," I said, heading toward the door. "I know the way."

"Oh, no, Mr. Carl, that's not allowed. You can't go back—"

"It's all right, Deirdre," said Torricelli, flashing his badge. "Official business."

"I don't understand."

"Of course you don't. Just make sure nobody leaves, please."

I opened the door to the hallway, expecting to see Tilda barring my entrance, but no Tilda, no bar. I could hear the whir of a drill in one of the examination rooms. The sound produced an involuntary shudder.

"Let's go," I said as Torricelli and I headed straight for the drilling.

The patient lay on the orange chair, wingtips shaking, his mouth agape, suction in place, as Dr. Bob, his back to us, mask on, cap on, rubber gloves tight, plied his barbarous trade.

"Robert Pfeffer," said Torricelli, "I have a warrant for your arrest on the charge of kidnapping."

The dentist extracted his hands from the patient's mouth,

turned to stare at the two of us. The patient lifted his hea
and stared, too, suction still in place, mouth still agape.

"I tried to stop them, Doctor," said Deirdre, rushing in be
hind us, "but they just barged in."

"What's the meaning of this?" said the dentist. I notice
that his voice had deepened and he had changed the style o
his glasses. "I'm in the middle of a procedure."

He pulled down his mask, showing off a bushy black mus
tache. Not Dr. Bob, not Dr. Bob at all.

"Uh-oh," said Torricelli. "Sorry about that. We're lookin
for Dr. Robert Pfeffer, also known as Robert Pepper. Do yo
know where he is?"

"I can't help you," said the other dentist.

"Where'd he go?" I said.

"I don't know," said the dentist. "I'm Dr. Domsky. This i
my office now. Pfeffer sold me his practice."

"When?"

"Yesterday. I had been trying to buy his practice for quit
some time, and suddenly he agreed on the condition I tak
over right away. I haven't had time to change the sign."

"How'd you pay?"

"He insisted on a cashier's check."

"I bet he did." I turned to Deirdre. "Where is he?"

"He didn't tell me anything," she said. "But he gave me
very nice bonus."

"No hint?" said Torricelli. "No nothing?"

"No, sir," said Deirdre. "But he did leave somethin
specifically for you, Mr. Carl. That's what I was trying t
tell you."

"He's gone," I said.

"Seems so," said Torricelli. "I wasn't sure I believed you
cock-and-bull story, but it looks like there might be some
thing to it. I'll tell Mia Dalton the news and put out an APB.

"You won't find him," I said.

"No, I don't think we will."

The patient still on the chair said, "Ahweehahooih?"

"Of course," said Dr. Domsky. "If you don't mind, gentlemen."

"No, that's fine," said Torricelli, reaching into his pocket. "Here's my card. If you hear from him, give me a call. Sorry to disturb you."

Dr. Domsky looked at the card appraisingly. "Torricelli, huh? And you're Carl. I seem to recognize those names. You don't happen to be patients of this office, do you?"

I looked at Torricelli, who looked back at me and shrugged.

"As a matter of fact," I said.

"I would really appreciate if you gave me a chance to keep your business."

"Dr. Domsky is a wonderful dentist," said Deirdre. "He has such gentle hands."

"Oh, I bet he does," I said.

Back at the desk, while I was waiting for Deirdre to retrieve whatever it was Dr. Bob had left for me, I noticed that the smile hall of fame had been taken down off the wall. It would be up somewhere else soon enough, I was sure, and I had a decent idea of where.

"Here you go, Mr. Carl," said Deirdre.

It was a manila envelope with my name on it, holding something small and rectangular. I ripped it open, slid the object into my palm. My tape recorder. I pressed play, and out came Whit's voice: "... *went through her neck. He said it was a nightmare of blood. He ran away and called Dr. Pfeffer, who said he'd take care of it, and he—*" I clicked it off.

"What's that?" said Torricelli.

"A parting gift, I suppose," I said.

I hefted the tape recorder in my hand even as I rubbed my

tongue across the inside of my new false tooth. Whatever righteous anger I held toward Dr. Bob seemed to bleed out of me just then, replaced by a perverse gratitude. Maybe it was because of my perfectly fitting bridge. There is something about a medical professional competently healing your maladies that leaves you in his thrall. But there was something else, too. In our own bizarre way, we had battled like two heavyweights, subject to some strange set of rules I had never figured out. Neither of us had won decisively, we had fought to a draw, but that suited me just fine. And by his leaving me the tape recorder, he was giving me a tip of the hat before he moved on toward another prizefight in another town.

"What are you going to do now?" said Torricelli.

"First I think I'll go over the calendar with Deirdre and schedule a cleaning and checkup for about three months from now. You can never be too careful with your teeth. And then tomorrow I'm going to march into court and win my case."

And that's just what I did.

CHAPTER 78

One final act of surveillance.

It wasn't such a tricky piece, this one. There was a sea of cars parked in a wide parking lot. I slipped my car between an Explorer and a red Dodge pickup and set it so I had a perfect view of the big gray door. Then it was just a matter of waiting. But no coffee needed this time, I had company to keep me awake.

"What are we doing here, exactly?" said Beth.

"Surveilling."

"Why?"

"Well, I can really use the practice. And I also want to know who he called to meet him on his first minute out."

"He told me he was meeting up with his daughter."

"That would be nice. But let's wait and see."

"I'm just relieved that the whole thing is over."

"You know who seemed really relieved?"

"Who?"

"Mia Dalton. When Torricelli told her everything about Dr. Bob in the courtroom, you could see her jaw muscles twitch. I think she would have dismissed the case right there, except for what it would have done politically to her boss. I never saw a prosecutor let out such a breath of gratitude at a not-guilty verdict."

"She offered me the job again."

"She's relentless."

"I told her it doesn't pay enough."

"It pays more than you're getting with me."

"But the benefits, Victor, the benefits."

"They get dental over there."

"Reason enough to stay put."

It was a hot, sunny day. Our windows were open, but still it was warm in the car. I took off my jacket. I took off my tie. If it had been seemly, I would have taken off my pants, too.

"I'm sorry," said Beth.

"Okay," I said.

"I never got a chance to apologize, and I wanted to."

"I accept."

"You don't even know what I'm apologizing for."

"It doesn't matter. Whatever you want to apologize for, I'll take it. It doesn't happen so often."

"Shut up."

"Okay."

"For being so unprofessional."

"That's what you're apologizing for?"

"Yeah."

"Come on, Beth, you can do better than that. Being unprofessional is what we do. Derringer and Carl, the unprofessional professionals. In fact, we should copyright that before the CIA steals it. If we had to go around in these stinking suits acting like professionals all the time, what would be the point? I'd quit the business."

"What would you do?"

I thought for a moment. "I'd like to try my hand at being a foot model. I'm told I have very lovely feet."

"Who told you that?"

"A very nice Vietnamese woman who was giving me a pedicure."

She sat back, stared at me for a long moment. "You never fail to astonish me."

"You want to see?"

"God, no." She turned to look out the front window for a moment, stared at the still-closed metal door. "So what should I be apologizing for?"

"I don't know. I don't do the whole accept-apology thing very well. I always want to say, 'Forget the apology and just give me cash.'"

"For doubting you," said Beth.

"Okay," I said. "I accept."

"I'm serious."

"So am I."

"You were taking care of me the whole time. Even playing those tapes in court. They were as much for me as for the jury, weren't they?"

"Can lawyers plead the Fifth Amendment?"

"No."

"Well, that's what we do, Beth. We take care of each other."

"I don't know where it came from, but I was just overwhelmed. I don't remember ever feeling so emotionally fragile, so emotionally invested. I don't ever remember feeling something that strong before."

"Oh, no?"

She laughed. "You think different? When?"

"Think about it."

"Victor, I don't—"

"Hold on," I said. "There's the door."

The big gray door opened a sliver. A guard walked through the opening. He took off his guard hat, wiped his brow with a forearm, put the guard hat back on just so. And then out stepped François Dubé.

I could sense Beth beside me, holding her breath.

François was dressed in a white shirt, open at the collar, and the pants from one of the suits he wore at the trial. He carried no suitcase; I suppose there was nothing inside worth taking with him. He shook the guard's hand, looked around for a moment, waited for the guard to go back inside and close the door behind him. Then he took a pack of cigarettes out of his pocket, tapped one into his mouth, flicked a match to life, cupped his hands around the flame. He cut quite a dashing figure, did François, almost as if he were posing, like something out of a Godard film, Jean-Paul Belmondo in *Breathless,* rubbing his lower lip with his thumb.

And it didn't take long for his Jean Seberg to arrive.

The black limousine turned in to the parking lot, passed right by us, slid to a stop in front of François. The back door opened from the inside, before the chauffeur could do it himself, and out popped—who else?—Velma Takahashi.

"I guess the papers got signed," I said as François tossed away his cigarette and the two embraced.

"I don't understand," said Beth.

"Her divorce papers with Takahashi," I said. "I suppose, after the verdict, she agreed to a quick settlement just to get it over with. Now there's no more reason to hide in the shadows. She loves him. She always loved him. She gave him to Leesa to keep him for herself while she married Takahashi and his money. And everything's worked better than she could have hoped. She's free of Takahashi, she's loaded down with Takahashi money, and Leesa's out of the picture. She can spend the rest of her life with François, at least until she gets bored again."

"That's why she tried to set up the fake story with Sonenshein."

"To get François out," I said. "Even though she thought he really had done it, she missed the big galoot."

"And he loves her," she said softly.

"So it appears, or her new bank account. It's hard to tell when looking into the lifestyles of the sick and self-absorbed."

We watched quietly as the two, still embracing, maneuvered themselves into the open door of the limousine. Doors slammed with resonant thunks, the limousine pulled away. Beth wiped at her eye.

"I still feel something. Is that crazy?"

"Yes. He has our bill, but it's her money, so I don't expect we'll see any of what he still owes us. Nothing has a lower priority than paying yesterday's lawyer."

"What about his daughter?" she said.

"You figure it out. His first call was to Velma. He's not the type to hang around for his daughter."

"The poor little girl."

"Remember Gullicksen, Leesa's divorce attorney? I sent him to the Cullens, along with copies of the tapes. They're going to fight for custody."

"Is he going to fight them back?"

"Let's hope not."

"Victor, you don't know. It's her father. She'll miss him forever."

"Probably, yes. I've spoken to the Cullens. They said the daughter is going to need some support. The Cullens were looking at the Big Sister program. I gave them your name."

"Victor."

"You stuck me with Daniel Rose. I'm returning the favor."

"I won't be able to help."

"Sure you will."

"She'll miss him forever. It will never go away."

"But you'll still be able to help."

"I don't think so. I'm all wrong for it." She paused for a moment. "Before, you asked about my father."

"Did I?"

"I don't think I ever told you about him."

"No."

"I don't think I ever told anybody."

"You don't have to."

"Yes," she said. "Yes, I do."

"Want to go somewhere?"

"No, this is fine," she said. "We might be a while."

"That's all right," I said. "But first, it's sort of hot. Do you mind if I take off my pants?"

Tommy's High Ball.

I suppose I had become something of a regular, because as soon as I poked my head in the door, the bartender shouted out, "Yo, Pork Chop, your factotum is here."

I looked at Whitey, standing stoop-shouldered behind the bar. "Factotum?"

"I call it like I see it," he said.

"I'm not even sure if I know what it is."

"You don't need to know," said Whitey. "But you sure is it."

"Thanks," I said. "I think."

I turned to the booth closest to the door. Horace T. Grant was deep into a game of chess with his usual whipping post. He looked up from his board.

"I'm in the middle of something here," he said. "Can you wait a minute?"

"We've got to go," I said.

"Simpson," he said to his opponent, "we'll have to resume this exercise in controlled mutilation when I return."

"Oh, no, we won't. You play or you resign."

"Resign?" Horace sputtered with indignation. "I have you on the ropes, old man. If you didn't take so long to plot your foolish moves, I'd have beaten you twenty minutes ago."

"Just taking my time, setting my traps. My position's got possibilities."

"And all of them calamitous," said Horace.

"Play or lose," said Simpson.

Horace looked up at me. I nodded to the door. His shoulders slumped as he tipped over his own king.

Horace's opponent let out a yap and raised his hands high. "I got you, Pork Chop, yes I did. Got you clean and fair. You surrendered to the overwhelming possibilities of my position."

"Enjoy it," said Horace as he stood. "It's going to have to last you another twenty years."

On the way out of the bar, Horace said to me, "This better be good."

"Oh, it's good," I said.

My car was parked outside. Isabel Chandler, the Social Services caseworker, sat in the front passenger seat. And in the back, in a car seat Isabel had provided, sat Daniel Rose.

When Horace was seated beside Daniel, I leaned in the car door. "Horace, do you know Daniel?"

"I've seen the boy in the neighborhood," said Horace. "How you doing there, son?"

"Okay," said Daniel.

"I haven't seen you around much lately," said Horace.

"I've been living somewhere else," said Daniel.

"Someplace good, I hope?"

"It's okay."

"Daniel, Mr. Grant's the one responsible for arranging to have me be your lawyer."

Daniel smiled at the old man. "Thank you."

"It's my pleasure. And I like them teeth of yours, boy. It's an improvement from what I remember."

"They're not real," said Daniel proudly.

"Neither are mine," said Horace.

"You were the one talking to my sister all the time."

"I might just be," said Horace.

"I remember."

"Have you seen your sister?"

"Not for a while," said Daniel.

"Okay, then. Well, it's nice to finally say hello to you."

Horace reached out his withered old mitt. Daniel slipped his small, pale hand inside, watched as it was swallowed whole. And then the gentle shake.

It wasn't too long a drive. We hit the Cobbs Creek Parkway, followed that down to Haverford and then up toward the golf course. A left and a right and a left again, and then here we were, in the neighborhood of small brick row houses, of children playing in the yards, of families. The house I was looking for was easy enough to find, what with the balloons all tied up to the light beside the door.

"This is it," I said as we stopped in front of it. "What do you think, Daniel?"

"It looks okay," he said.

"The Hansons are very excited to meet you," said Isabel. "This won't be like the last place, a short-term thing. They've promised to take care of you as long as it's required."

"What about Mommy?"

"She's working hard, Daniel," said Isabel. "When she's ready to take care of you the way you deserve, we'll go before the judge and figure out what to do. But until then this will be your home."

"I miss my mommy."

"I know you do, Daniel," I said.

The front door opened, and Mr. and Mrs. Hanson came out. They had big smiles on their faces, and they each held a wrapped present.

"Let's go meet your new family," said Isabel.

She got out of the car, bent over, and unhooked Daniel. The two of them walked slowly toward his new home.

"You want to get out?" I said to Horace.

"Nah, give the boy some time."

"This is going to work out for him," I said.

"It can't be no worse than what he had."

"You did a good thing for Daniel."

"It was nothing nobody else wouldn't have done."

"Don't bet on that," I said as I got out of the car.

The Hansons were leaning forward, talking to the boy as he clutched hold of Isabel's leg as if it were a life raft on a choppy sea. When they reached toward him, he shied away. When they tried to give him the gifts, he hid his face. God, it seemed so simple when Isabel and I were setting it up, it seemed so obvious. But it wasn't working out, there was no joy or excitement in Daniel's face. Just fear and disappointment, another stop on a train to nowhere.

"Daniel?"

We all looked up. Standing in the front doorway was Tanya Rose, dressed in her Sunday best, smiling nervously.

Daniel peeked at her from behind Isabel's leg.

Tanya reached her arms out.

Daniel shouted, "Tanya," and then ran to her.

Brother and sister, they hugged and jumped and fell into a heap and hugged some more, and suddenly Daniel couldn't stop himself from laughing.

In a very real way, this tender moment was brought to us by Dr. Bob. He fixed Daniel's teeth, he found for me Tanya's new family, he taught me to do more than the expected, to find a way to make the exceptional the norm. And maybe for the first time, I felt the pull of what he had been trying to find all his life, the almost painful satisfaction that comes from trying to do something good and seeing it work out better than you could have hoped. Dr. Bob was the ultimate do-gooder, unwilling to let custom or law get in the way of his attempts to help.